DOWN WIND
and
OUT OF SIGHT

D1415732

Douglas Richardson

ARCHWAY
PUBLISHING

This is a work of fiction. All of the characters, names, incidents, organizations, and dialogue in this novel are either the products of the author's imagination or are used fictitiously.

Archway Publishing books may be ordered through booksellers or by contacting:

Archway Publishing
1663 Liberty Drive
Bloomington, IN 47403
www.archwaypublishing.com
844-669-3957

Cover Design: Douglas Richardson
Cover Art: Nick Adams/Merion Art
Author Photo: Adrianne Mathiowetz

ISBN: 978-1-6657-1348-1 (sc)
ISBN: 978-1-6657-1346-7 (hc)
ISBN: 978-1-6657-1347-4 (e)

Library of Congress Control Number: 2021921088

Print information available on the last page.

Archway Publishing rev. date: 1/12/2022

Readers Respond to Doug Richardson's
Down Wind and Out of Sight

"Douglas Richardson seems to have created an utterly original stand-alone genre. *Down Wind and Out of Sight* occupies a place and space all its own, and I was repeatedly astonished by its unusual qualities. A dark book, yes, but consistently compelling, often deeply moving, and frequently very funny. The characters all were particularly vivid, and the plot was quite different from anything I have ever read before. I love that the author kept the tone highbrow and intelligent, while at the same time telling such an offbeat and gritty story."

Hollis Bentley, Professional Communications Consultant

"This contemporary work of fiction contains an extremely enjoyable story and a strong core cast, borne along by a supple writing style with dialogue that rings true to the ear. It features a striking protagonist with a slashing outlook and a rich inner life, supported by his surrounding circle of characters."

John Paine, Professional Editor

"*Down Wind and Out of Sight* is such a remarkable book. It's an offbeat, unforgettable thriller, full of dramatic action and surprising twists. But it's also deeply compassionate and often moving in its exploration of emotionally-challenged characters. Its utterly original plot features a cast of richly-wrought and often hilarious characters, taking readers to unexpected places and leaving them breathless at the end."

Pamela Heuszel, Author and Attorney

"Quirky but stimulating characters and quirky but stimulating science combine with an ingenious plot to add up to a consistently engaging read. *Down Wind and Out of Sight* is filled with rich detail about electronics, psychology, marine biology, and criminal investigations, and these small touches really help make the book."

James Diorio, PhD Engineer

"The story of 'The Hole in the Wall Gang,' an improbable cast of characters bonded by the drive to survive, is told so engagingly that you suspend disbelief and immerse yourself fully in the fun. *Down Wind and Out of Sight* takes you from the Australian Outback to the peaceful rivers of upper Chesapeake Bay, with visits to a sweeping country estate, a secret government research facility, and the mysterious electronics laboratory of an autistic adolescent savant. And the whale: *Don't miss the whale.* What a trip!"

V.J. Pappas, Founding Editor,
Dow Jones National Business Employment Weekly

Author's Note

BEFORE WE START OUR JOURNEY IN FICTION TOGETHER, LET ME shamelessly beg a favor: please rate and review this book once you've finished it.

When I completed writing my debut novel at age 75, I assumed that the world of fiction marketing was still anchored to longstanding conventions - traditional publishers, traditional bookstores, traditional publicity, and traditional book reviews from tradition book reviewers.

When I turned to marketing *Down Wind and Out of Sight,* I immediately discovered that everything - publishing, publicity and distribution - had become *digital.*

While traditional book awards and positive reviews still can give a book a boost, today *reader reviews* offer far greater visibility and clout. The opinions of actual end users have the ring of truth and can confer enormous marketing leverage and visibility.

In other words, dear reader, *your opinion really matters to other potential readers.* And, therefore, it really matters to me.

I would be extremely grateful if, after finishing *Down Wind and Out of Sight,* you would go on to Goodreads or Amazon or any other digital site and provide a review – good, bad or indifferent. I will read them all. More important, a lot of other people will read them, and this will be the most potent marketing currency I can have. Thank you for your help, and I'll see you on the internet.

For Pam, truly a circle 'round the sun.

"It is in the shelter of each other that the people live."
Irish Proverb

PROLOGUE

I. Miles from Nowhere

MY FIRST MEMORY AS A CHILD—NOTHING BUT A BLURRY VISUAL imprint, really—is of staring at dust motes drifting lazily in the afternoon sun. I am crouched in a corner, hidden in shadow, everything—arms, legs, chin, breath—pulled in as tightly as can be. I squint my eyes and stare, trying to fasten on a particular dusty dot and follow it as it drifts and vanishes.

When I lose track of one mote, I seek another, riding it across the trapezoidal sunlit square reflected on the floor from the window high on the wall behind me. There are stripes in the square, stripes of alternating dark and light and dark and light. Motes drift into the darkness and disappear. Motes emerge from the dark stripes and take a place in the sunny swirl ahead of me.

I realize now that what I was seeing on the floor were the patterns cast by venetian window blinds. And I know now what I was doing: *I was hiding.*

I cannot recall anything before this. Everything that came before is lost. Gone from my memory is anything about my parents, my history, my sense of person and place. If I knew joy and warmth and mother's milk, those recollections were lost—discarded, really—when I was plunked into the Moore River Native Settlement about eighty miles north of Perth, Australia.

The only record I have been able to find of my background is a smudged and wrinkled administrative form headed "Moore River Native Settlement Intake Processing Note." I have no idea where or how I acquired it. It notes a birthdate of February

7, 1944, and lists my father as Klissam Ordulu, "an Indigenous Person and Resident of Welladoola." His employment is listed as "general labor." It says my mother was one Clarice Kibbe, "a Caucasian woman of ill repute, emigrated to Australia from Los Angeles, 1944." Under employment, the word "prostitute" is scratched out, and the word "none" written over it.

The intake note states that my given name was William Ordulu (in parentheses they added "Urdooloo"). Curiously, whoever wrote the form then wrote my name again, but this time in reverse order—Urdulu Williams—as if unsure what my true name was or should be. In time, Urdulu became Hugh. William, probably through youthful mispronunciation, became Ullam. And there you had it: a hodgepodge creation of an identity. Clearly, no one gave a much of a shite what my name was.

The note describes me as a "medium-fair" half-caste Aboriginal child (hair: red) "voluntarily removed" from family in the Murchison region of Western Australia by the Australian Office of Children, Youth and Families in late 1949. That means I would have been five when the rug got pulled.

I remember nothing of being torn from my family, no mental images of Daddy and Mommy, no idea of whether my mother rent her garments in despair or just handed me over indifferently to my new "teachers."

I was assigned to the "young men's dormitory," a ramshackle bunkroom in the back row of housing, pushed back up tight against the barbed-wire fence that hemmed us all in. I was the third bunk in from the door; I got the bed on the bottom because I wasn't big or strong enough to climb to the top bunk.

The reason I think I was seven when I hid in the nurse's dispensary amid the dust motes—*who would look for me there?*—was because subsequent experience taught me that was the usual age of the little boys when the male caretakers at Moore River typically began "taking liberties." For the girls, the caretakers (all men; the only women were cooks, schoolteachers, and nurses) usually waited until there was a little hair between the legs or the budding of Aboriginal breasts. For the girls, rape came with age. But the boys they liked young. Young and weak and pitiful and defenseless.

Beyond the sheer physical pain of being repeatedly raped, I detested the helplessness I felt, the utter lack of power or control. I hated that I couldn't fight back, that no one cared if I kicked and screamed. I was seven, for Christ's sake. What was I to do?

The little boys at Moore River, at least the pretty ones like me—caramel-colored skin, hair that wasn't black, thin lips and dazzling white teeth—came in for a lot of unwanted attention. We were pinned down, violated, and subjected to other humiliations. Slapped. Choked. Forced to "dance the nigger jig," lick a manure-caked shoe or choke down shots of the cloudy, searing Turkish raki our caretakers so loved.

❀　　　❀　　　❀

THE MOORE RIVER NATIVE SETTLEMENT WAS OPENED BY THE government of Western Australian in 1918 under the auspices of A.O. Neville, the Chief Protector of Aborigines. If such a thing is imaginable, mixed-race children sat lower in the Australian social pecking order than pure-blooded indigenous "Aborigines." Neville claimed to believe that we useless mixed-race kids could be constructively repurposed, trained to work in white society. He claimed that as time wore on, we would marry white and be assimilated fully into society. This was rank hypocrisy: regardless of their skin hue and hair color—and indigenous Australians come in a broad spectrum of both—to Neville, all Abos were "blackfellas," and the infusion of some Caucasian genes was not going to turn them into whitefellas. What he really believed— what he called our "protection"—is that we should be interned, confined, marginalized, and ignored until, over generations, we all simply died off.

Although Moore River was intended originally to be a small, self-supporting farming settlement for about 200 indigenous people, by the 1920's it had abandoned any pretense of noble purpose and turned into a giant holding pen for alcoholic

Aborigines (there were many), orphans, the aged and unwell, unwed mothers, and, particularly, mixed-race children. Later, reformers would label us half-caste kids the "Stolen Generations," amidst much hypocritical self-flagellation by the social workers and the government bureaucrats. The truth was that Moore River was run as a segregation depot, a "solution" that Neville determined to run with the minimum expenditure of government funds.

The Moore River cemetery holds 374 bodies, broken people who died of diarrhea, "senile decay," bronchitis, enteritis, tuberculosis, and marasmus (that's science-speak for undernourishment). Of these, 203 are children; 149 were five years old or less and more than 100 were under the age of one when they died.

The kids who were "molested" to death in one way or another at Moore did not find their way to the cemetery and were never honored in the brief Abo funeral ceremonies where the departed were interred to the sound of survivors' ritual clapping sticks. They just disappeared. It was like that: I'd wake up one morning, and a bunkmate would be gone. Willie Melvin: here on Tuesday, gone on Wednesday. Barney Ballone? "Never heard of 'im." One of the earliest social skills we learned was not to ask why, how and where.

❖   ❖   ❖

I VIVIDLY REMEMBER THE DAY IN 1951 WHEN THE NAME OF THE MOORE River Native Settlement was changed to the more ethnic—and therefore more racially enlightened—Mogumber Native Mission.

"Mission" was supposed to sound nobler, more holy, less oppressive than "Settlement." In 1951, with a stroke of a pen, the "Stolen Generations" simply vanished, transported from the jurisdiction of the Chief Protector of Aborigines to the tender mercies of the Mogumber Heritage Committee, newly minted, committed to virtuous habilitation of indigenous children (henceforth, Australians were asked, please don't use the dismissive term, Aborigine. Or 'Abo.' If they had to use an "A" word, people were asked to call us Aboriginal Peoples).

In place of Moore's spartan facilities and legacy of childhood rape, one was to believe, Western Australia was determined to build a progressive educational institution that provided modern health facilities, a righteous Methodist church, and vocational training to prepare this useless pile of human garbage for socially beneficial employment in such roles as household servants, clerks, miners, and manure-muckers.

Since the name change came in 1951, and I recollect at least the beginning of this day so vividly, I must have been around seven. I remember we were all provided with new white short-sleeve shirts and dark blue pants (the girls too) and lined up in neat rows in the main courtyard for the name change ceremony.

We had been at attention in the broiling sun for over an hour when Commissioner for Native Affairs S.G. Middleton—known ironically to kids and caretakers alike as "Uncle Sam"—rode in on his splendid red roan, all oiled up for the occasion and shining dazzlingly in the sun as if cast from bronze.

Middleton, who had never served in the active military but wore still-fresh white gloves and a saber at his waist, feigned saddle fatigue and weary resignation as he rode back and forth before us. His stooped posture in the saddle was supposed to convey the world-weariness that comes with the challenges of dealing with various sub-human species. In fact, some older boys just back from the fields whispered to us, Middleton's Land Rover and horse trailer were parked less than a half mile away down in an arroyo. The ice cubes in the insulated silver tumbler of gin he had left perched on the armrest probably had not yet completely melted when Uncle Sam trotted into Mogumber, bound for duty.

Middleton was forty-ish, pale, a vivid carrot-top, lavishly mustachioed, lean as a leopard, straight as a rod. Only his eyes betrayed a chink in his command presence: they were pale and slightly protuberant, and they darted about nervously, as if he was on the lookout for assault or ridicule. The old Moore River caretakers regarded him as a cynical bastard, keen for power, wily but not bright, unconcerned with anything or anyone but himself.

On this day, those old caretakers, now facing imminent unemployment, slouched on benches in the shade of the headquarters veranda. They did not stand when Middleton rode in. The new teachers and staff, stiff in dark suits, starched shirts, long skirts, and severe blouses, rose and did their best to gaze hopefully toward the promise of the future. The more seasoned teachers alternated glances between their watches and the long table behind them on the veranda laden with bowls of fresh-cut fruits, assorted pastries, the teetotalers' punchless punch bowl, a huge silver bucket brimming with melting ice, and the neat rows of gin, scotch, Pimm's Cup, and bottles of beer.

Uncle Sam reviewed the ranks of the "pupils" and adjusted our lines, much as if we were Anzac troops headed off for Turkey to fight on the beaches of Gallipoli. He nearly succeeded in masking his disdain for this sad-sack multi-hued cohort of pathetic losers and surly malcontents. But truth to tell, we weren't fooling him. Nor he us.

We were indeed a motley crew. Contrary to the hackneyed stereotypes of short, frizzy-haired folks with coal-black skin, pot bellies, bandy legs and square faces blowing didgeridoos while covered in white chalk, my indigenous cohort included a broad spectrum of skin colors, hair textures and physical characteristics. I fell in the middle of the color palette, caramel-colored, the color of desert dust and clay. My hair changed color repeatedly over the years, sometimes muddy brown, sometimes almost red, always clamped to my head in tightly curled bristles.

Like many of my little chums at Moore, I defied stereotype and was configured as a future long-distance runner: wiry, long legs, lean torso, and hard, flat belly. My ears small, my eyes dark and widely-set, my smile forced and wary. Even as a kid I had deep furrows across my forehead, which probably made me look as if I was straining to peer into my future.

Although many of us had bright, infectious smiles, none of us now smiled. As taught—as disciplined—we lowered our gaze and averted our eyes. We knew that insolence was punishable. Corporal punishment was permitted and popular.

Middleton wheeled his mount to face the mixed bag of those assembled. "This is a splendid day for us all!" he suddenly declaimed. "Today we both honor the legacy and rededicate the mission of the original Moore River Native Settlement." He enunciated slowly, clearly, distinctly, with taut T's and sibilant S's.

He looked over his shoulder at the staff and teachers on the veranda. "I thank the loyal staff of the Moore River Native Settlement for their years of dedicated service, and welcome the additions to the committed staff of what henceforth will distinguish itself as the Mogumber Native Mission. Indeed, we are people on a mission. We will realize changes, modernization, normalization, social integration. We will depart from Rufus Henry Underwood's 'native settlement scheme' and build a relationship with Western Australia's indigenous peoples marked by respect and opportunity. Enlightened leadership will lead us all to a better day."

On and on Middleton droned. Our eyes glazed over, and our heads drooped in the searing sun. We only hoped that when Middleton finally stopped talking, we might get some Kool-Aid. Finally, Uncle Sam chopped his chin downward for closure and emphasis. He then wheeled his horse away, no doubt intending a dramatic pirouette to once again face his captive audience, thrust a triumphant arm into the air, and proclaim grandly that "the time had come," for us that being the time for the race to the refreshment table.

Opinions vary on what happened next. One report said Middleton's horse caught a hind hoof in a post hole that remained after the decrepit lean-to over the old hitching post had been removed. One of the caretakers told an investigator that in trying to spin back toward the lines of students and staff, Middleton cross-reined his mount and confused the poor beast.

In any event, the horse did not turn. Instead, he reared and backed up, staggering on his rear legs, front hooves pawing the air for balance. One rear hoof clipped the lower stair of the veranda. That's the stair I and my age group were standing on.

I recall no sound. I do remember seeing the horse's shiny flank twisting toward me. I remember seeing the burgundy monogram on Middleton's saddle blanket, growing larger and clearer as the horse's ass—literally—bore down on me.

And that is the last I ever saw, and certainly the last thing I remember, of the Mogumber Native Mission.

II. The Big One

I WAS AWAKENED BY A PINPOINT OF LIGHT BEING SHONE INTO MY eyes. It moved right, then left, then right again. It stopped in the center. Then a cold compress was placed over the top of my face.

"Hugh, can you hear me? Do you understand what I'm saying?"

I nodded my head. Slowly. It felt like it weighed five hundred pounds.

"Hugh, I want you to reach up and grip my hand with your right hand. Squeeze it as hard as you can."

Strange. It seemed to take about five minutes to lift my hand off the coverlet, which was white and smelled pleasantly of starch, and locate the proffered hand. Perhaps my reaction took only seconds, but time seemed to ooze like a soft slurry washing over me. I found the hand and squeezed. My grip felt surprisingly powerful. It did not feel like a little boy's squeeze at all.

"That's good." The voice was soft and female, but quite deep. "Now let's do the other hand." Her voice was like being bathed in a soft melody.

"Hugh, you had another seizure. A really big one this time. I am going to reach to your mouth and remove the rubber bite-bar. Please do not react. Please do not bite my hand."

Not until she touched my lips and tugged at a piece of rectangular hard red rubber did I sense how tightly my teeth had been clenched.

"Fine. Can you talk?"

"Can talk," I said. "But jaws hurt."

"Do you want to keep the compress over your eyes, or do you want me to take it off so you can look around and see my face?"

"See face."

At first her face was a blur, but when my vision cleared, I could see that hers was not a Caucasian face. It was chestnut brown. Not black. Wide across the eyes. Small, almost button nose. Smooth, shiny skin. Some black hair poking from under some kind of white cap. It wasn't a nurse's cap, somehow I knew that. It was a…straw sun hat with a wide brim.

She leaned close to look into my eyes again. Her teeth were startlingly white. Her smile was wonderful. *Wonderful.* For a moment, I swam in her smile. Then I recognized that smile. And froze.

"Do you know who I am?"

I nodded.

"Do you know where you are?"

I paused to consider: This clearly was a hospital. The head of my bed was elevated. I could hear beeping sounds. I realized that an IV drip is running into my arm, which meant that I knew what an IV drip was. I must be sick or injured. I was in a blue hospital gown. The sheets were fresh and crisp, and I liked the smell.

"Hospital. Fancy hospital."

"Very good. And can you remember my name?"

My focus sharpened, and suddenly, with a bang, sounds, sights, smells locked into alignment. An awful dread descended upon me.

"Your name is Giala Billimoria. You're a doctor, but you're not a medical doctor. You're a neuro-something or other."

"Very good, Hugh! What city are we in?"

"Well, Mogumber doesn't have a hospital, so we must be in Perth."

"No, Hugh, actually we're in Sydney. You have lived with me at the Akers Institute in Sydney for ten years."

I cannot adequately describe the sensation that coursed through my body at that moment. It felt like I was free-falling into some bottomless abyss, spinning, tumbling in a dizzying spiral. I have never experienced disorientation so complete, so sickening. I searched for facts I knew for sure.

"*No.* Can't be. My name is Hugh Ullam. I just had my seventh birthday. I live at the Moore River Native Settlement."

"*No,*" she fired back sternly. "Your name is indeed Hugh Ullam, and you have just turned eighteen. It is 1962, not 1951, Hugh. You are talking with me like an educated adult because you are, in fact, a very highly-educated adult."

I gaped at her.

"You are an educated adult whose cognitive circuits are a mess right now because you have just had another *grand mal* seizure. Be calm, Hugh. Just as before with your other seizures, some things will come back, some probably won't. There is a lot of residual brain trauma from your childhood. But most things will come back into focus, and you recovered quite nicely from your other seizures, even though you have indeed suffered some cumulative memory loss."

❂   ❂   ❂

WHAT ALL THIS MEANS IS THAT EVEN TODAY I CAN'T TELL YOU WHAT'S true and what's not true about much of my upbringing. I can only report what I was told and trust I have been informed in good faith. If over the lost years, my doctors and "caregivers" (as they are now called) chose to pin the tail on my donkey and spin me in circles, l have no way to dispute many of the attributes and events they have assigned to my life. In large measure, I remain their captive, their creation.

Until my recent unpleasant turn of cerebral events as I hit fifty, I have never had another "neurological event" since the Big One. No seizures, fits or fugues from age eighteen until recently. I have never taken anti-seizure medication.

At present, my memory seems pretty reliable for both current and not-so-current events, at least events that occurred after The Big One. I'm generally pretty sharp, my recent cerebral accidents notwithstanding. I'm organized, even hyper-organized. While my memory is no longer eidetic—not photographic—it's still pretty damned good. Talk to me and you wouldn't know that I suffered massive brain trauma as a child, that there are some gaping holes in my recollection of my past.

My knowledge of myself benefited from reconstructive pilfering: at some point I purloined my file from Akers. I hid in the electrical cabinet in Billimoria's lab late one Friday afternoon, and lay curled in a corner until all sounds stopped, and the line of light vanished from along the bottom of the door. I came out, ironed out the kinks in my joints and switched on the light. I stayed up all night and read everything.

Dr. Giala Billimoria's files occupied one full wall of the room, a bank of pale green filing cabinets, four drawers each, four feet high. And not one was locked. I easily found my "file." Actually, it was three full drawers, filled with reports, notes, test results and scores, X-rays, home-schooling scores, and, particularly interesting, a black leather notebook with page after page of Giala Billimoria's handwritten notes. All about me. All about her plans for me.

The formal Akers reports and notes were chilling. And, for me, unbearably sad. I learned that I was "the little Aborigine boy with the smashed head" who was regarded as a freak. In essence, I was made a test dummy, the subject both of inquiry into how such a badly bashed brain could still function and of experiments to perform dry-runs on untested neurological theories.

My comments and cries were recorded verbatim. Every time I said, "ouch," or "please don't" or "what happened?" or "I don't like that," someone dutifully wrote it down. Later, when I got more expressive and yelled, "Fuck you, bastards" or "I'll kill you," someone wrote that down, too. No doubt about my formative years: there was a lot of pain involved.

As I write this, I know that Giala Billimoria is dead now. First Akers fired her and then some bloke broke into her flat—not me, I swear—and killed her with a blunt instrument. Call it poetic justice. Karma. No, the killer wasn't me, but it could have been. After I read all her handwritten notes, which blend scientific detachment, casual sadism, and complete indifference to my pain over eleven years of calculated manipulation and experimentation, I would gladly have killed her if given the opportunity.

Through Giala Billimoria I learned the meaning of betrayal.

PART ONE
Found Family

1

Beginning at the End

THE SIGN AT THE END OF THE DRIVE SAID, "SLOW, WATCH FOR DEER," so Maryland State Trooper Arlon Santunas touched the brake and glanced right toward a stand of tall lodgepole pines and then left, across a vast expanse of brass-colored fields extending down to the Bohemia River. Not a deer in sight.

Ahead, the smooth asphalt drive pointed arrow-straight toward the sinking western sun, down a long aisle of gnarled Osage orange trees which formed a solemn, silent arch, a cathedral of cooling shade. In the distance, Santunas could just make out a flash of red brick peeking from behind a stand of dense, carefully groomed hedgerows. Although he often tucked his Crown Vic into the end of Bohemia Manor's private drive to surprise speeders hurtling south down Route 13, Lon Santunas had never previously ventured on to the Bayard family estate, had never seen the imposing house at the end of the lane.

The entry drive ran just short of a half mile, then opened into a large circular courtyard paved in rough-hewn Belgian block. Santunas made a Y-turn and slid his unmarked puke-tan cruiser backwards into one of the marked parking slots directly across the courtyard from massive front door.

1

This was a true manor house, a worthy rival to the various DuPont mansions that dotted northern Maryland and Delaware. This iteration of Bohemia Manor—historically called Bohemia Mannor Farm with two 'n's—had been built by the Bayard family in 1920 following the destruction of its predecessor in a fire set by a butler who had gone around the bend and chosen a class-conscious form of suicide. The architects of the manor's reconstruction had strived to create a Teutonic monument of tradition and substance, a fitting residence for a family of tradition and substance. Bo Manor, as the locals called it, was a U-shaped Georgian mansion with powerful symmetrical wings, the residential side, and a garage side, flanking an imposing entry, the overall effect proclaiming, "Here there be money."

Many of Cecil County's other great houses were gone now or had fallen into disrepair and decrepitude. Large estates had been carved up into developments and subdivisions, and once-grand family seats now stood empty, awaiting historic preservation that would never come. Almost daily there were mercy killings, historic Greek revival manses simply bulldozed and obliterated. Other gracious beauties were shoehorned on to half-acre lots and surrounded with scores of little single-family stick-builts in tan and gray and taupe.

Yet even as many once-fine Cecil County estates withered in their death throes, fading, rusting, warping, sagging on their foundations, awaiting foreclosures and tax sales, Bohemia Manor remained in magnificent condition, a tall and proud monument to wealth and power. Someone was really putting the time in on this place, thought Santunas. It sure as hell wasn't Hermann Bayard, asshole aspirin king and globe-trotting vagabond.

Santunas opened the door of his cruiser cautiously because the mysterious invitation note he had found on his desk had labeled this a crime scene. He reached into the back seat and pulled out his scene kit, a dark blue fanny-pack with "FBI" embroidered in bright yellow letters. This had been his graduation prize when he had completed the FBI Advanced Field Investigation Program, and he was very proud of it. He belted the pack around his waist and crossed the courtyard to the front door. There he found a note, printed in large bold type, fastened with red push pins.

TO ANY POLICE AUTHORITY OR INVESTIGATIVE PERSON:

Do come in. The door is unlocked. No alarms are set. No one is here, so to speak. You have my permission to explore any and all parts of this property (although I know you will explore them with or without my consent). The court orders and powers of attorney granting me authority for all business, financial and operational matters of Bohemia Manor, as well as Power of Attorney for matters pertaining to the body and affairs of Hermann Bayard, are in a binder on the desk in the second-floor office.

You also will find a journal, written by myself in recent months, that should be of considerable interest. I regard this as more than just a recap; it is my legacy, a talking document, my voice calling out from the infinite darkness of death, recounting hard facts and telling cold truths. That said, while the journal will explain almost everything, I must keep some secrets to protect the innocent and the blameless.

What you probably should look for first, and the reason you are standing at the front door, will be found in the third-floor bedroom at the back of the house. My bedroom.

Have at it, guys. Figure it all out. Assemble the pieces. All of you folks at the

Maryland State police, Elkton Sherriff's Office, FBI, Aberdeen Military Intelligence: ask yourselves what you should have done differently. Imagine what will happen when the truth comes out. And I have made sure that it will—at a time of my choosing, in a way of my choosing.

Sincerely yours,

Hugh Ullam

PS: I would not lift the lid on this to the press until you have your act together, all your fact-finding is wrapped up and your PR flacks are dressed in body armor. This will be a big, messy story, with great potential to make you all look like jackasses. By all means, get your stories straight. Here's the good news: there's nobody to sue you for screwing up so spectacularly.

Trooper Santunas flipped open the top flap of his scene kit and pulled out a pair of green latex gloves and a pair of blue fabric booties with elastic tops. The guys at the Academy called theses "eebs," short for Easter bunny booties. Once gloved and booted, Santunas squeezed the heavy brass door handle and pushed open the door. It moved easily and silently. Well-oiled. He stepped in, looked around and immediately smelled death. Not the sharp, coppery smell of fresh blood or the sweet revolting stench of advanced putrefaction, but rather the distinctive aroma of decay well underway. Something around here definitely had been dead awhile.

He found himself in a soaring vestibule that stretched to a high ceiling with carved wooden vaults arching above the second floor. On each side, a wide stairway rose to a mezzanine landing and then split left and right to two more ascending stairways.

These stairs were very impressive, which was, of course, the architect's intent.

Santunas yelled with his deepest, most forceful voice. "State police! Is anyone here?" His hail echoed through the house and was met with silence.

Santunas turned left and headed into the high-windowed great room. The room's décor was surprisingly austere: three distinct but identical conversation bays, all facing west across hundreds of acres of farmland, looking out toward the Bohemia River. Each bay was anchored by a large couch covered in a muted green-blue embroidered fabric, flanked by two wooden-armed chairs in dark green leather. A deep fireplace with a simple stone mantel dominated the north wall, over which hung a large portrait of a thin, pleasant-looking man in a dark business suit. Santunas had never met Hermann Bayard, but it seemed logical that the owner of Bohemia Manor would be accorded a prominent place in this house.

The room was musty, but the smell of decay was much less pronounced here than in the front hall. Finding nothing of investigative interest, Santunas turned back to the front hall, paused briefly to sniff the air, and, following his nose, headed up the stairs.

At the left side of the second-floor landing, an open door led into large study with tall windows providing a panoramic view of the river. A small modern desk, rather like a secretary's workstation, had been placed in the middle of the room. Centered neatly on the desk lay a thick volume about three inches thick: a metal pin-binder, a bunch of loose-leaf pages bound tightly by four long screws extending through to the back cover.

Santunas carefully lifted the cover of the journal. The cover page was blank except for an adhesive sticker, bordered in red. Neatly hand-lettered, straight, and centered:

HUGH ULLAM, GENERAL MANAGER
BOHEMIA MANOR FARM, ELKTON MARYLAND
PRIVILEGED PERSONAL WORK PRODUCT

Santunas turned to the next page. Ullam's handwriting was neat and legible, rather spiky. Ullam had used a fountain pen with a calligraphy nib, creating an overall effect that was graceful, yet confident, masculine, purposeful. *Such smug handwriting,* thought Santunas. *Just what you'd expect from that arrogant prick.*

Unlike the rest of the journal entries, the first page of the journal was not pinned into the binder. To Santunas' surprise, he saw his own name in bold block letters on the top of the page.

TO THE ATTENTION OF MARYLAND STATE POLICE TROOPER ARLON SANTUNAS

Santunas read the first few paragraphs and felt a wave of dizziness sweep from socks to skull.

> Santunas,
>
> I trust and hope you're the first one to read this. It's why I had the mystery message delivered to *you.* Was the delayed delivery clever, or what? In my invitation note to you, I called this a crime scene. That was both to make you hasten out here ASAP and because I think it's a crime that I won't be here to see your reactions when you rummage through my house and find what I left for you.
>
> In *Little Caesar,* the late, great Edward G. Robinson supposedly once said, "You'll never take me alive, coppers!" Well said, Ed. And so it is with me: if you are reading this, it means that I trundled off for the Big Sleep before you and your minions could catch me, and that you have missed your chance to take me down, impose retribution for my evil deeds, make me kneel in humiliation before the townspeople with their torches and pitchforks, and impose your unique brand of Cecil County frontier justice. Now that I

am done with the history of my time at Bohemia Manor, I hereby claim victory.

I will be at the controls as I fly out of here. Although I am dying absurdly young, *I have remained in control of my destiny,* and that's a big win for me. A slug of scotch, a few pills, and that will be it: *Game Over.* I admit the chase sure got hot at the end. But that's because Suits and his brownshirts were on their game, not because you clowns were doing anything right. You remained the Keystone Kops right up to the end.

Santunas, the binder you are holding in your hands is the original of my journal, *but it is not the only copy.* If you were an honest cop, you would, of course, give this original to your superiors so they could unwind all the details—what the crimes were, who the criminals were, what happened to Deirdre Callas, all that. Oh, but hold! *You* were one of the criminals! Because the journal often paints you in an unfavorable light, I suspect that you will steal it, try to make it vanish as if it had never existed (if you choose to do that, at least read it before you shit-can it; it's an interesting story, even the parts that aren't about you and Callas).

Theft will not work, Trooper Lon. Unfortunately for you, I have photocopied several other copies of the entire journal. And using my skills at orchestrating delayed delivery—it's really not hard—I have arranged for those copies to fall into other hands at some point in the future. Hands that will find the journal *very* interesting and who will want to shine a bright light on all the events described therein. An investigative journalist, say, perhaps working for a major broad-distribution periodical. Lots of notoriety for you, Lon.

The fun part is that you don't know who is going to get the copies or when they are going to receive them. All you know that at some point you and your sidekick Callas are going to take a hell of a beating (rest in peace, Deirdre). Oh, I wish I could be here to see it!

Must go now. I bid you adieu.

Hugh Ullam

As if it were a bomb, Santunas gingerly closed the journal and placed it back on the center of the desk, exactly where he'd found it.

He walked out of the office into the hall and then shouted again, "State police! Anybody here?" He got the silence he expected, but somehow he now felt safer. The single stairwell to the third floor was hidden behind a full-height blind wall at the east end of the hall, so that the stairs remained hidden to anyone coming up to the second-floor landing from below. Santunas headed up.

The moment Santunas reached the third-floor landing, he knew he was close to the locus of death. Here the pervasive odor was strong, sweet, pungent. It seemed to ebb and flow in waves, as if blown by wind. Four bedrooms on the front side of the house were open and empty. A fourth, which the placement of its door suggested was a much larger room, was locked.

On the river side at the back of the house, a final bedroom door stood ajar. He realized a window was indeed open: in addition to the variations in the intensity of the smell, Santunas felt a gentle breeze tease the front of his uniform and ruffle the sharp creases in his pants.

Santunas reached into his pocket, pulled out a small jar of Vicks Vapo Rub and smeared a mustache of ointment over his upper lip, wincing at the pungent scent. He then inhaled deeply, held his breath, and stepped in.

It was a pleasant room, quite large, with a fireplace fronted by a small dark red couch and two craftsman-style easy chairs covered in taupe corduroy. A dormer window, now open with the sheer curtains being drawn in and out by the breeze, looked out over the fields and river.

The bed was flanked by a bedside table and a dark-shaded lamp on each side. There was a crystal tumbler and a half-empty bottle of Johnny Walker Red scotch on the left side table next to an empty orange prescription pill container tipped on its side. Santunas rolled it with a gloved finger until he could read the label: *Percocet.* Next to it sat a small square prescription bottle. *Ambien.*

The bed had been completely covered with a bright blue plastic utility tarpaulin. On the bed lay something Santunas knew well: a black heavy-duty crime scene body bag, the kind with a clear plastic inner liner and a clear plastic window in the center-zipper outer cover that allowed a view of the occupant's face.

The body bag was occupied. And it smelled, densely, intensely. Santunas stared. The bag was zipped closed, from the bottom almost all the way to the top. Then he saw a ribbon of dark green peeking out at the top of the zipper. He realized it was an athletic coach's whistle lanyard, the kind with the metal spring clip at the end to connect to the whistle. Only this lanyard's clip was clicked not to a whistle, but to the pull-handle of the zipper on the front of the body bag. From there the lanyard ran to the top of the bag and disappeared down inside.

It took a moment for Santunas to grasp what he was seeing. Then it struck him: the occupant had climbed into the body bag and zipped the clear inner bag as high as he could while still being able to reach out with his arms to grab the lanyard. Then he had pulled the lanyard up from inside, closing the zipper and leaving only a couple of inches open to the outside air.

The occupant had zipped himself inside the body bag while alive.

Hugh Ullam had killed himself and done everything he could to leave as neat and tidy a death scene as possible.

Santunas walked to the bed and looked hard at the body bag.

From its shape, it was clear that the occupant's elbows remained arched over his head, still tugging on the lanyard in the repose of death. Santunas looked down through the plastic window in the body bag. He could see the outline of a head, but the face was blackened and unrecognizable.

The smell permeated everything. Santunas knew it would saturate his uniform and cling to his hair. He'd had to throw uniforms away before when working other death cases after it proved impossible to eliminate the peculiar odor of death and decay. It would take three days of showers to break down the scent, a week of cover-up deodorants and splash-on fragrances to eliminate Hugh Ullam's stink from his life.

The death scene spoke for itself. *Move along, folks, there's nothing more to see here.* Nothing more for me to do here, thought Santunas. From here on, it's just Hugh Ullam and the forensics guys. He started for the door, then paused. *Shut the windows, or leave them open? Trap the stink or risk scene contamination from stuff the wind carried in?*

After Santunas closed the window, he headed back to the library where he carefully picked up the journal. As he turned to leave the room, Santunas noticed another typed bold-faced note, this one scotch-taped to the front of the rolltop desk.

How about it, Santunas? Am I considerate, or what? Your forensics guys owe me thanks, even if I am dead. How about some posthumous praise?

Santunas removed the note from the desk, folded it and stuck it in his pocket, tucked the journal under his arm, and headed downstairs.

He breathed deep and long when he stepped back out of Bohemia Manor into the late afternoon sun, relieved to be away from the smell, glad that with luck, he would never set foot in this house again except maybe to point out the death room to the forensics techs. He turned and tore the taunting note off the front door, then stripped off the latex gloves and absurd-looking booties, balling them angrily in his hand as he headed back to his cruiser.

Now he felt a sickly dread, heard the far-off whisper of dangers lurking out of sight in the future: *Hey, where did this journal come from? Who is this Santunas guy? Is this stuff for real?*

Once the gloves and booties were stuffed in a baggie in the trunk and the journal placed into a plastic sleeve hidden beneath the spare tire, Arlon Santunas slid behind the wheel and fingered his radio.

"Dispatch? Santunas, 4145. Please log time of call. I am at the Bohemia Manor Farm on Route 213 about three miles south of Chesapeake City. Apparent suicide. Unusual circumstances. No other parties present. I'll stay here until the crime scene forensics unit can get here. I'm not sure it's a crime scene, but I think it should be treated like one. And tell 'em to hurry it up because this place gives me the creeps."

2

Santunas Reads

SANTUNAS REALIZED HE'D HAVE TO READ THE ENTIRE JOURNAL, cover to cover, not just hunt for the parts that referred to him or to Deirdre Callas. Ullam could have trumped up a whole lot of bullshit, and it would be up to Santunas to set the record straight if necessary.

The binder opened smoothly on its tiny piano hinges. It held several hundred pages of light gray paper traced horizontally with faint pink lines. It looked...professional, expensive, durable, meant to be shelved and preserved. It was virtually new, with no signs of wear, worn corners or dog-eared pages. He read a few of the first pages, then turned to the middle of the binder and read a few more, trying to orient himself to the journal's form and organization.

Immediately he realized that this was not a diary—a contemporaneous description of events written in chronological order. It was meant to be read by other people, not to jog the writer's memory or serve solely as a historical scrapbook. This was a look back in time, not a journey through it.

Clearly the binder represented stylized recollections, probably written over a fairly short period of time: the handwriting was of consistent style and strength, the ink color uniform, the conventions of formatting, margins, and layout consistent were the same throughout the binder. And the entries were...careful: they showed evident attention to word choice, style, impact. This fucking thing was...a *production*.

The only deviation from the binders' carefully controlled consistency was the occasional insertion of a newspaper article. These were laminated and fastened into the binder with Velcro, rather than glue, which allowed the articles to be removed easily and turned over if an article continued beyond the initial page. Most articles were from the *Cecil Whig,* the weekly local paper published in Elkton and serving Cecil County, Maryland, as well as northern Delaware and southern Pennsylvania.

He realized he had skipped over the chapter titles. Now he went back over them, trying to see what they promised, what they threatened.

They threatened a lot.

"Oh, man," said Arlon Santunas aloud. "This is gonna be bad."

3

Out Back in the Outback

ON A BEAUTIFUL SPRING DAY IN OCTOBER—REMEMBER THAT IN Australia, the seasons are reversed—I was sitting in my office in Doobibla, Queensland, looking out the front window and soaking in some of the last cool and clear weather we would have before winter set in with scorching temperatures and perpetually dusty skies.

A man walked by, stopped, glanced up at the sign over my front door, peered in the window at me. I looked back at him and smiled.

Hermann Bayard looked just about as I expected. Quite pleasant, in a Teutonic, all-tucked-in sort of way. Early forties was my guess. About six feet tall, trim, toned, a somewhat pinched face, a full head of sandy hair brushed straight back from a pronounced widow's peak on his forehead. A little gray at the temples, small ears, firm chin.

Overall, the first impression he conveyed was of...*brownness.* Or, more precisely, camel. He wore camel-colored slacks that were the same color as his hair, a brown belt, a white shirt open at the neck but clearly heavily starched, and a camel-colored tweed sport coat, impeccably tailored. When he opened the door to step in, I could see expensive light brown loafers and a flash of brown socks. Perhaps he had his blue days or gray days. On this day, he was as brown as Doobibla.

"Hi," he said pleasantly. "I wonder if I could get a little help."

"Most likely not," I replied, smiling back at him. "At least not as your accountant."

"Excuse me?"

"I mean no offense, Mr. Bayard, but I know who you are, and I'm pretty sure I know why you're here, and I think what you want is probably not something I think I should step into."

Bayard clearly was nonplussed. "I beg your pardon? You are Ullam the accountant, yes?"

"I am," I said brightly. "Certified by the certifiers to be the equal of any accountant in Australia. And probably the best indigenous chartered financial accountant in the country."

"Okay, I'm confused." His voice took on an edge. "Are you in business or not?"

"I am indeed, but I don't think yours is a matter I'm inclined to take on."

"What do you know about my matters?" Now he appeared visibly upset.

I put on a soothing tone. "Quite a lot, I'll bet. I'm not trying to be an asshole, Mr. Bayard. I'm just trying to get to the point and not waste your time. Please, please, do sit down."

He took the chair across from me and crossed his arms across his chest.

"Okay," I said with a deliberateness that probably sounded melodramatic. "Here's what I think I know. You are Hermann Bayard, American bloke, absentee owner of the Sister Creek Sheep Station, which you inherited from your father when you were about twenty. You've never given much of a shite about it, with no great love of sheep, so you delegated its operations and finances to local overseers, blackfellas from the same families your da had used for many years."

I leaned in toward him, in response to which he leaned back and recrossed his legs the other way.

"You've had every reason to believe your sheep station was profitable, having long enjoyed a modest but constant flow of free money from down under. Now you've trekked out here from Sydney, actually all the way from Maryland in the U.S., because one day you took a moment out from your globe-trotting to dig deep into your Sister Creek financial reports and found things didn't add up. Suddenly you became aware that you were being fleeced by the locals, if you'll forgive my pun."

I paused for effect, "By the way, it was very virtuous of you to continue to use indigenous people to run your enterprise. Won you a big gold star hereabouts."

I paused again. "How am I doing?"

"How do you know all this, Mr. Ullam?"

"Hugh is fine."

"How do you know all this, Hugh?"

"Well, I hoist a pint now and again with Benny, Ruggo and Sam at the Doobibla Arms. Blackfellas' pub. Abos trust Abos, Mr. Bayard—may I call you Hermann, or would I overstep?"

"Yeah, Hermann."

"Hermann, your guys know they have a good thing going, and they're happy to talk about it with people they trust. They trust me, so they talk to me. They also brought some ledgers for me to look at on the sly, not in my business capacity. Quite impressive they were, too, quite well done for something put together by a bunch of rustics. Well-cooked books, you might say."

"So, what did you tell them?"

"I told them—off the record, with no fees changing hands, see—that they were committing fraud and theft. They were doing it quite cleverly, with a whole bunch of nips and tucks that didn't scream out but that would add up nicely over time. I should note that at the same time, they were doing quite a good job of running the station. Better than most blokes around here could, and I'm in a position to know, because I do almost every station's books hereabouts."

"Why didn't you inform the police?"

"Not my place, Hermann, not my responsibility. No business

relationship. No fiduciary duty. I don't know how it is in the U.S., but down here in Oz there is no affirmative obligation to report a crime. And in addition, probably because of the way we blackfellas have been treated for a few hundred years, indigenous people tend not to be good Samaritans – at least not where white people are concerned."

"What else did you tell your friends?" Bayard said sarcastically.

"I told them that one day you would figure it out and come roaring down here and raise hell and threaten them with jail."

"What did they say?"

"They said they really weren't much worried. They said they knew you didn't give a damn about sheep, and that this property was just a small pimple on your very rich American ass—forgive me, but I'm quoting here—and that you would probably be inclined toward an...*arrangement*. Something where you would threaten legal proceedings but really did not want to take on the expense of lawyering up, would try to get back as much as you could, and then cut and run."

Bayard sighed. "Yeah, well, they were pretty much right."

"I know."

"And since everyone says you are far and away the best accountant in the area, I thought you might be the right man to confront the blackguards."

"Blackguards, is it? That's a starchy British term, Hermann. Well, down here we don't use that term. We just call them thieves or crooks.

"In any event, I'm not inclined to confront Benny and Ruggo—Sam's just along for the ride, by the way. I live around here, my clients are mostly indigenous people—sheepers and cattle grazers and small business owners, a few surprisingly wealthy investors—and so I'm not inclined to be seen as a side-shifter."

"Well, without 'side shifting,' can you tell me exactly how they have been stealing from me?"

"The lads at Sister Creek have used a whole bag of tricks, some on the revenue side, some on the cost side. They pay too much for new stock and then take a kickback. They pay inflated prices for feed equipment, services. They under-report shorn fleece volume and revenues. They then sell the unreported product to a blind man—I think you'd call him a fence in the US—who markets it on the shady markets down south in New South Wales. It's a shame, Hermann, because your flock is highest quality, and Sister Creek's fleece is always premium graded. Sad to see it peddled down south as if it were poodle clippings. Also, the lads pay themselves bonuses that are expensed as phantom products on phantom invoices. Stuff never really ordered, never really received."

"They're smart enough to do all this?" He shook his head dismissively.

"Don't be elitist, Hermann. These guys are plenty smart enough to run a profitable enterprise. Been doin' it for years."

"Jesus fucking Christ," Hermann Bayard sighed, looked up at me. "If you had to guess, how much would you say they've stolen from me?"

"Hard for me to say for sure, Hermann. These guys are the sons of the blackfellas your father hired, what, twenty years ago? If everybody's been playing the same games the whole time, your family has been shorted perhaps a million bucks. Benno and Ruggo? Into you for maybe two-hundred fifty grand."

"Okay, what happens if I report them to the police?"

"I'm not really sure, Hermann. Maybe you get a lot of indifference from the local constabulary, as in 'Gee, sir, we'll certainly look into that, sir. Can't have foreign investors being defalcated, can we, sir?'"

"Defalcated?"

"You don't know defalcation, Hermann? A man of your means? It means robbed. Embezzled. Misappropriated. Screwed over."

"So, your cops would just turn a blind eye?"

"Well, they're not *my* cops, Hermann, and up here they are a mix of whitefellas and blackfellas. But I don't really know what would happen. Maybe there would be a hell of a mess, with investigations and trials and jail time. *Maybe.*

"I can tell you that Benny and Ruggo are highly regarded around here. And I can tell you that Sister Creek has a reputation for being well-managed. Still, we're not barbarians in this country, and not all the white folks are descendants of convicts. We still believe in the rule of law. So maybe if you allege a crime, all the legal machinery will...lurch into action. At least as long as you are down here. As soon as you hop the plane back to the US, likely you would find that it would...de-lurch."

I gently pushed my hands, palms out, toward him. *See? Truth-teller. Nothing up my sleeve.*

"But what if you looked at it a different way, Hermann? What does siccing the law on your managers really get you? Yeah, you might make the bad guys suffer, maybe even send them to jail. Put their families in financial straits. But do you really want to do that?"

"What do you think I should want?"

"I should think that you would want to get your money back."

"You're goddamned right I do!"

"But that's not what's going to happen if you blow the whistle, Hermann. Best case: you file a criminal complaint, you hire and pay a forensic accountant—not me, by the way—to build your case, you drop a ready-made theft case into the district constabulary's lap. What happens? Benny and Ruggo instantly plead guilty. Maybe they get two-to-three-year sentences, likely no more.

"And they are assessed a huge fine, Hermann. Maybe they get spanked as much as a couple of hundred thousand each. Wow! Justice! And for a second there, you feel great. 'I'm being made whole!' And about then it will dawn on you that these two blackfellas are judgment-proof. They won't pay a big fine because they can't pay a big fine. You'd be lucky to see $5,000. These guys will claim they can't rub two nickels together."

"But they've been...*defalcating*...hundreds of thousands of dollars from me. We take that money."

"What money?"

"All the money they've stolen from me over the years!"

"Hermann, I must say that for a very wealthy man, you certainly are a very naïve man. Where do you think the enforcement authorities are going to find all that money? Down at the Mighty Rich Aborigine Savings Bank? Hermann, whatever part of their ill-gotten gains haven't been spent keeping families alive and children fed, whatever huge piles of cash are sitting around in shoeboxes hidden in lizard burrows or something—do you think for a moment you would ever find it? Your chances of restitution from these guys are zero. They know it. And they knew it when they entered into their life of prosperous petty crime.

"Oh, and another problem, once you've rid yourself of these indigenous vermin. Now you've got a giant sheep station on your hands, a real cash sink, with no one running it—and no one willing to run it because you've roughed up a couple of locals who were, the story will go, just trying to provide for their families and clan.

"So, what are you going to do, Hermann?" I continued. "Come down here and run it yourself? Hire some hotshots from Sydney or Canberra or Alice Springs to come manage it? Anyone you hire would soon be amazed at the number of things going wrong—late deliveries, no credit from local vendors, poisoned sheep, unavailability of shearers, tractors with sugar in the gas tank, maybe a couple of semi-destructive fires. Blah, blah, blah, Hermann. Yes, indeed, a *lot* of blah. Is that what you want?"

"No, God damn it. I just want to get out of this mess as fast as I can. I want to cut my losses."

"Well," I said brightly, "as I suggested a moment ago, I do have an idea. And maybe there is a way I could help put that idea into action."

"I thought you said you wouldn't take me as a client."

"I meant that I wouldn't serve as your accountant and collection agent. But for an appropriate broker's fee, I might be willing to serve as a seller's agent."

"I don't get what you're suggesting."

"I'm suggesting you make Benny and Ruggo an offer they can't refuse. You, or your seller's agent, let them know they've been found out. And you, or your seller's agent, suggest that they buy the Sister Creek sheep station from you."

"*What?*"

"You tell them that you no longer want to be in sheep ranching, that you want to sell the property, and since they already are so familiar with its operation and finances, they would be highly-qualified and highly-motivated buyers."

"That…is the craziest…fucking…idea I have ever heard."

I stood up, walked around my desk and leaned back against it, and stood with my arms crossed, looking down at Hermann Bayard.

"Hermann, consider this: Let's say you have the property and the operation appraised. I am qualified to do that, and I would be willing to conduct an appraisal, charging you an appropriate professional appraisal fee. We establish a fair market value for the property. Straight up. No hokey pokey. My rough guess is about two and a half million dollars. We offer the property to Benny and Ruggo for that fair market value…*plus*, say, $250,000. Sort of a 'seller's premium,' if you catch my drift."

Now Bayard was sputtering. "B-B-Benny and Ruggo?"

"Yep. We get a local lawyer to incorporate them. Something like the Benny and Ruggo Indigenous Owners New Wave Sister Creek Sheep Station, Ltd. A large, locally owned profitable enterprise. It would be written up in all the papers, maybe even make the national business magazines. A true inspiration for indigenous people."

"You're kidding, right?" Now Hermann Bayard's face was scarlet, his lips tight, colorless.

"Nope. I'm in dead earnest. Look, it's a going concern. Benny and Ruggo and Sam have proved it's manageable, because they're managing it. And it would run even more profitably now because they would have no incentive to steal from themselves. And also, because they'd be watching each other like hawks."

Hermann waved his hand dismissively. "And since they're

so dirt poor they can't rustle up more than $5,000 among them, just where do they get the money for this multi-million- dollar purchase?"

"Simple, Hermann. *From you.* Purchase money mortgage. You fund the purchase, take back the financing. Super reasonable down payment, thirty-year note, nominal interest rate. We swing the whole thing to the up-and-up, and basically, in addition to payments against principal, they pay you in interest in about the same amount they've been stealing from you."

Hermann Bayard was flicking his left thumb against his forefinger, shaking his head slowly. "Oh, man, I can't believe this."

"It's just an idea, Hermann. No one's forcing you. You can always try to sell Sister Creek on your own. But you'd just be selling land. And then fixtures, and then stock. Huge hassle. It's worth far more as a going concern, but it has to be going, don't you see? This could be a better solution overall."

He looked hard at me, as if trying to divine my true intentions. His head was cocked slightly. He sniffed. He was still flicking his thumb with his forefinger.

"Look at it this way," I continued. "You get out from under. You add a modestly performing but socially virtuous asset to your financial portfolio. If Benny and Ruggo fail to perform, if they go into default, you can always foreclose. That helps keep them motivated—and vigilant."

I smiled. "Meanwhile, they 'own' the property, which makes these proud entrepreneurs big dogs among their peers hereabouts."

Hermann was still flicking his thumb.

"Hermann, this is as good a solution as cashing out, and there is no way to cash out without taking a big hit. As for me, the services I provide will be on a strict fee-for-service basis. I do not take a piece of the action, and I do not cover up any chicanery. I file quarterly financial reports with you, and they will be accurate. You have them audited by someone else annually. At least you will always know where you stand."

I let silence settle over the room. Hermann walked over to my front window and stared down the dusty distance of Dindalloo Street. He turned and glared at me; his brow deeply furrowed.

"Did you just now come up with this great brainstorm?"

"Nope, I've been kicking this idea around for some time now, once I saw you were being taken for a ride. I knew you'd probably drop by at some point."

"Have you discussed it with Benny, Ruggo and Sam?"

"I have not."

"I mean it, Hugh. Have you ever talked this over with any of them?"

"I absolutely have not. There is no conspiracy afoot here. This is not a set-up."

"Would they go for this deal?"

"I don't know. Probably. Particularly if I explain it to them, Abo to Abo."

Hermann Bayard sighed deeply. "Man, I cannot believe this."

4

An Invitation from Hermann

BOHEMIA MANOR FARMS
Hermann H.R. Bayard von Norden
5551 Augustine Highway Earleville, Maryland 21919

February 13, 1989
Hugh Ullam, Chartered Public Accountant
Rural Free Delivery 16
Doobibla Queensland W4338
Australia

Dear Hugh,
Please excuse the length of this letter. Weighty matters, both personal and business, are discussed herein.

As you know, I have been very pleased with the Sister Creek Sheep Station outcome, as well as very impressed with your financial and accounting expertise and your general business judgment. You're a weird duck, but I trust you and enjoy working with you. I also know that you have been receiving harsh public criticism from some of the indigenous clients you ceased to work with when you took up the various affairs of Sister Creek. I know your practice has suffered, largely on my account.

Perhaps the current situation creates an opportunity for both of us. Or perhaps not. You tell me.

Hugh, I need someone like you right now. I would like you to consider emigrating to the United States to become my accountant, financial advisor, and manager of all my personal affairs, as well as to serve as the General Manager of all Bohemia Manor Farm operations. I am asking you to make a permanent pilgrimage to Maryland, to join and lead our offbeat band—me, my handicapped daughter, Ulricke (Rickey), and her caregiver and our cook, Nora Dadmun. As far as I'm concerned, this represents an offer of permanent lifetime employment. If you accept, you will be overpaid. Name your price.

And if you accept, Bohemia Manor will become for you what it is to us—a rather unlikely island, but one that will be a place that can provide you with stability, security, comfort and perhaps above all, privacy. We do not have to let anyone in; our contacts with the world "out there" can be limited to business interactions and dealing with vendors and service people.

As for me, I now travel most of the time, and I like it that way. I won't be around much. I want Bohemia Manor to be my pied-à-terre, basically just a place I can return to when I want and leave when I want. I want it to be well-maintained and well-run, but I do not wish to be captive to it. I do not want to be its face. I do not want to have to take care of a lot of mail addressed to me. I do not want people to rely on me.

Specifically, here's what I'll want you to do: run all Bohemia Manor Farm business operations and assume full P&L responsibility for the enterprise, serve as my agent and surrogate in all business matters, handle all banking, manage my investments, keep the Sister Creek crew honest, give Nora Dadmun and Rickey anything they need, provide me an allowance when I ask, and tell anyone who asks that I am not available.

Simple enough, and certainly well within your capabilities. Basically, you run the show. Keep me solvent, keep me out of day-to-day details, keep me free to do what I want. Keep the ship on an even keel. Keep nosy people away and at bay. For this I will pay you very handsomely and provide a generous benefits package.

Now, in the spirit of full disclosure, I must raise a caveat. All your life, you have been treated, at least by everyone Caucasian, as a second-class citizen, with all sorts of barriers, biases, and discriminations aimed at you and your mates. I respect how well you have stood up to it, how you have maintained your dignity and integrity. Maybe you think that by emigrating, you will be putting a lot of "shite" behind you.

Some maybe, but certainly not all. When you move to Cecil County, Maryland, you will continue to be treated like a second-class citizen. In the US, things are better than a couple of decades ago, but racism lives on in various forms, and you are bound to be at the receiving end of some of that. It could get nasty.

When you come to Earleville, Maryland, I expect that you are going to encounter three problems. First, you'll be a "colored" man in an area that is still overtly racist. Second, there aren't many indigenous Australians in Cecil County, and the locals will simply not know what to make of a colored man who is not African American. Equally important, I think, is what will happen the moment you open your highly educated mouth. At that point, some of the locals are going to feel very threatened. They will call you "uppity," and I think they will be inclined to "teach you a lesson" in various ways.

Finally, once word gets out that you are General Manager of Bohemia Manor Farms, a multi-million-dollar enterprise, you will not only be an educated indigenous Australian with a strange smile, you will be a colored Australian *with power*. Your presence, appearance and role are going to make you a challenge to the well-entrenched and very self-protective local power structure. You may think that these days we're past all that Jim Crow stuff, but, as I said, you're going to find that racism is alive and well in Cecil County.

That's how it's likely to be, Hugh. And so, I ask you: Do you want to put up with that kind of grief? Can you put up with that kind of bullshit?

I do not make this offer as some sort of existential challenge. I make it as an offer. So, what do you think: do you want to make a lot of money running a farm and watching over a band of escapist people?

RSVP.

With warm regards,

Hermann

5

Well, That Went Well

IT WAS RAINING LIGHTLY, AND MY FIRST SIGHT OF BOHEMIA MANOR Farm was accompanied by the thwock-thwock-thwock of the station wagon's wipers. The long driveway glistened, smooth and black, and the trees were showing the silvered undersides of their leaves in the brisk breeze. So, this was my grand entrance, Hermann Bayard driving, me clocking my head around, trying to take everything in.

We turned into the courtyard, and I saw two figures sitting on the front steps, each under a large dark green umbrella. One was youthful, rail-thin, with shockingly red hair. She was staring at the Ford—at me—intently. The other, obviously older, my guess was in her mid-thirties, sat with head bowed, her face shielded by a sweeping cascade of dark hair.

As Hermann pulled the car to a stop next to the front door, Ulricke Stuhlmann Bayard, tall, skinny, barefoot, and dressed in a loose-fitting peach-colored shift with large armholes on this warm May afternoon, stood and walked toward the car as I climbed out, her bare feet splashing in the warm puddles. She reminded me of Little Orphan Annie, the movie one, not the blank-eyed comic strip one. She was quite beautiful, but somehow...*off*. Her striking green eyes were looking in my direction but didn't seem to be focusing on anything. She looked like she was blind.

I stood, stretched, and held out my hand to her. When she made no move to take it, Nora Dadmun, the upper right part of her face disfigured by a dark port-wine birthmark, reached out from under her umbrella, reached across Rickey Bayard, took my hand in both of hers, and smiled warmly. "Hugh, I'm Nora, and I am very happy to meet you. Welcome. I hope this is the start of a rewarding time for you. Hermann says quite flattering things about you."

Nora's voice was quiet and warm. When she spoke, even her declarative sentences ended with a rise in pitch, as if there was a question mark after every statement. The effect was to make Nora sound as if she was unsure of herself and eager to please.

There was something else: Nora apparently could not hear or pronounce the "th" sound, a trait common to people from Ireland or Wales. Both her voiced and unvoiced "ths" sounded like softly-inflected "d's" or "t's": *"I hope dis is duh start of a pleasant dime for you? Hermann says quite flattering tings about you?"*

In a soft, breathy voice that mimicked Nora's, Rickey, her umbrella cocked back so that it didn't get tangled up with Nora's, said, "Hugh? I'm Rickey? And I tink you are...probably duh funniest-looking human being I have ever seen?"

"Mind your manners, Rickey," said Nora.

Behind me, Hermann guffawed "I warned you, Hugh. This is the way it's going to be."

I smiled at Rickey. "Funny ha-ha, or funny peculiar?"

Rickey cocked her head, furrowed her brow, and began slapping one hand theatrically against her hip. She stopped imitating Nora, and her voice took on a steely edge. "We don't get many Aboriginal Australians in Cecil County. Are you going to try to play the father figure?"

"You've got a father. My job is to manage the farm, not manage you. Still, I will be living here, and we will be seeing a lot of each other from now on. Ours is an unusual situation,

Rickey, and I am going to do everything I can to make it work for both of us."

"Well," said Rickey, slapping her hand on her thigh again, "*that* should be interesting." Then she spun on her heel and walked back into the house. Nora moved to apologize. I put on my brightest, most reassuring smile. "Nora, no need. Hermann briefed me on our way down from New York. I think I know what I'm getting myself into."

Nora Dadmun covered her face with her palms and pulled her hands slowly down her face, distorting her features as if they were modeling clay. Her large port wine birthmark was revealed for a moment, and she shook her hair back into place to cover it. She lifted her head wearily.

"Oh, no you don't, Hugh," said Nora. "No, sir."

❂   ❂   ❂

HERMANN CLOSED THE LAST LEDGER VOLUME AND PLACED IT ON THE top of the stack of files, books and other ledgers lying in front of him on the desk. He stood, rested his weight on his hands next to this pile of facts and figures, lifted his head to fix me in his gaze.

"So that's it," he said with evident relief. "We've been through it all. Everything's here: farm operations and P&L, household ledger for the last umpteen years, my investment portfolio, tax returns and preparation notes, bank records, trust distribution documents, correspondence with my dipshit relatives in Munich. Anything you can't find, just call Augie Pabst in Elkton. He's got almost everything on his computer. If you want to hire him for accounting services, feel free. There's also a complete medical file in Rickey in that maroon binder. All the shrinks, the docs, her whole developmental plan. Which hasn't worked, by the way."

He stepped from behind his desk, gestured for me to have a seat in his large burgundy leather chair. "What is it pilots say when handing over control to another pilot? 'You've got the airplane.' Well, Hugh, you've got the airplane. Going forward, except in the broadest terms, I don't want to have to trouble myself with my finances. I just want you to keep me rich, keep me well-stocked with walking-around money and funds for all my purchases, take all the concerns about this goddamned estate off my shoulders. I'm tired of all the bullshit, and I can afford to walk away.

"And I am going to walk away now. Away to a life of my own pleasures and devices. I wish not to be called, contacted, tracked, chased, hounded, sued, or indicted. Your job is to make that wish come true. Do that, and you will have, if not a warm friend, at least an intensely loyal employer. I know how to give thanks."

I seated myself: clearly it is what I was supposed to do. Hermann walked toward the door of the study and was surprised to find Rickey standing there, absently scratching her forearm, listening, silently and intently, to everything we'd been saying. "Guten Tag, Ulricke," Hermann said as he brushed by her. "Guten Abend, Vati," replied Rickey. *Good day, Rickey. Good afternoon, Father.* When Hermann was gone from the room, she added, "Arschlocht." *Asshole.*

Rickey ambled across the room in her strange mechanical gait and seated herself across the desk from me. She was wearing photochromic sunglasses, the kind that change color in response to the intensity of ambient light. Right now, in the relatively dark study, they showed only a mild tint, and I could see Rickey's eyes behind the copper-toned lenses. She was fastening me with what I'm sure she thought was a steely gaze. A pair of headphones with enormous black ear cups circled her neck. The plug and connection wire draped across her chest in a sweeping loop, making her look like she was wearing a bandolier of ammunition.

"Didn't know you spoke German," I said.

"You have to in order to be a real Bayard," Rickey said dismissively.

I found her intensity unnerving. Her appearance, too. Her age seemed indeterminate, indeterminable. She could have been twelve, could have been thirty. Her skin was pale, almost translucent, her hands and arms heavily veined. Her collarbones protruded, her breasts didn't. Her hair was wild and red.

"So, I wonder what else Hermann hasn't told you about me," she said coldly.

"We discussed the basics of your care, feeding and maintenance, but we did not talk about you personally."

"You make me sound like a dog that has to be kenneled."

Oh, shit. Now I have put her on the defensive. I spoke softly, deliberately. I needed to calm her, not alarm her. "Bohemia Manor Farm is hardly a kennel. We talked about you in the way your father wants to talk about you—from the perspective of my employment and my responsibilities. He pretty much danced around the personal details. Said I should get to know you myself, without being influenced by his opinions."

"Smartest thing he's said in his whole fucking life," spat Rickey. "And please don't refer to him as my father. That's a disagreeable fiction. From now on, just call him Hermann, if you've gotta call him anything at all."

"Wow," I said. "That's harsh."

"Get used to it," she replied. "That's the way I am. Nora calls me rude, I call myself a truth-teller. You'll see soon enough. Now, if you want to know the 'official 'version of the way I am, Mr. Hugh Ullam, just read everything in that maroon binder in the middle of the stack there. That's the official Ulricke Bayard playbook. It's all there, all the physical exams and the mental exams and the intelligence tests and the poking and prodding and 'how do you feel about that?' questions. All the progress reports reporting no progress, at least in the opinion of all the great experts. Bunch of garbage, all generated for Hermann's edification at the cost of enormous pain to me."

"You've read it?"

"Every word."

"What did you think?"

"All that crap doesn't describe anybody I know. It's all so cold and distant and almost totally lacking in empathy, just like the nerds who wrote it. It all makes me sound like an autistic zombie."

I knew exactly how she felt. Pictures of my childhood at Akers flashed in my mind: Billimoria with her clipboard, clicking her ballpoint in and out. The fat electroshock tech shoving the red bite-piece between my teeth. The prissy agent from Children, Youth and Families who turned his back when I begged for help. These flashes were upsetting, because here, years later, they threatened to disarm me, disable me. I felt my gates close, my walls come up.

Rickey did not seem to notice my discomfort. She was not looking at me; she had her eyes squeezed tight shut and was shaking her head mechanically, left to right, left to right.

Everything those reports say about my 'flat affect' and 'diminished emotional range' is just a crock. I got plenty of affect, plenty of emotional range. You'll see."

"You sound like a...complicated person, Rickey." God, I sounded so pompous, so patronizing. *Why in the world was I talking like that?*

"Bet your ass. Think it's my job to be simple?"

"I don't know what your job is, Rickey."

"My job is to learn stuff and be left alone. Why is that so hard for neurotypicals to understand?"

"What's a neurotypical?" I asked.

"Anyone who isn't autistic. You know, 'normal' people."

Now Rickey opened her eyes and looked hard at me. "So, let's cut to the chase. Are you going to send me away? Pack me off somewhere?"

Taken aback, I almost said, "Why would I do that?" But I knew the better answer. I looked firmly into those frightened eyes opened wide behind the tinted sunglasses. "Absolutely not."

"Hermann wants to be rid of me."

"Hermann wants to be rid of the pain you two cause each other. But Rickey, he's going to be the one doing the traveling. You're staying here."

She relaxed, unclenched her palms. "I was afraid you'd think the easiest thing to do would be to send me away."

"Rickey, I am not looking for the easiest way. I'm looking for the best way."

"Talk is cheap, Mr. Hugh Ullam. My mother bailed on me.

My father has long since given up on me. Who's to say you won't?"

"*I say*. That's not what I came here for. I came here to manage Hermann's business affairs, and that's what I'm going to do. I'm not a social worker, Rickey. I'm not your judge, I'm not your jury. I just want to settle in and get along with everybody, okay?"

"You're Nora's boss. You call all the shots. Why shouldn't we be afraid of you?" I was floored at the notion of me being in charge of other peoples' lives. *What an utterly novel notion!*

"Rickey, when I was growing up, I went through more shit than you will ever know, and for my whole life I have been pretty isolated. Just like you in many ways. I'm not looking to repeat that here. I just want a calm, stable life, okay? So why don't you give me a break?"

Rickey smirked. "See? You're already getting impatient with me."

"Rickey, are you testing me? Well, here's my bottom line. You know you can trust Nora, and I will prove to you that you can trust me. May not always be pleasant, but we will always have your best interests in mind."

"Yeah, well, I trust Nora, although she always has her own agenda. The jury's out on you, Hugh."

⚙ ⚙ ⚙

RICKEY WALKED INTO THE LIBRARY AS I WAS DEEPLY IMMERSED IN the maroon binder. She came over to the desk where I was seated and lifted the binder out of my hands. She riffled through the tabs and stopped at a tab about halfway through.

"Here," she said. "Read this."

"I have."

"Learn anything?"

"I learned that you have synesthesia, which might help explain the unusual way your brain works."

"Have you ever met anyone whose senses all blend together?"

"As a matter of fact, I have."

"Tell me about them."

I felt like I had been handed a grenade whose pin was pulled. "No," I said flatly. "Other people don't need to be part of this conversation."

I had been synesthetic ever since that horse fell on my head. I knew its costs and benefits. Synesthetic people have blended senses. They see numbers as colors or shapes. They smell sounds. They see noises. When it comes to computations, even now I am amazed at how effortlessly sights, color, sounds, and even smells spin and whirl and then automatically converge to screen the correct answer up before my eyes. Always the correct answer. Synesthesia comes in handy if you're an accountant.

My own synesthesia is not a "gift" I divulge, because doing so always makes people relate to me strangely, makes them wonder if I can read their minds. Looking at Rickey Bayard, I decided against self-disclosure, unsure how Rickey would use the knowledge that we were wired much the same.

"But I am familiar with synesthesia, yes."

"Then you know how I do all my math tricks. No computation, I just sit back and watch the numbers turn to colors and reform automatically into the correct answer. 'Look! She's a savant!' It's magic. I love my synesthesia."

Rickey shifted in her chair, changed gears, handed the maroon binder back to me. "Okay, I went first. I've told you about me. Now it's your turn. Tell me all about the great Hugh Ullam."

Again, I said no, gently, but firmly. Rickey recoiled in surprise. "First you say that you just want to fit in. Now you're playing the mystery man?"

"I'm sorry, Rickey, but self-disclosure comes hard to me. Over the years, I've been taught the hard way that revealing too much information can be dangerous, tips the scales against me, turns me into a victim. Let's just take it slowly, okay?"

"I didn't think this getting-to-know-you thing was a competition." Her voice dripped with sarcasm.

"It's not, and I am not trying to be difficult, Rickey. You will get to know me through my actions, and soon you will learn what

I told you is true, that I am trustworthy. That's basically all you need to know at this point. That you can trust me."

Ricky had paled. I suspect she was afraid she had divulged too much, ceded advantage. She popped to her feet, whispered, "Fuck you, Ullam," and marched toward the door. Her departure left a slight vacuum in the room, a rush of air departing after her, a little zing of static electricity.

I spoke out loud: "Man, this is going to be a trip."

⚙ ⚙ ⚙

NORA, GARBED IN A FESTIVE YELLOW SUN DRESS, WAS FILLETING A

monkfish, kind of dancing around the cutting board, slicing adroitly at its insides and outsides. I sit down across from her.

"I would welcome a little help, Nora. I'm worried that I'm not connecting with Rickey. I wonder if you can give me a short course on 'Rickey Bayard 101.' At this point, some basic do-this-don't-that principles would be very helpful."

Nora shook her head ruefully. "What? You really think it's that simple? Just get the Cliff's Notes version and ace the exam? Well, I've got news for you."

I raised my hands in defense, in protest. "I'm only trying to…"

Nora interrupted me sharply. No soft-spoken uptalk now. Nora was *pissed*.

"I have spent years working to understand Rickey, to get along with Rickey. Not to be her friend, because Rickey doesn't do friends, but to be her advocate. I've worked with all the 'experts' to try to put the pieces together, and that has proved to be a fool's errand. I've spent endless hours trying to build a relationship with Rickey and ease her pain and teach her some social skills. It's exhausting, Hugh. And now you waltz in here thinking that a 'short course' is all you need? God, are you ever in for a surprise."

"Hey, I'm just trying to get some traction, Nora. I'm not taking you or everything you do for granted. I just need an initial grounding…"

"There is no 'initial grounding!' No dipping your toe in the water. When you signed up with Hermann, you signed up for a deep dive, Hugh. Unless you intend to ignore Rickey and just play accountant, it's time for you to dive.

"You want a 'short course?' Here's your 'short course:' there is no owner's manual for Rickey Bayard, no guidebook for navigating her intellectual genius, her autism, her Asperger's Syndrome, her synesthesia, her hypersensitivities, her isolation, her constant pain. The only way to learn to live with Rickey Bayard is to live with Rickey Bayard's gifts and handicaps up-close and personal. Forget about diagnoses and treatment plans and all that warm and fuzzy bullshit about 'maximizing potential.' You're going to have to shit or get off the can, Hugh. Either just check out on this troubled child like her parents did or get involved. It's that simple."

She paused, out of breath. Her eyes still flashed.

"Holy smoke," I said quietly. "Did I deserve that?"

Nora took a cleansing breath. "You're right. You did not deserve this, did not ask for this, because you had no way of knowing what you were getting yourself into. Obviously, you touched a nerve. But Hugh, when it comes to 'do's' and 'don'ts, 'you're going to have to build your 'do's' with Rickey on your own, create your own relationship with her. Won't work to piggy-back what I do because you're not me."

Nora marched on. "As for 'don'ts,' okay, there are a couple of things you must know. First, don't think that you can 'fix' Rickey Bayard, Hugh. She's not in neurological or psychosocial rehab. Everything you see about her is permanent. Yes, she is mastering better social skills, but this is not insight-driven growth. These are routines she's rehearsing, rote behaviors that respond to specific triggers.

"Sometimes Rickey can masquerade quite successfully as a little adult. At times, you're going to think that she is witty, funny way beyond her years. But that's either because she has memorized something someone has told her is funny or because she unknowingly says something that is clever. She does not basically understand irony or humor. That means she really doesn't get her own jokes, so there's no follow-up, no continuity. Just one-liners."

I found myself resenting Nora's patronizing tone. It sounded like she was trying to build biases, to fog my lenses. I was not at all sure I could take what she was saying about Rickey at face value.

"Her appearances can be very deceiving," Nora continued. "Just when you think you can relate to her on an adult level, she'll revert to being a little id-creature, driven by her impulses, emotionally totally out of control. You'll get used to being screamed at, Hugh.

"You'll also see that Rickey often gets fixated on detail and little repetitive rituals, her routines and rat-runs. Don't mess with those.

"A lot of autistic kids do repetitive behaviors to stimulate or calm themselves. Neurologists call it 'stimming.' These days, Rickey has only one notable stimming behavior. And that happens only when she is really frightened. If Rickey starts head-banging, Hugh, you have to intervene immediately, because when she loses control, she slams her head against things. Fortunately, that doesn't seem to be happening as often anymore."

Nora was clutching her arms across her chest, as if experiencing, or re-experiencing, some intensely unpleasant memory.

"Then, there's her hypersensitivities. Rickey's senses punish her, and I mean, like, real pain. Constant discomfort. She is extremely photosensitive. That's why she wears sunglasses all the time. Also, loud, or sudden sounds trigger a violent startle response, make her cover her ears, make her cry out. That's why the headphones. And she has such an overdeveloped reaction to touch that she will take a swing at you if you inadvertently brush up against her or try to hold her hand. She says, 'touch burns.' You've got to be careful about that. No touching, no hugging, not if you know what's good for you."

Now Nora smiled and inhaled deeply, like a children's storyteller turning a page.

"I'm sure Hermann has told you that she really is a genius,

right? They can't measure her IQ. Don't try to match wits with her; she'll outthink you every time. It's like Rickey has special circuits in her brain that spark these enormous mental leaps. You'll be having a fairly normal conversation with her, and suddenly *whoosh!* she's just way out there, out in some other universe. And when Rickey goes out into hyperspace, sometimes she just stays there. She'll be totally oblivious to you or what's going on around her. Don't try to pull her back. She'll just go ballistic on you.

"One last thing. Her recent medical exams suggest that Rickey is going to go through puberty early. God, what a treat that's going to be, watching the effect of a huge hormonal dump on all her other behaviors. Some fun, hunh?"

"It's okay. I asked for it."

Nora gave a wan smile. "No. No, you didn't. As I told you out in the driveway, you don't know everything you're getting into at Bohemia Manor Farm. I'm sure Hermann didn't warn you, at least not fully. After all, he really wanted you to come, so naturally he wouldn't say anything to scare you away."

I sensed that Nora had been trying to wear me down, trying to overwhelm me. Now maybe she thought she had gone too far, broken the camel's back, because both her expression and her voice softened.

"There is a bottom line with Rickey, Hugh. Consistency, predictability, stability. These aren't just important to Rickey, they're essential to Rickey. So, stay calm. If you overreact, Rickey will overreact. When things get out of control, Rickey gets out of control."

Later, as I replayed this conversation in my mind, I wondered if I had just learned more about Rickey or more about Nora.

6

Job Interview

"MISTER SLETLAND."

"Mister Ullam."

"I'm happy with Hugh," I said.

"Tryg's fine with me."

We shook hands and sat down across from one another at the card table in the south end of the living room.

How to capture Trygve Sletland's appearance? Obviously Nordic, but there was more. There was...*something unusual.* He was totally and completely "put together," like he had been "detailed" by one of those auto service places that washes and waxes your car. Tryg Sletland radiated attention to detail. *Impeccable.*

His open-necked off-white shirt was heavily starched. His watch was a simple Seiko—no chronograph, no diver's dial, just a basic silver watch with a white face and a black leather band. His gray flannel slacks—pleated, heavy material, a "fine hand," as a tailor would say—were sharply creased. His shoes were shined and unscuffed. I couldn't tell if he was fit, but he was trim, and he had good posture. His smile was relaxed, his gaze direct but not confrontive. He was, I supposed, in his early 40's. When he spoke, he limited his syllables, talking in short sentences, speaking in short staccato bursts of sound. He communicated as if he was trying not to use up too much air. I liked him immediately.

"So, welcome to Bohemia Manor Farm," I said.

"So, it is a farm, then."

"Well, yes. We are very much a working farm, a profitable going concern. We contract with a variety of tenant farmers for a variety of crops. It's a sizable operation. What did you think it was?"

Tryg looked a bit embarrassed. "Well, I didn't know, you see. If I may say so, your ad was pretty vague about what the position was really about. 'Rural facilities management' could mean a whole lot of things. Warehouses, marinas, schools, strip malls—they all can be rural. If I had known this was a farming-related position, I would have written you a somewhat different application letter that emphasized different things. Sent you a different resume. I would have highlighted different things. Talked more about my farming experience."

"Well, this position definitely is heavy on farm management. Does that rule you in or out?"

"Oh, it rules me in. Big time. But before I talk about my qualifications, can I ask you something?"

"Fire away," I said.

"Why did you post your ad—and such a vaguely-worded ad at that—in a job-posting board for ex-convicts? Did you advertise elsewhere, as well? Farm journals, maybe?"

"No. Just there."

He looked at me curiously. Raised his eyebrows and cocked his head.

"Fair question. Tryg, I believe I have a unique situation here. So, even before screening for relevant expertise, I'm screening for a certain kind of personality. For character. This position will reward extreme loyalty—the kind of loyalty a convicted felon would likely feel if someone offered him respectability, stability, security, and a relatively hefty paycheck. Perhaps for the rest of his life. I wrote the ad that way because I wanted to see what kind of responses I would get. What kind of people I would attract.

I could always weed out candidates who didn't fit the bill. You know—hardened criminals, moral failures, like that."

He threw back his head and laughed. "Wow. That's heavy."

"Tryg, in most job interviews, first the interviewer screens for relevant skills and experience, then, if the applicant makes it through the screen, they turn to the 'soft' issues of 'fit' and motivation. For reasons I'll explain, I'm going to do it in reverse. Is that okay with you?"

"Well, it's your interview," he said matter-of-factly. "You can organize it any way you prefer."

I picked up his resume, glanced at the most recent entry on the first page.

"It's courageous to list your...tenure...at Allenwood State Prison right at the front here, but most people would tell you to take it off. It's not really an occupational qualification, they'd tell you."

"I didn't want to have to explain a fourteen-month gap in my employment history."

I burst out laughing. "Oh, so you thought it was easier to explain a felony conviction than a gap in your career?"

"It states the truth. Brings a thorny issue front and center. I'm okay with that. Take me as I am, or don't take me."

"And that kind of candor is why you're sitting here today."

He shrugged.

"May I continue?" I said.

He nodded.

"So, what were you in for?" I asked.

"New York state charged it as negligent homicide. When they flipped my case to Pennsylvania, they gave it their name, involuntary manslaughter. Same thing. State charge, not federal. I pled."

"What did they give you?

"Eleven-and-a-half to twenty-three months. Served fourteen months at Allenwood, minimum security. The country club. You heard of the place: no rapes and you can order your hamburgers medium-rare."

I laughed again, then got serious. "Felony record, of course."

"Oh, yeah. But that's not the worst part. Neither is the fact that my then-wife finished a divorce in record time while I was in the can. I don't give a damn about her at this point. This was all her fault, after all. No, the worst part is that the felony rap means I'm immediately screened out of consideration for any job where I might make a good living. Can't use my certification as a jet aircraft mechanic because airlines ban people with felony records. Can't be a bank teller. Can't even be a security guard, for Christ's sake. I honestly hadn't realized what a career killer the felony conviction would be. The fact that it was a manslaughter rap just makes it worse. People worry that I'm an axe-murderer."

"Are you an axe-murderer?" I asked.

Now it was Tryg's turn to laugh. "Jesus, you are direct, aren't you? No, Hugh, I am not murderous in any way. This 'involuntary manslaughter?' Wasn't even in the heat of passion. Wasn't even a fight. My living room. Third time I'd found him in my home. Not even punches thrown. He pushes me, I push him back. He trips, hits his head on the edge of the desk. Just above the ear. Freak thing. Massive skull fracture. Died within hours, uncontrollable swelling. But he sure did die, and Elissa was happy to paint me to the cops as an out-of-control crazy man."

"Sounds like an accident to me. Or maybe self-defense. Why did they take you down so hard?"

"Dead guy's family had a reputation to protect in the community and the political connections to protect it. Elissa's uncle is a federal judge. I hired a lawyer, good guy, and he says, 'Champ, welcome to the land of the stacked deck. Don't spend a lot of money on a fruitless defense. Take your lumps and then get on with your life.' So that's what I'm trying to do, Hugh."

"Well, if I don't have to worry about being murdered in my bed, do you have any weaknesses or vices that I should worry about, Tryg?"

He paused just long enough to suggest that he was seriously pondering how best to answer the question.

"Hopefully without sounding like I'm tap dancing here, I can say with a straight face that I have no disqualifying vices, Hugh. My worst weaknesses, if you want to call them that, are that I am an introvert, that I have been called a 'neat freak,' and, to most people I probably seem like pretty boring company. Lots of stuff goes on inside that doesn't show to the people outside. It's my style, but I don't regard it as a weakness."

If he had been watching carefully, he would have seen my fists clench momentarily.

"Maybe your extreme candor is a weakness," I said.

"Maybe. Maybe not," Tryg replied. "Not to me, anyway."

I let that answer hang in the air for a long time, then switched gears.

"Let's say I am convinced that you're trustworthy. And very, very discreet. Let's talk about farming. Are you just a farmer or truly a farm operations manager?"

"Both," said Tryg, smiling. "Hugh, if all aspects of farm operations—and not *rural facilities management*—are really what you're interested in, you just lucked out big time. As it says on the second page of my resume, I was raised on a family-owned farm in Neshkoro, Wisconsin. We were a Conagra affiliate, meaning it was a mega-farm, not a mom-and-pop farm. Twenty-two hundred acres under cultivation. Crew of twenty-two, not including my father. Tons of heavy machinery and irrigation equipment. State of the art, big bucks to buy and maintain.

"We ran a top-notch operation, Hugh. I know the farm part and the managing people part. I know crops, I know seeds and seasons, I know farm markets. I know loans and costs and profits. But most important, I just know how to manage things, keep every damned detail under control. I am possibly the best organized person you will ever meet. In Neshkoro, we were classic Midwestern hicks, Hugh, but we made a *lot* of money."

Now I was the one grinning broadly. *Could I really be this lucky?*

"So why aren't you in Neshkoro, Wisconsin making a lot of money?"

He shrugged. "In a word, *Dad*. Without going into a lot of

unnecessary detail, let's just say that when I moved to Milwaukee to get my MBA at Marquette, Dad knew I'd never be back."

"So, what you're saying is that for the farming operations management job I have here, you'd be competent, but not motivated."

"Obviously, my circumstances have changed. I assure you, if I come to work here, motivation will not be an issue."

"Tryg, when I sent you the directions for getting to Bohemia Manor, did you happen to do any research on this place? Any chance you know who Hermann Bayard is?"

Tryg shook his head. "No idea."

"Bohemia Manor is an ancestral estate now owned by Hermann Bayard. If you've ever heard of Bayer aspirin, you've heard, at least indirectly, about Hermann Bayard. You could say he's the American black sheep of a very, very wealthy family in Bavaria. That is, Southern Germany."

Tryg cocked his head, pressed his steepled hands more firmly together. "Is Hermann Bayard very, very wealthy too?"

I had to laugh. "No, Hermann Bayard is merely...very wealthy. I am Hermann's accountant, financial manager, and general manager. Also shield and protector. I have full legal authority and power of attorney to do anything I want around here. As long as he has enough spending money for his own pursuits, Hermann doesn't seem to care how I spend his money. So as far as your potential employment goes, he is relevant, but I am...*instrumental*. It's my show, Tryg. I call the shots."

"But here's a farm to run, and I am an accountant, not a farmer. Also, I am a person of color. And Australian. That's a tricky combination here in Cecil County, Maryland. On one recent occasion I heard myself described as 'that weird nigger with the goofy smile.'"

I showed him the smile.

Tryg sat up in his chair, nodded knowingly.

"So, you need a beard."

"No, I need a loyal competent overseer of farm operations who also knows when and how to serve as my beard."

"Okay," he said.

"Okay what? Think you're game?"

"Okay," said Tryg.

He really did have a most agreeable smile.

I moved to close the deal. "Housing is in the guest cottage or in the main house, your call—but you must live somewhere on the farm. You'll have use of the farm's cars. Free gas from our tanks. Absolutely terrific meals, courtesy of the magnificent Nora Dadmun. Cable TV. Also, if you want, I can serve as your investment advisor. I'm very good, if I do say so myself."

I paused for perhaps ten seconds. I wanted to sound *seriously* serious. "And perhaps of particular importance to you, Trygve Sletland, I offer you respect. Where else are you going to get all that?"

Tryg turned his head away, looking out the French doors down toward the Bohemia River. I thought maybe he might be tearing up. He turned back to me and, his voice husky, said "How's the pay?"

"How 'bout a base of a buck-forty with an annual cost of living adjustment? Health coverage, full benefits, blah, blah, blah."

He caught his breath. "Well, can't hardly argue with that."

"I can write you an offer letter, if you want."

"No need."

"One more thing, and it's a big deal."

From my expression and tone, Tryg knew I was in deadly earnest here. "In case I haven't made it abundantly clear, discretion, confidentiality, and even secrecy are of highest importance to me. We are doing nothing illegal, but I don't ever want to play defense. Ever, if I can help it. We will keep to ourselves, and we will keep our business to ourselves. Can you do that? Will you do that?"

He scratched the underside of his nose with his thumbnail. He pulled his upper teeth hard over his lower lip. He coughed softly.

"Can you do that?" I repeated.

"Me? Mr. Introvert? No worries, Mate, as you Ozzies would say. Count me in. From day one, you will see that I can be trusted."

7

Bunnies in the Grass

WE CALLED OUR LITTLE SELF-CONTAINED COMMUNITY THE HOLE IN the Wall Gang, a reference to the notorious bunch of bank robbing outlaws who lived in a cave in Johnson County, Wyoming in the wild west days. Nora, Tryg and I knew we had a good thing going, and, to the greatest extent possible, we were careful not to blow our cover or put our arrangement at risk. We strove to fly under the radar, attract no attention, make no waves, operate as independently from the outside world as possible, and breathe easy. In this we largely succeeded.

The basic, although unspoken, principle of our *modus vivendi*—our tacit arrangement for coexisting in peace—was to stay politely and respectfully superficial. Except for Rickey, who was clumsy about boundaries, we were careful to avoid emotional trespass, to approach border crossings only at agreed-upon checkpoints. We operated in the present tense. That is, we confined ourselves to the here-and-now and pretty much steered clear of historical research, archeological digs, or trying to unearth channels of common life experience.

We settled into a comfortable division of labor. Tryg, whom we jokingly labeled "Mr. Normal," was the outside guy, both running the farm and serving as our umbilicus to the world outside the farm. Nora was fully occupied cooking for all of us and tending to all of Rickey's many needs, including overseeing her progress through the graded home-schooling curriculum of the highly respected K12 International Academy. Initially Nora also cleaned the house, an impossible additional burden on her time and energy. I promptly hired a cheerful Brazilian woman, Rosa De La Torre, to run the Hoover, dust the artwork, iron the sheets, and keep us all dressed in clean clothes. Her twice-weekly visits and lengthy to-do lists were supervised by the meticulous Mr. Sletland, and the house always looked impeccable. You could eat off the floor.

I, of course, was the numbers guy: dollars, budgets, ledgers, ' taxes, bookkeeping. I appropriated Hermann Bayard's den, turned it into my private business office, and could be found working there pretty much nine-to-five every day.

While never shouldering primary responsibility for acting as Rickey's caregivers, Tryg and I got better and better at distracting Rickey, getting her off Nora's back and modulating her more excessive periods of acting-out. Once she was given some time to breathe, Nora's tense and beleaguered demeanor eased somewhat, and a witty and sensitive side of her personality began to peep out from behind the protective curtain of hair over her face.

Tryg's thing with Rickey was to get her to build things with him. Electronic things were high on the list, and they spent hours out in Hermann's unused airplane hangar, tinkering with circuit boards and soldering guns. As for me, I came to enjoy engaging Rickey in idea jousts, in which I was dazzled at the astonishing breadth of her knowledge about a myriad of subjects. She relished the give and take of ideas, our frequent battles of wits, our word games. I usually lost. Fortunately for my self-esteem, Rickey never took this competition personally, never seemed to try to hurt or humiliate me. Her frequent insults were merely ritual banter, and we both knew it.

Gradually, I came to believe that Nora's "101 Lecture" about life with Rickey was off the mark. Rickey was not simply a talking dog responding to the pokes and strokes of operant conditioning. Nor was she a rigid, emotionless "locked-in case." It became clear to me that her inner emotions, like mine, were muffled under layers of self-protective insulation.

❁   ❁   ❁

NORA DADMUN WAS NOT BIG ON SELF-DISCLOSURE. SHE JUSTIFIED this on the basis that I was not either, sort of a 'you hide yours, I'll hide mine' standoff. After months at Bohemia Manor, here is exactly everything I had learned about Nora Dadmun: She was born in Cardiff, Wales. Moved to Whitewater, Wisconsin when she was eight. Whitewater, coincidentally, is about fifteen miles from the Sletland family's mega-farm in Neshkoro. Nora was the younger of the two daughters of a cold and self-righteous father who owned three seed mills. Behind his back, the whole family called him Captain Ahab. Nora was laughed at in school because of her birthmark. Her sister was perfect. Nora graduated from the Fanny Farmer Cooking School in Boston, that's why she cooked so well, although she did not really enjoy cooking. Her perfect sister was trained at the Cordon Bleu in Paris. She no longer cooked anything.

Nora never discussed her earlier career with me. "Not relevant," she said.

In hiring a cook, Hermann Bayard had staged a contest among five applicants, three of them restaurant chefs. They each presented Hermann and Marte with a variety of dishes— breakfasts, lunches, and some quite exceptional evening meals. Nora won this contest easily and was installed in Bo Manor's massive kitchen, a restaurant-grade stainless steel palace Hermann had recently renovated.

When Nora first came to the farm, Marte Bayard was still trying to figure out what to do with Rickey, who, at seven, was becoming an increasingly frustrating challenge. Marte began asking Nora to help out with Rickey's "activities of daily living," and gradually but steadily the entire mantle of childcare slid over on to Nora's shoulders.

Nora told me Marte went downhill from there. She became a sloppy drunk; fights with Hermann became frequent. One morning just after Rickey turned eight, Nora resolved to resign after Marte, juiced to the gills, stumbled into the kitchen, and stared at her at length. Finally, she said, "Jesus, Nora, ninety percent of you is just so beautiful. And the rest is just a complete train wreck. You are sickening to look at. Have you ever thought of just committing suicide?"

The next day, as Nora pulled out her luggage to pack, Marte took matters into her own hands, climbed into the Mercedes and left. Neither Nora nor Rickey ever saw her again. The divorce was completed by mail. Nora told me that a week after the divorce was finalized, Hermann placed thirteen million dollars into a Chase Manhattan Account, which Marte promptly cleaned out. Although, for various legal and accounting purposes, I have to tried to locate Marte Bayard since then, I can find no trace of her, in the United States or abroad. Marte simply took the money and ran.

❁   ❁   ❁

AFTER I HAD BEEN AT BOHEMIA MANOR ABOUT EIGHT MONTHS, WE had another add to staff as Tryg made another hire that would have later major unintended consequences. For him, particularly, but also for all of us.

Hermann Bayard had employed a yard service whose work was uniformly terrible. Bohemia Manor Farm always looked… unkempt, as if the yard work was never complete. Whatever equipment these clowns didn't break, they stole. Tryg promptly fired them, and their replacement was Simone Hadley and her younger brother Ray, late of Christchurch, New Zealand.

Simone was tall, blond, extroverted, with an infectious laugh and a droll sense of humor. She had studied landscape architecture at Victoria University at Wellington, then emigrated to the U.S.

after her parents moved back to England. At loose ends, Ray tagged along. Ray Hadley, nineteen, was dark-haired, shy, and soft-spoken, with a poet's soulful face, large solemn eyes, and the body of a mountain climber. I had no doubt that when he walked the aisles of Walmart, legions of adolescent girls swooned in his wake.

Upon arriving in the U.S., Simone saw the elegant estates in northeast Maryland as a land of opportunity. She took out a loan, bought an old pickup, a decrepit utility trailer and an antiquated golf course lawn mower, and began knocking on doors. She knocked on ours, Tryg answered, and the rest became history.

I was very pleased with Simone's landscaping work. Tryg soon became very pleased with Simone. She did not push or presume, but after a while it was not unusual for Simone and Ray to stay for dinner once or twice a week. Simone promised that she would not hold Tryg's obsessive-compulsive tendencies against him, nor the fact that I was Australian against me.

Nora also was quite taken with Simone and was pleased at how helpful she was in the kitchen. When Tryg and Simone soon became intimate, it was never in his room or elsewhere at Bo Manor. Tryg would simply tell me he was going to do a "sleep-over" at Simone's house in Galena, assuring me that he would be on the job first thing in the morning. He always was.

Young Ray, he of the somber mien and penetrating gaze, was a frequent presence, ghosting around in the background, polite and taciturn. We joked that Ray said all of about fifteen words a year. He made himself useful in various ways, always willing to run an errand or give Tryg a helping hand with machinery maintenance. He basically played for meals and tips, but he gave off an earnest, positive vibe, and we enjoyed having him around. Nora pronounced him "pretty serious, but a good kid."

Still, Nora and I worried: As Rickey roared into puberty, Ray could not take his eyes off her. Simone saw it too. At first, she would just smack Ray playfully across the back of the head. "Ray," she would say, "eyes front." Or "Thumper, what did your mother say to you?" These lighthearted warning signals soared over Rickey's head, but Ray got the point, blushing a telltale crimson that betrayed that he had been caught ogling once again.

Later, Simone got more serious. "Ray," she said in front of us more than once, "do not fuck up. You can be replaced. Do you hear me?"

Once, when Ray failed to acknowledge her, failed even to blush, Simone grabbed him by his shirt collar and thrust her face inches from his. "I said, *do you hear me?*" Ray lowered his head and nodded, embarrassed to be bawled out by his sister in front of us, embarrassed that his sneak peeks at Rickey had been detected again.

But Christ, who could blame him? Rickey Bayard had become the stuff of teenage boys' fantasies. Her tits, her ass, the ginger carpet that matched the drapes—all were on frequent display through her revealing clothing and uninhibited poses. Rickey had become gorgeous and sexy in a gaunt magazine-model kind of way. Ray was nineteen. Nora and I agreed: here there were dragons.

When it seemed that Simone's warnings might not be getting through, I volunteered to have a guy-talk with Ray about self-discipline and the perils of exploiting the vulnerable.

"Ray, let's take a walk."

Once we were outside and out of earshot of the women, I said, "do you know what *in loco parentis* means?"

"Hunh-unh."

"It means that someone stands in for the parents when the parents aren't around, has full authority for rules and discipline. At Bo Manor, that's me, when Hermann isn't here, which is almost always. Around here, when someone has to play the heavy, that's me. So please listen up, so this can be a short walk."

Ray's eyes grew big as saucers.

"Ray, with her revealing clothing and sensuous poses, a lot of which seem to be directed your way, I honestly don't know whether Rickey is consciously trying to flirt with you or is just oblivious to the vibes she's sending out. It doesn't matter which. Our rules about Rickey are the same either way.

"I do see that you have tried to play it cool, and I know it's not easy having Simone jerk your chain every time Rickey catches your eye."

Ray looked away. He did *not* like this conversation.

"So, let me make it simple. Here's where I, *in loco parentis,* lay down the law. Ray, you are, not now or ever, to regard Rickey as an object of sexual attention. I know she can be a turn-on, but you must never allow yourself to be turned-on, to wonder if there's romance in the air. Believe me, there's not. Rickey does not understand the idea of romance."

Ray was still looking away, so I slapped my fist into my palm. *"Never!"*

His head jerked up angrily. I put my hand up in front of his face to still his reaction. "I know what you're thinking, Ray. 'Yeah, yeah, yeah, I got all this.' You're thinking I'm beating up on you. But I need to draw the firmest possible line here. Rickey is off limits, now and in the future. It's not just that Rickey is underage, which of course she is right now. Even when Rickey reaches the age of consent, she will not be capable of granting meaningful consent. She is a vulnerable, socially handicapped person who does not know her own limits. So, you must provide the limits. This is a zero-tolerance policy, Ray. Nora and Tryg and I—and now, I think, Simone—are fiercely protective of Rickey. So, please, Ray, please. Be very vigilant, very careful in how you relate to Rickey."

⚙   ⚙   ⚙

AS FAR AS HOUSEHOLD GEOGRAPHY WAS CONCERNED, I TOOK THE large bedroom at the back of the third floor, the one with windows overlooking the river, and I found it both comfortable and comforting after the barren confines of my digs in Doobibla.

After Marte's departure, Nora Dadmun had decamped from the third floor to what had been the maid's quarters off the kitchen. Hermann had subsequently enlarged this space and converted it into a comfortable apartment with a private outside entrance. Given the choice of a furnished room over the garage, which would have given plenty of privacy, and a bedroom in the house, Tryg Sletland chose to take one of the remaining bedrooms on the third floor, leaving two vacant rooms between his room and Rickey's.

Rickey declined an agreeable guest bedroom on the second floor and joined Tryg and me on the third. "It feels safer to be with you two up here," she said. Her bedroom, at the south end of the hall, was spartan and dark. The windows were covered with double-lined curtains, generally kept closed, that blocked all light, and the bulbs had been removed from the ornate three-bulb ceiling fixture. All illumination came from a dim bedside lamp. There were no toys or dolls in Rickey's room, no pictures, or posters on the walls.

Many autistic people are compulsive organizers and neat freaks, using rigid environmental rituals as a means of maintaining a sense of control. They arrange things and line things up in neat columns and rows, becoming intensely uncomfortable if their sense of order is disturbed. This was not how Rickey maintained her space. The only thing that kept her room from being a typical adolescent disaster area was that she kept so few possessions in it. Hooks and shelves were pointless; most of what was in her room ended up on the floor.

Tryg Sletland couldn't stand to go near it.

⚙ ⚙ ⚙

WHEN HERMANN BAYARD PASSED THROUGH TOWN, AN OCCURRENCE that became increasingly infrequent, he found nothing to annoy or trouble him and pronounced himself satisfied. The farm's affairs and operations were in good order, the finances were well-attended, the house and grounds were in impeccable condition, his automobiles were in fine running order, and all his favorite foods and liquors were available in ample supply.

Only once did I risk querying Hermann about his lifestyle and his fractured relationship with his daughter. After a splendid

Nora dinner one night, Hermann and I were enjoying a fine brandy in the library. Man-to-man vibes coursed through the room, and I waded in.

"Hermann, can I ask you something?"

"Sure, Hugh, anything."

"What's *with* you? And what's with you and your daughter?"

Hermann eased himself slowly into an armchair, lifted his snifter to admire the warm chestnut glow of the VSOP. Then he cupped it in his hands to warm the brandy. Hermann's modulated voice, precise diction and firm sentence stops spoke of fine prep schools and excellent English teachers.

"You mean, why do I escape? I was not always an irresponsible derelict, Hugh. Before Rickey was born, Marte and I had a solid marriage. Compatible, good communication, all that. My autistic daughter changed that. Completely destroyed that. Rickey destroyed Marte, and Marte destroyed our marriage. Ever since Marte bailed out on us and left me to deal with Rickey on my own, I have felt... at loose ends."

"In my case, not only was I deprived of the love and company of a supportive wife, but I was cursed with...Rickey. Rickey's autism and all her other...traits...are made doubly cruel by the fact that as she has grown, her physical resemblance to Marte has become really eerie. Obviously, Marte's genes dominated the field, and mine ran and hid somewhere. These days, it's hard for me to even look at Rickey."

Hermann's self-pity annoyed me intensely. I, who had never had a family of any sort, simply could not relate to a person who described his flesh-and-blood as a curse, a person to be shunned simply because she looked like her mother. Now Hermann proceeded to make it worse.

"Forgive me for saying this: *I hate being around Rickey.* I know she's autistic. I know that she can't help what she is and how she behaves. But when I try to interact with her, I am just infuriated by all her anger and surliness and indifference to affection. Indifference to *me*.

"I guess I should feel guilty about saying this, but I really don't feel much of anything for Rickey anymore. I'm sure you think me hard-hearted. But so is my daughter. Rickey was eight when her mother abandoned her. Rickey appeared not to care that her mother had vanished. Marte was never discussed, never mourned, never missed. Me, I was hurting big time, but of course Rickey, who is absolutely incapable of empathy, provided no support. Me? I'm different from Rickey. I am not a strong enough man to love without being loved, Hugh. Can you understand that?"

I lifted myself from my chair, turned my back on Hermann, and walked over to the cold, long unused hearth. I kicked at an enormous, blackened andiron with my toe. I turned back to him.

"No, Hermann, actually I can't. Okay, so your need for love was unreciprocated when Marte left. Wasn't it pretty goddamned harsh to take out your pain on an emotionally- handicapped little girl?"

Hermann remained seated, dropped his head, and spread his hands in a *what-can-ya-do?* gesture.

"Well, actually she started it. When she was ten, Rickey looked at me one day, and I swear to God she said, 'Can't you all just leave me alone? I'm tired of being poked and prodded. I'm tired of people talking about me as if I am not there. You're rich. Make everybody leave me alone, Father. Can't you just hide me, make me disappear? If I can just have food, I can take care of myself better than anyone else can. Let me do that, and I'll let you off the hook. I will release you from all the responsibilities of being my father.' *I swear to God, Hugh, that is really what she said.* This was a ten-year old saying this, like she was calling my bluff.

"So, I called *her* bluff. I was angry. I admit I was very deeply hurt. So...I granted her wish. I just cut the strings, switched off the power, checked out. We have both been backed into our angry corners for a long time now. I cannot think of any way to reconnect. I guess I should be ashamed for saying this, but at this point, I don't want to. Reconnect, that is.

"Fortunately, I have enough money to make sure that all Rickey's physical and medical needs are met, and, of course, she has no emotional needs. I am very blessed to have found

Nora. She makes it possible to avoid institutionalizing Rickey. I investigated all the possible options and found that there are no facilities for people with Rickey's unique mixture of handicaps and gifts. Nora made it possible to grant Rickey's wish to live in splendid isolation at Bo Manor."

Hermann lifted his head and looked hard at me, his expression dead and distant.

"Is that enough for you, Hugh? I hope so because I would rather not talk about all this again."

8

Languages

I WAS SIPPING MY MORNING COFFEE AND ONCE AGAIN GAZING across the fields at the ever-lovely Bohemia River, at that moment gilded in the rising sun, as Rickey ambled into the kitchen. Nora had tried to talk with Rickey about her exhibitionism, and now Rickey was wearing an enormous gray hoodie and sweatpants. It looked like there was room for two in there. Her sleeves were pushed up and held with safety pins. Her muffled voice issued from the depths of the hood. It sounded like its coming from far back in a cave.

"Where's Nora?"

"She took the golf cart out to get the mail."

"But it's time for my breakfast, and my bacon isn't ready."

"She'll be back soon, Rickey. You'll get your daily bacon."

Rickey took her deep white cereal bowl from the antique glass-fronted cabinet, positioned it precisely in the middle of her place mat, measured the proper distance out from its rim—exactly three fingers width—and placed a soup spoon in perfect parallel with the edge of the place mat. She placed a paper napkin, folded diagonally in half, on the placemat crosswise above her bowl. It formed an arrowhead, pointing directly at me.

She took her special mug from the Rickey peg on the wall, shuffled over to the coffee maker—we have coffee flowing 24/7—and poured her precise portion, right up to where the purple stripe met the aqua stripe. She picked up the tiny crystal cream pitcher with both hands, like a surgeon lifting a kidney ready for transplant, and held it at eye level. I don't use cream, so the cream was exactly at the level Nora has poured it. Exactly where Rickey insists it be ready each morning at coffee time. Eight thirteen, Eastern time.

Next, she took a postal scale and placed it next to her cereal bowl. She centered her tin cereal loading cup in the middle of the scale. "Fifty-two," she said. The same number of grams it weighed, empty, every morning. Then she poured exactly thirty-nine grams of Kellogg's Sugar Frosted Flakes into the cup, followed by twenty-four grams of Kellogg's Grape Nuts. "One hundred fifteen. *Okay*," she murmured quietly. Now Rickey counted out fourteen blueberries from the dish Nora had left on the counter and dropped them one-by-one on top of her dry cereal, placing each carefully.

She picked up the milk pitcher, poised it above her cereal bowl, then stopped, evidently annoyed. She put the pitcher down and folded her hands in her lap.

"Don't mind me, Rickey," I said. "Dig in."

"I can't. Nora isn't here."

"You can't eat your cereal without Nora's supervision?"

"Fuck you, Hugh."

The screen door banged in the butler's pantry, and Nora breezed into the kitchen, riffling through the mail. "Hugh," she said. "The golf cart is really acting up. The meter says it has a charge, but its bucking and hiccupping like crazy. Will you have Tryg look at it?"

"Your wish is my command, mem-sahib."

Nora laughed and moved to the oven. She removed several ramekins of shirred eggs and a flat baking pan of bacon she had cooked earlier and weighted down with a tinfoil covered brick.

She poked the top of the eggs. "Perfect," she said. "Rickey, will you be trying eggs this morning?"

"I'd rather eat cow manure," said Rickey. "Just give me my bacon, so I can start my cereal."

"Your wish is my command," said Nora, and we both laughed. Rickey didn't laugh.

Nora took three flattened strips of bacon, cut each strip into three identical pieces, and placed them on a small flat plate so that none of the pieces touched another. She placed the bacon plate three inches to the left of Rickey's cereal bowl.

"Chow down," she said.

Watching Rickey eat was like watching the Japanese tea ceremony. Her moves were slow, deliberate, practiced. Each move had a controlled start, a full stop, and a pause before the next. She alternated: bite of bacon, spoonful of cereal, slurp of coffee. Inhale, exhale, repeat. As usual, she was murmuring to herself as she ate. Nora and I know this ritual must not be interrupted. It takes Rickey Bayard nine and a half minutes to consume her bacon, cereal, and coffee. No eggs. Ever. Rule breakers will be punished by verbal abuse.

As Tryg walked in and poured himself a cup of coffee, Nora lifted a large eleven-by-fourteen envelope from the stack of mail, read the mailing label and burst into a smile.

"Rickey, if this is what I think it is, you're in for a happy surprise."

"I hate surprises."

"Oh, you'll like this one, I think."

Nora pulled out a sheaf of papers, flipped through them quickly. There was a thick report, also a beautifully hand-lettered certificate mounted on heavy framing stock and a personalized cover letter from the school's director in Oslo.

"What is all that?"

"It's your final report from the International Baccalaureate Correspondence Academy and your certificate of graduation. Congratulations, Rickey, you're a high school graduate. And the school director has some very nice things to say about your performance."

Nora handed Rickey the cover letter and Rickey read excerpts out loud. "Extraordinary achievement in STEM curriculum...blah, blah, blah...second-youngest person ever to receive certification from IB...blah, blah, blah...welcome to our distinguished international alumni ...blah, blah, blah. What's STEM?"

"That means science, technology, electronics and math courses," said Nora. "You blew STEM away, Rickey."

"Congratulations on that, Rickey," said Tryg. "Although I'm not surprised."

Rickey gestured at the papers in Nora's hand. "Those my grades, there?"

"Yep. Hugh, in Rickey's program they grade 'Superior,' 'High Pass,' 'Pass,' 'Low Pass,' 'Fail,'" and Incomplete. Rickey, your STEM courses were all Superior. Your English and social sciences courses were...not as high."

"Well, that figures," said Rickey disdainfully. "All that soft shit. Poetry. Modern European history. Novels about feelings. Essay questions. Not for this kid."

Nora waved the letter. "They say you've won an achievement award based on your STEM grades, which in your case is a fully-funded correspondence program, two semesters, from Drexel University in Philadelphia. You can choose mathematics, electronics, or computer science."

"No, thanks. I'll pass."

I was floored. "*What?* My God, Rickey! What could be better than that?"

"My own electronics lab down in the hangar. That would be better. I can teach myself better than Drexel can teach me. Give me a lab. I can always do Drexel later."

"I could help with that," Tryg ventured.

"Help with what, exactly?" I said.

"Well, Rickey and I have been talking about this. She's put together a list of electronics equipment she would like. I could source it for her, doesn't have to be brand new. There's a strong secondary market for stuff like that as new generations of technology come out."

This was moving pretty fast for me. "A...*lab*. Rickey, what are you going to do with an electronics lab?"

Rickey set her jaw defensively. "Stuff," she said.

"And Tryg, just how much is a lab like this going to cost Hermann?"

"Depends on who's selling, how old it is, like that," Tryg said. "A good set-up could run twenty, thirty thousand, even more. That's why I haven't mentioned this to you up 'til now."

"Well, if *that's* all!" I said dramatically, waving at the ceiling in a 'sky's-the-limit' gesture. "Well, okay, man, go for it. Rickey, let's call it a graduation present from your father."

"Let's not," said Rickey.

⚙   ⚙   ⚙

I HAD JUST COME BACK FROM DOING SOME KAYAKING UP THE FAR reaches of Bohemia River, and as I marched up the hill toward the house, Nora, animated and urgent, caught me on the patio while I was still soaked in sweat. "You gotta see this," she said, and shoved a newspaper under my nose. I sat down at the patio table, still toweling off.

"Okay, it's a *New York Times* crossword puzzle. From the looks of the handwriting, it's Rickey's work. I know she likes crosswords. Looks like she nailed this one."

"Look at the date," said Nora.

"Okay, it's yesterday's. So what?"

Nora shoved a second page under my nose. "This is today's puzzle page. There's the solution to yesterday's puzzle. Notice anything different?"

It took a moment to see her point, to compare Rickey's solutions with the *Times'* solutions. "The solutions are entirely different," I said.

"Sure are," laughed Nora. "Every single one. She solved the

puzzle using her own set of words. She came up with a whole alternative set of solutions, horizontal and vertical. Okay, now read the clues from yesterday, see if her solutions make sense, or if she was just cramming random words into the spaces or fudging the intersections."

"I don't get it."

"Here, look at this one. Their clue was 'skilled stripper.' Their answer was 'Gypsy Rose.' Rickey's answer was 'ecdysiast.' Her answer is actually better. All of her answers are like that. Think you could ever do that?"

I looked at a few more of the *Times'* clues, a few more of Rickey's answers. "Amazing," I said.

"I just spent an hour with a dictionary, looking up her words. Here, here, look at this one!" exclaimed Nora. "Their clue was 'Noted for Looney Tunes.' Their answer was 'Bugs Bunny.' You know what Rickey's answer was?"

I looked up Rickey's answer. "Theremin." I counted up the letters: seven for Bugs, seven for Rickey's answer.

"What's Theremin?"

"A theremin is an electronic musical instrument invented in 1920 by a Russian named Leon Theremin. It has two electrical fields, one for volume, one for pitch. You play it without touching it, you just wave your hands over it. The BBC has called it 'the strangest instrument ever invented.' Does this sound like Rickey, or what?"

❁   ❁   ❁

AS FAR AS SPOKEN LANGUAGE WENT, THE VARIOUS MEMBERS OF THE Hole in the Wall Gang talked and sounded very different from one another: Tryg's clipped sentences, Nora's careful, breathy uptalk, my polysyllabic verbosity – all resulted in a kind of communications Babel at Bohemia Manor. Then there was Rickey.

In her "normal" speech, Rickey alternated between pressured speech, when it seemed that she could not get the words out fast enough to keep up with her racing thoughts, and slow, almost painful-sounding articulation that made it sound as if she was doing simultaneous translation from some foreign language. Then we discovered that this is exactly what she is doing.

Rickey frequently sounded as if she was murmuring or muttering to herself; she was surrounded by a soft, constant and almost inaudible rustle of sound, a continuous, breathy rising and falling of tones and inflections.

This ever-present background noise came to annoy me. Several times I turned to Rickey and asked, "Did you want to say something, Rickey?" Each time she shook or lowered her head; one time she looked up and said, "No, not to you." Still the constant gentle hum continued. I raised the issue with Nora, she looked at me with smiling exasperation. "Why don't you just ask her, Hugh? Instead of carping or speculating, just ask her."

I was not sure this was a good idea. If Rickey's muttered "language" was an attempt to assuage emotional tension, a form of stimming, I worried that asking her about it would trigger a defensive firestorm, an urgent request that I fuck myself and leave her alone.

I finally found a way to ask her one afternoon when as I watched Rickey work through a bewilderingly complex mathematical problem. "Playing around," as she put it. Her answer, my calculator showed, was absolutely correct—down to five decimal places. Of course it was: that's synesthesia in action.

"My God, Rickey," I blurted, "your mind really is a marvelous thing."

"Why, thank you, Hugh. How kind of you to say that."

I knew this was a learned response, a product of Nora's constant tutelage on how to win friends and influence neurotypical people. With patient guidance and correction from Nora, Rickey had mastered a repertoire of stock phrases and could apply them more or less appropriately to interpersonal interactions. As she waded into adolescence, to some degree Rickey had learned to appreciate the effects, positive or negative, her speech and body language had on people. In this case, I considered her response to my compliment to be a high-order response. *Maybe Rickey is learning nuance.*

"Rickey, I notice that often while you are working or lost in thought..."

"I am never 'lost in thought,'" she snapped. "I always know exactly where I am."

"Excuse me. I have noticed that when you are deep in thought, you often seem to be speaking to yourself, but I can't understand what you were saying."

"Well, of course you can't. That's because it's *my* language. I am speaking to myself in my mother tongue. I do it all the time, as I am sure you are aware. I'm also aware that sometimes it pisses you off, but, well, tough darts."

So much for getting along with the neurotypicals.

"Does this language have a name?" I ask.

"Well, it doesn't to me, because it does not need a name. But I suppose you could call it...*Susurrus.*"

"That means whispering or rustling."

"Right," she says. "Doesn't it sound like that to you?"

"How long have you spoken Susurrus?"

"Since forever."

"How did you learn it?"

"Well, I made it, Hugh. I'm still making it."

"Is it random?"

Her face instantly reddened "Are you asking me if it's just gibberish? If I'm just sitting around muttering nonsense, if my language is just *noise*?"

"Whoa, Rickey. I am not insulting you—not intentionally, anyway. But you said you make it up as you go along. That sounds sort of random to me."

"That would only be true if the sounds had no meaning or if I forget things as soon as I create them. But I don't. I remember everything I add. This isn't any of your goddamned business, but I love my language. I *swim* in my language."

"Can you translate it into English?"

She shook her head in mock despair. "How prosaic, Hugh.

'Does it have a grammar?' you're going to ask. Does it have a vocabulary? How fucking predictable. It's *my* language. You, as a locked-down, self-involved person, should know better than to ask me a question like that. Susurrus is shaped by form and flow and situational context. Also, to some degree, by my perception of colors. Susurrus is like a painting of my mind, my world, not yours. It just gets bigger and more detailed and more colorful."

I'm not sure why I asked the next question. "Will you sing me a song in Susurrus? I don't want you to translate, I just want to hear it."

Rickey cocked her head and smiled at me. "There's hope for you, Hugh Ullam. Susurrus has only five tones, so in pitch you might think it resembles a chant more than music. But when I 'mutter,' as I've heard you and Nora ridicule it, I really am singing. Here, I will sing you a song, in this case, my origin song."

And so, Rickey sang, and it was quite haunting. Not beautiful, exactly, but somehow both soft and intense at the same time. It was a bit like hearing poetry read by someone who cares about it. I thought it sounded like Gaelic, with a continuous flow of sound and steady breathiness. Rickey's inhalations were undetectable, her exhalations long and fully voiced.

She stopped after about a minute. "How's that?"

"Well, it's really quite wonderful. What was that about?"

"It's about how hard it is to live in two worlds at the same time, how it makes your brain hurt. About all the many things that hurt, and how few things comfort and soothe." She paused, then looked at me intently and said, "Surely you must know about that, Hugh."

Nora and I decided to have Rickey's language aptitude checked out, engaging an expert in discourse analysis at Penn's Annenberg School of Communication to come to Bo Manor for an interview with Rickey. She acquiesced grudgingly: "But that's it. This is the last one. After this, no more tests, no more interviews, no more useless reports, or diagnostic summaries. I am what I am. You guys can just live with it."

Two weeks after he spent an afternoon alone with Rickey

in our living room, Dr. Klaus Krippenberg, a referral from the Center for Autism, called and asked Nora and me to drive up to Philadelphia to get his impressions.

Krippenberg, a pleasant, engaging personality framed by the bushiest eyebrows I have ever seen, was refreshingly direct. "Let's cut to the chase. Do you want to know about Rickey or Rickey's language?"

"Both," said Nora.

"Okay. Let's start here: Rickey really is unique. She is capable of astounding levels of ideation. Her capacities as a savant are actually more striking than her Asperger's symptoms, which are pretty standard. Her thinking is turned inward and focused on two all-important goals: minimizing her own pain and stimulating her own brain.

"That's where Susurrus comes in. Like she says, Susurrus is hers, hers alone. With Susurrus, Rickey is in a constant secret dialogue with herself. She's not trying to communicate with you or anybody else, and she does not want her language to be understood by neurotypicals."

"But *why* is she doing this?" asked Nora.

Krippenberg clearly was excited by all this. "Because it gives her an internal sense of place and direction. *Susurrus is a map of Rickey's mind.* As Rickey is murmuring, which you've noticed she does almost constantly, she is trying to correlate the outside world she must accommodate—*inadequately, always inadequately*—and her inner consciousness. Put differently, Rickey's Susurrus world is her primary reality, and her life among you is a secondary reality—for her, a very badly compromised reality."

Nora clunked her head down on the desk.

"What's to become of Rickey?" I asked.

Krippenberg bowed his head, hiding his face behind his steepled fingers. Then he looked up at us.

"Honestly? Nothing. Nothing will become of Rickey Bayard. Unfortunately, she is not here to *become.* She is here just to survive. That's how she experiences it. Nora, Hugh, Rickey is like the boy in the bubble—although Bohemia Manor is a pretty nice bubble.

"Please don't get me wrong, I'm not saying you should just give up on her, only that you have to manage your expectations. She is certainly a part of your unique 'family,' but she will never assimilate fully into the family *because she simply can't.* Much of her lives in another world."

"So, what should we do?" whispered Nora.

"My advice is, unless or until you have to, *don't change a thing.* What should you do? *Nothing.* Let her live on at Bohemia Manor, doing her thing. Let her be. For her, surely it can't get much better than it is now.

"The bind, of course, is going to come when any or all of you leave or die or otherwise abandon her. Then, unless I am mistaken, I think she may become lost. The savant aspects hide a lot of gaping holes, huge problems with both her judgment and her resiliency. In my opinion, Rickey is not incidentally handicapped, she is fundamentally handicapped. I wish I could say otherwise."

Krippenberg rose to indicate the meeting was over. Then he turned to me. "Oh, but I must tell you something else, Hugh. Rickey knows that you also have synesthesia, and she wonders why you have never discussed it with her. Rickey identifies with your own synesthesia. She sees it as a kind of bond, a link. But she also thinks you don't use it very well. She thinks you're ashamed of it. And she can't understand that because she loves her own synesthesia. Maybe you should think about how to try to capitalize on that shared gift."

I was stunned. My mind was flooded with all the things I might have said to build a bridge, all the things I might say in the future. This would be hard. One thing I knew for sure: it was going to be harder for me to hide from Rickey now.

9

Making Waves

INTERESTINGLY, GIVEN HER SUPERIOR STEM SCORES IN correspondence school, our new high school graduate did not seem particularly interested in computers. In fact, she seemed almost insulted by them. We bought her an Apple Macintosh, and she fiddled with it a little bit, but she really did not use it to tap into the outside world. I asked her about this. "It's just a fucking toy. My head is a better computer than an Apple Macintosh. My software is better than their software."

Tryg tried hard to open Rickey up to the potential of personal computing, but she rebuffed him. "Tryg," she said patronizingly, tapping her forehead, "I do my personal computing up *here*."

On the other hand, Rickey's obsession with a personal electronics lab continued. In addition to her Principles of Electricity and Electronics course from the International Baccalaureate Correspondence Academy, Rickey polished off a series of college-level texts and industrial manuals, and Tryg, no slouch when it comes to circuits and capacitators, told me she talked a mean electronics game and could go detail-for-detail with him.

Following up on our promised graduation gift, Rickey

presented Tryg with a series of shopping lists, demanding that a bewildering variety of electronic equipment be purchased and assembled down in the old airplane hangar. Perhaps her most curious request was for a high-powered military-specification radio signal generator capable of producing radio and acoustic signals across the full range of the electromagnetic spectrum. She also said she wanted transmission equipment "that can move mountains. I want to make big waves."

Tryg, God love him, started to source it all, bit by bit, purchase by purchase. He actually found a signal generator, as well as all the other monitors, oscilloscopes, consoles, breakers, conduits, transmitters, and power handling cabling Rickey was accumulating. This he did without question or complaint, and Rickey seemed grateful.

Then Washington College, a little liberal arts college down in Chestertown, decided to give up on its electronics curriculum and advertised that all its electronic lab equipment was for sale. Tryg bought it all for $18,500—an enormous steal, he said—trucked it all up to the hangar, conducted a complete inventory, organized, and shelved all the parts and pieces. Rickey was up to her armpits in electronic gear, and the positive effect on her affect was most agreeable.

Rickey stood by as Tryg assembled the equipment and wired everything together. When he was done, Rickey disassembled it all and reassembled it in the way she wanted, rearranging the generators, cabinets, keyboards, panels, monitors, and instruments into an entirely new configuration.

When they eventually lit up the huge industrial generator, everything in Rickey's Rube Goldberg lab worked smoothly. Rickey then moved pretty much full time down to the lab, stuffed a cot into a storage room, connected a cheesy Radio Shack intercom to the house intercom circuit so Nora could call her for meals, and began her new life as a radio scientist, sending and receiving, sending and receiving. There were no words, of course, to Rickey's transmissions, but her message was clear: *Rickey calling. Rickey calling. Can you hear me? Do you read me?*

Tryg and I suspected that at some point all this random radio activity was going to get noticed by the government spooks at the Aberdeen Proving Ground over on the other side of Chesapeake Bay, but if they were alarmed or interested, they didn't track us down to complain. At least not initially.

10

Brunching and Bonding

DESPITE LIVING IN A HUGE HOUSE WITH COUNTLESS ROOMS AND vast living areas, the Hole in the Wall Gang tended to hang out in the breakfast room adjoining Nora's enormous kitchen, both to eat and to fraternize. The French doors on one wall provided a majestic view of the Bohemia River; an alcove on the opposite wall housed our television, stacks of magazines and books, ceramic cups filled with assorted ballpoint pens and random personal articles and junk, mostly Rickey's, never Tryg's. Our long, rustic dining table extended into the dim far corner of the breakfast room, providing Rickey with a darkened hidey-hole where she could avoid being exposed to bright light and either avoid or participate in conversation as she chose. All of us, even Rickey, grew fond of this warm and friendly room where we would gather, gossip, gripe, and pass time together.

Sunday brunch became special, a weekly event to be anticipated and savored. Nora often sought an international flair to showcase her culinary skills: Belgian waffles, German sausage, Thai dumplings, French pastries, Spanish rice, even some English pudding monstrosity called—cue the laughter—spotted dick. We had a few earnest conversations, but mainly the brunches were a goof. We did mimosas and bloody Marys, and our Sunday mornings often became loose and boisterous.

Shortly after she passed thirteen, Rickey insisted that we have the first Sunday Brunch Talent Show. After the plates of waffles and thick-cut bacon were cleared, Ricky insisted on going first. She stood on a chair, draped a makeshift bedsheet toga over her shoulders, and then brought us to our knees with a stirring rendition of William Ernest Henley's Victorian poem, *Invictus*. "It means unconquered," she advised us patronizingly, and paused. Her speech started soft and built to a forceful crescendo, her voice clear and confident:

> *Out of the night that covers me*
> *Black as the pit from pole to pole,*
> *I thank whatever gods may be*
> *For my unconquerable soul.*
>
> *In the fell clutch of circumstance,*
> *I have not winced nor cried aloud.*
> *Under the bludgeonings of chance*
> *My head is bloody, but unbowed.*
>
> *Beyond this place of wrath and tears*
> *Looms but the Horror of the shade,*
> *And yet the menace of the years*
> *Finds, and shall find, me unafraid.*
>
> *It matters not how strait the gate,*
> *How charged with punishments the scroll,*
> *I am the master of my fate:*
> *I am the captain of my soul.*

When she finished, there was an astonished silence, which Rickey felt obliged to fill with commentary. "The fourth stanza alludes to a phrase from the King James Bible, Matthew 7:14.

'Because strait is the gate, and narrow is the way, which leadeth unto life, and few there be that find it.'

I felt myself choking up, saw Nora bow and shake her head. Simone gave Ray a firm hug from the back, and then Nora went over and gave Rickey, still standing on the chair, a long hug around the waist. Rickey did not flinch or resist. "I've been practicing," she said.

Tryg stood and said, "And now for something completely different," and pulled out a stack of quarters and a box of ping pong balls. "I am a magician with crop yields and fixing broken tractors. And I also am a magician with ping pong balls." He flashed his bare arms and imitated Bullwinkle the Moose: "See, Rocky, nothin' up my sleeve."

Tryg Sletland proved an adept sleight-of-hand artist: ping pong balls popped up between his fingers, then disappeared with a flick of his wrist. He made quarters appear from our ears and made them vanish even while holding them in his open palm. Over and again, white orbs and shiny objects appeared and disappeared as Tryg swept his hands in smooth arcs and Rickey cried, "How do you do that?" over and again. Finally, Tryg clapped his hands, and all the quarters and ping pong balls flew into the air at once. In a single gesture, Tryg made a sweeping arc with his arm, caught them all, closed his fist, and made them vanish.

"In honor of the Hole in the Wall Gang," he said. "Good vanishers, all."

Nora's turn. "Time to do *my* thing," she smiled. "I am about to show you knife skills the likes of which the civilized world has never seen."

Mimicking the screechy voice of Julia Child, Nora croaked, "First we take the dipping sauce, prepared last night, and put it aside." Now Nora opened a plastic crisper and pulled out a multi-colored mix of vegetables and fruits: radishes, oranges, a turnip, celery, carrots, some green beans, apples, green, orange and red peppers, parsley and other herbs, cherry tomatoes. She arranged two knives, a paring knife and a nine-inch butcher's knife, on her thick cutting board. Then she took one knife in each hand, banged the butts of the handles on the board, and with a flamenco flourish shouted, "Arriba! Andale!"

Nora leaned low over the pile, paused momentarily, and then cut loose, if you'll pardon the pun. Her hands moved in a blur, swept in dramatic arcs, slicing, dicing, stabbing, mincing, all at phenomenal tempo. She threw a carrot into the air, stabbed its base with the paring knife and then slashed back and forth with the butcher's blade, dropping neat little orange discs on to the counter. "Aha!" she cried. "Eat your heart out, Zorro!" We all burst into delighted laughter.

Within five minutes, Nora had assembled a fruit and vegetable sculpture, a rosette of colors and shapes that looked like a Tibetan monks' mandala. Arcs of tomato. Chevrons of jicama. Carrots carved to flowers, cucumbers sliced into an assortment of shapes and sizes. Edible art.

She looked up and, smiling broadly, flipped her hair off her forehead with a flick of her head. "First in class at the Fanny Farmer Cooking School," she said proudly. We applauded and dug into her dip. Like her performance, it was marvelous.

"I cannot match that," I said. "Instead, I am going to take you back to the Moore River Native Settlement in, say, 1950. I need you to imagine a group of aboriginal five-year-olds singing this song in unison."

I began to sing. I am not sure I had sung a note since I was at Moore River, but my pitch was pretty decent. *"This is the story of Eddie Koochee Katchee Kama Tosaneera Tosanoka Samakama Wacky Brown. Fell into the well, fell into the well, he fell into the deep dark well. Suzie Jones, milking in the barn, saw him fall, ran inside and told her Ma that Eddie Koochee Katchee Kama Tosaneera Tosanoka Samakama Wacky Brown fell into the well..."*

And so, the song continued, seemingly interminably, each person—Suzie's Ma, who was baking crackling bread, Old Joe, who pushed aside his plough, picked up his cane and hobbled into town, all the townspeople—telling the next that young Eddie had fallen into the well. The punch line is that when the crowd finally gets back to rescue Eddie, it has taken so long for so many people to say his name that he has drowned.

More loud applause. Simone was dancing around, waving her arms for attention. "Bloody hell!" she screamed. "We had that song in New Zealand! Only ours was a different kid! Our kid was an Indian kid! *Nicky-ticky-tumbo-no-sah-rumbo-bari-bari-boos ki-perri-pan-do-nikki-pom-pom-chimiendo-dom-bori-ko!* What a small world!"

We all laughed uproariously. Then Ray Hadley said quietly, "I'd like to try one, but I need some help. Can anyone here carry a tune?" Surprisingly, Tryg said, "I can. I used to sing in the church choir."

"What I need you to do, Tryg," said Ray, "is to become a drone, just like a bagpipe, or more specifically, the Irish version called the Uillean pipe. I need you to sing, and just keep singing, a single note. You don't need any words, just sing 'aaaah," like this."

Ray sang a single tone, harsh and nasal and piercing.

"I can do that," said Tryg, and he mimicked Ray perfectly.

"That's great," Ray grinned. "We're going to sing 'Raglan Road,' an old Irish ballad of unrequited love." Ray affected a soft Irish brogue. "It'll tear yer bleedin' heart out."

And it did. Ray began to sing, his first notes stabbing deep as Ray's voice, sweet and full, with a slight vibrato, caromed off Tryg's metallic keening. *"I saw the danger, and yet I passed along the enchanted way, and I said 'Let grief be a falling leaf and the dawning of the day.'"*

I was surprised at my involuntary emotional reaction, and Rickey and Nora appeared to be struck just as powerfully. Both were blinking rapidly. *"The Queen of Hearts still making tarts, and I not making hay, oh I loved too much, and by such and such is happiness thrown away."*

Ray sang softly, but with a striking innocent openness, as if he was reaching into his own soul. He certainly was reaching into mine. *"I see her walking now, away from me so hurriedly, my reason must allow, that had I loved not as I should, a creature made of clay, when the angel woos the clay, he'll lose his wings at the dawn of the day."*

Ray's last words were almost a whisper, and Tryg let his drone trail off, like a bagpipe run out of wind.

Rickey stood on her chair, trembling. She had turned as pale as the sheet still draped over her shoulders. Her eyes glistened with tears. She bit hard on her lower lip, let her makeshift toga fall from her shoulders, lurched off the chair and stumbled from the room. Nora moved to go after her, but I caught her elbow, restrained her. "She's okay, Nora. Overwhelmed, but okay. Let her have her feelings by herself. I think this may have been a first."

Ray Hadley looked bewildered. "Have I done something wrong?"

"No, Ray, you certainly haven't. In fact, you may have done something wonderful. I think you may have broken through a wall."

✦   ✦   ✦

SOME TIME AFTER OUR MEMORABLE BRUNCH, I SOUGHT OUT RICKEY in her room. Judging from her dismissive posture, she was evidently in ill humor. "FYLMA, Hugh."

This was an evolved and now shared joke, a bit of humor that we also employed as a warning of an imminent Rickey storm.

Initially, FYLMA was just a bit of shorthand between Nora and me. It stood for, "Fuck you! Leave me alone!" This was an instruction Rickey unleashed frequently, a signal that she was experiencing frustration or pain. One afternoon, when Rickey was percolating about something or other, Nora said to me, "Please, Hugh. Don't push her. Don't trigger another FYLMA, okay?"

Rickey looked at me, looked at Nora. The light bulb went off. "You fucking bastards," she said. "You're making fun of me."

"Not so," said Nora. "Hugh and I simply use it to signal that it looks like a flash point is near. We're trying to avoid unpleasantness, because it's not pleasant to be told to fuck yourself over and over again."

"Yeah? Well, if you can use it, I can use it. Hugh? Nora? FYLMA!" Then she laughed.

On this particular day, I asked Rickey if she knew who Temple Grandin was. She didn't.

"Temple Grandin is the foremost expert on livestock handling equipment in the world. She has a Ph.D. and travels around and consults with meat packing companies about the most humane, and also the most efficient, way to move cattle through stockyards. She's the inventor of the modern cattle squeeze chute."

"And this matters because…," said Rickey.

"Three reasons," I said. "First, because she is autistic, and she sees the world in a unique way. In her case, she says that she sees things as if her eyes are a video camera, literally recording her sensory perceptions, no editing, no filling in blanks. Also, she says she sees the world the same way cows do. That's how she understands what will soothe cows and what will agitate cows. So, she can design pens and chutes that will not alarm the cattle. It has made her famous."

"Interesting," said Rickey flatly.

"Second reason is because she lectures and writes a lot about how hard it is to operate in the world of neurotypicals. She says autistic people perceive the world distinctly differently from neurotypicals."

"I could have told you that," said Rickey.

"Grandin is very funny when she lectures, but she admits that she has simply memorized a lot of humorous lines. She admits she has no idea why people find them funny. She just knows they work to loosen up the audience."

"Hey, I do that," said Rickey. "Sometimes I even get people to think I'm a real adult with a real sense of humor. *Suckers*"

"Third, she invented the squeeze machine. Temple Grandin is an extremely anxious person. She saw how the cows relaxed when they were put in squeeze chutes, and she wondered if the same principle would work on her. So, she designed an anxiety-reducing 'squeeze machine' you lie down in and then use hydraulic pressure to squeeze you hard from the sides. It's made of plywood, and she has given the plans to the world. No patent."

"And so?" Rickey was making this unnecessarily hard.

"And so, how would you like to work with me to build you a squeeze machine in here? My idea looks different from hers, but it's the same principle. It's simple and I think it would work."

Now I had Rickey's interest. "I'm game," she said, swinging her legs off the bed.

"Get me some stuff from the toolbox in the garage, please. We'll need an electric drill, a sabre saw, a couple of small pulleys, and some bungee cords. Oh, and some long lag screws. Also, while you're in the garage, please poach the vinyl pads from the golf cart."

We removed the door from the spare bedroom, keeping the hinges mounted. With the sabre saw, we cut a square hole about eighteen inches wide and eighteen inches high in the bottom of the door for Rickey's feet to stick through. Rickey was very good with the sabre saw, very precise. Then I measured the distance from the floor to the bridge of Rickey's nose, and we cut a square opening that would let her face protrude through the door from behind.

We used a stud-finder to find a strong place to fasten the door and mounted the modified door on the wall with long lag screws so that it could swing freely. We tacked one vinyl golf cart pad to the wall behind the door and the other on the back of the door. We mounted pulleys on the wall and the door and fastened the bungee cords in such a way that Rickey could stand behind the door with her feet and face sticking through the holes, and then pull the padded door firmly in toward herself, pressing it against her body from knees to shoulders. Rube Goldberg would have been proud.

Rickey's enthusiasm built as our home-grown squeeze machine took shape.

"You ready?" I asked.

She actually smiled. "Test pilot Ulricke S. Bayard reporting for duty."

Rickey positioned herself behind the door and pulled on the wooden handle we'd mounted on the end of the bungee cord. "Can't pull hard enough," she said. "Can't get enough pressure."

"We added two more bungee cords and arranged them in a sort of block and tackle arrangement. Rickey tried again, pulling the door in on herself.

"Oh, *yes!*" she cried excitedly. Through the top hole in the door, I could see her face relax, her tensed shoulders droop. "Oh, yes, Hugh. This thing really works. *It really works.*"

"For what it's worth, Rickey, Temple Grandin said she never used her machine longer than about twenty minutes. After all, you are pinching off circulation. She also said she was afraid that if she stayed in longer, she might never come out."

Rickey squeezed out from behind the door, and then she shook my hand, as if we were completing a solemn business transaction. "Thank you, Hugh. This means a lot to me."

"My pleasure, Rickey. We're all here to help each other."

"I didn't know you cared," said Rickey.

11

The Question of Sex

NORA TOLD ME TO CHASE DOWN RICKEY TO HELP SLICE VEGETABLES
for a dinner salad. I found her in Hermann's library reclining on
the couch, her head propped up on a throw pillow wedged against
one arm, her legs dangling over the other arm. She was bouncing
her feet in a tense rhythm, right-left-right-left-right-left, against
the side of the couch, punching shallow dents in the corduroy.
She was wearing her yellow indoor sunglasses. A thick volume on
was propped on her thighs, and she appeared deeply engrossed.

Before I could relay Nora's request, Rickey looked up at
me. She showed me the cover of the thick hard-bound book she
was reading: *Human Sexual Response* by William H. Masters and
Virginia E. Johnson. Hermann Bayard sure had some interesting
stuff in his library.

"You ever read this?"

"Can't say that I have. I've heard about it, and I know it
caused a big stir when it first came out, but I have to say that
reading about academic research on peoples' sexual habits is not
of particular interest to me."

"Well, I'm not surprised," said Rickey. "You don't seem like
a real sexual guy."

I felt myself flare.

"I know tact is not your long suit, Ms. Bayard, but even by your standards that comment was rude and uncalled-for. And nosy. I don't think the realities of my sex life are any of your goddamned business."

I expected her to back off—*wouldn't anyone?* Not Rickey. She bored in.

"So, what are the realities of your sex life?"

I tried to sound firm without coming across as defensive or prudish. "As I said, I don't think that's any of your business."

Ricky put on her serious adult 'let's talk' voice.

"But it *is,* Hugh. Don't you see? In case you haven't noticed, I'm in the middle of puberty. I'm at the age where adults are supposed to be telling me stuff, educating me about the birds and bees. Uncloaking all the mysteries of sex and hormones and fucking and getting off. But other than Nora telling me about maxi-pads and the monthlies, what guidance have either you or Nora given me about this transition from child to adult? Zilch. *Nada.*"

Caught utterly flat-footed, I said the stupidest of all possible things.

"What do you want to know?"

"Well, *duh,* Hugh. How 'bout *everything?* You know it's pretty isolated out here in the sticks, and I don't have a lot of little junior-high friends to tell me all the secrets. And somehow, I don't think Masters and Johnson are going to be all that relevant. I'm finding it quite interesting and educational and all, but it is pretty dry. So far all its really showed me is that there is a long distance between your brain and your genitals."

Where in the world was this coming from? I forced myself to remember that I was talking to an autistic developmentally disabled adolescent, not a mature adult. Maybe I can reset the context, I thought. *Maybe, if I get lofty, I can fly out of the top of this storm.*

"Actually, you put it quite well, Rickey." *Just strike the balance,*

Hugh, not too parental, don't get all pompous. Don't try to be falsely chummy. Just, you know, helpful.

"Studying sexuality scientifically like Masters and Johnson do is a lot different from actually experiencing the physical satisfactions of sex. It's one thing to study intimacy, another thing to share intimacy."

At that moment, I was rather proud of that answer.

"'Well, I *like* the rational," Rickey said. "You don't have to *do* something in order to understand it."

Rickey took off her sunglasses, looked me straight in the eye, spoke matter-of-factly. "Look, as an autistic person, I know I'm officially incapable of understanding intimacy. But my guess is that Nora Dadmun isn't either, and as for you, I can't imagine that you've experienced a whole lot of intimacy here at Bo Manor. Or even before, unless there's some part of your life that I have totally missed. My guess is that around here we're all pretty much restricted to the pleasures of masturbation."

I struggled to find footing. "Well, masturbation can be very satisfying."

"Oh, I know," Rickey said, brightly. "Orgasms are *totally* excellent. I think they are especially beneficial for autistic people."'

"I can believe that," I said. "For most people, actually."

Now Rickey furrowed her brow, as if contemplating weighty ideas. "Is masturbation better than sexual intercourse? I've never had sexual intercourse, you know, and I'm trying to figure out whether I should give it a try. I think it might be very problematic for someone who's as sensitive to physical touch as I am. Touching myself? Okay. Others touching me? Not sure I want to go there."

I was caught in quicksand, sinking surely and steadily. I said to Rickey, "They're both very pleasant, Rickey. They're alike in that orgasm is orgasm, regardless of what triggers it. It's a pleasant physical release, you know that. Three cheers for our hormones and nerve endings."

Rickey didn't laugh or smile.

"Masturbation is kind of your present to yourself. Intercourse has a wonderful extra dimension. Involvement with someone else, the sharing, the special kind of touching. Sometimes even playfulness. It has an emotional reward as well as physical excitement."

"That sounds like trouble for me," said Rickey. "I'm not sure I can get completely on board with all that touching and intimacy. And wow, all that submission and aggression stuff Masters and Johnson talk about. A lot of moving parts going on there."

I still couldn't believe what I was hearing. At her age, she was supposed to be a sea of raging hormones. Instead, she was s talking about 'aspects of submission and aggression.' I said, "True, with intercourse there are a lot of things that can derail things or get in the way, but when it's right, it's pretty damned pleasant."

"Probably not for me," Rickey said, a little dismissively. "I'm not sure I could even tell the difference between fucking and rape. And then there's *Love*. I really have no idea what *that's* all about. I read that Carl Jung called love 'the over-idealization of the other.' Like, *hunh*? When people call having sex 'making love,' it just goes right over my head. And while we're defining our terms, so what's lust?"

"I'm not sure how Masters and Johnson would define it, but I'd say lust is having the hots, only directed at a particular person."

Rickey said, "Is that bad?" And I said, "By no means. When experienced and expressed appropriately, lust is very cool. Very natural. And yes, often very fun."

Now Rickey said, calm as can be, "What if I had lust for you?"

To my credit I did *not* say, "What!" or "Holy Shit!" or "Are you crazy?" I said, as calmly as I could, "There is a lot to unpack in that question, Rickey, and I want to give you a respectful answer and not just blow you off. First of all, although I'm flattered to be thought of as attractive, I am not an appropriate sex partner. I am your surrogate parent. My mission is to protect you, not exploit you. And that's especially true given your age and your sexual inexperience. Given your autism."

Rickey exploded. "God damn it!" she yelled. "It's always about my autism, isn't it? How I'm so emotionally handicapped and 'mind blind' and I'm so naïve and vulnerable and all that other crap everybody's always laying on me. Well, let me tell you, Mr. Hugh Ullam, *the part of me that isn't crippled, isn't crippled*'"

"Rickey," I said, "this isn't just about what you feel about me or the way I feel about you. And it's not just about appropriate behavior, It's also about *the law*. When people my age have sex with people your age, it is not just sex, Rickey, it's a crime. It's rape, whether you consent to it or not. And people go to jail for that."

Rickey's face assumed a cagey squint, like someone about to spring a trap. "Well, what if I had lust for...*Nora*? That wouldn't be a rape thing, would it?"

"You're playing games with me, Rickey, and I do not appreciate it. Imagining Nora as a sexual partner is every bit as off-base as thinking of me as one. Inappropriate, simply inappropriate."

When I said this, Rickey assumed the face of innocence. "But I've read articles that say a lot of autistic people are gay. One even said that most of 'em are gay."

"I must say that I do not regard myself as an expert advisor on the subject of sexual orientation. Now, if you're telling me you think you might be gay, if you say you are more attracted to women than to men, you and Nora and I can certainly talk about that, or arrange for you to talk confidentially to a professional counselor about that, if you like."

I was beginning to feel dizzy. My thoughts were scurrying frantically around in my head, trying to find purchase. "Look. I know sexual preference is a big issue for kids your age, especially someone who doesn't have a group of friends or peers to compare notes with. Hell, all aspects of someone's identity, not just sexual preferences, can get real jumbled up when adolescents go through puberty. And that's particularly true when it relates to people they care a lot about."

"God, you make sex sound like such hard work." Her tone brightened unexpectedly. "You think Nora's gay?"

"I really have no idea. I don't know her preferences, I don't know her past, we haven't ever discussed the subject."

"Well, I'd say that's a little strange, you two being adults and all."

"I'd say it's respectful. I'd say we mind our own business."

"Are you gay? Or bisexual or pan-sexual or anything else forbidden or interesting?"

"God, Rickey! You are a *trip*. For the record, I am absolutely straight. I prefer my sex with women. I am not gay, but that doesn't mean I can't care deeply for people who are. I just prefer not to have sex with them."

"But you're not having sex with them! Or with anybody! And Nora's not. We're all just stuck out here alone in the boonies, so how am I to *'explore the issue'* of whether I'm gay or not?"

I exhaled. Long. Slowly. Deeply. "Look, the all-alone-out-here thing doesn't have anything to do with being gay or straight. It has to do with *isolation*. And in each of our cases—you, me, Nora—it has to do with personal...issues...that make it hard for us to form intimate relationships, sexual or otherwise. Okay? Tryg is the only one who really has something going with someone else, so I guess we should just envy him and Simone."

"Yeah. Suppose so." Rickey put Masters and Johnson down and walked out of the room.

✿   ✿   ✿

LATER I TOLD NORA ABOUT MY REALITY SESSION WITH RICKEY. SHE let her head drop and pressed her fingers against her eyes.

"Christ," she said. "I don't know whether to laugh or cry. I don't know if your little chat ended something or started something. But it sure brings something home to me."

"And just what is that?"

"That our goofy little Hole in the Wall Gang works fine in some ways, but it probably looks pretty abnormal in others. We're all hiding things—*hiding behind things*—and it looks like Rickey is going to begin calling us on it. And when Rickey calls bullshit, you know it's been called."

"Probably. I guess it goes with the adolescent territory. But in my case, Rickey can call until she's blue in the face. You're free to tell her anything about yourself that you want., but when it comes me, certain areas are going to remain private property."

Nora stiffened, as if I were insulting her.

"You've repeatedly made that perfectly clear, Mr. Ullam. Well, fine. Keep your guard up if you want, Hugh. No one's going to force you to bare your breast."

Since this conversation was already going downhill, I decided, *Fuck, why not? Let me just push it off the cliff.* I cleared my throat. "Look, Nora, on the subject of sex, I want to clear the air on one other thing."

Nora was staring darts at me.

"You know as well as I do that when I first got here, and we were trying to figure out who was who and what was what, we had a couple of near misses. Here's two isolated people, both feeling a little sexy after a good bottle of wine, some suggestive glances and *double entrendres*. I think we were pretty close to hopping in the sack, am I right? At least I was. Did I fantasize about some hot lustful sex with you? Indeed, I did. You are a very, very attractive woman. I don't think you appreciate how sexy you are.

"But I'm glad we pulled back. This isn't just about not having sex with the boss, about 'don't get laid where you get paid.' It's about placing a higher value on trust than on pleasure. So, for what it's worth, I assure you that in the future I will never take advantage of you or seek sexual favors from you. And I don't care what you do with your sex life, as long as I don't have to watch you being victimized by somebody."

There was a long silence. Then Nora said, "Well, gee, how could I possibly argue with that? Here you are, 'the boss,' all logical and practical, announcing *your* decision. You just want to be the boss. You just want to call all the shots.

"Remember when you asked me for the Cliff's Notes version of how to get along with Rickey? Well-intentioned, but extremely naïve. *But at least you asked, right?* Well, here we are again, dealing with Relationships 101, only it's me this time. Only this time, you don't even bother to ask what *I'm* feeling. What *I* want. What *I* need.

"The thing about you, Hugh Ullam, is that you don't even know when you're being an asshole. 'Don't get laid where you get paid.' God, Hugh! Don't you see how insulting that is, even if your intention is good? I suppose I should cut you some slack, because you've had all the compassion and empathy knocked out of you over the course of your horrific upbringing. But that doesn't mean I wouldn't appreciate some now and then. All business, all the time, that's Hugh Ullam. Well, good luck with that, Hugh. I think you need to think more about the difference between a business and a family."

12

Status Check

I DID NOT STOP TO TAKE STOCK AT THE TIME, TO UNDERTAKE A detailed appraisal of our life and times. At this point, the events of the Hole in the Wall Gang at Bohemia Manor did not seem to have a plot or chapters. Time just passed. If we lacked direction or a sense of momentum, at least we were stable and generally companionable. At this point, a suitable motto for our actions and choices would have been, "It seemed like the thing to do at the time."

We still were more 'found family' than intimate friends. Yet in hindsight I see that we now were connected not only by our mutual dependency, but also by a frail nervous system, an evolving network of dendrites and synapses—reaching out, connecting, sending miscellaneous soul queries.

Rickey, now a full-blown adolescent, still was volatile and emotionally all over the place, and the shouts of FYLMA remained frequent. But I thought she was trying harder to become an integral part of our collective consciousness. Rickey, whose existence when younger seemed little more than a series of frantic gestures communicating her cerebral static, had begun putting out feelers to each of us: *Can you find me in here? Will you reach in for me?*

There was no reason to believe that our lives were approaching a major inflection point. If you had asked me how things were going just then, I would have said that everything was pretty much hunky dory.

PART TWO
Everything Changes

13

This Can't Last

SHUNRYU SUZUKI WAS A SOTO BUDDHIST MONK AND TEACHER WHO sought to popularize Zen Buddhism in America by founding the San Francisco Zen Center in 1970. There he led cheery but interminable teaching sessions attended by scores of devoted followers sitting for hours in the full Lotus position—*sitting Zazen.* By all accounts, it was a painful experience: beyond the physical discomfort required, Suzuki's wisdom was arcane and convoluted, his fractured English nearly incomprehensible.

Legend has it that one day a frustrated student who had experienced more pain than enlightenment cried out, "Suzuki-roshi, I love listening to you, but I can't understand a thing you say! Is it possible to capture the entire heart of Buddhism in a single paragraph?"

Suzuki is said to have paused and smiled.

"Yes," he said.

"Everything changes."

And so it was to be with us.

14

Holy Crap!

NORA, ELBOWS PROPPED ON THE KITCHEN ISLAND, WAS IDLY turning the pages of the *Cecil Whig*. Tryg had his soldering gun out and was carefully rewiring our malfunctioning toaster, Simone was doing her nails, and I was balancing the household checkbook. Rickey was staring off into space, probably running complex mental math problems in some alternative universe.

Suddenly Nora bolted upright, spread the newspaper with her hands, and exclaimed, "Holy crap!" Tryg dropped this soldering iron, which immediately burned a neat chevron into the island's birch cutting board. "God damn it, Nora!" he barked. "What the hell?"

"These two guys caught a shark off Turkey Point! Holy crap!"

We all moved to look over Nora's shoulder at the photo of two paunchy locals kneeling proudly on Schaeffer's dock behind a very large shark. The picture clearly showed a large bullet hole in the middle of its head, right between its black, beady eyes.

Nora read aloud. "Two local fishermen had a real fish story to tell when they landed a seven-foot bull shark in their john boat off Turkey Point yesterday. Errol Flemons, blah, blah, blah, and Alonzo Brito, blah, blah, blah, wild thirty-minute struggle, blah,

blah, blah, twenty-pound test line, 'good thing I had my .38 with me,' blah, blah, blah, 'nearly dropped my teeth when I saw that big flat head and them evil eyes staring up at me.'"

Nora looked up, shaking her head. *"Ho-oh-oh-ly cah-rap."*

Tryg looked bewildered. "Why? Is this unusual?"

"You're not from around here," Nora said, "or you'd know better than to ask that."

She continued reading. "Cecil County Extension Agent Aaron Youngquist has estimated the shark's weight at over 250 pounds. 'These men are lucky,' Youngquist said, 'because bull sharks are one of the three most vicious sharks in the world. If they'd somehow gotten that fish in that little boat alive, there would have been a lot of excitement, for sure.'"

Rickey had stood and now was leaning on Nora's back, reading over her shoulder as Nora continued to read aloud.

"Experts from Maryland Department of Natural Resources expressed great surprise that the shark had ranged so far north of the bay's salt line. Jane Abbott, a marine census expert at the Chesapeake Bay Foundation, said, 'This is very, very strange. This is the first bull shark we've ever recorded this far up Chesapeake Bay, and we have to wonder what brought it way up here. While it is well known that bull sharks are shore feeders and sometimes stray into brackish water or even freshwater streams, historically they just haven't done it around here. Bull sharks don't mate in shallow water, so we don't think it was responding to a mating urge. He was swimming right into the freshwater flood of the Susquehanna River, so he must have been lured up the bay by something he found very attractive. You have to wonder if all those underwater experiments they're always doing at the Aberdeen Proving Ground aren't somehow creating an attraction. Sharks have very sensitive electrical sensors called Ampullae of Lorenzini, so if Aberdeen is experimenting with underwater transmissions, it may have affected this shark. We're going to be on the lookout for other sharks or deep-water marine life in the Sassafras, Bohemia, Northeast, and Elk Rivers. I'd sure love to know what brought him up to our neck of the woods.'"

Nora looked up. "Like I said, *ho-oh-oh-ly cah-rap*. Now there's something you don't see every day." Rickey had edged back to her chair and was now looking down at her feet. She glanced up, and I saw Tryg catch her eye. He cocked his head and raised an eyebrow. Rickey nodded, smiled, and looked back down at her feet.

15

Bohemia Plane Crash Kills Two

From the *Cecil Whig*
"The Independent Voice of Cecil County"

Bohemia River Plane Crash Kills Two, Triggers Marina Explosion

Galena, MD. A Schenectady, New York couple was killed early Thursday evening when their twin-engined Cessna 310 aircraft crashed into the Bohemia River and then caromed into the docks at the Bohemia Vista Marina. Barney Schooley, 54, and his wife, Mary Folsom, 48, were killed when the pilot apparently became disoriented in heavy fog and flew the plane into the water several hundred yards west of the Bohemia River Bridge. According to an eyewitness, the plane, which appeared to be inverted when it crashed, skipped into the marina's outer T-pier, cartwheeled over the end of the dock, and crashed on top of the fueling shed.

Huge Explosion

The impact ruptured gasoline and fuel hoses on the dock and triggered an explosion which engulfed the fueling shed, two cabin cruisers and three sailboats berthed at the marina. Fortunately, marina manager Dorothy Sepic, 31, was standing near the main fueling storage tank and valve manifold on shore when the explosion erupted. She was able to immediately close the master fuel flow valves and cut the supply of gasoline and diesel fuel to the fueling shed on the dock. Even after being starved of further fuel, the fire raged on for over three hours, prohibiting first responders from reaching the wreckage of the aircraft until after 10:00 PM.

The five boats destroyed in the blaze all sank at their berths. All were unoccupied at the time of the crash. Fourteen other boats were moved by courageous first responders to safe berths away from the blaze. Five other boats appeared to have suffered smoke and flame damage, but were in no danger of sinking.

A total of 14 fire engines converged on the blaze, representing the Cecil Country Volunteer Fire Department, Singerly Fire Company, North East Fire Company, Cecil Country Emergency Services, and the Bear, Delaware, Fire Company. In addition to hoses run down the main marina dock to fight the blaze with water, firefighters, working under banks of spotlights, fought the fire with both foam and water from atop the Bohemia River Bridge, which was closed until midnight Tuesday night. The Marine Response Spill Corporation, based in Chesapeake City, had oil and spill containment barriers in place within two hours of the crash, even as the fire continued to burn itself out. Region Three of the EPA will be conducting a site audit before the end of the week and will announce procedures for further containment and clean-up as soon as possible.

The bodies of Schooley and Folsom were recovered from the charred remains of the airplane at 10:30 PM by Singerly Company EMT volunteers. They were pronounced dead at the scene by Cecil Country Medical Examiner Bernard Bloehn and were transported to the Cecil County Morgue. Schooley, the Managing Partner of the law firm of Crowley, Schooley & Weiss in Schenectady, was an experienced pilot, reportedly with about 750 hours of flight time, an instrument flight rating, and a twin-engine rating. However, according to his brother Armand Schooley, he had only recently purchased the twin-engine Cessna 310 involved in the crash, and the planned trip from Schenectady to Bear Delaware for his daughter's wedding was his first cross-country flight.

Eyewitness Saw It All

Schooley's crash was witnessed by Hugh Uland, General Manager of Bohemia Manor Farm, located directly across the Bohemia River from where the plane hit the river. "I was standing on my patio overlooking the river" said Uland. "The fog was very heavy, which is unusual for an afternoon in June. It blanketed right down to the river, and I could not see more than about a half mile down the river. Suddenly the plane shot out of the fog, and I was very surprised because it was no more than about a hundred feet off the water, and it was almost upside down. It took several seconds for the plane to descend down to the water. Then it hit and skipped once and then dug in its right wing and cartwheeled into the marina. It was like slow motion, and it certainly is the most sickening sight I have ever witnessed."

Pilot Disoriented, Mysterious Forces Reported

The *Whig* has learned that several minutes before the crash, the tower of the New Castle County Airport in Wilmington received an urgent radio call from Schooley, who reported that all his instruments had suddenly malfunctioned and that he was completely disoriented. "He [Schooley] was very frightened," said Glen Levy, who received the radio transmission. "He said that while flying across the upper Chesapeake toward Summit, he had become completely enveloped by fog and could not see the ground or landmarks. He said he was instrument rated, but that all his instruments had suddenly 'gone crazy, like they were being jammed' as he approached Turkey Point, including his altimeter and artificial horizon.

"I told him that Aberdeen Proving Ground sometimes runs tests of various kinds of electronic systems, and that his instruments might have been affected that way. I told him to get the sun to his back and climb until he was out of the fog and could see the Delaware River. Then he should fly east until the fog cleared or his instruments reset. Several minutes later, I tried to raise Mr. Schooley again, but he did not respond."

16

Meet Deirdre Callas

"LET ME SPEAK TO HERMANN BAYARD."

These were the very first words Trooper Deirdre Callas ever spoke to me. She said them while pointedly looking away from me, as if looking at me was distasteful or uncomfortable. When I responded to the doorbell and swung the heavy front door open, she did not greet me, did not state either her name or her purpose. I stepped out onto the landing and closed the front door behind me, a gesture that apparently irritated her. I tried to make eye contact, but she continued to stare at her clipboard.

In her training as a state trooper, someone had obviously taught Deirdre Callas the "two straight trees" pose for projecting apparent authority, because that's how she stood now on Bohemia Manor's front porch, weight firmly and equally planted, her strong stout legs vectored straight and strong down into tall, polished trooper boots. She was studiously looking down at the clipboard in her left hand, pen in her right hand, poised for action. Her name, Deirdre Callas, State Trooper, was engraved on a gold bar pinned atop her left breast. Her flat-brimmed trooper hat shadowed her face, but from what I could tell, it appeared to be a very attractive face.

"I said, let me speak to Hermann Bayard." I found her tone arrogant, hostile.

"I'm sorry, Trooper Callas, but I cannot do that," I said quietly.

"This is official state police business. I insist on speaking to Hermann Bayard immediately."

"Mr. Bayard is traveling abroad. He is not here, and he is not available."

She bristled. "What do you mean, he's 'not available?'" She spat out the last two words, her hissing tone suggesting that what I had just uttered was ridiculous beyond belief. "You're telling me you cannot get in touch with your own employer?"

"That's exactly what I'm telling you. I don't know his present whereabouts, and I have no idea how to reach him." *This wasn't true, of course, but who was to know?*

"Well, who the hell does?"

"No one. When Mr. Bayard wishes to communicate, he contacts us. He prefers that we do not contact him."

Deirdre Callas did not like losing, and evidently she felt she was losing. Finally, she looked up and made eye contact. She was indeed very pretty, with high cheek bones, a delicate nose and small, symmetrical lips. Light brown hair, cut in a bob, protruded from under her Smokey-the-Bear trooper hat. She had deep brown eyes. I was surprised to see that she was wearing makeup, although not lipstick. This trooper definitely sent mixed messages.

In state trooper training, they had attempted to teach Callas the "I'm-in-control steely eye-lock," and she tried it on now. I was supposed to be withered by her stare, but she could not know that I had spent eleven years at the Akers Institute in Sydney, Australia, learning how to frustrate authority figures. I had forgotten more about passive aggression than Trooper Deirdre Callas would ever know.

I simply stood there, my face blank. Then I smiled. My smile, which I know has been called both dazzling and off-putting, obviously rattled her composure.

"Well, what happens if there's an emergency?"

"I handle it. I have been given the authority to handle all emergencies."

She slapped her clipboard against her left leg, a gesture more petulant than powerful.

"And just who...the hell...are you?" I loved the way she drew it out for effect. She was trying to regain ground with verbal stunts. I had to respect her for that.

"My name is Hugh Ullam. I am General Manager of Bohemia Manor Farm. I am legal head of the Bayard household and the person in charge of all of Hermann Bayard's finances. I am, as they say, the Big Kahuna around here. The Rajah. If you wish to buck with me, the buck stops here."

Trooper Callas' jaw dropped. "You expect me to believe that Hermann Bayard left a nig...a black man in charge of this whole place?"

To ease the mounting tension, I put some slack in the line. "Mr. Bayard and I both realize that this is an unconventional arrangement, especially in a region where it is unusual for people of color to be in charge of things. To spare people embarrassment and confusion, he left me with these documents."

Of course, I had brought the Constant Binder—that's what I call it—out with me. It is my sword and my shield, and it is never far from my side. It is made of aluminum front and back panels connected to the spine with piano hinges. In other words, indestructible. Inside it had several vital documents, all heavily laminated on both sides, as if it was expected that they would be passed around and thumbed a lot. All were held in large chrome loops that allowed them to be flipped easily.

"The first document is the basic 'To whom it may concern,' letter," I said, "explaining who I am and granting me authority to do what I do. The second is a durable power of attorney, empowering me to conduct all Hermann Bayard's business affairs, without reservation. The third is a medical power of attorney for decisions relating to his daughter, Ulricke Bayard, who is developmentally disabled and severely handicapped. In effect, she is my ward."

I turned the binder one hundred and eighty degrees, so the writing would be right side up for her and extended the binder to her for inspection. She took the binder and rested it awkwardly on top of her clip board, flipping to the first document. It was on Bohemia Manor Farm, Inc. letterhead, and the signature at the bottom had been notarized. She didn't read it out loud, but I saw her wince when she came to the operative sentence: *PLEASE ACCORD MR. ULLAM EVERY COURTESY.*

The change in Trooper Deirdre Callas' demeanor upon reading this document took me quite by surprise: she completely lost her composure, shaking her head in disbelief.

"Well, I will be goddamned," she said softly. Strong southern drawl, heavy emphasis on the *damned.*

"I hope that won't be necessary, Trooper Callas, but I also hope that this letter will convince you that I am in fact in charge, and not just some field hand who was stealing food from the kitchen when the doorbell rang. It doesn't get you anything to give me a lot of attitude, and so far, your attitude toward me has been strikingly unprofessional. I am trying to decide whether to lodge a complaint with your superiors."

Whoa, she did not like that. The war was on, but I had the tall horses. My tone had not been warm, and I kept her locked in eye contact until she looked down to glance over the other documents in the binder. Round One to the indigenous blackfella.

"Would you be so kind as to tell me the reason for your visit today?"

"They told me the owner of Bohemia Manor had seen the plane crash at the marina two weeks ago, and I was assigned to get a full statement."

I took a step back in order to power down our personal space a bit.

"Well, they were partly right. Someone here saw the whole crash, but it wasn't Hermann Bayard. It was me. I'm the one who called 9-1-1. I'm the one who helped direct traffic on the bridge after the fire trucks arrived."

"The person who took the dispatch said it sounded like a white guy."

"Do I not sound like a white guy? Maybe an Australian white guy, but a white guy nonetheless?"

She had no choice but to give ground.

"Yes, I must say that you do. Obviously, I jumped to conclusions."

"That happens quite a lot with me, Trooper Callas. It's the cross I bear."

Deirdre tried another gambit to assert authority. "Can we go inside so that I can take some notes?" She stepped to my right and headed toward the door.

It took only half a step for me to block her way. She recoiled to catch her balance, her left hand windmilling awkwardly.

"I cannot permit that, Trooper Callas. As much as I would like to be hospitable, we do not permit visitors into the house unless we have had ample prior notice so that we can move Rickey Bayard to a protected setting and give her time to adjust.

"You see, Rickey is an autistic child with multiple developmental disabilities. She panics easily and reacts violently—and I do mean violently, Trooper Callas—to unexpected events or changes in her regimen. She is very, very sensitive to noise and touch, even light. She needs to be kept isolated, and she wants to be kept isolated. Right now, Rickey is in the kitchen having lunch, and I'm not about to upset her by bringing visitors—she calls them 'aliens'—into the house. I trust you'll understand if I suggest that we sit in your cruiser instead and talk there."

This really did not sit well. Deidre Callas, sighing with exasperation, lifted her head to the heavens and slapped her clipboard against her thigh once again.

But we did end up sitting in the car, facing each other. Deirdre Callas really was attractive, and I enjoyed looking at her. She made it clear that the reverse was not true. She got all businesslike and plunked her clipboard on her knee—the Crown Vic did not have a console or armrest.

"Please tell me about the crash and what you saw."

"It was late in the afternoon of July sixth, and I was on the back veranda trying to locate Tryg Sletland. We were going to drive into Elkton for seed supplies. I did not see him, and he later told me he did not witness the crash. Anyway, it was extremely foggy, which is unusual for that time of day. There's often fog off the river, but usually it's first thing in the morning or after dusk, when the air temperature inverts from the water temperature."

"Inverts?"

"Changes so that one is cooler than the other. That's what produces fog."

"How heavy was the fog?" she asked.

"It was unusual on several counts. It was very dense, but it did not go all the way down to the water. I could see all the way across the river to the shore over there, across to Long Point. The fog was like a floor...or a ceiling, or whatever, hovering above the water. It was about, I guess, fifty or sixty feet above the water. Above that height, it was completely opaque. You couldn't see a thing above about sixty feet. I suppose a meteorologist could explain it, but I can't recall ever seeing fog like that, before or since. The surface of the water was absolutely still, absolutely flat, like a mirror."

"Then what?"

"Then the plane burst into sight out of the fog, just about abreast of the Long Point Marina. It was pretty much upside down. The plane was reflected in the surface, so that it looked just like there were two planes. I will never forget that sight. It's like this all was in slow motion. The plane settled down toward the water and then hit the surface right on the windshield, but the nose did not dig in. The tail dragged like it was a big fin, leaving a wake. The plane sank down, skipped off the water and then bounced back up, like a kid skipping a flat stone. I guess it bounced back up twenty or thirty feet. Then the plane veered toward shore. The wing on that side caught the water, and everything just went crazy. There was a huge ball of spray, and the nose dug in, and it began cartwheeling toward the dock at Bohemia Vista Marina."

"How many times did it cartwheel?"

"Two. The first time I could see the whole bottom of the plane in silhouette. It bounced back up into the air and then cartwheeled again as it crashed on to the tee-head on the dock at the marina. Just before it hit, the whole tail assembly broke off and flew up into the air.

"Everything was silent for a second. I could feel my heart pounding. I remember I started to say, 'My God! My God! My God!' but before I finished saying it the third time—my memory is clear on this—there was a huge 'Whoomph!' sound and a big cloud of flame and smoke shot up. There was a bright reflection of the flames on the river. Then I suppose the heat burned the fog off, because suddenly the flames and smoke shot up into the air. There was a sound like wind blowing in a series of waves. It went 'whoosh, whoosh, whoosh!'"

"Could you see the plane?

"No, by then all there was smoke and flames."

"What did you do then?"

"I ran into the house, through the butler's pantry and into the kitchen to get to the kitchen phone. I called 9-1-1. It connected into emergency at the Galena Fire Department. Before they could ask 'what is the nature of your emergency?' I screamed, 'A plane hit the gas dock at Bohemia Vista! Big explosion! Get every available fire company over there!'

"She asked me to repeat myself, if you can believe that. I said, 'Plane crash. Bohemia Vista. Huge explosion. People killed.' She asked me my name and where I was and whether I was on a cell phone or a land line."

"You're sure it went down like this?"

"Trooper, let me explain something. I have almost perfect memory, and no, it doesn't fade with time. I really do remember just about everything. Every detail. If you listen to the 9-1-1 recording, you will find it is exactly, word-for-word, what I just told you. If you find other witnesses to the crash and talk to them, their stories will be exactly like mine, except mine will be more accurate."

Callas spoke noticeably more carefully after that. We talked for a few minutes more about how I raced down to the Bohemia River bridge and found I could not get across because of the flames, which were blackening the bridge in soot, and the heat, which melted the glass out of the windows in the bridge control tower. I talked about how I tried to help direct traffic and how some people actually sped up or veered toward me as I waved my hands at them.

"Okay, we're done," she finally said. She inserted her ballpoint across the top of her clipboard and gestured me out of the car. No thanks, no goodbye, just a dismissive wave of the back of her hand. She drove off slowly.

I'm certainly no stranger to racial discrimination. Every day of my life in Australia I had been on the receiving end of systematic, automatic disdain and oppression. To say that I was marginalized, even in "our" region up in Queensland, would be an understatement. We blackfellas outnumbered whites, yet whitefellas overpowered us every day, in every way. But there— how can I explain this?—although we hated how we are treated, we don't take it personally, because every white person in Oz demeans every black person. It's universal.

In my short time in Cecil County, Maryland, I had discovered that in many ways American racism was pretty much the same. But Trooper Deirdre Callas had brought a sharp and deliberate edge to our interaction. Despite never having met me before, she seemed to dislike me personally, to find me uniquely offensive. Her demeanor seemed different—angrier, more direct—than the garden-variety racism that pervaded life on the upper Chesapeake.

What was it? Did she find me particularly "uppity?" Did the fact that I was educated and articulate threaten her? Was she reacting to the differences in appearance between indigenous Australians and African Americans? Did she find my role and station at Bohemia Manor offensive and outrageous? Was it something I said...or failed to say?

This much was clear: I was not on Trooper Deirdre Callas' good side.

17

Do Me a Favor

"HELLO, SAILOR."

Lon Santunas thought Deirdre Callas' voice always sounded different on the phone, deeper and huskier than in person. The southern drawl was less pronounced, the voice less forced. Sexier.

"Deirdre, hi. I was just thinking about you."

"Clean thoughts or dirty thoughts?"

"Well, actually I was planning out next week's duty roster, but I'm not above sneaking a few racy ideas in here and there. You know that my mind is never far from the gutter."

"What about next week's duty roster?"

"Well, I just got back from the barracks, and I see on the board that you're scratched from our shift on Wednesday. Everything okay?"

"Relax, Lon. Just my annual mammogram and annual fun and games with my gynecologist. Got to make sure the equipment is in good working order. Speaking of which, you busy?"

"You do get to the point, don't you? Never too busy for you, Deirdre. Visitors are welcome if that's what you're getting at."

"That's exactly what I'm getting at. Long time, no dick."

"My dick or anybody's dick?"

"Trooper Lon, I know you think I am nothing but a cock-thirsty tramp, but I am a completely monogamous cock-thirsty tramp. Yes, I like to screw a lot, but I don't like to screw around. You're not going to catch somebody else's clap from me."

"Well, then, I guess I can breathe easy. How far away are you? I can have some Chablis chilled in thirty minutes. Or hearty burgundy. Name your poison."

Lon always found Deirdre Callas' transformation from locked-and-loaded state trooper to unbuttoned fuck buddy surprising. In uniform, Trooper Deirdre Callas always looked edgy, like maybe her boots were a bit too tight. She wore formal authority uneasily, as if she needed to display it as much as wield it, as if her Glock and her flat-brimmed trooper hat conferred self-confidence that was absent without these emblems of power. As a cop, Deirdre struck most people—colleagues and citizens alike—as wound tight, as artificially and unnecessarily officious.

Sex—the anticipation of sex, the sex itself, the languid after-effects of sex—relaxed Deirdre Callas, eased her tensions, temporarily banished her demons. She seemed to breathe easier and deeper, to unsnap the checkrein so she could toss her head, step out from behind the screen, and allow herself to be fully seen.

Deirdre Callas looked as if she had been assembled from two different people. Both athletic, both in great shape, but different. From the waist up, she was petite – small boned, with small hands, narrow shoulders, and small breasts (in fact, Lon knew, she was self-conscious about her breast size). Her upper body was that of a gymnast.

From the waist down, Deirdre was distinctly pear-shaped. Her thighs were thick, her buttocks full and rounded, her calves prominent and powerful, her ankles thick and strong. She looked like a powerhouse. Deirdre worked out diligently to "trim down," as she put it, but she and Lon both knew that her fundamental architecture could not be changed. Deirdre called her upper body Yin, and, with a slight grimace, labeled her lower body Yang.

Lon had earned considerable brownie points—and some extra-exuberant sex—by pointing out that in Asian iconography,

Yin and Yang complemented each other and formed a perfect circle when joined. When they coupled, he loved the strength of Deirdre's powerful legs, the delightful momentum provided by her generous hips. With Deirdre Callas, when you got on for a ride, you got a ride.

Lon had long since learned that Deirdre was deeply and profoundly multi-orgasmic. Fortunately, Lon had considerable staying power himself. Deirdre's repeated trips to ecstasy would have exhausted and humiliated a one-and-done sex partner. Lon smiled—with both anticipation and a little self-satisfaction—as they left the starting gate.

They never spent the entire night together. Typically, they would snuggle for a half-hour or so after sex, "spooning," Deirdre called it, then Deirdre would arise, assemble herself unselfconsciously, kiss Lon lightly on the lips, and head out into the night.

◈ ◈ ◈

THIS PARTICULAR NIGHT'S 'MEETING' WAS PARTICULARLY pleasurable. The lust river was running fast and deep as Lon smiled at Deirdre. "Frank Sinatra?" he said. She smiled and kissed him on the top of the head. "Definitely Mr. Sinatra. Maybe Frank Sinatra squared."

This was a little private joke. They had been sitting in McAvoy's Tap one evening, rather idly stroking each other's genitals under the table, when Frank Sinatra's "The Best is Yet to Come" crooned out of the jukebox. "Maybe this should be our song," Deirdre had whispered. "It seems to be all about coming."

"And you know what Ava Gardner said about Frank Sinatra, right?" Santunas whispered back. "'Twelve pounds of man, hundred pounds of dick.'"

"It can be our secret code word," Deirdre had smiled. "Frank Sinatra. And Frank Sinatra squared? That means watch out for friction burns."

As the evening neared its mellow conclusion, Deirdre Callas

turned to Lon Santunas, reached over, and stroked his forehead. "Lon," she said. "I want you to do something for me." He reached over and cupped her diminutive breast, pleased at the prospect of Act IV. "Sure, babe."

"Not that," she laughed. "Enough, already. No, I need you to help me out with something."

Now the timbre of her voice turned hard, her tone urgent. He propped himself up on his elbow to look at her.

"What's this about?"

"I'd like you to do a number on someone, to put him in his place, teach him some fucking manners."

"What did you have in mind?"

"Nothing major, but more than a speeding ticket. A real wake-up call. Taillight, maybe."

"Who we talking about?"

"That weird black shithead who runs Bohemia Manor Farm. This asshole needs to be taken down a notch or two."

"And just what did he ever do to you?"

"Last week I was sent over to Bo Manor by our Galena people to do a follow-up interview on that plane crash. The *Cecil Whig* said someone there had been an eyewitness."

"And...?"

"And this black asshole gave me this enormous attitude, all arrogant and patronizing. Flashes all these papers that appoint him general manager and tell everybody to 'accord him every courtesy,' and bullshit like that. He was really doin' the dozens on me, Lon, and trying to jerk me around. No respect, none at all. I tell you, I was sorely tempted to pop a cap right in the middle of that shit-eating grin of his."

"Let me ask you something without you getting all pissy with me. Is this all about this guy being colored, or is it about some guy giving you an attitude?"

"They go together."

"Well, maybe they shouldn't, at least not so much. Deirdre, this...*thing* you got about black people is kind of over the top. I know you had a tough childhood and all..."

She cut him off, turning to confront him, slapping his hand away from her breast, and bunching the sheets tightly up around her throat. Her eyes had become slits, her normally pale face suddenly blotched with vivid red patches on her cheeks and throat. "*Tough?* Tough? What the fuck do you know about tough? Your father didn't sell you as a sex toy for rent money."

She was shouting now. "You think I should be okay with being fucked by some hoity-toity Nigerian college professor *every goddamned week* for three years? 'Oh, yes, my dear, that's right. Thursday is fuck day. We must stay on schedule.' Is three abortions before I was sixteen *okay* with you, Lon?"

Lon Santunas inhaled hard and caught his breath, throttling the powerful urge to shout back at her. He waited a moment until he could control his voice. "Okay, okay, *okay.* Yes, you're right, that was some very heavy shit, and no, I'm sure I *don't* know what you feel. I can't imagine what that was like, Deirdre.

"But we've been over this before. Okay, you feel justified in resenting black people. Look, I don't like the coloreds much either. But is doing a number on this one person going to make up for all the shit you went through as a kid? What's it going to get you?"

Deidre Callas' shoulders began to shake, and she hid her eyes with her hands, letting the clutched sheet drop. "Lon, this guy down at Bo Manor was so *sarcastic.* He was deliberately putting me down. It was so...*wrong.*" She was sobbing now. "Lon, we can't let that kind of shit go without fighting back."

"We?"

"Look, are you going to help me or not?

"Why not just do it yourself? Stand up for yourself directly? Do a show and go? Your baton can smash a taillight just as well as my baton can. And the local police at the Elkton jail are probably happier doing you a favor than doing me a favor."

"I would, Lon, but I can't risk it. I got two complaints against me already, some people bitching about how I treated some 'citizens of color' on traffic stops. They're complaining about profiling or 'civil rights violations' or some such crap. Anyway, one more complaint and I go to Disciplinary Board, probably suspension with no pay. Maybe termination."

"*What?* You got two yellows? You never told me that! Why didn't you tell me?"

"You want me to spread the word that I hate uppity black people? I don't need the word going around that I'm some kind of racist nut-case."

"You think telling me about getting cited twice is 'getting the word around?' Thanks for your trust in me, Deirdre."

"Okay, okay, I'm sorry. It's my problem to deal with. Except I need this particular asshole to get what's coming to him, and I need help to do that. Being cited was embarrassing, Lon. For years I had strong marks and a clean record, and now I gotta walk on eggs every time I talk to a black person. Also, I admit, I didn't tell you because I didn't want you getting on my back."

"Oh, but you think it's okay to make me your tool of revenge?"

"Yes, Lon, I do, or I wouldn't ask. I'd do the same for you, you know that."

Deirdre's complexion had returned to its normal porcelain-white glow. She reached over and stroked Lon's flaccid penis. "That's what friends do, Lon. That's what friends do."

18

Show and Go

I HAD GOTTEN NO MORE THAN A HALF MILE FROM THE FARM IN THE station wagon when I heard a brief blip—the sound a siren on a state police cruiser makes when it's not turned fully on but just flicked on and off—and saw a single flashing rooftop bubble light in the rear-view mirror. I pulled off immediately, shut off the engine, reached over for the ever-present Constant Binder on the passenger's seat, and rolled down my window. I kept my hands in plain sight on the steering wheel.

I watched a short state trooper climb out of his olive drab cruiser and walk slowly toward the Country Squire. As he passed the rear of the car, I heard a sharp crack and the splintering of plastic and knew immediately the trooper had just bashed my taillight with his baton. I remember thinking, *they do this trick on blackfellas in Australia all the time. You mean they do it here too?*

The trooper walked up to the driver's door. His identification tag said Arlon Santunas, State Trooper. Drawing on years of Australian experience, I said nothing, but merely looked up at him, cocked my head politely, and raised my eyebrows in inquiry.

"Out of the car," Trooper Santunas said.

I reached for the binder, which contained my driver's license and the car's registration and insurance documents, but Santunas stopped me. "Leave it. I know all about your fancy binder. Don't mean shit to me. Now get out the car."

Without saying a word, I very slowly opened the car door, very slowly lifted myself out, very slowly turned to the car, and very slowly placed my hands on the roof.

"Well, what do you know?" laughed Santunas. "They can be taught! Know why I pulled you over?"

I kept my voice low, calm, and steady. "I cannot say that I do, sir."

He mimicked my answer, mocking my words and tone: "'I cannot say that I do, sir.' Well, I pulled you over because your Ford—oh, I shouldn't say 'your,' because you sure as hell don't own it—because *the farm's* vehicle has a broken taillight lens, in violation of the Maryland Motor Vehicle Code. Can't have that now, can we?"

Facing away from him, I could sense his smile as he spoke. "Now you're thinking, hey! What's the big deal? Broken taillight, that's a warning or at worst a summary offense. Is that what you're thinking?"

"It is not, sir."

"So okay, mister smart guy. And I've heard you are a real smart guy, right? Just what are you thinking?"

"Now I am thinking that this stop is in retaliation for offense Trooper Deirdre Collins took when I declined to let her enter Bohemia Manor."

God! Did I really just say that? Hugh, Hugh, Hugh, where is your self-discipline?

"Well, Mr. Ullam," (he pronounced it You-Lamb) "aren't you just a goddamned genius! Yes, I know who you are. I know that you think you got all this clout, that you can just make up your own rules here in Cecil Country. And right now, you believe yourself the victim of police abuse, right? The famed racial profiling you black folks are so upset about? Do I have that right?"

I had years of experience responding to just such abuses of power by various authority figures. I knew the rules here. I knew that confrontation would be unwise and unsuccessful. I knew that any response would be treated as a provocation. I knew to shut up and take what came.

"Do I have that RIGHT?" Trooper Santunas screamed into my right ear.

"That is not for me to say, Trooper Santunas." *Uh, oh. Mistake, Hugh. Now he knows that you know his name.*

Santunas' voice suddenly changed utterly. He adopted a slow, exaggerated southern draw, soft and menacing, like something out of the movies. "You forgot one thing, mister victim. Around here, when colored smart-mouth their betters, they know they gonna be some 'percussions, one way or 'tother."

I said nothing. I kept my head tucked between my arms outstretched on the car roof, because I knew that posture reduced the potential for a skull fracture if that's where I was struck. Looking down between my arms, I saw Trooper Arlon Santunas cock the wrist holding his black baton. And then he gave me a sharp wallop across my upper leg. He did not swing; he just snapped his wrist. He was careful not to hit my knee; his shot smacked off the taut hamstring muscle. He certainly knew how to do this, short and snappy. And extraordinarily painful. I gasped deeply, and sagged, suppressing an urge to vomit.

"How you like them apples, hunh? Now that I have your attention, Mr. You-Lamb," came the same slow drawl, "I hereby inform you that you are under arrest."

Now his voice reverted to his usual nasal twang. "Know what for, asshole? Resisting arrest, mister plantation manager. You are about to learn about how justice works down here, and you are about to get a personal tour of our local penal facilities. Put your fucking hands behind your fucking back."

Neither I nor Santunas spoke during the fifteen-minute ride to the Cecil County Detention Center. The only conversation was a radio call Santunas made as we passed over the C&D Canal bridge.

"Deidre? Santunas. I got a good black buddy of yours sittin' in the back of my cruiser, admiring the scenery on the way to CCDC. His resistance to authority got him in a little trouble."

"Put up a fight?" Callas' voice crackled over the radio.

"Nope, didn't say a thing when I told him I was arresting him for resisting, didn't do a thing. And now he's just sitting here, giving the back of my head the hairy eyeball."

"You gonna do the full show and go?" Callas asked.

"Well, that's the plan. Just a night to think things through."

⚙   ⚙   ⚙

ALTHOUGH THE MARYLAND STATE POLICE HAD DETENTION FACILITIES

in other counties, it had none in Cecil County and had contracted with the Cecil County Sheriff's Office to process and house people the state police arrested from Galena up to the Pennsylvania state line.

I was unfamiliar with the criminal justice system in the United States, but based on what I'd seen on TV, I expected to be booked, searched, and fingerprinted and that my belt, shoelaces, and contents of my pockets would be taken from me before I was locked up. But there was no processing and no searches. My six-inch buck knife remained in my pocket, and my beloved Australian alligator belt was still cinched tightly around my waist.

I was walked straight through to the holding cell, unsearched and untouched, by a young blond deputy with a military style buzz cut and pant creases sharp enough to cut diamonds. His name tag said 'Tinglestad.' No first name or rank.

The paint was barely dry on the new Cecil County Detention Center, and even the windowless holding cell smelled antiseptically fresh. I was spared the stink of urine, stale beer and vomit I had expected. The only other person in the cell was a tousled boy in his late teens who kept wiping the tears out of his eyes and saying, "I'm sorry, I'm sorry, I'm sorry" over and over again. He did not acknowledge my arrival or presence, uttered no "Hey, what are you in for?" or "Lawd, ain't this just the shits?" He sat facing away from me, shaking his head, and wringing his hands.

"Am I entitled to a phone call?" I asked Maroney.

"Why yes, sir," the deputy said politely. "You most certainly are. Yes indeed, you most certainly are." He smiled.

After two hours—I still had my watch on—the whiny kid's mother, a neatly coiffed women in her thirties dressed in tight blue jeans, high-stack heels, and a white frilly blouse, was ushered in and the delinquent was sprung into her custody. He cowered as she cuffed him across the back of his head.

"Curtis, you little piss-ant!" she fumed. "Just how'd you manage this? None them other boys even got brought in. Now you sittin' in a jail cell with some goofy-lookin' nigger, and now you got a rap sheet with B&E and public drunkenness on it. Did you enjoy havin' beers for lunch, you little rat's ass? If I was your real mother, I'd really do a number on you. But I don't have to break my nails because your father gonna tan your hide so dark they could make a La-Z-Boy out of you. You payin' your own fine, mister gang member."

She dragged him by the sleeve down the corridor, banged on the locked door and stood there slapping her other hand impatiently against her thigh. There was a loud metallic clack, the door sprang open, and they were gone.

After three more hours, the young deputy appeared with a cellophane wrapped sandwich—white bread, a piece of yellow processed cheese, a single piece of lettuce—and a can of RC cola. "Sir," I asked said politely. "About my phone call?"

"Oh, we're workin' on it. We be workin' on it. Don't you be worryin' none. Oh, and your car's safe in the impound." He smiled broadly, made a sharp military about-face, and headed out of the holding compound door. Then he spun back abruptly.

"Hey, I jes' realized. They ain't no toilet here in the holding tank. You must be getting a mite uncomfortable. Let me just move you down the hall to a reg'lar cell with a toilet and blanket and toilet paper and all. And don't worry, it's okay to drink the water."

❂   ❂   ❂

THAT WAS THE LAST I SAW OR HEARD FROM ANYONE FOR THE NEXT fourteen hours. As far as I could tell, I was the only resident of the Cecil Country Detention Center. By the time the lights clicked off at 11:45, I was sure I was not going to get my phone call, so I crawled under the blanket—brand new, forest green, still in its clear plastic wrapper—and put myself to sleep.

I know how to do this. During my formative years at Akers, I had learned how to turn sensory deprivation into relaxation, rest, and eventually sleep. As a kid, I knew nothing of meditation or finding one's center, but I learned these skills empirically through years of trial and error at Akers. I found out how deep breathing provides release. I did not dream of warm and wonderful places; I did not fantasize about sugar plum fairies. I learned to take myself nowhere, wrap myself in emptiness, and sleep dreamlessly until the morning buzzer sounded.

And therefore, I was sound asleep when a klaxon sounded in the CCDC at seven the next morning. At the foot of the bunk someone had placed a camper-pack of Captain Crunch cereal and a half-pint of two-percent milk. No spoon, but I made do.

At nine-thirty, the cell block door opened, and a gaunt figure appeared outside my cell. He was not a state trooper. He was, as we used to say in Australia, 'regular army,' a term that had nothing to do with actually being in the army. He was dressed in a neat dark blue tunic with black slacks. Again, the killer creases. The pencil pockets on his chest were a lighter shade of blue. His black name badge, engraved in white, said 'Maroney.' No rank, just 'Maroney.' His glossy black oxfords reflected the fluorescent ceiling lights. I placed him at about fifty. He stood tall, arms crossed over his chest. He had pronounced wrinkles at the corners of deep-set eyes that squinted as if he were in pain. They were set deep behind a single bushy eyebrow that ran uninterrupted across his forehead.

"Time to go," he said in a soft, reedy voice.

"Go where?" I said.

"Out the door, to the great out-of-doors," he said. At this he smiled. "Time for us to clean out the riff-raff."

"I'm sorry," I said. "I don't know what's happening here."

"You never heard of a show and go? Well, you done seen the show, and now you gonna go the go."

"What about the charges?"

"Charges? Ain't no charges. Ain't no records. Ain't no *nothin'*. That's why there was no phone call. That door opens, you walk out, and none of this little sleep-over never happened, do you follow me? Be grateful: we ain't gonna charge you for dinner and breakfast.

"And Mr. Ullam? (He pronounced my name correctly). I know who you are, and I know that you think you're some kind of privileged white hat around here, all because you work for that rich horse's ass Bayard. I know you are Australian and not African American, but I don't give a sweet damn about what brand of colored you are. That don't make you anything but a curiosity around here, and I don't think you should want people to be curious, follow me? With that in mind, may I make a constructive suggestion?"

"Absolutely." I stood with my head lowered slightly, my hands clasped behind my back. Akers had taught me the value of showing deference.

"Learn your lesson. Learn who has the power around here. Learn to fit in, the way the other colored folks do around here. If you get all self-righteous and try to make a stink about your show and go, you will learn a whole lot more about who's got the power in Cecil County. You lost a night's sleep, courtesy of the Maryland State Police, who we respect and help out whenever possible. You wouldn't want to lose anything more, if you catch my drift."

"I catch your drift."

"The impound lot is two blocks down and two blocks left. Your car and keys are there. Because you're new to town, we're going to waive the impound fee, but you're going to have to pay Larry Bindow his towing fee. That'll be twenty-five bucks. If you don't have the cash on you, Larry will extend you credit, but whatever you do, don't forget to come back in and pay him back. Am I clear?"

"You are absolutely clear, Officer Maroney."

"Sergeant Maroney."

"You are absolutely clear, Sergeant Maroney."

"One last question, Mr. Ullam. Off the record—'course this whole little adventure is off the record, right? I was off shift yesterday when the State Police dropped you off for your little visit. I'm curious: who was it, Callas or Santunas?"

"Santunas, but I think it was because I had a run-in with Callas. Does it matter who violates my civil rights?"

Maroney shook his head in mock dismay. "See? Now there you go, getting all uppity again. Mr. Ullam, here I am just trying to give you some helpful tips, and you just keep pushin' back at me. I'm giving up on you. Let me see you out."

⚙   ⚙   ⚙

THE IMPOUND LOT WAS RIGHT WHERE MARONEY SAID IT WOULD BE, and Larry Bindow, a huge genial goof whose belt was buried beneath an enormous floppy gut, was happy to extend credit. Turns out I didn't need it: I had twenty bucks in my pocket, and Larry said he'd drop the price five dollars for me. He brought the Ford around, left it with the door ajar and the engine running, and wished me a good day.

To my considerable surprise, the Ford's left rear taillight now was intact, and it still had the parts department SKU sticker from Kedlow Ford on it.

When I climbed into the Squire, the Constant Binder was sitting on the passenger seat. It was encased in a heavy-duty clear plastic envelope, the kind with two paper circles and a string that you wound around them in a figure-eight pattern to hold the envelope flap closed. This was not my envelope.

19

Crossing the Rubicon

ALTHOUGH I HAD CERTAINLY HEARD OF PEOPLE SUCCUMBING ALMOST immediately to some major myocardial catastrophe, I never believed the old saying that "he was dead before he hit the ground." A body just can't die that fast, I thought, the heart spontaneously ceasing all work without even a twitch or a last futile push, the lungs collapsing utterly and instantly, the brain cutting all power like a tripped circuit breaker.

Leave it to Hermann Bayard, age forty-seven, fit and trim, an athletic type, moderate in his habits, descended of long-lived German stock, to prove me wrong.

We were in a loose, lazy mood. Simone was off on a yard job elsewhere, but the rest of the Hole in the Wall Gang, Nora, Rickey, Tryg, and I, plus Hermann (who we never thought of as part of our reclusive club), were out on the patio, taking in a lovely sunset over the Bohemia River, watching Turkey Point disappear in featureless silhouette.

Nora had whipped up a pitcher of some killer sangria, and we were feeling pretty mellow. Hermann had hit the pitcher heavily and was clearly quite drunk. Rickey sat at the patio table, ignoring us as usual, reading a heavy volume of something or other, murmuring quietly under her breath.

In the distance we could hear the intensely irritating howl of what we called a "Little Richard," a high-powered ocean-racing speedboat beloved of the macho set here on the Chesapeake. We agreed that the over-moneyed owners of these flashy phallic forty-foot multi-engine boats were obviously compensating for genital under-endowment, that is, for having a little dick.

The sound finally abated, and the burr of cicadas and crickets reclaimed the soundtrack.

"Someone should just shoot those motherfuckers," said Tryg amiably. "My, how they offend the human ear. Which is what I'm equipped with."

"Gas prices will kill them," Hermann slurred. "With marine gas over three bucks a gallon and those things burning sixty gallons an hour, a round-trip up the bay from Middle River and back will set somebody back five hundred bucks. That and their giant monthly payments should cause mass extinction in a couple of years. Sailboats are silly, but at least they don't make noise."

"Oh, it's not just the decibels." This was Rickey, breaking in with a pressured rush of words, her tone confident and professorial. "At full throttle those unsilenced engines will have a noise level of over 120 decibels, which is enough to damage your hearing. But also, the noise comes in a frequency range that exacerbates the acoustic impact of the sound waves. Even without the high volume, those frequencies will damage the inner ear. Those assholes are not only going to go broke, they're going to go deaf."

There was a moment of astonished silence. Rickey smiled brightly.

"I know all about this because, you know, I have been doing a lot of research on acoustics, both in the air and in the water. I'm experimenting with frequencies all across the radio spectrum. That's what my lab is for, you guys. Did you all think I was just listening to AM radio top 100 hits with all my equipment down there?"

"And just why have you been doing all these experiments, Rickey?" asked Hermann.

Rickey acted as if she hadn't heard him.

"And why are you doing that?" asked Tryg.

"With the water experiments, I want to understand the characteristics of acoustic waves," Rickey said. "How to propagate them, see how far they'll go and how long they remain audible. I'm also learning how much power it takes to generate them. Like, how a single whale can generate acoustic waves that go hundreds of miles."

"And tell me, Rickey, what prompted this interest?" I asked. Everyone had turned to Rickey, and she was relishing the attention.

"Two things kind of connected up," she said. "In the *Cecil Whig* last year, there was this article about this guy over at the Aberdeen Proving Ground who specializes in listening to ULFs—that's ultra-low frequencies. Very slow acoustic waves with long wavelengths. The ones he listens to are underwater because water is a very good acoustic propagator."

"Why does he bother?" Nora said.

"Couple of reasons. First, ULFs travel enormous distances without dissipating. You can hear some of 'em a couple of thousand miles away if you have the right receiver. Second, submarines have distinct ULF signatures. Supposedly this guy can identify and track every submarine on earth, from right here in Aberdeen, Maryland. Is that cool, or what?"

"Oh, puh-leeze," said Hermann.

"I read the same article," I broke in, trying to avert a father-daughter pissing match. "The guy had been a sonar operator on a hunter-killer sub, right, Rickey? And he was a genius at recognizing different signatures. Got so good they sucked him over to Aberdeen to be their human sonar. Now all he does is track subs."

Rickey was nodding vigorously.

"So, you want to track submarines from Bo Manor Farm?" Hermann asked.

"No, no, no. Here's the second thing. You guys ever hear about Humphrey the whale?"

Blank stares.

"Back in 1985, a forty-foot humpback whale veered away from his migration route from Mexico to Alaska. For some reason he swam into San Francisco Bay. He went further and further in until he was all the way into the Sacramento River, which is brackish, more fresh water than salt water. Just like here on the Bohemia River.

"Anyway, he ended up in a dead-end *forty miles* from the ocean, and they could not coax him out or scare him out with loud banging noises. He got listless and changed color, and they thought he was gonna die.

"This acoustics professor, Dr. Bernie Krause, thought they might lure him out with recordings Krause had made of humpback feeding songs. But to get the sounds into the water they had to have speakers and amplifiers only the Navy had. So, the Naval Postgraduate School in Monterey lent them some fancy transducers, which they mounted on someone's private yacht. They played the songs on and off to keep Humphrey interested, and it worked! *He followed the yacht! He followed the underwater signals!* As the water got saltier, Humphrey got all jiggy and finally swam out of the Golden Gate bridge. True story. There are Humphrey the Whale children's books about it."

Rickey was grinning at us, sitting on the edge of her chair.

"Okay, here's the thing. Krause's recordings had ULF signatures. *Whales speak ULF.* For years people have listened to whale sounds with hydrophones, and now we know that individual whales have individual songs. All whales and dolphins communicate using sound they produce by forcing air through a sort of a pair of internal 'lips.' Then they re-cycle the air for more vocalization, more 'oomph.' Dolphins' click-click-clicks don't go very far, but whales send powerful messages. They have phrases and repetitive call-and-response patterns. Isn't that *wild*?"

I'm sure we all looked skeptical. But Rickey's eyes were

bright; she was making an emphatic shoving gesture with her palms pointed out toward us; she was literally pushing back.

"So, here's what: I'm working to see if I can communicate with whales or orcas or porpoises in some way. And maybe not just mammals. Maybe sharks and certain fish, too, the ones with electrical receptors. I want to attract them. Right up the Chesapeake. *Up here on the Bohemia River.*

"But I don't know what frequencies to use, so I need to study those signals, to experiment with what kind of receivers you need to hear them and what kind of signal generator you need to send them. And getting enough power to push the signals, especially in water, is proving a problem. So, I'm seeing if I can stack frequencies and piggy-back power profiles. I'm having a hard time with that part."

"That's just the water stuff. While I'm learning about the whole radio spectrum, I'm also experimenting with airborne frequencies. That part is pretty easy. It's really just like a radio station, broadcasting radio waves. I have my own AM 'station.' I call it WRKY, hah, hah. I got 30,000 watts clear channel, but unlike a fixed-frequency station, I can move my transmissions all over the spectrum. That's why all the antennas and dishes on the hangar roof."

None of us knew enough to ask for details.

"But the air stuff is completely different from all my underwater signal generation, the whale stuff. Very, very different. With the signals I'm sending into the air, *we be jammiin'*!"

We looked at her blankly.

"Bob Marley," said Rickey. "You know, the Rasta guy?" When her attempt at humor failed to get a rise out of us, Rickey grew impatient.

"It's kind of a variation on jamming technology, like when the army screws up the enemy's instruments and communications with huge bursts of radio noise. Real spy stuff."

Rickey looked at us with that seriousness only an adolescent can muster: "Anyway, all this work with specialized signal generation...*is my quest.*"

"Bullshit," said Hermann. "Bullshit science fiction. On my dime."

Rickey popped to her feet. "What did you say?"

"I said, 'bullshit.' To which I might add 'horseshit' and 'chicken shit.' Most kids your age get by with thirty-dollar Gilbert home chemistry sets, and I have forked out tens of thousands of dollars so that you can fiddle around in fantasyland."

Rickey's face turned beet-red, and Nora moved to defuse the imminent explosion. "Okay, Rickey," she smiled. "Suppose you succeed, and you get a whale all the way up here. What then?"

"What do you mean, what then?"

"I mean, what happens to the whale once he's up here? Do you give him a name and make a pet out of him? Scratch him on the head? Feed him sardines?"

"Nothing happens! I stop the signal, and he just goes away. I'm not trying to *capture* him, I'm just trying to do some operant conditioning on his normal response patterns."

Hermann still wanted to fight. He stood and walked unsteadily over to Rickey. "Well, I think that's animal cruelty. You are exposing that whale to a one-hundred-and-forty-mile round trip in a busy waterway. You are exposing that poor whale to great danger."

Rickey slung her book at Hermann's head with both hands. It missed, and Hermann, laughing now, leaned down to pick it up. While still bent over, he suddenly coughed loudly, a single strange animal bark. His eyes widened in surprise. "The fuck!" he said thickly. His tumbler fell from his hand, and he toppled face-first onto the patio. His collapse was slack and uncontrolled, like a marionette whose strings have been cut. He didn't throw out a hand to break his fall. He just plopped, his left leg bent under him, his right leg splayed off the edge of the patio. He came to rest in heap, like a pile of soiled clothing tossed into a laundry basket. No twitching or agonized gasping. He lay utterly inert, his face pressed into the pavers.

I knew instantly that Hermann was gone.

⚙   ⚙   ⚙

AND INDEED HE WAS. WE RUSHED TO HIS SIDE, UNFOLDED HIM, AND turned him onto his back, tore open his shirt, and pried his mouth open. His eyes were fixed, his pupils dilated. His mouth gaped. A trickle of blood ran from his right nostril. Tryg, who knew CPR, pinched Hermann's nose, and attempted mouth-to-mouth resuscitation. Clearly it wasn't working: air was going in, but nothing was coming back out. His chest did not rise and fall; looked like Tryg was shoving on a sack of flour.

Hermann Bayard was totally unresponsive. He was indeed a dead man, obviously a completely dead man.

Rickey now stood beside him, looking down at his chalky white face. Her own face resembled his: ashen, expressionless. Her arms were crossed tightly across her chest. She exhaled loudly.

"Nora!" cried Tryg. "Run in and call 9-1-1!" Nora stumbled to her feet, making strange rowing motions with her arms.

"*Stop!*" I roared, freezing Nora in her tracks. "Do *not* call 9-1-1! Whatever you do, do not bring other people in here!"

"Are you crazy?" Tryg shouted. "We have to get him some help."

"Tryg," I said firmly. "We do not have to get him some help. He is beyond help. Hermann Bayard is dead. You call 9-1-1 and in twenty minutes some EMT team from Cecilton will pronounce him dead."

I paused, surprised at the calm that had come over me.

"And then, my friends, the shit will really hit the fan. The medical examiner will be called. Our good friends with the State police will arrive and take witness reports. They will cart Hermann Bayard off to the morgue. They will want to know all about how we have been living here. Some press flack who covers the ME's office will catch hold of the story and flog it to the *Cecil Whig*. Hermann Bayard's untimely and unexpected death will probably not be big news...but it will be news: 'Mysterious German Recluse Drops Dead.'

"And friends," I continued softly, "when that happens, we will all be shit out of luck. Our cover will be blown. A little follow-up investigative action will soon reveal our secret little coven. Sooner or later—and I think it will be sooner if my good friends Santunas and Callas have anything to say about it—we will be thrown out of here. Maybe we won't be charged with anything, maybe we will. But we sure won't be allowed to stay here and live off Herman Bayard's money anymore.

"And Rickey...it very much pains me to say this...if that happens, you stand a good chance of being placed in a facility for severely autistic young adults. Probably it would be a private institution, because you stand to inherit Hermann's money, so the social workers probably wouldn't put you in a public facility. But you sure as hell won't be living here."

Rickey Bayard dropped to her knees, her body collapsing and her arms thrusting in front of her—a perfect rendition of what is called the child's pose in yoga. Nora moved to hug her and help her up, but Rickey shook her shoulders violently—like a wet dog shaking off after a bath—and she stayed locked in place, her head hidden between her arms.

Now that I had up a head of steam, I kept talking. "So, friends, here's the bottom line. We have a decision to make, and we have to make it *right now*. If we want to save ourselves, we are going to have to lay low. We're going to have to stay down wind and out of sight. From now on. *For good.*

"Look, there's no need for our lives to be different from what they are now. *We... just...don't...tell...anyone...that...Hermann... Bayard...is...dead.* We continue to live the way we do, do things the way we do, keep below the radar. Nothing's really any different: when asked, we say, 'we have not heard from Hermann Bayard in a while, and we are not able to contact him.' Nothing's really has to change, except that I sign his name to the tax returns."

"Except that we'd all be felons!" Tryg exploded.

"Mr. Sletland, let me remind you that you are already a felon—a felon that right now has a lifetime tenure in a job that pays you over a hundred and forty thousand bucks a year. Tryg, do you really want to screw that poochie?"

FOR OBVIOUS REASONS, WE COULDN'T GO THE FUNERAL HOME ROUTE

for a proper embalming, but we all decided we could bury Hermann in the time-honored American way, in a simple pine box, with folks paying their respects by saying some kind words at the grave site.

In almost no time, Tryg built Hermann quite a fine pine coffin, with neatly mitered corners and even a slight bow in the top, rather like the back of violin. It was neatly varnished, and it had brass hinges rather than simply a lift-off top. We used a throw pillow off one of the living room couches to support Hermann's head, and, after *rigor mortis* had relaxed its grip, we dressed him in a dark blue Lacoste alligator polo shirt and a pair of light gray slacks. Loafers, no socks.

We buried Herman Bayard about thirty yards from the water on the little point that overlooks the Bohemia River Bridge. We would have preferred, as tradition dictates, to plant him fully six feet down, but we were in a hurry, and I confess that we cut corners. Hermann ended up adequately interred, but far less than six feet down.

We asked Rickey if she wanted to attend the "funeral," and to my surprise, she said yes.

We all stood silently around the grave for a minute or two before saying our words. Nora went first. "Hermann, I can't say that working for you was always a pleasure, or even usually a pleasure. But I thank you for your kindness and fairness to me, and I hope you recognized my commitment and dedication to Rickey. I can't help but think that our current arrangement amused you and perhaps pleased you. As Hugh Ullam so often says, 'Living well is the best revenge.' Goodbye, Hermann."

Then Tryg said, "Hermann, what can one say about such a strange end to such a strange time? For us all. I know that both before and after you died, we were taking advantage of you. Still, in light of how it all played out, I can't feel terribly guilty. As Karl Marx put it, 'From each according to his ability, to each according to his needs.' There's no telling where things will ultimately go from here, but I will always be grateful to you. *Auf wiedersehen,* Hermann."

I nodded to Rickey, her face a stony mask. Her final words to Hermann were typical of her communication style, punctuated with pauses and gaps. "You died...laughing at me. How typical, father. How typical of you...to dismiss me and abandon me. You weren't here mostly, and now you won't be here...entirely, so no big difference, right? I hope no one...expects me to feel grief and loss. Still, I hope they... never find you and...that everybody just leaves your grave alone, just like I hope everybody...*just leaves us alone."*

Now that it was my turn, I found myself at a loss for words. I felt no more inclined toward an outpouring of emotion than Rickey was. *What was my relationship with Hermann Bayard all about?* It then struck me that it really was all about business.

"Hermann, we struck a good deal, you and I, and each of us held up our end. I think you died knowing that in hiring me you'd made a decent choice. Your net worth now is greater than when I signed on. I will continue to do the tasks I have been doing. We will continue as long as we can continue, until fate overtakes us in some way. Our various violations of law really aren't hurting anybody, and they are providing the best possible life for your daughter.

"I also must say, somewhat to my surprise, my own role has moved beyond making sure that Rickey is taken care of. It has evolved into caring about Rickey."

"When I moved here from Australia, I did not expect this... this...extra dimension. Thought it would just be easier to just run the business end of things, to let Nora do all the hard work with Rickey. Now I think we—Rickey, Nora, Tryg, Simone and me—have all been touched and connected in unexpected ways. I am sorry you are not going to be here to see what comes of it."

20

All Ears in Aberdeen

PETTY OFFICER SECOND CLASS EZRA PRASCHKE, SONAR TECHNICIAN/ Surface, was known as "Ears." He enjoyed the nickname, and when introduced to visiting Navy brass, which was often, he would always say, "Yup, I'm all ears."

Praschke had earned his nickname because he could hear things other people couldn't. He had the finest hearing the U.S. Navy audiologists had ever tested. While his perception of very high frequencies was acute—he could actually hear a dog whistle—what surprised the hearing experts most was his ability to detect and distinguish the lowest frequencies in the electromagnetic spectrum, the ones with the long, long waves.

Scientists break electromagnetic waves into twelve categories, the lowest four of which are Extremely Low Frequencies (ELFs), Super Low Frequencies (SLFs), Ultra Low Frequencies (ULFs) and Very Low Frequencies (VLFs). These four are of particular interest to marine scientists, climatologists, meteorologists, and, particularly, the U.S. Navy.

The Navy tech guys have long fooled around with all these frequencies, hoping for breakthrough communications technologies with submarines. At Aberdeen, the "radio guys" spent years working with various kinds of new-tech transmitters for ELFs. SLFs and VLFs, none of which ever proved worth a damn.

Praschke didn't care much about anything but ULFs, and his bailiwick was receivers, not transmitters. His clout at Aberdeen—the reason he was a Petty Officer and not still just a Seaman—stemmed from the excellence of one pair of receivers: his incredible ears and their ability to detect and decipher ULFs.

Heard by the average person, ULF noises sound like a random collection of swishes, hums, thrums, squeaks, and whistles. To Praschke, ULF signatures were the whispered notes in a constant, splendid symphony. ULF sounds could be made by various kinds of machines, ships on and below the surface, electronic technologies, animals big and small, even peculiar weather events. Praschke particularly loved to listen to the ULF signatures generated by whales, fishes, underwater seismic activity, and submarines.

Praschke's singular skill was in interpreting the patterns of what he heard. Though a high-school dropout, he was blessed with a keen memory and a mental filing system that allowed him to interpret, categorize, store, and retrieve hundreds of distinct "acoustic signatures." Like the kind that humpback whales created when singing songs that others of their kind could understand. The deep, distant rumbles that underwater eruptions made. The unique kind that propellers made when spinning through the water, particularly submarine propellers spinning in very deep water. The kinds of noises submarines made when they were trying to make no sound at all.

Although thought by many to be nothing more than a huge firing range shooting prototypes for new types of artillery shells out over an off-limits area in northern Chesapeake Bay, Aberdeen was in a fact a babel of distinct classified research and application projects sponsored by different military branches and agencies. At Aberdeen, Praschke participated in what they called ASRP, the Acoustic Signature Research Project. ASRP had been around for decades, but its role, budget and sophistication changed dramatically as new types of super-silent submarines—ours and theirs—slid down the ways of military shipyards.

Praschke had served four tours of duty in Los Angeles-class and Virginia-class nuclear-powered fast attack submarines. He started as a sonar operator, but soon displayed an uncanny ability to identify the distinct sound signatures of different boats and ships: recreational craft, power boats, luxury liners, freighters, destroyers, carriers (they could be heard a *long* way away, like across oceans), and, especially, submarines. Praschke could recognize and remember the acoustic signature of every submarine on earth. Not just the type—the specific submarine. "Oh, that's the *Tovarich*," he'd say. "That's the old critter with the bent propeller." Or, "Hear that? It's the *Cellini*. Italians sold it to the Chinese, who renamed it *Fei Dan* and put a new diesel in it. Sounds like lightning hitting a Quonset hut."

Praschke supplemented his natural gifts with intense study of the world's navies. He knew about how the Israelis modified and updated their boats. He knew that countries most people didn't even know had navies had submarines. He knew that one third world pygmy nation somehow managed to keep an obsolete Russian nuclear killer sub operating, albeit with a total of only four available torpedoes.

The primary frustration for Praschke's handlers was that his was a unique, and uniquely human, skill. Praschke's gift could not be duplicated, replicated, deconstructed, or manufactured. Such was the irrational structure of the capabilities of a physiological freak. There was no way to back him up. If he croaked or turned up deaf one day, it would set their research and development back significantly. Accordingly, Praschke was treated with kid gloves, if not respect.

On this particular evening, Praschke was working the evening shift. His research leader was interested in learning if his faculties waxed or waned depending on time of day or his level of fatigue. He had excelled at the graveyard shift; now they wanted to know how well he operated earlier in the evening. He was sitting in a cushy leather desk chair, trying out a new set of noise-cancelling headphones, clicking the noise cancellation feature on and off to see what effect it had on detecting low frequency rumbles. At about 7:30 PM he was toggling between a pod of humpbacks off the Azores (two calves!) and eavesdropping on the obsolete and incredibly noisy Russian diesel-electric submarine *Zaphorodzets* banging around the outskirts of Gibraltar.

Suddenly he heard a strange, unfamiliar clicking through his phones. He sat upright in his chair.

"Wuhzzat!?"

Then he heard a mysterious kind of sizzling. The bank of VU meters on his console abruptly pegged at maximum, then dropped back to background surface noise levels. The green wave on the twelve-inch oscilloscope in front of him danced wildly.

Praschke was reaching to check his headphones when his head exploded with an intense bursting pressure and a single, shrieking tsunami of sound. The VU meters pegged again, the decibel monitor maxed out and tripped its breaker. The oscilloscope went black. In rapid sequence, *click-click-click-click-click*, all the other breakers on the main panel tripped as well.

Bellowing with pain, Praschke shot back in his chair until it tripped on a floor outlet and tipped him, writhing and kicking and clawing at his headphones, to the floor.

Sergeant Bruno Thomas had been working at the adjacent console, programming wave profiles. He certainly heard the screech, but it was muffled by Praschke's headphones. He heard the simultaneous *clack!* of whole banks of circuit breakers tripping. Thomas sprang to Praschke's side. Praschke was spastically thrashing his arms over his face, keening a panting woof-woof-woof sound.

Thomas reached down and pulled Praschke's headphones off. Streams of crimson poured from both of Praschke's ears. His eyes were wide, his pupils dilated like large black marbles. He uttered a choking whimper and blacked out.

21

Rickey Blows the Lab

NORA DADMUN AND I WERE IN THE KITCHEN WATCHING A RERUN OF
Mission Impossible. The dishes were still on the table. Rickey's
chair was empty. She had eaten a couple of bites of noodles,
but otherwise her plate of congealing molé chicken appeared
untouched. She never ate green beans, so Nora had not even put
any on her plate.

"Again?" I said, shifting sideways so that I could put my feet
up on Rickey's vacated chair. "What kind of diet is this? I know
most teenage girls are picky eaters, Nora, but Rickey is not
exactly trying to make herself look good for the boys, is she?"

"When she's hungry enough, she'll eat, Hugh. Don't pressure
her, or she'll just go to FYLMA again. I just can't stand that again
tonight."

On this night, Rickey had announced that she was going out
to work in the lab to work on a "major trial." After she'd been
gone a few minutes, the TV suddenly flared, and the picture
shrank into a single dot in the middle of the screen before the
screen went entirely black. The house lights flickered for a
moment, then steadied, as the auxiliary generator outside clicked
on automatically and reset the house power.

I looked at Nora. Her hair, normally a soft helmet of fine light brown, stood out from her head like a fright wig. I looked down at my arm: the hairs were standing on end. I ran my hand over my scalp. My hair, of course, remained tightly curled, but a spark of static electricity jumped from my hand to top of my ear—a big spark.

"What the hell?" I said.

"Must be some of Rickey's high jinks," said Nora.

"Can't be. Her lab has its own power source."

"Well unless we're being invaded by electric aliens, this surge has got to be something about Rickey's fun and games."

"I'll go check on her in the lab," I said, "make sure she's all right. Grab me some Twinkies for her out of the drawer, Nora."

❁   ❁   ❁

RICKEY BAYARD'S "LAB" HAD ONCE BEEN THE FARM'S CINDER BLOCK airplane hangar, set into a hillside about sixty yards from the back of the main house. The Hangar-cum-workshop had gone unused for many years, and was dark and dank until Rickey and Tryg commandeered it for "scientific purposes."

Rickey's "lab" wasn't really a lab at all, not in the Dr. Frankenstein-men-in-white-lab-coats sense. It was actually a long bank of tan consoles, cabinets, and instruments about twenty feet long. The bank contained numerous screens and oscilloscopes, a chart plotter, an antiquated computer monitor, a couple of keyboards, and rows of switches, levers, and circuit breakers, all connected with neatly bundled runs of wires and cables of various colors running out in the open. A thick black cable ran up the wall behind the cabinets and disappeared through a hole punched through the cinder block near the ceiling.

This, I knew, led to an array of three dish-type antennas on the roof, two about a foot and a half across, the other about four feet wide. Rickey's lab had two "stations," as she called them, each fronted by its own office chair rolling on a ratty square of green indoor-outdoor carpeting. One was Rickey's listening installation; the other was her signal generation and transmitting equipment. At one end of the bank of equipment, large black cable the diameter of a python was attached to its own heavy red industrial generator, old and grimy, but major-league powerful. A similar-sized cable ran out of the hangar door from the console and disappeared down toward the Bohemia River.

Tryg and Rickey had collaborated on the sourcing, installation, and testing of all this gear, but Tryg was the one who designed the unique transducer that would allow the huge signal transmitter cable that ran down from the lab to be immersed in the Bohemia River without electrocuting every fish in the upper bay.

And so it came to pass that one day Rickey flipped the switch, the meters peaked and settled, everything hummed, and bingo, Rickey was ready to listen to the electromagnetic universe and to generate a bunch of signals on frequencies across the entire spectrum.

☙   ☙   ☙

WHEN I GOT TO THE HANGAR, THE LARGE OVERHEAD DOOR WAS OPEN, and tendrils of wispy gray smoke were curling out. The space inside was dark. The cinder block building usually was flooded with light because Rickey ran her bank of equipment off three generators— the "house generator" for routine lab power and the two large commercial generators, the largest a huge industrial castoff from an obsolete Dupont manufacturing facility—around the clock. "Plenty of juice," she said often, "I gotta have plenty of juice."

On the left, a door led into a janitor's closet that Rickey had converted to a minimalist bathroom and shower. A door to the left of that led to the sleeping quarters. Over our objection, Rickey preferred this tomb to her bedroom in the big house. Floors, walls, and ceiling were pitch black; to the walls and ceiling, Rickey had glued anechoic foam blocks to cancel out noise. The only light source was a small Tensor lamp perched on a plastic milk carton and aimed at the floor. I found this makeshift bedroom to be a very creepy place.

☙   ☙   ☙

AS I HASTENED TOWARD THE LAB AND THROUGH THE OPEN HANGAR

door, I saw Rickey standing in front of the consoles, backlit by the emergency lighting fixture that glowed red high on the wall. She was wearing a black industrial welder's apron, a pair of worn flip-flops, aviator sunglasses, and rubber latex gloves. Her newest acquisition, the latest model of noise-cancelling headphones, hung around her neck and were not cupped over her ears. Like Nora's, her hair now was electrified with static and standing on end. It looked like a tumbleweed. Her arms were clasped tightly under her diaphragm, not in pain, but in evident frustration.

There was a tremendous stink in the lab, the combined smell of burning electrical insulation and superheated machine oil. A haze of smoke hung in the air. All three generators were emitting snap, crackle and popping noises and shooting arcs of sparks. It looked like a mad scientist B-movie.

"Rickey!" I shouted. "Are you all right?"

Rickey turned toward me. She was not crying or frightened. She was furious.

"Hugh! Fuck! Fuck, fuck, fuck. I screwed up. I so fucked up. I was so close, and then I blew it all up. Huge surge. *Huge.* Everything is fucking fried. It's all junk, all toast. I can't believe I was so goddamned stupid. One well-placed circuit breaker could have saved everything. God damn it! God fucking damn it!"

Rickey clapped her hands angrily against her thighs.

"It all has to be replaced, Hugh. I'll need the whole lab replaced, at least all the electrical stuff. Let's get better stuff next time. We're rich, we don't have to settle for this old primitive shit."

With that she spun on her heel and walked out of the lab, out into the evening breeze and out toward the fields, out through the acrid smell of burned insulation, fried circuit boards, and small electrical fires flickering in the cabinets of a variety of once-pristine components.

22

Tuba in a Phone Booth

WE TOLD RICKEY TO GO BACK TO USING HER BEDROOM IN THE MAIN house. The burnt electrical stink of the burnt-out lab was intolerable, and besides there was nothing left down there for Rickey to tinker with; everything was fried.

Tryg did a quick survey of all the lab equipment and found that anything that either generated power, used power or directed power had been completely destroyed by some enormous and uncontrolled surge of current. All three generators were beyond repair, the windings having melted, the field coils reduced to molten blobs, the rotors warped and blackened, the cabling and power cords shriveled.

All nine radio signal transmitters and all fourteen receivers had literally blown up, their guts blackened and burned, their circuit boards melted, their metal cabinets blown and twisted. It looked like they had been slammed by a giant electric tidal wave. The circuit breakers had been overwhelmed and destroyed before they even had a chance to trip. All the porcelain in-line fuses had shattered. All the oscilloscopes and VU meters, their faces now blackened and warped, showed needles pegged at the maximum. Many of the component cabinets, some of which seemed to have catapulted from their racks, showed soot stains where front and side panels joined, suggesting there had been fire inside.

It was, as Rickey had so succinctly put when I found her standing the smoldering ruins of her lab, "all junk, all toast."

Then Tryg told me of something he found very surprising. "I'm no electrical engineer, Hugh, but I know a little about circuits and loads. I was really shocked to see that all the transmitters had, in effect, been hard-wired in series to create a single massive collective circuit. Some sort of giant transmitting machine. It was very strange to see them linked in tandem, like a series of elephants holding each other's tails. The only thing I can guess is that Rickey had been trying to create some sort of giant multi-frequency amplifier to push her signals. This was crazy stuff. And this was certainly not the way Rickey and I had configured the lab."

☼ ☼ ☼

NOW I STOOD IN THE DOORWAY TO RICKEY'S BEDROOM, TAPPING lightly at the jam to get her attention. She was lying on her bed, looking at the ceiling.

"So, talk to me," I said calmly.

"My burns hurt," said Rickey.

"Rickey, I know I sound like an over-protective parent, but it's a miracle you weren't killed out there—electrocuted or burned to death. Christ! Until now, we've given you free rein to invent things and experiment as you see fit, but now I really need to know what was going on out there."

"Great idea, terrible execution. Equipment failed to accommodate project design parameters," said Rickey.

I held up a folded newspaper. "Did you see the article in this morning's *Whig?*"

"You know I never read the paper."

"Well, let me read something to you. It's short, so I won't bore you too long. Second section, metro news. The headline is *Power Surge Short-circuits County*. The article says, and I quote, "A massive unexplained power surge threw the northern and western Cecil County power grid into chaos about 7:30 last night, causing a series of localized power outages, blackouts, brown-outs, and blown transformers, Delmarva Power and Light has reported.

"Delmarva Chief Regional Engineer Warren Spahn told the *Whig* that reports of the event came in from various callers within the county. Spahn said the surge was not created by any equipment that was part of the Delmarva power grid, and that it had many of the characteristics of an enormous lightning strike. 'There was a single huge spike, a massive burst of energy coming from out of nowhere. Our whole grid tripped momentarily and then reset and restored power almost immediately. All Cecil County residents now once again have residential service. One of our engineers said this event reminded him of somebody blowing a tuba inside a telephone booth—a huge uncontrolled blast taking place in a confined space. We immediately dispensed crews to examine our transformers and substations, and we found no site that showed evidence of a lightning strike or transformer explosion, or any other externally caused event or sabotage. We have contacted the state police to see if they heard or observed anything that might be linked to the event. Any citizen with relevant information is urged to call Delmarva Power and Light's office in Elkton.'"

I paused to see if Rickey was following this or had checked out. She was listening intently. I read on.

"'There were several other very strange things about this event,' Spahn said. 'First, for those people thinking that it was probably something involving Aberdeen, we contacted them and they said it wasn't them, they were dark last night. Second, the surge didn't just affect residential power. We've already had reports from some boaters on the bay that their instruments—compasses, depth sounders, chart plotters—suddenly stopped working or began giving erroneous readings. And we've just had a phone call from American Airlines' regional administrator informing us that a flight crossing the Elk River on the way from Charlotte to Philadelphia suffered a sudden and complete instrument failure. They were flying blind up there. Autopilot wouldn't engage, no altimeter, compass spinning like a top. The problem resolved itself after several minutes, thank God. One of the relieved pilots joked that it felt like they had been caught in a death ray.'"

I slapped the paper loudly against my thigh, which caused Rickey to jerk upright.

"So, what about that, Ulricke Stuhlmann Bayard? Should we be renaming you Benjamin Franklin?"

To my surprise, Rickey, now standing, was smiling broadly. "Well, yeah, call me Benjamin Franklin if you want to be a smart-ass. Sure, my piggy-backing test went haywire, but the basic architecture worked. That puppy was pumping out some serious power. I'm sure Aberdeen could match it, but for a home-built lab, this was crazy power, and it was spread across the whole spectrum. Imagine if I focused this juice just on generating ULFs!"

❂   ❂   ❂

WHEN WE ALL—RICKEY, NORA, TRYG AND I—CONVENED IN THE kitchen an hour later after I had cooled down a little, Rickey was defiant. "Do we really have to talk about this now?"

I began to rise from my chair, only to find Nora's hand clasping my wrist firmly. "Sit down, Hugh. Now then, what exactly is this meeting all about?"

I began to sputter, and Tryg, God bless him, took over. "Rickey, we need to know exactly what you've been working on in your lab."

"I told you guys! The whale project! How many times do I have to tell you? What do I have to do to make you understand?"

I utterly lost it. "Yeah? Well, it seems you didn't understand it too well, either. This great 'project' blew up and nearly killed you!"

Rickey finally realized how serious we were. How serious this was.

"Okay, okay. The whale project requires me to transmit powerful ULF radio signals underwater, right? The signal has to get from my signal generator in the lab down to the water—that's the big black cable you've all been making jokes about—and then into the water. Kind of like a microphone stuck into a bathtub, all right? I can't just drop a big, electrically charged cable into the water, right? Like, *boom!*, a big short circuit? So Tryg built this wonderful watertight transmission head—a transducer. That part works great."

Despite the tension of the moment, Rickey still was smiling. "And I've been generating some gorgeous low-power ULF wave forms. Long and deep and alluring as hell, if you're a humpback. Or maybe a bull shark."

Rickey paused dramatically. "Yes, that was me. I have been sending various signal profiles for some time now, and I regard having that bull shark show up off Turkey Point as 'proof of concept.'

"So, the signal generators are working great, but the problem is *power*. What good are beautiful ULF signals if I can't push 'em beyond Baltimore? I need to get out into the world's oceans! So, to amp up the power, I needed the generators to work together. To *aggregate*. Simple concept, really."

Tryg suddenly got it, and his eyebrows shot up. "So that's why you had linked all the different transmitters."

Rickey spread her hands in an ain't-it-obvious? gesture. "The challenge was *focusing* all those connected signal generators. They sucked up all that interconnected power but then they just sprayed it all over every frequency across the whole electromagnetic spectrum. In the water, sure, but also in the air from the transmitters on the roof. It was like carpet bombing using electricity. I just didn't know how to focus it."

Nora stood up, walked over to where Rickey was sitting, and pushed her face close to Rickey's. This kind of gesture was most unlike Nora.

"Rickey, for God's sake, what destroyed the lab?"

Rickey paled, recoiled from the unexpected confrontation. "I know *what* it was, but I don't understand *why* it was. I inadvertently created a phenomenon that got out of control. It multiplied itself in the blink of an eye. Many times over. What destroyed the lab was *acoustic resonance*."

Clearly Tryg got it. Nora and I did not. "Something like harmonic resonance?" Tryg asked.

"Yes!" Rickey exclaimed. "Exactly like that. Only this was electrical resonance, electrical resonance that took off and ran wild."

"What's this resonance?" asked Nora.

"Oh, wow," said Rickey. "Let me put it as simply as I can. You know how an opera singer shatters a wine glass with her voice? That's acoustic resonance – an escalation of the glass's natural resonant frequency that comes from adding more...*power*.

"On my whale-attracting machine, I was adding more power, step by step, to really blast out those ULFs. Okay, I knew that unless you damp it or change the frequency of the added power, the whole system can become resonant—just... *take off*. I thought I was being careful. But that's what it did—*it took off.*

"But," said Tryg, "we built your lab around a whole bunch of different signal frequencies. Why would the whole system suddenly go resonant?"

"Dunno," said Rickey. "Our generators were pretty powerful, but nothing that, even working together, should have produced a huge surge like that. There I was, working in my lab, linking my transmitters, adding my frequencies together, one plus one plus one, and so forth. Like assembling Legos. The wave forms were gorgeous, the oscilloscopes were nominal, the VU meters were right in the middle, safe and stable."

I had to remind myself that this was a thirteen-year-old saying this.

"But obviously, when I added the final signal generator, the signal went from being the sum of a lot of separate frequencies to some giant resonant...*thing*. When that resonance began, I had zero time to react. I noticed the needles jump once, twice, and then ka-boom! and I'm covered in soot, my hands are singed, and my ears are ringing." She shrugged.

"You seem pretty blasé about something that could have killed you." This was Tryg.

Rickey affected unconcern. "Look, something unexpected

happened, and the overall frequency form got away from me, and yes, I was burned a little bit, but obviously I wasn't killed. It's just an electrical problem to be solved, that's all."

I felt myself losing control. I was about to really tee off on this kid when Tryg beat me to it. He had turned deathly pale and has hands were trembling uncontrollably in a squeezing motion, as if he were pressing on a basketball with all his might. He hissed through clenched teeth.

"Rickey, when and if you ever grow up, I hope you find a way to get your head out of your ass. You triggered a near catastrophe."

Rickey jutted her jaw defiantly. "It wasn't a catastrophe. It was merely an unforeseen event. This is how science moves forward."

Tryg raised his hand to slap Rickey across the face. She cringed as his hand swept downward toward her cheek. His hand jerked to a stop perhaps two inches from Rickey's nose. Tryg was positively vibrating. Then, without taking his eyes off Rickey's surprised face, he dropped his hand to his side, bit his lip hard, and backed out of the room.

23

At the Auction

WHEN RICKEY FINALLY WALKED OUT THE FRONT DOOR, I SIMPLY could not believe my eyes. She looked utterly stunning. More than that. She looked like a super model. I was floored.

Nora had fitted Rickey out from her own closet in a pair of loose-fitting linen slacks, a lavender silk blouse, and a deep purple vest embroidered with Chinese calligraphy. Rickey was a couple of inches taller than Nora, so the slacks were slightly too short, which added to the Asian look and showed Rickey's elegant ankles and Nora's patent leather Dansko clogs to splendid effect.

Rickey wore her usual sunglasses, and Nora had lent her a dramatic broad-brimmed sun hat which shadowed her face and added to the air of distance and impenetrability Rickey always projected. If suitably photographed here on the entrance to Bohemia Manor, with deep shadows and stark contrasts, Ulricke Bayard's striking beauty was worthy of a *Vogue* cover, complete with the expression of utter detachment, even disdain, so favored by its models.

Rickey, of course, did not give a damn what she looked like, and she had agreed to be clothed like a human being only because we told her she would not be allowed to attend the equipment auction in her customary attire. And yet her wardrobe change was somehow transformative, in effect if not in intent. Usually, Rickey kind of shuffled along, her head down, her arms held slightly out from her sides to avoid the friction of cloth against cloth. Now she appeared to be gliding. Wrapped in Nora's threads, this same movement and posture suggested a muted momentum, a flowing, irresistible force, a complete absence of self-consciousness.

"Jesus, Mary, and Joseph," said Tryg.

Nora laughed happily from the top of the steps. "Yeah, she cleans up pretty good, doesn't she? An entirely new look for our mad scientist."

Rickey spun and took a step back toward the house. "Is this funny to you, Nora? Do you think I enjoy this fucking Barbie doll dress-up? I don't see you dolling up in all this ladies' magazine crap you keep hanging in your closet. Why do you even have it, anyway?"

The fact that Rickey was not malicious did not keep her from being hurtful, deeply, and often. Nora recoiled like she'd been slapped. She turned on her heel and disappeared back into the house.

Tryg gestured Rickey to the waiting station wagon. "That comment showed really bad judgment, Rickey, in addition to being just plain shitty to Nora. I know that sensitivity comes hard to you, but Nora is trying to help you out, and she doesn't deserve to be dumped on. Now get in the goddamned car."

To my surprise, Rickey looked up at Tryg and nodded. "You're right, Tryg. I should have just kept my mouth shut. I'm always just shooting off my mouth, I know. But I'm sure she doesn't know how silly I feel wearing someone else's clothes and trying to come across as a neurotypical."

Rickey opened the rear door and started to climb in. She looked at my green Dickies and work shirt—clean but wrinkled. "Speaking of clothing, Hugh, what's with the field hand look? You trying to fly under the radar or something?"

"Actually, Ms. Bayard, that is exactly what I am doing. You and Mr. Sletland are going to ride in the front, like white folks should do, and I, your humble servant and social inferior, will take the back. You are the bidders, and you should look like the bidders. No need to raise eyebrows with my appearance. Just don't forget who is carrying the letters of credit and the cashier's checks. I'm the one with the money, children."

❖   ❖   ❖

AS HARD AS THIS MAY BE TO BELIEVE, WE HAD DECIDED TO ALLOW Rickey to reconstruct her lab. This decision had not simply been a matter of giving in to Rickey's entreaties—at first angry and insistent, then pleading and tearful. Rickey seemed genuinely shocked when she realized that her signal aggregation experiments had led to a plane crash that had snuffed out two innocent lives and created hundreds of thousands of dollars of damage. Her reaction to the tragedy was not guilt or remorse, but rather a peculiar kind of confusion. She regarded the confluence of circumstances leading to the crash as an "improbability" in which she was as much a victim as a cause.

Nora and I agreed that because Rickey did not comprehend the concept of accountability, there was no way to hold her accountable for events she did not intend and could not control. Tryg dissented. "She needs to be punished."

Nora shook her head. "How? And for what? What standard of responsibility would you impose, Tryg? Inform her that she has to become an adult now?" To my great astonishment, Trygve Sletland gave Nora Dadmun the finger. "Misguided," was all he said.

After a lot of heated debate and a couple of protracted pissing matches in which Tryg argued that those who do not learn from history are doomed to repeat it, the "Council of Elders," as we referred to ourselves in our discussions, consented to let Rickey continue the whale project. We agreed that it kept Rickey motivated, and that the chances of it actually succeeding seemed remote. We decided that the airplane crash was a fluke, and that the world was much more likely to ascribe the cause of the crash to the skunkworks at Aberdeen than to anything going on at Bohemia Manor. Our considered judgment was that we had dodged a bullet and that Rickey was likely to dodge the law.

We therefore agreed to allow Rickey to reconstitute the lab, subject to certain strict conditions. First, no more airborne signals; Rickey was to play only in the water and only with ULFs. We convinced Rickey that we did not want Aberdeen's Gods of the Radio Waves getting a search warrant and bursting into Bo Manor to see who was competing with them on the upper end of the electromagnetic spectrum. No more flummoxing Delmarva Power and Light. No more Big Bangs.

Our second condition was a demand for oversight: acting as a committee of the whole, Tryg, Nora and I would vet Rickey's choice of projects and supervise her activity. We expected her to rail at any intrusion on her autonomy, but to our surprise she said she would welcome evaluation of her work and ratification of her ideas and progress, even if it was conducted by scientifically illiterate idiots.

❖　　　❖　　　❖

IT WAS PURE SERENDIPITY THAT WE ENCOUNTERED THE PERFECT opportunity to reconstruct Rickey's fried lab, maybe even upgrade it substantially. Buried deep in the 790-page *Government Surplus Catalog and Guide* was the notice for an auction at a facility being closed, the Naval Arms Research Laboratory's Eastern Shore Counterintelligence Substation in Stevensville, MD, just at the eastern foot of the Chesapeake Bay bridge that led over to Annapolis.

Tryg and I had driven down to the site on a recon mission and drove by the facility twice before finding it hidden at the back of a deep unpaved parking lot off Route 50. It looked like a warehouse: faded cinder block, two office stories over four large loading dock bays. A simple sign at a windowless front door read "United States NARL Stevensville Substation. Authorized Personnel Only. Premises Under Surveillance. Trespassers will be detained and prosecuted." Not many taxpayer dollars at work on security here, no chain link fence, no razor wire. No whirling radar antennae, no dish receivers on the roof. If there were surveillance cameras, they were well hidden. As far as secure national defense installations go, this one was unlikely to attract attention or raise suspicion.

The building appeared deserted. A two-by-three-foot poster was glued sloppily to the front door, and Tryg and I went over to check it out.

NOTICE OF ABSOLUTE AUCTION

This facility will be closed as of January 1, 1993, and its operations transferred to Newport News, Virginia.

Pursuant to Government Notice GAO 34-9737, as described fully at Pages 494-529 of the *Government Surplus Catalog and Guide*, as revised 2/15/93, the contents of this building will be placed for public auction on August 3, 1993, in 116 lots to include office furniture, telephone equipment, typewriters, adding machines and calculators, certain computer equipment, and a large supply of unclassified commercial-grade electronics and laboratory research equipment, Including generators (5), receivers, transceivers, misc. broadcasting equipment (FM, SSB, Short Wave), signal generators, consoles, monitors, oscilloscopes, circuit boards, racks, VU meters, gauges, circuit breakers and breaker assemblies, 23 spools of misc. electric and electronic cabling, all as described fully in catalog.

All bidders must pre-register at least two weeks before the auction date. No unregistered bidders will be admitted. 10% cash deposit or certified payment required at time of Auction; all balances must be fully paid before removal of any items. All sales as-is, where-is. For more information, call Lt. Denver Pullen, 301-723-5577.

"Bingo," said Tryg.

As we started back to the car, a dark blue Ford Crown Victoria rolled slowly out from behind the warehouse and came to a stop behind our car, effectively blocking us in.

A slender young naval officer—whites, badge bars, a few ribbons over his left tit—opened his door and stood behind it. He wore no name tag. He stepped out, and we could see that he had a Glock at his hip. The effect was incongruous, but it got our attention.

"Help you guys?" he said pleasantly. I was pleased he said "guys" and not "boys."

I let Tryg do the talking. "We're going to be bidding on some of the electronics stuff, and we wanted to be sure we could find the place. Good thing we came down for some recon. This ain't exactly the Portsmouth Naval Base."

"Sure ain't," he laughed easily. "That was the whole point. While we were open, we kind of operated off the map. Everyone's map if you catch my drift."

"Are you Lieutenant Pullen?"

Pullen nodded.

"Were you stationed here?" I asked.

"I was and am…right up 'til the last pirate is hung."

"Pardon?" Tryg said.

"Navy jargon," he smiled. "Until we finally turn the lights out."

"Who'd you piss off to draw death watch duty?" asked Tryg.

"Well," Pullen smiled broadly, "I could tell you but…"

We all finished the sentence together: "…then I'd have to kill you."

❂   ❂   ❂

ON THE DRIVE DOWN TO THE AUCTION, RICKEY SAT IN FRONT,
nervously flipping her bidder's paddle back and forth like a fan,
silently rifling through the lot list over and over again. I could see
that she had highlighted the lots she wanted to bid on; a couple
of items had large check marks in the margin. Each lot item had
a recommended bidding minimum in a column off to the right.
I thought whoever put those estimates together was clearly a
wild-eyed optimist.

"Okay, what's my budget, Hugh?"

"Your budget is whatever you need it to be, Rickey. Sky's
the limit."

She turned and smiled broadly at me. "No shit?"

"No shit, Rickey. Tryg will help you with the bidding, so you
don't get carried away too soon and piss money away needlessly.
But yes, we are here to get you what you want. He's the registered
bidder, but you're going to be waving the paddle. It's your lab.
You bid until you win. The bank is open."

"What are you going to be doing?"

"I am going to be standing at the back of the room, hanging
my head and avoiding eye contact, doin' the aw-shucks thing with
my foot in the dirt, trying to be as invisible as I can. When the
auction is done and you and Tryg take your chits up to the cashier
for payment, I will magically appear, produce the Constant Binder
so they will have to talk to me, and tender the vendors the money
they want, in whatever form they want—cash, cashier's checks, a
certified letter of credit. Whatever. I will pay, Tryg will arrange
delivery with whomever they've hired to handle that, and we
should be home by early afternoon."

"You're carrying cash?" Tryg said, surprised.

"I certainly am. I suspect this whole thing will be run by
a private auctioneer, not a navy gang. Sometimes those private
guys—they're real junk yard dogs—will negotiate a percentage
discount if you offer cash."

"Jesus, how much you got with you?"

I paused, unsure how much to disclose in front of Rickey.
Aw, what the hell.

Eighty-five thousand dollars, nestled neatly in my trusty backpack."

Tryg twisted to look at me, sending the car veering over to the shoulder. "*What!?* Hugh, that is batshit crazy, carrying that kind of cash around!"

"Tryg, it's a U.S. Navy military facility. There will be security. I do not expect to be robbed at gunpoint. And it's not like I'm going to be displaying greenbacks on my hat."

Tryg shook his head, whether in disapproval or disbelief I could not tell.

"But doesn't bargaining a cash discount skim proceeds due the navy?" This question came from Rickey. I admit I was surprised at this display of integrity, but the increasing font of Rickey's knowledge never ceased to amaze me. For an adolescent kid, Rickey's mental database was huge and seemed to be growing exponentially. I had, however, never expected her to develop a moral compass.

"That's between the navy and their agent, my dear. Their relationship is not our concern. And if the guy says no, we got other ways to paper the deal. Remember, Rickey, that these guys want to sell all this stuff. They want the deals to work, not crater. They're driven, but we're driving."

"I hear you. And don't call me 'dear.' I am nobody's dear."

⚙   ⚙   ⚙

BY THE TIME WE ARRIVED—AND WE WERE FORTY MINUTES EARLY— the parking lot was almost completely filled with cars, vans, box trucks and flat-beds. A state police trooper waved us over on to the left shoulder, into a line of cars inching toward a bidder check-in point. This took the form of a narrowing funnel of six official vehicles that ushered traffic up to a long folding table, behind which were seated two naval officers with clipboards. Three of the cars were white government-issue pool sedans, and three were Maryland State Police cruisers in front of which slouched a cadre of troopers, casually waving bidders up to the check-in table.

I felt a stab of alarm. I was instantly afraid of what I was going to see, and instantly sickened when I saw it: there, chatting calmly, were Troopers Arlon Santunas and Deirdre Callas. Because we were in the Country Squire and not the Bohemia Manor pickup truck with the name on the side, neither Santunas nor Callas recognized us until we were several cars away from the registration table.

Santunas saw me first, sitting low in the back seat. He stiffened and gestured to Callas, who registered surprise and then placed herself in front of our car while Santunas moved to Tryg's window. His demeanor was not friendly.

"Just who the hell are you, and what are you doing here?"

"I am Trygve Sletland and this is Ms. Ulricke Bayard. We are registered bidders for this auction." Rickey leaned across the seat and waved her bidder's paddle at Santunas in greeting.

"And what is *he* doing here?"

"We are here to buy certain equipment for Bohemia Manor Farm, and as I think you know, Trooper Santunas, Mr. Ullam is both general manager of the farm and Mr. Hermann Bayard's financial and business representative. He is attending the auction in that capacity."

Santunas slapped his hand on the station wagon's hood, creating a sharp report that launched Rickey back in her seat and made Callas spin and reach for her sidearm. Tryg appeared unruffled.

"Oh, he is, is he? Well, we'll just see about that."

Santunas strode up to the registration table and conferred briefly with one of the officers, who handed him his clipboard. Santunas riffled through the pages. Behind us, horns began to honk, and Callas walked back down the line to shut them up. Santunas handed the clipboard back to the navy guy and walked – swaggered is a better word – back to our car. He pointed through the window at me. "*He* can't go in."

"I don't understand," said Tryg. I noticed that a vein on his left temple had begun to pulse.

"He ain't registered," sneered Santunas. "You and the girl are on the bidders' list, so you may pass—although I'm not sure we should be letting a kid in. But Mister You-lamb ain't registered, so he ain't going nowhere. This is still a secure United States naval facility, and entry is denied."

Tryg's voice was flat, hard, restrained. "The flyer on the door says this substation was closed on January first, Trooper Santunas. No secure activity is going on here. It's just a warehouse filled with old equipment and in a couple of hours it won't even be that."

Santunas puffed his chest up self-importantly, to almost comic effect. "The Maryland State Police," hissed Santunas, "has been requested by the United States Navy to provide assistance at this U.S. Naval installation. And we say unauthorized persons are not permitted on-site. He's not getting in, and if you keep slowing up my line, you two won't be going in either." He spread his legs and put his hands on his hips, a slightly ludicrous and overdramatic gesture.

Tryg started to protest, but I put my hand on his shoulder. "Tryg," I said. "This is another form of show and go. Don't rise to the bait. I'm going to step out. I will wait for you on the other side of the highway until the auction is over. When it's time for payment, put Rickey in line to hold your place and come out and see me. I will provide you with whatever you need. Please, let's just get this done."

Tryg inhaled, long and slow and hard. "Roger that," he said softly.

◉ ◉ ◉

I FOUND A COMFORTABLE PLACE TO SIT BENEATH AN ENORMOUS OAK tree and sat back to watch the proceedings. The rest of registration went quickly and smoothly, and I noticed that the State Police troopers played no further role in screening and check-in; the navy guys simply asked for names, consulted their clipboards, and waved the bidders in. Santunas and Callas leaned against one of the cruisers and, with their eyes all squinty and their Smokey-the-Bear hats cocked straight, proceeded to give me the evil eye from across the highway.

At 9:45 AM, the navy guys folded up their table and headed into the building to supervise the auction. Santunas got into his cruiser, made a Y-turn, and headed east back up Route 50. The trooper in the second cruiser drove away toward the Bay Bridge. Callas dusted the car smudge off her butt and walked casually into the warehouse. By 9:47 there was no security whatever at the entrance to the United States NARL Stevensville Substation.

I sat quietly until 10:30. A couple of latecomers had driven in, hustled out of their vans, and disappeared into the substation. Now there was no visible activity of any kind, and I soon got bored.

Restless now, I stood and crossed the highway. I wound my way toward the substation, half expecting the door to fly open and storm troopers to pin my unregistered ass to the parking lot gravel. I headed around to the side of the building, then further around to the back. Here grass had grown long and tangled. There was no trash and debris, as you'd find with most abandoned buildings in low-rent commercial areas. There was just...nothing. Nothing except long grass, parched brown by the August sun.

There was a door. I tried the handle and was surprised to find it unlocked. I opened it quietly and found that it led up a walled stairway. The stairs were steel, with open treads, looking as if they'd been made for installation out-of-doors.

What could I do? Of course, I headed up, pressing my steps softly but firmly and placing my feet as quietly as a cat burglar. The steel steps stayed silent. As I neared the head of the stairwell, I heard a strange murmur that resolved, ever louder, into a human voice. The timbre and cadence were strange, as if this was not English. Then I realized what I was hearing: it was the voice of the auctioneer, asking for bids, cajoling, confirming, and finally shouting out a done deal.

The stairwell led out onto a catwalk that fronted a series of glass-walled offices. I found myself on a balcony, looking down at a gaggle of bidders, milling and moving from lot to lot, muttering to each other, shaking their heads when their reactions were negative, occasionally waving their bidding paddles, which looked like the stunted wings of baby chicks.

The throng moved from lot to lot, all stacked on separate pallets, led by the auctioneer as if he was giving a walking tour of the White House. He worked fast, and he was good, his prompts and his prices sharp and distinct. He moved rapidly down the lots, usually spending less than a minute on the presentation, the prance-and-dance, and the closing shout.

I saw Tryg and Rickey near the front of the group. To my surprise, Tryg's arm was wrapped protectively over Rickey's shoulder, and she was not recoiling or shrugging him off. There was no sense of warmth, but their postures were conspiratorial, collaborative. It looked like Rickey was doing most of the talking, Tryg doing most of the nodding. Wherever the throng went, Tryg and Rickey forced their way to the front, staking a firm claim to the heart of the action. The crowd tended to part as Rickey, looking every inch the fashion model, pushed her way through.

Tryg had given Rickey the paddle. I had argued against this, not because I didn't want Rickey to have a moment of enjoyment or a sense of control, but because I thought the auctioneer was likely to respect Tryg's stature and demeanor more than Rickey's enthusiasm. But now it was clear that Rickey had been a visible and active bidder, and with each lot that came up, the auctioneer now looked her way, checking to see if she was in. And there was no question about when she was in: when Rickey pulled the trigger, her paddle would shoot up and then wave, like a giant hand waving hello.

I could see that Tryg had taught her discipline. When a new lot came up with stuff that she wanted, I could see her vibrate with anticipation, but Tryg kept a hand gently on her arm: *not so fast, Rickey. Not so soon. Let's see how the wind blows. Steady... steady...NOW!*

I watched the action for about forty minutes, and Rickey seemed to be getting most of what she wanted, her main competitors being a plump, bearded guy in a hideous copper shirt and a skinny rat-faced guy in a sleeveless wife-beater tee shirt. I was enjoying the show and enjoying watching Rickey Bayard enjoy herself. I was relaxing, leaning on the balcony rail, when I sensed something moving behind me. Then I sensed something press into the back of my head. I had never had a gun barrel put to my head, but believe me, when it happens, you know what it is.

A voice, a female voice whispered softly: *"Do...not...move. Do...not...make... a...sound. Do...not...raise...your...hands. I... want...you...to...place them...behind your back. Now...turn toward your right...and – verrry slowly...head back to the stairwell."*

❂   ❂   ❂

WELL, IT WAS CALLAS, OF COURSE, HER FACE FLUSHED WITH TRIUMPH from having caught someone in the act of.... of...well, *something*. We reached the bottom of the staircase and stepped back out into the sun. My hands remained behind my back. I felt the cold clunk of the cuffs across my wrists, and the pressure of the gun barrel was removed from the back of my head. I realized that State Police troopers are trained to cuff someone one-handed while simultaneously keeping a gun pressed to their skulls. Callas did this quickly and smoothly.

"My, my, my. You really *do* think you're special, don't you?" I said nothing.

"You, mister arrogant asshole, are well and truly under arrest."

"What would the charge be?" I asked. Flat. Calm. Non-confrontational. *Whatever you do, Hugh, I thought, stay non-confrontational.*

"We'll start with trespass. Then we'll talk to the intelligence guys about whatever security violations they want to hang on your ass."

We walked around to the front of the building. Callas' pistol was holstered, and she was walking by my side, close, sure I was not going to try anything. The front door of the building opened, and out stepped Lieutenant Denver Pullen. He glanced at me, his eyes lit up in recognition, and then his brow furrowed in confusion as he saw that my arms were cuffed behind me and that Deirdre Callas was smiling like a Cheshire cat.

Pullen was nonplussed. "Deirdre, what the hell is this?"

"This," she said, "is an arrest for defiant trespass and whatever security breaches you guys got. Caught him up in the balcony, spying on the auction."

"And…" Pullen said quietly.

"The 'and' is, Denver, that he's not registered."

"What do you mean he's not registered? I know this guy. Met him here a couple of days ago. Of course, he's registered, for Chrissake."

"Nope, he's not. I checked. The other guy and that teen-ager—they're on the registered list, but not Mr. Hugh You-lamb, here. We turned him away at the gate an hour ago."

"You're shitting me." Pullen paused. "Wait. Do you know this guy?"

"Sure do. We had to arrest him a few weeks ago up near Chesapeake City. It was Lon's collar."

"What charge?" asked Pullen.

"Ah…resisting arrest," said Callas.

"Show and go," I said. "The old smash the taillight trick. Throw the black guy in the slammer overnight, teach that uppity boy a lesson. No charges, no phone call, just shake that black motherfucker up."

"Hoo, boy," sighed Pullen. He paused again. "Deirdre, I think you and Santunas have gotten yourselves into some deep, deep shit here. As in false imprisonment, abuse of authority kind of shit."

"Hell, no!" Callas exclaimed. "It's a breach, Denver. He was up there, unregistered, spying on the auction in a high-security facility. *Unregistered!*"

Pullen ran his hands through his hair. He looked down, and

then lifted his head and looked Trooper Deirdre Callas square in the face. Then he spoke very deliberately.

"*You. Dumb. Fuck.* This wasn't a security registration, you idiot. It was a public auction registration, for billing and bookkeeping purposes. *Public Auction.* As in, 'open to the public.' If Bozo the Clown had wanted to come and watch, you were supposed to let him in and help him park his clown car! The State Police were asked to help direct traffic, not play CIA.

"And, by the way, this man is *not* Bozo the Clown. He is the general manager of Hermann Bayard's farm. Do you have any idea how much torque Hermann Bayard has in Cecil County? He ain't popular, but his name still has a lot of juice. Christ, I'm not even from around there, and even I know that! And Mr. Ullam came down here with his farm manager, and he politely introduced himself to me, and now you've gone and arrested him.

"You know, Callas, you think people don't know about you and your little sidekick Santunas. Well, you got a reputation. Even the navy MPs down here talk about your vigilante racist bullshit. You and Santunas are bad news, Callas."

Pullen squeezed one fist with the other and looked up at the sky. "Man, I'm just trying to think what to do about this."

"I have a suggestion," I said.

They both turned to me.

"Let's not do anything," I said. "I'm not eager to be at the center of a shit storm, and I'm sure neither of you are, either. I'm not about to press charges or raise a stink. And why would either of you guys want to raise a stink? Let's call this a misunderstanding. No harm, no foul."

Deirdre Callas was visibly trembling, but whether from anger, fear or relief, I couldn't tell. Pullen gathered himself, became a naval officer again.

"I do have one request," I said, and both Pullen and Callas raised their eyebrows expectantly.

"Trooper Callas, in the future *please, just leave me alone.* I am an Australian Aboriginal person, come in peace. I am not an African American radical out to destroy your supremely white social order, I am an employee just trying to run a farm for my boss. Unless you catch me red-handed in the midst of a felony that falls directly into State Police jurisdiction, and I assure you that is never going to happen, please...*just leave me alone.* Live and let live. That goes for Santunas, too."

✿   ✿   ✿

RICKEY HAD GOTTEN EVERYTHING ON HER WISH LIST. IT TURNED OUT that there were a number of duplicate lots at the auction, and what copper shirt and rat face did not score, Rickey Bayard scooped up—often by bidding the second or third lots, which were a lot cheaper. Before the auction, Rickey's pre-auction planning had included scoping out all the duplicate lots and creating a tactical bidding plan to optimize her chances of getting what she needed at the lowest possible cost. She had briefed Tryg on her approach during the first few lots of the auction, and he was awestruck.

"Hugh," he said later over drinks on the patio. "It was unbelievable. She had a war plan, a contingency plan, all built around the sequence of the lots. There were only three items—the lot of assorted signal generators, the big commercial generator, and the gas chromo scope thing—that were unique, and she bid the sky to get those. The other stuff? She was just standing there, keeping tabs on when to swoop in and bid low. We keep treating Rickey like she's naïve. Well maybe in some regards, but she sure wasn't naïve when it came to getting what she wanted at that auction."

We had deliberately let Rickey overhear this entire conversation. We did not expect her to spontaneously develop a smiley personality, but we thought she might relate to us differently if she felt we respected her gifts. This proved true.

Rickey's entire lab cost us $57,700. We paid cash, plus another $4,400 for white-gloves delivery.

Several weeks later, Tryg came to dinner with a huge grin on his face. "Rickey," he said. "I have a really great surprise for you. I thought about your story about Humphrey the whale, and that led me to get in touch with the Naval Postgraduate School in Monterey. To my surprise, they were very helpful. Turns out there were only five J-11 underwater transducers in the country in 1985, back when they saved Humphrey. It was not an item you could buy from your local Radio Shack. But, at least for the Navy's purposes, the J-11s are now obsolete. The Navy is now all the way up to J-23s. The point is, they surplused all the old J-11s. And one is on its way here right now. For the cost of shipping, $1,250. This will work better than the one I made by a mile. Rickey, you are really in business."

❂   ❂   ❂

WITHIN TWO WEEKS, RICKEY WAS BACK AT WORK TRYING TO LURE whales to Bohemia Manor, dressed in her loose shift, flip-flops, dark glasses and headphones. If she was unhappy about the rigid oversight the Council of Elders had imposed on her, she did not show it.

As for us, with the benefit of hindsight, I must say that we rather stupidly blinded ourselves to the probability of still more disaster. We thought that if we steered Rickey's experiments away from anything that directly involved people, the likelihood of either disaster or detection would remain remote. It was not until much later, when things began to unravel, that it occurred to me that by insisting on supervising Rickey's work on the whale project, we had become complicit in its consequences. We had rowed ourselves even farther up the criminal creek and tied our fates even tighter to Rickey's.

24

Demise of an Osprey

I WAS OUT KAYAKING. TO RELAX, TO STAY FIT, I DID A LOT OF KAYAKING, often after dark, because I sometimes attracted unpleasant attention from Caucasian mariners if I kayaked around the northern bay during the day. On this particular evening I launched my one-man sea kayak from the beach at Bo Manor shortly after 8:30. I was feeling strong, feeling good. In no time, I had zipped out of the Bohemia River, made a right turn up the Elk River and was nearing the approach to the Chesapeake and Delaware Canal.

Chesapeake Bay, being shallow and wide, can develop a vicious chop when the wind pipes up. Even up on the upper eastern shore, where the bay is narrower and Turkey Point sticks down past the Elk and Bohemia Rivers to interrupt the fetch of westerly winds, a moderate breeze can kick up short, mean waves that bash boaters' brains out.

Ah, but not this night. Instead, this was one of those striking Chesapeake nights in early September, one of those strange séances that sometimes happen in late summer and early autumn, when the winds tiptoe offstage, the crickets go still, and the whole northern bay turns into a vast mirror. On nights like this the stillness is so pervasive, so intense, that it feels like the whole world is holding its breath. Not a wave anywhere. Not a ripple. Just a broad expanse of perfect glass, silvered tonight by a quarter moon.

Near the mid-channel tower marking the entrance to the C&D canal, I glided to a stop to catch my breath and plop my feet into the water, a sweet coolness, almost a caress. Now I sensed a slight change: the faintest of breezes lightly touched my cheek. A murmur. The mirrored surface of the Elk River broke into a vast field of silver-stippled chevrons.

A sudden shocking scream jolted me upright. My paddle went sailing out of my hand, and I pawed frantically around the side of the kayak to try to grab it back. Another shrill scream rent the night. It sounded like an infant being thrown into a wood-chipper. I finally settled the kayak and shouted into the darkness,

"Hannah! You goddamned bitch!"

Hannah the Hawk was an osprey, also known as a fish hawk or fish eagle. The bird books will tell you that ospreys, with their white heads and M-shaped wingspans, are common sights patrolling along shorelines and waterways and guarding their huge stick nests, often built on buoys, channel markers and towers. Ospreys are unique among North American raptors for their ability to dive into water to catch their diet of live fish.

Ospreys are large hawks, and Hannah was big for an osprey. She was also a giant pain in the ass. Hannah had become both famous and notorious in Cecil County, and each spring she was written up in the *Cecil Whig* as if her story was new. Hannah had nested atop the tall solar panel on the mid-channel marker of the Elk River five years before, routed all other ospreys competing for her real estate, staked a permanent claim to her huge bundle of sticks and branches, and each spring produced a brood—three chicks every time—in the absence of any apparent mate.

When she had chicks in the nest, Hannah, who had won her name in a *Cecil Whig* "Name Our Famous Osprey" contest, became viciously protective. Ever vigilant, she perched on her giant nest like a mechanical automaton, rotating back and forth, jerking and bobbing her head as if suffering from a combination of electroshock and St. Vitus dance.

Hannah looked mean, and she acted mean. When she felt threatened, Hannah would soar into the sky and then dive on boats and boaters that came too near her tower, often rising fifty feet above the water before collapsing her large wings against her body, extending her talons, narrowing her bright yellow eyes into malign slits, and plummeting toward terrified interlopers. She dive-bombed me in my kayak one evening, and believe me, it got my attention.

Now Hannah stood perched in her giant nest on the top of the mid-channel light, illuminated every two seconds by the flashing red solar-powered beacon. Though silent for the moment, her head clocked left and right, as if she was searching to hear something. The combined effect of the flashing light and her ratcheting head made her look like some giant black forest clockwork cuckoo bird.

Yet at first, I saw nothing, heard nothing.

Then, as my pulse settled, I heard a peculiar sigh. When the night is so still, sound amplifies and carries across water, so there was no telling either where this sound came from or how close it was. Hannah and I both went silent and stayed still, Hannah now moving to high alert. Half a minute later, I heard it again— louder, closer, definitely coming from downriver, a sort of a cross between an "umph" and a deep "phoosh."

My first thought was, *I know what that sound is. God almighty, Rickey, you really did it.*

I looked out into the channel and suddenly a large, smooth circle appeared. The silver chevrons on the surface disappeared, replaced by a solid glassine slick. I saw now that this strange circle was domed, that there was something rising out of the water even while moving toward me.

Then the dome sank. The shining circle closed over, and the silver chevrons reappeared as if nothing had interrupted their march across the Elk River.

I was perhaps forty yards from Hannah's tower when I both

heard and felt an enormous impact, amplified through the water, and transmitted through my kayak and up through my butt. It sounded like someone had hit a flagpole with a sledgehammer.

Some huge underwater force had hit the tower.

In the beacon's flashing red glare, I could see that Hannah had been catapulted high into the air by the impact, surrounded by a storm of sticks and twigs from her nest. Two seconds later, the next flash showed Hannah plummeting, inverted, toward the water, her wings thrashing wildly for aerodynamic purchase, finding none. As she hit the water the surface beneath her suddenly churned and lifted.

Slowly, gracefully, a huge horizontal platform rose from beneath the Elk River in a rush of cascading water. This... this *thing*...rose three, six, eight feet above the surface, froze momentarily in the still night, and then crashed violently down on the churning eddy in the water where Hannah struggled to regain flight.

Then...silence. Actually, kind of a vacuum of non-sound. A strange kind of nothing. The silver chevrons closed and again chased over the surface as the impact ripples dissipated across the river. The sliver of moon illuminated a couple of feathers that had popped to the surface and now floated silently at the base of the mid-channel marker, surrounded by remnants of Hannah's nest.

My kayak bobbed quietly on the river, awaiting instructions.

Slowly, very slowly, I eased my paddle into the water and pushed the kayak forward, sliding quietly back toward Bohemia Manor.

Jesus Christ, Rickey. You actually did it.

25

Hawaiian Progress

"HALLO, WIKTOR."

Victor Portochenko spun in surprise, believing he was alone on the wing bridge of the *Hawaiian Progress* as it made its way through the last several miles of the Chesapeake and Delaware Canal. Now he squinted into the darkness and realized that there was someone behind him, smelled him as much as saw him in the shadows: stale diesel fuel, stale sweat, stale cigarette smoke.

A figure stepped forward into the green glow of the starboard running light, stooped, slight, wiry, smelly, a genial grin on his rat-like face. "Hallo, Wiktor. How you are?"

"Vlad! Christ! Shit! You scared the hell out of me! What in God's name are you doing up here? How did you get up here?"

"I am climbing up outside escape ladder from cargo deck. *Five stories,* Wiktor. Five stories, but for me, is piece from cake. Am not afraid from height. Anyway, am just having cigarette and looking at moon." He spoke rapidly, blurring his words. Portochenko felt as if he was always half a sentence behind in deciphering the Romanian's fractured syntax and thick accent. *Chust hevink tsig-rat yend lookink yat moan.*

Despite his Russian name, Portochenko, having been born

169

in Chicago, had no discernible accent except for a Midwest nasal twang. "Oilers can't be up here. God, you know that. I can put you on discipline, and if I do, you know Matson's going to dock you wages."

Vladim Ceaudescu spread his wiry arms, palms up in supplication. "Wiktor, Wiktor. Having some heart. Giving me break." *Gevyink meh brek.* "You are not officer, don't have to be big tough power guy. You just helmsman, taking all the times orders, just like me, yes?

"Anyway, is last trip this wreck. I am on here *six years,* lots time down boiler room with black gang. No windows, no view, Wiktor. So, I am loyal guy, yes? What I am hurting here? I not bothering no one, not planning no mutiny. So, giving me break, okay?"

Portochenko sighed. Vlad was right. This wasn't the time to play hard-ass for no good reason. Not the time for strict rank and discipline. The *Hawaiian Progress,* now pushing fifty, had become little more than a tramp steamer, a near derelict lugging a final load of lumber to Baltimore before heading to the scrapyard in Norfolk. Soon she would be razor blades.

The *Hawaiian Progress's* peeling paint was faded so badly you could hardly make out the blue Matson 'M' on her yellow stack. Rust streaks resembling brown icicles ran from deck to waterline from bow to stern, making her look like she was dressed in a brown hula skirt. Now she pulled herself painfully through the C&D Canal at less than twelve knots, her warped propeller shaft making a deep cyclic moan that resonated throughout the ship.

"Okay, Vlad. I say you can stay up. But keep yourself in the dark in that back corner and whatever you do, don't let Robison see you. And remember, we've got the canal pilot on board, so for Chrissakes don't let him see you or we're both fucked."

"Tenk you, Wiktor. Not vorrying. I am being good boy."

❂   ❂   ❂

SINCE HE HAD BOUGHT SCHAEFFER'S CANAL HOUSE RESTAURANT

and Marina three years earlier, Gunther Senkler's demanding management style had "turned these slackers into a well-oiled machine," as he liked to put it. He had once again turned the sagging restaurant under the towering Route 213 bridge into a destination for boaters and non-boaters alike. A splendid chef himself, Gunther had lured Taki Economaki down from the Silk Bass restaurant in Philadelphia to become head chef, set up new supply chains that provided the very freshest food and produce, even hired a pastry chef from Savannah.

And it had paid off handsomely. Although Schaeffer's decor still had much of the rough-edged ambiance of local crab shacks and fried-food restaurants, it was now earning strong reviews from as far north as Philadelphia and as far south as Norfolk. The barbecue pit on the outdoor patio struggled at first, but when he hired the steel band from Jamaica to perform on the outside deck on Friday and Saturday nights, it took off and attracted an entirely different weekend clientele, the roasted chicken and fried shrimp basket crowd. Gunther had created his own little vertically-integrated mini-conglomerate, and as he stood looking down at the docks, he felt a rush of pride.

❂   ❂   ❂

GUNTHER'S SELF-SATISFIED MUSING WAS INTERRUPTED BY DEWEY

Berghauer's mellifluous voice over the PA system. Dewey was only an average bartender, but somebody had evidently once told him that he had radio pipes, and he took heartily to his ship announcement duties. Dewey gave each and every sentence a sonorous gravity and extended every announcement far longer than the diners would have preferred.

"Ladies and gentlemen, if you look out the windows facing the canal, in three minutes you will see the *Hawaiian Progress* passing from left to right. Built in 1944, the *Hawaiian Progress* is a Type C3-class ship. She is 492 feet long and displaces 12,500 tons. As she passes, we will be turning on our spotlights so you can see her clearly in the dark. If you like, you may move out to the balcony while she passes and give a friendly wave to the crew, who come from all over the world."

Dewey had uttered the last few sentences without pausing to breathe, and now he ran out of air and his throat closed up. His labored gasp, whistled distinctly over the PA system, triggered laughs both from the indoor dining room and the folks on the outdoor deck. Dewey dove back in.

"As she goes by, you will see one of the 36-foot orange launches of the C&D Canal Pilots' Association tied to her starboard side next to the boarding ladder. The launch stays with the *Hawaiian Progress* for her journey through the C&D Canal to the Elk River. There are presently nine C&D pilots helping guide ships through the canal. Tonight's pilot on the Hawaiian Progress is George Townes.

"Why do we need pilots? The C&D canal is not just a calm, straight channel. Not only does it twist and turn, but the water levels of the upper Chesapeake Bay and the Delaware Bay are inherently unequal. That's why the canal originally had locks. At mean low water, the water level on Chesapeake Bay is nine inches lower than the Delaware River. That means a tide rip runs through the canal, east to west, at up to six knots. That is very fast, very powerful. When the tide goes out on Delaware Bay, the level of Delaware River suddenly becomes lower than the Chesapeake, and the tidal flow shifts and rushes the other way toward the Delaware River. To put it mildly, navigating the C&D canal is very hazardous, and our experienced pilots are all that keep large ships from being pushed into the banks by the current."

A young boy seated in front of Gunther and squirming uncomfortably in his dress-up clothes, turned to his father. "Can I go look, Dad?"

"Yes, Stevie, you and Andrea may be excused. And after you look at the ship, if you want to go down and check out the steel band, just don't lose your sister. Please be back in in a half hour."

GEORGE TOWNES, WHO HAD BEEN A C&D CANAL PILOT FOR EIGHTEEN
years, stood six feet five inches tall and looked like a giant gray
heron. He stood next to the junior helmsman in the inside
bridge of the *Hawaiian Progress*, staring down the Canal toward
the Elk River. At night both sides of the canal were lined with
bright yellow halogen lights on tall poles. These were supposed
to improve canal visibility at night. Instead, they created night
blindness that made it hard for pilots to see forward more than a
few hundred yards.

A Sea Cadet from the Pilot's Service, his white pants sharply
creased and his slam-cap cocked perfectly on his adolescent head,
appeared in the doorway leading out to the wing bridge. "Mr.
Townes, sir, the launch is roped in tight, riding smooth and safe
alongside. We're ready to take you off when you're ready, sir."

"Very good, Cadet Tomarchio. I tell you what, the current is
running real strong east to west tonight, and we've got a southeast
wind that wants to shove our ass over toward the north bank. I'm
going to stay aboard until we get down to the Moran ocean tug
docks down past the bridge."

At six knots, the *Hawaiian Progress*, with George Townes now
commanding the helm, thrummed past the railroad lift bridge at
mile ten, down toward the Coast Guard Station and Museum in
South Chesapeake City, directly across the canal from Schaeffer's.

The radar operator suddenly pushed his face down into his
viewer, reared back, pounded the side of the radar console with
the palm of his right hand, and leaned back down into the green
light of the circular radar display.

Dispensing with any formality in addressing the officers on
the bridge, he croaked, "Hey! There's something big in the canal!"

"Big what? A boat? A ship? We've had no notification of any
ships coming up." Townes was leaning toward the front windows
of the bridge, straining to see down the canal past the bridge
abutments.

"The radar return has no shape and it's kind of blurry. Most
of it is buried in the grass. I don't know why my scope can't grab
it unless it's riding real low."

Captain Georgi Simonescu strode to the ship-to-shore handset and dialed the pre-set number for the Coast Guard station in South Chesapeake City. "Ship in canal to Coast Guard, most urgent. Do you have any notice of a submarine coming up the canal?"

The response was immediate and flat, as if an inquiry about submarine traffic in the C&D canal was unsurprising. "Negative, ship in canal. We have no notice of military vessels anywhere on northern bay or in canal. I repeat, negative on a submarine. Please state your calling sign and situation."

Before Townes could answer, a heavily accented voice echoed across the bridge in a sing-song shout. "Excusing me!"

They turned to the door to the wing bridge and to their surprise saw a scarecrow figure dressed in a greasy blue oiler's uniform.

"Excusing me!" the man shouted again. "*Is whale!* Is whale in canal!"

"What the hell?" cried Townes. The pitch of his voice had climbed several registers, but betrayed no panic, just confusion.

"Is whale!" cried Vladim Ceaudescu again. "I am smelling him! Used to be working on Japanese whalers! I am know! And I am just now hearing him blow!"

Townes did not stop to ask himself how an oiler covered in diesel stench and cigarette stink could smell a whale hundreds of yards away—or even what such a man was doing on his bridge. Instead, his years of training triggered immediate responses and calm, staccato orders. "Engine all stop! Do not, repeat, do not, reverse engine! Rudder hard to starboard! Captain, please broadcast brace for collision through whole ship. There is not room for this ship and a whale in the same canal."

The pitch and timbre of the warped propeller shaft changed abruptly from its grinding groan to a deep whisper—*shoosh, shoosh, shooooosh*. Townes knew that the propeller's revolutions—its "turns"—had slowed, but that the movement of the ship through the water would keep the propeller turning even though it was now freewheeling and no longer being powered by the engine.

"Lookouts to the wing bridge! Both sides, I don't care who, just get out there, goddamn it! Get a spotlight on and find that son-of-a-bitch!" Both Townes' hands were tightly clenched by his sides. "Helmsman! Is the rudder hard to starboard? We've got to try to get the current pushing the stern toward the north bank."

The ship's giant spotlight, mounted on a tall pole on the left-side wing bridge, popped on and threw a blinding pencil beam far out in front the *Hawaiian Progress's* rusty bow. "Go to flood!" yelled Townes, and the beam flared and spread, illuminating the canal in front of them from bank to bank.

Just at the border of illumination, they could see a bump—a kind of ridge surrounded by a halo of smoother water. Then it disappeared, leaving a slick circular patch.

"You there! Comms!" Townes yelled. "Quick, call down to Moran Tugs. See if they can get their little coastal ranger up here, pronto. If we hit something and are disabled, we're gonna be in deep shit, and this ship's going to be parked in some diner's lap at Schaeffer's. And someone tell me what the hell that really is out there! *We cannot have a whale in the C&D canal. That is not happening.*"

But it was.

There was a bump—a muffled impact felt the length of the freighter—a pause, and then a lighter bump-bump-bump. Something had crashed into the ship and now was bouncing down the starboard side. This was followed by an unearthly *moo-ah!* sound from beneath the ship, the sound of something soft hitting something hard. Then there was a screech of tortured metal. The men on the bridge felt the stern of the *Hawaiian Progress* lift and then settle.

The rev-counter on the helmsman's console indicated that the propeller had stopped turning. "Turns zero, Mr. Townes!" An awful groaning vibrated up through the floor of the bridge, a wrenching, grinding, protesting groan. Then it abruptly stopped. The silence was deeply unsettling.

"Mr. Townes," the helmsman now said quietly. "The rudder is jammed on something. I cannot turn it in either direction."

The *Hawaiian Progress* continued to move, pressed on by the powerful current. The stern now slowly started to drift toward the Coast Guard station on the south bank.

Townes shook his head. "Rudder's clearly jammed to the left and the current is pushing on it. Gentlemen, this ship is seriously screwed. We either are going to block the whole canal, or we are going to crash into Schaeffer's. Sound the siren."

"We don't have a siren," said Captain Simonescu. "Only foghorn."

Townes grabbed the ship-to-shore microphone. He knew that most VHF radios in the area would be tuned to standby channel 16, and he spun the dial on his own radio to that channel. *"Dewey Berghauer! Dewey Berghauer! Schaeffer's, Schaeffer's, Schaeffer's! We are out of control, and we are going to smash into you! Get everybody out of there!"*

Dewey Berghauer and Gunther Senkler stood side by side in the bar, transfixed as the bow of the *Hawaiian Progress* began to shift out of the channel and point toward the marina's gas pumps. The turn was slow, steady, almost serene. It was terrifying. Seconds ticked by, and the rate of turn increased: the *Hawaiian Progress* was now turning faster and going faster as the current fed its momentum.

As Gunther raced down the back stairs, through the ship's store, and out onto the dock, his entire field of view was suddenly totally obscured. He glanced up and could not understand why he could not see the sweeping arch of the Route 213 bridge high above him. Then his mind processed what he was seeing: the rust-encrusted bow of the *Hawaiian Progress* was no more than two hundred feet away, sweeping swiftly toward Schaeffer's. Toward *him*.

Now he heard screaming: yelling adults, terrified children, shouts of warning and alarm. Over it all he heard Dewey Berghauer's booming voice on the PA yelling, "Get out! Get out! Get out!" over and over again.

Gunther saw that he could not possibly reach the pier that connected the fuel dock back to the ship's store before the collision, so he ran in the other direction, down toward the end of the pier nearest the Pilots' Association building. Now he stopped, prepared to jump—he knew the water would only be a few feet deep—and turned.

To his horror, he saw the *Hawaiian Progress* continue to spin in the channel as the current shoved on her jammed rudder and pushed her stern toward the Bayard House restaurant across the canal. His heart skipped as he saw her inexorable forward movement, slow, majestic, horrifying, heading directly toward Schaeffer's gas dock.

Often one notices unexpected details at fraught moments. What Gunter saw, reflected in the bright orange light on the edge of the canal, was a smooth sheen under the stern counter of the *Hawaiian Progress*. It looked like an oil slick, calming the surface, and spreading steadily. And in the middle of the slick was...a something. A big something. Then it moved, spun spastically in the air. And Gunter knew what it was. Incredibly, it was the fluke of a whale. Gunther Senkler felt his neatly-pressed woolen slacks warm as his bladder betrayed him.

◉ ◉ ◉

ANDY SHANER NEVER KNEW WHAT HIT HIM. TOTALLY WRECKED ON Margheritas, he had danced himself silly with Veronica to the tunes of the steel band and then suddenly had bolted to the edge of the dock and vomited his collection of sweet fruity cocktails into the canal.

Gesturing to Veronica that he was going back to the boat, he had weaved down the dock to where his impeccably restored wooden cabin cruiser, *Alpha Waves,* was tied up at the gas dock. Andy had staggered aboard, losing his footing on a gunwale slippery with evening dew, and fallen hard into the cockpit. Cursing, he had lurched through the main cabin and thrown himself into his cruiser's luxurious V-berth and passed out about five minutes before the *Hawaiian Progress* caromed off the cement bridge abutment and drove her bow straight through the side of

Alpha Waves, over her bridge, over the gas pumps, through the dock, over the restaurant's dumpsters and up onto the parking lot.

Andy never heard the panicked screams, never heard the thump, the crash, the splintering of wood and fiberglass, the groan of steel twisting as the ship forced itself up the shore embankment. *Alpha Waves* was sheared in half, crushed, and shoved to the bottom of the canal in moments.

Her bow now planted firmly in Schaefer's parking lot, the *Hawaiian Progress* now pivoted as the current grabbed her stern and swept it faster toward the Bayard House. There was a deep, metallic thud as the ship was pushed sideways into the cement abutment supporting the Route 213 bridge and pinned there, powerless, and helpless. The current, suddenly blocked by this huge and immovable dam, now rose in a tumbling wave that pushed ten feet up the side of the ship until collapsing and falling back on itself, creating a steady frothy roar that sounded like rapids during spring flood.

In sick fascination, Gunther Senkler watched this slow-motion tableau unfold at the end the dock in front of him. He heard screaming and yelling coming from various directions—from the deck of the ship, from the patio deck, from behind him on the gas dock—but to his shocked ears, the sounds seemed muffled and indistinct, as if being filtered through cotton batting. He felt strangely calm, realizing that absolutely nothing he did could change the course of events at this point.

With a curious detachment, he pondered three questions that popped unbidden into his mind: Are the gas pumps going to blow? Is the Route 213 bridge going to fall a hundred feet into the C&D Canal and crush hundreds of people? Will my insurance cover this?

26

Aftermath

NORA DADMUN HAD DRIVEN ALL THE WAY TO THE TRAIN STATION IN Wilmington to buy every local, regional, and national paper she could find, and now Nora, Tryg, Simone and I were winding up a high-speed exercise of compare-and-contrast, both to see how the whale incident played generally and to look for one particular bit of information. We decided to exclude Rickey until we could assess the likely consequences of the events on the C&D Canal.

The crash of the *Hawaiian Progress* was grabbed by the wire services and within a day was front-page news in papers large and small across the country, a typical curiosity story of the "Well, here's something you don't see every day" variety.

The UPI photo would become an award-winner. In the picture, shot from a helicopter directly above the *Hawaiian Progress*, the ship spans the entire width of the C&D canal, her stern shoved deep into the mooring basin in South Chesapeake City, having pushed a number of pleasure boats up on shore. She is pictured wedged up against both abutments supporting the Route 213 bridge, which threw spooky striped shadows across the ship's deck.

On the north side of the canal, the ship's bow has ridden

179

twenty feet up the embankment behind Schaeffer's chicken-frying tent and now is perched on top of a BMW sports car in the first row of the parking lot. The ship's searchlight shines down on the remnants of the gas dock, down on two dockside fuel pumps knocked askew and with their black hoses trailing into the water, where splintered white remnants of the good ship *Alpha Waves* bob on the surface.

The picture has enough action to delight the most jaded city editor: Here is a cascade of water breaking like a rapids down the length of the right side of the ship as the westbound current, now at high tide, shoves the freighter hard up against the base of the bridge. Here are three men, one clearly dressed in white, two in darker uniforms, standing at the edge of the starboard wing bridge, looking down at the crowds of gawkers looking back up at them. Here are two pilots' launches circling near the aft boarding ladder leading up to the freighter's deck.

And here, at the upper edge of the photo, is trooper Lon Santunas' state police cruiser turning into Schaeffer's parking lot. If you look closely, you can see Gunther Senkler in the lower right of the picture, bathed in a feeble overhead light at the far end of the gas dock. And if you look hard to separate shapes from shadows at the stern of the *Hawaiian Progress*, you can make out a huge mound of muck floating on the surface of the C&D canal, the remnants of one very dead whale.

It's a terrific picture, and it would later run on the cover of *Time* magazine for a feature article entitled, "Is Nature Going Crazy?"

Different papers played the story very differently. The *Cecil Whig*, in full page-width headlines, adopted the breathless shriek of a supermarket tabloid: "CRISIS IN CANAL! HUNDREDS BARELY ESCAPE DEATH IN WHALE COLLISION!" *The New York Times* thrust tongue firmly in cheek and ran a tease banner—"Whale of a Tale"—over a two-column headline, "Freak Accident in Maryland Canal Grounds Freighter on Restaurant." The subhead in the first edition read, "Casualties include one boater and one humpback whale." This attempt at humor was removed in later editions following complaints that it was tasteless and irreverent.

The New York Post screamed, "WHAT THE HELL?" *The Washington Post* took the dry and understated approach: "Strange Incident in C&D Canal." *The Philadelphia Inquirer* carried the headline and a lengthy story that was picked up by AP and run broadly coast-to-coast in other papers: "Bizarre Collision Between Whale and Freighter in Maryland Canal." The subhead said, "Explosion Narrowly Averted; Scientists Mystified." A second subhead said, "One boater known dead, 16 diners missing."

Additional photos inside the *Inquirer* story showed a headshot of Gunther Senkler, a humpback whale breaching in the Atlantic off the shore of Delaware, a close-up of the *Hawaiian Progress's* bow perched atop the crushed sports car, a grisly surface shot of floating whale blubber with the tip of a giant fluke protruding toward the sky, and a picture of the ruined gas dock and twisted pumps.

The moment the tide turned in the canal, the pressure pinning the Hawaiian Progress to the bridge had eased. The ship had then freed itself and began drifting stern-first eastward back toward the Delaware River. Unable to proceed under her own power, the freighter had been taken in tow by two Moran tugs, the ocean-going tug *Big Chief* and the coastal rescue tug *Papoose*. They were going to tow her all the way to Norfolk and straight into the scrapyard. They would collect hefty salvage fees.

By the time we had waded through the entire stack of papers, we had answers to all the predictable questions. Luckily, there had only been one fatality, Andy Shaner, crushed on the *Alpha Waves*. All other "missing" diners were now accounted for and had become the subjects of countless interviews in local TV and media.

Finally, a sidebar on the third page of the lengthy *Philadelphia Inquirer* article got to the part I was most interested in, an interview with Jane Abbott, a marine census expert with the Chesapeake Bay Foundation.

"We are utterly at a loss to explain this event. This is the first known example of a whale coming into the upper Chesapeake Bay, and—given how shallow the bay is—the fact that it arrived at the canal without being spotted suggests it moved up the bay very quickly. Our guess is that it entered Chesapeake Bay from off the coast of Delaware or New Jersey.

"The question is, why was it moving so quickly, and why did it make a sharp turn from the ocean into Chesapeake Bay? We are well past mating season, and that takes place in deep water anyway. Whales that have become disoriented because of parasites in their inner ears or have some other illness that affects their sense of direction, tend to meander or go in circles. We're assuming a linear migration path for this whale, which was a male, by the way, and that means only one of two things: he was swimming fast away from something he was afraid of, or he was swimming fast toward something that attracted him.

"We need to investigate whether this was a unique incident or is part of some trend, some…something…that is drawing atypical fauna into the brackish water of the upper bay. You may remember that a large bull shark was recently caught in the mouth of the Bohemia River. That's not quite as unusual as finding a huge mammal in a ship canal, but it is an anomaly. This whole situation needs some intense investigation, because I do not think it was just a fluke event—no pun intended."

❖   ❖   ❖

A WEEK LATER, A HEADLINE IN THE SUNDAY OUTLOOK SECTION OF *THE Washington Post* caught my eye: "Scientist Links Whale Mystery to Radio Waves." The subhead read "Aberdeen Silent on Experiments."

The gist of the story was that Nathaniel Aranguren, Ph.D., a professor of acoustics and oceanography at the University of Maryland's Eastern Shore campus, was claiming that the whale had been enticed up the length of Chesapeake Bay by ultra-low frequency (ULF) radio waves being transmitted through the water from somewhere in the northern bay.

"I don't know if it was deliberate or accidental," Aranguren was quoted as saying, "but I think someone somehow *summoned* that whale. I don't know why, or what technology was used, but the only answer I can think of that fits all the facts is that some deliberate acoustic signal really caught that whale's attention."

Aranguren pointed a finger straight at the Aberdeen Proving Ground. "Most people think that all the Aberdeen Proving Ground does is fire off different kinds of artillery shells, but actually the place is a skunkworks that conducts all kinds of classified research and intelligence. They do a lot of projects involving acoustics. They are reported to have been developing all kinds of sophisticated underwater broadcast and receiver technologies for decades, most, I suspect, related to submarine warfare. I think the whale accident investigators ought to talk to them, because there is simply no other possible source of ULF transmissions in the Upper Bay."

In response to Aranguren's charges, Lauren Holz, Chief Public Information Officer for all US military marine research activity, issued a formal statement from her office in Washington, DC that was quoted in its entirety in the *Post* article:

> The Aberdeen Proving Ground in Aberdeen, Maryland is not now pursuing, nor has it ever pursued, any form of research in inter-species marine communication by way of underwater radio frequencies, ULF or otherwise. While the incident in the C&D canal is indeed highly unusual, we do not accept the hypothesis that the whale was somehow lured into the canal by some form of underwater messaging, and we strenuously deny any implication that our site or our research activities were in any way associated with this incident. We will have no further comment on this unfortunate accident.

❖ ❖ ❖

I CALLED RICKEY ON THE INTERCOM. "RICKEY, I NEED TO SEE YOU IN the study *immediately.* We have a real emergency on our hands. Please get over here now."

I was leaning against Hermann Bayard's huge carved Victorian desk—now my desk—arms crossed, when Rickey sauntered in. "So, what's all this about, Hugh?"

"It's the ultimate good-news-bad-news story, Rickey. The good news is that your acoustics experiment worked. The mad scientist scored a hit—a big hit. The bad news is that because of your home-grown acoustics shenanigans, it is highly likely that we will all be spending decades in prison."

"What the...hell are you talking about, Hugh?" Again, the pauses in her speech made her sound as if she was translating some other language into English.

I kept my voice as calm and matter-of-fact as I could. "Rickey, I'm assuming that you don't read the papers or listen to the radio, so I gather you haven't heard about our recent excitement."

"What are...you...talking about, Hugh?"

"On Tuesday night, a large humpback whale made its way up the bay, past the Bohemia and up the Elk River. I know that first-hand because I saw it when I was out kayaking. It scared the absolute crap out of me. That whale collided with a mid-channel marker not fifty yards from where I was stopped."

Rickey gasped in surprise. Her eyes grew wide, and she reached her arms in front of her, as if playing blind man's bluff. She whispered hoarsely, "A whale? Really? A whale? A whale!"

"Yep," I said, "big as houses."

"Well, where is he now?"

"Well, Rickey, here is where the problems start. Swimming against the current, the whale went up into the C&D canal."

"No shit!"

"Oh, yes. Yes, he did. He got as far up as Schaeffer's, when he was struck by a freighter going toward Baltimore."

"Oh, man!"

"He—if it matters, it was a he—he was pulled into the propeller and got chopped to pieces."

"Oh, man!" Rickey wasn't whispering any more.

"Two things happened, Rickey. He broke the propeller, and he jammed the ship's rudder."

"Oh, MAN! How big was the boat?"

"Just under five hundred feet long."

Rickey's jaw dropped. She looked up at the ceiling, as if trying to picture something five hundred feet long.

"The ship went out of control. The current pushed it sideways into the 213 bridge. It blocked the whole canal. It also drove up over Schaefer's docks and pushed up to the parking lot."

Rickey's voice dropped to a raspy whisper and trailed off. "Holy..."

"The good news, Rickey, is that although the ship drove right over the top of the gas pumps and tore them all to hell, they didn't explode. They didn't even spill into the canal."

"Whew," said Rickey.

"The bad news is the crash killed a guy. Crushed his cruiser at the dock. He was young, Rickey. Had a kid. Oh, and his family is worth millions...and they are rather upset. They have said they will be suing anyone and everyone connected with his death. They'll sue everybody, up to and including God, to get an answer."

Rickey moved over to the dark leather loveseat and sat heavily, resting her arms on her knees, and looking down at the floor.

"And we're just getting started, Rickey. This is not just a bunch of civil lawsuits, it's a potential criminal case. There's a laundry list of things one Ulricke Bayard could be charged with if they find out what she did. How about wanton and willful negligence? As in negligent homicide. That's a crime, Rickey. Better still, how about manslaughter—maybe not intentional, but it's still manslaughter. And it'll get worse when they figure out that you were probably responsible for the plane crash at the marina and still you kept at it. That's two more people killed. Maybe they'll let you off as a juvenile, but they could charge you as an adult if they really get a stick up their ass.

"Rickey, they do not have special prisons for autistic people.

No one is going to cut you a break or give you special treatment. So, we have to do everything we can to make sure we don't get caught. I say, 'we' because I'm an accessory. An accessory before the fact because I knew what you were doing out in the hangar. An accessory after the fact because I know what happened, and I'm not going to tell anybody."

I paused. Rickey looked down at the oriental carpet, and then she looked up at me. "Hugh," she said her eyes wet, "Does it make you…feel good…to lay it on so heavy?"

    ⚙   ⚙   ⚙

THE FOLLOWING MORNING, I FORMALLY MADE ACCESSORIES-AFTER- the-fact of Nora Dadmun and Tryg Sletland by bringing them in on the action plan. "Accessory or not, doesn't make no never mind to me," said Tryg. "I'm already an ex-con. I'll never get to vote again anyway. Outrageous story, though."

Bathed in warm sunlight, we sat together by the tall windows in the living room, a rare occurrence. I convened the planning meeting there to underscore the gravity of the situation.

I stood. "We are going to be questioned," I started. "Don't know when, or whether it will be by the state police or the FBI or some other government investigators, but for sure we are going to get a visit.

"We're already on the radar," I said. "I don't know how high on the radar, but we're on a list somewhere. Look, this investigation is sure to expand and they're going to try to connect the dots. 'Why did we have a shark off Turkey Point?' 'Why did that guy whose plane crashed report that all his instruments had gone crazy?' 'Why did that whale make a beeline up the bay?'

"Remember, I witnessed that plane crash. I've already been interviewed by the state police. And when I told them that they could not interview Hermann Bayard and refused to let them in the house, they definitely got snake-eyed. They don't have anything on us yet, but as you saw at the auction, the Santunas guy and his bitch-goddess sidekick sure would dearly love to bust my chops.

"The Aberdeen people, they're denying they had anything to do with all these transmissions, but they sure as hell are going to investigate. Their ass is on the line, because everybody thinks that they are the only ones who fool around with all sorts of voodoo radio stuff. And they can investigate better than anybody. Everybody knows that they do all these secret...experiments. They're spooks, and somebody has lifted the rock off their dark little world. You're gonna see them scurry."

I turned to Rickey, who was staring at her hands and moving her right foot around in little circles on the carpet.

"Look, Rickey, if that shark and that whale heard your siren call, Aberdeen did too. It's a safe bet somebody recorded them. It's also a good bet they can tell exactly how those signals were created, what it took to broadcast them into the bay. And then that big surge that blew your lab? They sure as hell recorded that signal or signals or whatever the hell it was. Maybe they tracked them, used radio direction finders to get a fix on their location, their source.

"I wouldn't be surprised if we may already be in the crosshairs. And another thing to remember, friends, is that we bought some of our original equipment from Aberdeen. I don't know if the Aberdeen investigators will have enough brains to talk to their own surplus sales depot, but if they ever do, the investigators are going to come storming over here. And they won't be polite.

"The only thing that's going to save our bacon is that it is so completely outrageous to imagine that some teenager, working in an abandoned airplane hangar out in the sticks, could assemble a machine that could broadcast underwater come-hither signals to whales. At least we got the 'highly-unlikely' factor on our side."

"Okay, Hugh," Nora said crossly. "You've had your moment of drama, so let's all just bring it down some. What are we going to do about this?"

"Okay," I said. "There's stuff we all have to do to survive

a visit. We're going to go to ground. And that means cleaning everything out, pronto."

Rickey's head shot up. "What?" she said sharply. "What are you talking about? You're going to take my lab away from me?"

"That is correct. We've got to get all the electronic stuff out of here."

Rickey leapt to her feet, spitting and sputtering. "Well, fuck that! That lab belongs to me! We just built it!"

Time to grab the reins. "What we all are trying to do," I shouted, "is to *keep ourselves from going to jail*. Like it or not, you are included in the plan. Once things all calm down for a few months, we can discuss what to do about the Rickey Bayard Show. For now, *please sit down, shut up, and pay attention.*"

I paused to gather my thoughts. Tryg was absolutely deadpan, looking off into space with his head cocked slightly. Nora had lowered her head, masking her face and her expression.

"First thing, Tryg, we need to break up Rickey's lab equipment so it's not all in one place. We're going to rent a couple of storage lockers in different places. You will need to rent a fifteen-foot moving truck from U-Haul, the kind with a forklift piggy-backed on the back. You'll need it at the storage locker to unload the generator and the rest of Rickey's shit. We'll stash all the cabling and outdoor stuff in one place, the big generator and the big consoles in another. We'll keep the little generator here, because it's not unusual for a farm to have one generator. Two generators—now that would trigger warning bells."

"Don't you call my stuff shit," Rickey shouted. "You think you're so smart, Mr. Aborigine smash-brain, but you never could have designed and built that transmitter."

I felt Rickey's pain, but we had to get real here.

"Rickey, you are completely right. I am truly amazed at what you accomplished. I really am. *But your experiments have killed people!* So, I am fairly stressed out right now because we are playing with some very serious fire here. Rickey, you had better cool it with me, because you are in all this up to your neck."

Rickey did not respond, simply switching to her I'm-not-showing-any-emotion channel.

"Next, Tryg, use the tractor to drag that rusty old combine sitting down in the lower field into the hangar. Disassemble the cutting bars and jockey wheels and spread the pieces all over the place. Next, take the shop-vac and reverse the hose and suck a lot of dirt in from outside and blow it all around inside of the hanger."

Rickey lit up again. "Oooh, no! No, sir! You can't fuck up my lab like that!"

I was about to speak when Nora stood and walked over to Rickey. She sat down next to her on the couch and put her hand firmly on Rickey's knee. Rickey flinched but let the hand stay.

"Rickey." Nora's voice was soft, but absolutely firm. "This really is an *emergency*. You accomplished what you set out to do with the ULF stuff, but we are really, *really* up against the wall here. You were part of the cause, now you have to be part of the fix. You have to grow up. *Right now.*"

Now Nora began rattling off orders like an emergency room nurse.

"Rickey, please move back into the big bedroom at the back of the third floor," commanded Nora. "You need to get all your personal stuff out of your sleeping place in the hangar. Everything. It cannot look like anyone has been living in there. Tryg, you start using the second-floor bathroom. The third-floor bath will be Rickey's alone. And add another dead-bolt to Rickey's bedroom door to make her feel as safe as possible."

"What if this is all just a false alarm?" said Tryg. "Maybe no one's ever gonna come around. Maybe we're just jerking ourselves around for nothing."

"Well, we can certainly hope for that," I said. "I certainly do not want to have to try to bluff my way past a bunch of military investigators. But we have to be ready. And Tryg, you should be the only one who will talk to them, okay? Polite, but kind of a rube, get me? If they insist on talking to me, I'm going to be the dimwit who is barely smart enough to chew gum, much less to act as a caretaker. I'm hoping they will underestimate me, talk down to me, whatever.

"Nora, you're the nervous-Nellie cook with the cast-down eyes who can't bear to talk to people. You don't know *nothin'*. Rickey, we may have to call on your acting skills. You've just been promoted from being an Aspy to being profoundly autistic and completely non-verbal. Best case is that no one will ever even see you unless they come with a search warrant.

"And Rickey, we're going to call this 'Plan B.' If I, or Nora or Tryg, ever say to you, 'Rickey, go to Plan B,' it means you are to pretend to be severely handicapped, and maybe even a little scary. You can make some sounds, but do not utter any words. Use Susurrus, if you like. Do not respond when someone talks to you. Do not make eye contact. Shrink behind me or Nora or Tryg. Shake your head. Snap your fingers. Stamp your feet. Can you do that?"

"Sounds like fun," said Rickey.

"Feel free to practice. Just don't get too into it, okay? With any luck, we'll all be able to stick to Plan A, which is us being who we are. The Hole in the Wall Gang."

27

Plan B

I PRESSED THE "ALL HOUSE" BUTTON ON THE INTERCOM AND SHOUTED loudly. "Plan B! Plan B! Nora, Tryg, Rickey, Plan B! This is not a drill! Bad guys coming down the driveway!"

After we had disassembled Rickey's lab and moved the rusty old combine into the hangar, Tryg had installed a closed-circuit surveillance camera system with a camera out at the end of the driveway, another on the driveway halfway to the house, and a third overlooking the courtyard, pointed toward the front door. We had monitors in my office, in the kitchen and in the hangar. Tryg also added an electronic eye on the front gates which emitted a long horn blast in the house, garage and hanger whenever the beam was broken by an entering vehicle. We figured it gave us about forty-five seconds to get to battle stations.

As I sat at my office desk on this Wednesday afternoon, the horn had beeped twice: two vehicles. I looked up at the monitor and saw a light-colored Ford Crown Vic sedan turn into the drive, followed by a white Ford Econoline window van. "It's Aberdeen!" I called into the intercom. "It's not the cops, it's the army. Nora, get headphones and sunglasses on Rickey and get her into your apartment. Tryg, can you hear me?"

"Loud and clear," said Trygve Sletland.

"Where are you? How fast can you get to the front door?"

"On my way. I was in my room, reading. I'm dressed, good to go. Where are you going to be?"

"I'm going to be standing behind the front door. After you greet them, call me, and tell me to show them around the outside. You and Nora have the inside."

"Roger."

Tryg met the visitors on the front stoop, leaving the door ajar. I was behind the door, and I could hear the conversation clearly and see the Aberdeen people through the slot in the door above the middle hinge.

"Good afternoon. I'm Colonel Bailey Suits. I'm head of Security and Military Police at the Aberdeen Maryland Research Center." Colonel Suits appeared calm, his voice pleasant. At the moment, he was playing the Good Cop. Full uniform, ribbons spread across his chest to command respect, sort of a weight-lifter's physique, but not aggressively macho or pushy, like you might expect of a senior military police officer.

"Good afternoon back to you," said Tryg agreeably. "Ah'm Tryg Sletland. I head up farm operations around here at Bohemia Manor Farm."

"We want to see Hermann Bayard."

"Ah'm sure sorry," said Tryg, "but we can't help you there, Colonel Suits. Mr. Bayard is outta the country. Raht now we don't have no way of getting' in touch with him."

Tryg's sodbuster act had me convinced. I thought he was striking a fine balance between ignorant clod and deferential lackey. "S'mattera fact, we don't even 'zactly know where he is."

"I find that hard to believe," said Suits.

"Ah'm sorry if you don't believe me, sir, but it's still true. That's the way Hermann Bayard likes it. He's away from the farm most times, Comes and goes when he wants to. As for not being able to contact him, well, he calls the shots, not us. He calls us, we don't have any way to call him. So, we just carry on and take care of the house and run the farm when he's not here. Which, like I said, is most times."

"Who's we?"

"Four of us live here. I head up farm operations and maintenance. Mr. Bayard has a handicapped teenage daughter with mental problems. Her name's Ulricke. Rickey. She lives here. She's took care of by Nora Dadmun, who also cooks for us. Mr. Bayard's bookkeeper is Hugh Ullam. He's a colored fella, lives on the property too and looks after Mr. Bayard's financial 'fairs."

"I see. And just how long has Bayard been away?"

"On his current trip, it's been some months now. We sorta track where he's been by all the receipts come in for all the stuff he buys. Looks like this time around he was in Bali for a while and now maybe is somewhere in Indonesia. But we're not really sure where he be or when he be back."

"Was he here when the ship collided with the whale?"

"Oh, no sir. And he was gone several months before the ship hit the whale. In fact, I'd be surprised if he even knows that a ship hit a whale."

Suits cleared his throat and pulled himself up to his full height. "Do you know why we are here?"

"I got a good guess, Colonel Suits. I been talking with some of our neighbors. They say since that ship accident, investigators been going all around properties on the Bohemia or the Sassafras or the Elk—places right on the water—interviewing the owners and searchin' around. And I read the newspapers. They been saying you fellas are looking for the source of mystery signals that you think lured that whale up here. So, I guess it's our turn for your visit."

"Well, it's not a visit, Mr. Sletland," said Suits, cocking his head slightly and touching the bill of his military hat. "Our job is to do site inspections. Searches. We have been asking property owners to allow our searches voluntarily, but in several cases where people have demanded that we obtain search warrants, we have had no trouble getting those from the United States District Court for the District of Maryland."

"I'm sure you haven't," said Tryg. "But that won't be necessary here. We'll be more than happy to help—*here Tryg said 'hep'*—you in any way we can. We got only one request, but it's important to us."

"That being…"

"Well, you're welcome to look around the house, but I told you Mr. Bayard's daughter has serious mental problems. Nora Dadmun can give you all the details, but the point is that if the girl gets agitated or upset, she can get real violent and sometimes tries to harm herself. She's super-sensitive to noise and to bright light and to touch; that's why she almost always has sunglasses and headphones on.

"If you insist, we can let you see her for yourselves, but we gotta ask that you do not confront her or get real loud or fire a lot of sharp questions at her. Whatever you do, please don't touch her. I gotta ask that you respect us on this. At the moment, she is in Nora Dadmun's apartment with Nora. Our thought was to keep her there while you people look around the house."

I noticed that Tryg, now on a smooth roll, did not give Suits a chance to respond.

"As for me, Nora Dadmun, and Hugh Ullam, well, we'll all be pleased to help you any way we can and to guide you around the house and the property, if that's what you need to do. How do y'all go about this?"

"As the ranking officer in this detail, I usually conduct the inside inspection. I regret if this seems like an invasion of privacy, but we do regard this as an urgent matter. That means our search must include living areas, bedrooms, offices, and attached garages. Can you guide me through the house?"

"No problem," said Tryg affably.

"Sergeant Heim and his squad will conduct the inspection of the grounds. Our plot diagram indicates that there's an airplane hangar and a number of outbuildings. We certainly will want to inspect those, both inside and outside."

"'Course," said Tryg. "Lemme ask Mr. Ullam to help y'all with that. And one other thing probably help, too. As you know from your map, Bohemia Manor is a helluva big farm, and it's bound to take your guys a while to look it all over. I'm not sure your van or Crown Vic are the right vehicles for muckin' around in our fields. If you want, Hugh Ullam can drive your people all around the property in our pickup truck. It has all-wheel drive and Hugh knows the whole property good as I do."

"That would be much appreciated," said Colonel Suits. "And thank you for your cooperation. Obviously, it makes our assignment much easier."

◉ ◉ ◉

THE BOTTOM LINE IS THAT EVERYTHING SEEMED TO GO FINE. AT LEAST as far as we could tell, we met muster, passed with flying colors, avoided detection or suspicion, didn't make any incriminating gaffes or admissions.

The Aberdeen people spent over four hours probing every nook and cranny of Bo Manor and the farm, leaving as the shadows grew long across the fields. We were patient, and they were patient. In the hallway, Tryg took me aside and asked if there was anything they couldn't see in my office. The answer was no, I said, give 'em *carte blanche*. Tryg made it clear to Suits that we could not approve having them read through my books and papers or make any copies on my Xerox machine; we were fine with a general premises search, but for confidentiality reasons, we would object to a document review without a warrant with some statement of probable cause.

Suits backed off quickly at this point: No, no, no, that wouldn't be necessary. That's not what they were looking for. Interestingly, Suits never did say what it was they were looking for. In any event, the house inspection seemed to go fine, without anyone having to get their back up.

Suits met Rickey, or at least saw Rickey. Nora later told me that Rickey stood up abruptly from the couch in Nora's apartment, clasped her arms across her chest and shook her head so violently that her headphones flew off. Nora moved to calm her, and Rickey—playing her role perfectly—then simply stood stock still, clasping and unclasping her hands at her sides. Nora said that the only sounds Rickey uttered were when she stared at Bailey Suits' wiry red hair and shouted "Fuzzy wuzzy!"

Nora then calmly asked Colonel Suits if he would like to interview her, Nora, that is, and when he nodded, she asked Tryg if he would stay with Rickey for a few minutes. Tryg moved behind Rickey, quietly put his arms on her shoulders and exerted a gentle pressure. Rickey exhaled deeply, dropped her head to her chest and stilled her hands. A wonderful, utterly convincing performance. Rickey later beamed at our rave reviews.

Nora led an obviously relieved Colonel Suits into the living room, where she later told us, she gave, polite, naïve and somewhat obtuse answers to his questions. She said that Suits was polite and respectful, but she noted how his questions seemed to move randomly from one topic to another. Nora did not think this was an accident or lack of preparation.

"How long have you and Tryg and Ullam worked here?"

"How long has Hermann been a world traveler?"

"Why did you have a closed-circuit TV system on the driveway?"

"How did Hermann come to employ an Australian accountant?"

"What is the hangar used for?"

"What is Ulricke Bayard's level of functioning?

"Did you know that Trygve Sletland was a convicted felon?"

"How much are all of you all paid?

"Is it really impossible to contact Hermann Bayard?"

And so it went, like a pinball caroming around a flashing game deck. Nora told us that even while smiling pleasantly, she kept her answers simple, if not completely monosyllabic:

"So, what did you think of that whale coming into the C&D Canal?"

"Oh, that was bad. The whole thing was very bad. I was very surprised."

"Do you think somebody lured the whale up into the Northern Chesapeake?"

"Oh, heavens, I couldn't say. Now, why would anyone want to do that?"

"Do you or Mr. Sletland or Mr. Ullam have any background in electronics?"

"Well, certainly not me! Tryg is very talented with mechanical things, like fixing tractors, does that count?"

"We were particularly interested in electronics or equipment related to radio frequencies or technical things like that."

"Oh, there's nothing like that around here."

"Does Ullam have any expertise in electronics?"

"I don't think electronics are his thing. Numbers, yes. He's a whiz at numbers. Oh, my God. But, like, look at him. He's an Aborigine from the Australian outback. Where's he going to learn about electronics?"

"What about Ulricke?"

"What about Ulricke?"

"Does she have any…gifts…we ought to be aware of?"

Nora said she had tried to make her laugh sound incredulous. "Rickey? Like is she some kind of genius or something?"

"Well, it's been known to happen," said Suits curtly.

"Not with Rickey it doesn't," said Nora, shaking her head in apparent disbelief. "With Rickey, what you see is what you get. And believe me, a little of it goes a long way. Sometimes she may act like Frankenstein, but she doesn't make anything in laboratories or anything like that."

❂　　　❂　　　❂

MY OWN TOUR WITH SUITS' SQUAD WAS BORING, NOT NERVE-
wracking. They seemed pleasant young guys, just doin' their job. My race didn't seem to register on them, perhaps because two of them were black. They seemed rather unguarded for employees of a giant spy facility, and I found it easy to strike up a conversation with them.

"You fellows been doing this house-to-house investigation long?"

"Since about three days after that ship accident, but I know there are some other guys who've been detailed to find out about some strange radio-frequency goings on for a few months now, even before the whale thing. They think all these mystery waves things may be connected. Like, didja hear about that airplane crash at the marina where the guy's instruments went all haywire?"

"Hear about it? Shit, I saw it happen!"

"Get the fuck outta here! Man, that must have been some sight!"

"When that plane came flying out of the fog, *it was upside down*!" I opened my eyes wide; they shook their heads in awe.

"So," I said, changing back to a lower key, "what do all your radio experts say about all this stuff that's going down?"

"Shit, that stuff's way above our level. They got the techno-spooks workin' on all that. We're just MP grunts who got told to go search a whole bunch of houses. We're about half-done."

I was relieved to hear that. It was better to be just another number in a long, repetitive process than to be at the beginning or at the end, where the level of scrutiny was likely to be more intense.

"You guys getting a little bored with all this lookin' around?"

"Oh," said the short kid with the buzz cut, "it's okay. Better'n a lot of stuff we have to do. Some people give us a hard time and demand warrants 'n' shit, but most people are pretty cooperative. Like you. I say this, though, searching the big farms like this, man, that's a pain in the ass."

"Sorry," I said, smiling.

"Hey, man, not your fault."

"You think you're getting close to anything?"

"There's two other squads making the rounds around the upper bay, and I don't know what they've found, but we've come up with squat. Zilch. Me, I wouldn't suspect the Bohemia River anyway. If they find anything, it's gotta be up the Elk."

One of the squad, a strikingly handsome athlete-type in his mid-twenties, hadn't yet said anything. Now he spoke up in a kind of stage whisper.

"Hell, they ain't going to find nothing in no house."

"Well, what then?" asked buzz cut. "What's your theory, Brainiac?"

"Boat," the jock said. "Simple. Obvious. *Transmitter was on a boat*. Movin' all around. Look, first they get that shark off Turkey Point—open Chesapeake Bay. Then there's the plane crash on the Bohemia. Then that big boom that blew out the eardrums of our best radio guy. He's mainly deaf now. End of his career, that's for sure. Then the whale in the Elk and the C&D. Somebody was movin' around, transmitting *from a boat*," he said firmly.

"You think all those events really were *connected*?" I asked, trying to sound incredulous, like it was the craziest idea in the world.

"Well, I can tell you the brass at Aberdeen sure as hell think they were connected. I heard three of 'em talking after our duty briefing. They said that while maybe all the frequencies were different, the signal signature—intensity, wave profile, all that—sure looked the same. Suits, for one, he thinks it's one person, or at least one transmitter."

"God almighty," I said.

⚙   ⚙   ⚙

THE SEARCH SQUAD SEEMED PRETTY CASUAL WHILE WE WERE riding around the farm and along the shore of the wetlands (including right past the point where Rickey had fed her huge "radio snake" into the Bohemia River), but they gave the hangar a very thorough going over.

Tryg's stagecraft had worked to perfect effect. All the signs of disuse were in place: the place looked dusty, the air was dank and musty, and—thanks to Tryg's skilled application of corrosive acid on the hinges—it took three squad members to force the garage door up. The combine had been stripped and turned into various piles of rusty parts, wheels, nuts, and bolts. There was no sign that anyone had been actively working on it in some time.

"We've been pretty busy with plowing and planting and

weeding," I said. "Tryg—he's the farm manager guy who also works on our cars and tractors and machinery—he just hasn't had any time to do his thing, you know?"

They checked all the equipment, they explored the room that had been Rickey's sleeping quarters and even moved the cylinders of welding gas we'd stored there around. They went through all the drawers in the long work counter. Nothing. I stood in the background, next to the hanger door, fearing I would hear a sudden shout, "Hey! Looka this!" But the shout never came. *No sir, they would report, there wasn't no electronics laboratory in that hangar.*

⚙   ⚙   ⚙

COLONEL SUITS THANKED US FOR OUR TIME AND COOPERATIVE

attitude. He shook Nora's hand politely, Tryg's firmly. He turned to his squad before he had a chance to shake mine. "Mount up, you guys," he said brusquely. "Let's leave these people to get on with their lives."

"Colonel Suits," I asked. "Will we receive any kind of report or summary of your search here today?"

"Nope. That's not how we operate."

"Well, will there be any kind of public report on whatever you all find?"

"Mr. Ullam, let me remind you of something. This is Aberdeen we're talking about, not the Elkton Sheriff's Department. We do not hold ourselves out for public scrutiny."

"I see."

"We'll see if you do."

PART THREE
Cut to the Chase

28

Goodbye, Deirdre

TRYG HAD TAPPED LIGHTLY ON THE DOOR OF MY BEDROOM, THEN stepped in. "Hugh," he said, "I think we have a situation."

I was at my small wooden bedroom desk. I closed the ledger I was working on, pushed the hood of the desk lamp downward toward the blotter and turned to him, gesturing for him to sit down. He remained standing.

"Did you hear the electric eye alarm go off?"

"Nope. Did it go off?"

"Well, it must have if it's working right. Because I was heading out the driveway to go up to Chesapeake City to have crabs with Simone. At the end of the drive there was a reflection, a taillight reflection, from a car parked about twenty yards up the McKees' dirt lane across from our driveway. The car was sort of angled into the underbrush. I pulled in behind it and found that some old wire fence strands had been pulled across the back of the car. Man, this was real amateur camouflage. It was a state police cruiser, Hugh, and it was empty. My bet is that we are being watched. Whoever it is must have walked around the electric eye."

For a moment, my wheels spun without getting any traction. Finally, I said, "Tryg, I'm pretty sure this is a tipping point. Some shit is going to hit the fan, and while I can't completely protect you, maybe I can at least insulate you some."

"I don't understand," he said. But he did understand. He just needed to have it spelled out.

"Ever since Hermann dropped dead, we've all been living on borrowed time. I don't know what legal charges they'd use, but if they catch us, we're on the hook for things like fraud, theft by deception, embezzlement, larceny, Christ knows what-all. We all have a lot to lose, and desperate times may call for desperate measures."

"This is not news to me, Hugh. Where does this put us right now?" Tryg looked calm enough, but his breaths were coming long and slow.

"That car probably belongs to Santunas. I think he's on to us. He's looking for Hermann, or at least looking for something to take us down. There could be a lot of heat. A *lot* of heat. You should get ready for that, starting now. But let's be clear: I am the leader of the pack, and this is my show. At least for tonight, if the bad guys are prowling around, I want to get you out of harm's way. If I have to take some pre-emptive action, I do not want you here as an accomplice.

"And so, Tryg, the first thing is that I want you to forget you ever saw that police car and forget you ever mentioned it to me. I want you to climb in the pickup and drive up to The Waterman's Tap and meet Simone. When you see her, I want you to apologize for being late and ask her exactly what time it is. Do that as soon as you get there. *Get her to say the time.*

"I want you to tie one on tonight, Tryg. Have a pitcher of beer, order at least two mudslides. Get buzzed, get a little loud. I want them to notice you, make Grick, the owner, wonder what the hell is up with you. Don't be an asshole, just be highly visible. Memorable, okay? Tell Simone you're all pissed off because the Sawyer Brothers screwed up repairs on the tractor, something like that, you gotta blow off some steam. One way or the other, do not get back here before 1:00 AM. Do I make myself clear?"

Tryg looked down at his boots, then up at the ceiling. He

inhaled deeply. "Why should you be the one to take action?" he asked wearily.

"Because I'm the right one to take action. Maybe nothing is going on here, maybe we got this all wrong. But I don't think so. If the authorities are coming after us because of me, then I'm the one who should be the point man."

Tryg shook his head. "I don't agree. We all should be in this together."

"Nothing to be gained by group martyrdom, Tryg. Get your ass to the goddamned bar. I want to get you out of the line of fire, literally and figuratively."

"Thank you, Hugh."

"Don't mention it. And I mean that, Tryg. *Do not mention it.*"

      ◉   ◉   ◉

WE KEEP A VARIETY OF GUNS IN HERMANN'S GUN CABINET IN MY office, but I went for the little chrome-plated Browning .25 caliber semi-automatic. I'm not sure why. It doesn't have a lot of stopping power, and it is wildly inaccurate at anything more than about ten feet. But I knew Hermann had been fond of it, it fit my hand well, I was comfortable with it (frankly, Hermann's .357 magnum scared the hell out of me). It also was easy to pocket and conceal.

It turned out that Deirdre Callas was our visitor, not Lon Santunas. And she was a remarkably inept cat burglar. Her tracks were visible in the dew on the driveway and on the Belgian block in the front circle. She clearly had walked down the length of the drive, moved past the garage, and headed down toward the hangar. She must have barely missed Tryg as he drove out to meet Simone. Her footprints were clear on the damp lawn, and it was easy to see where she had pushed her way through the privet hedge.

A silent Indian tracker she wasn't. I could hear her snapping twigs and stepping on sticks and generally making quite a din. I, on the other hand, know how to move soundlessly, anytime, anywhere, thanks to Akers and my need while there to observe while not being observed. I followed her, perhaps twenty yards behind, risking, but not seeking, detection. Callas never turned, never looked around, never stopped to listen. On a state police field surveillance exam, Deirdre Callas would have flunked big time.

I saw Deirdre reach the hangar and pause. I felt a stab of alarm because the light coming through the entry door and the glow coming through the large translucent overhead door made it clear that Rickey was in there. From my vantage point on the rise above the hangar, I could see clearly in through the jalousie window mounted low on the eastern wall

And there was Rickey. She was wandering from one pile of combine junk to the next. She'd pick up the biggest piece she could heft, lift it over her head, and then furiously throw it down on the floor. Although noisy, all this was also perfectly innocent. But it was also pretty creepy, supporting the impression that Rickey was not firing on all cylinders. And I worried, because when Rickey gets surprised, she can get very wiggy. I was afraid if she detected Callas' laughably bad surveillance that all hell would break loose. *Was Callas careful with a gun? Who knew?*

Once Deirdre moved to the tarmac in front of the hangar, the sound of her steps grew quieter. She couldn't see anything, of course, so she continued around to the side of the hangar and approached the jalousie window. I couldn't see everything she was seeing, but something obviously caught her interest because she arched up on to her tiptoes and pushed her face toward the window.

Deirdre reached into her pants pocket and pulled out what her gestures made obvious was a small camera. I could tell that she shot four pictures, because this was the old kind of cheap drugstore camera where you advanced the film by twisting a dial on the top, and I could hear the soft scraping of the advance mechanism: *Click. Scree, scree, scree. Click. Scree, scree, scree. Click. Scree, scree, scree. Click.*

Deirdre was still staring through the window when the big

green outside generator suddenly kicked on. These days, the only thing it was hooked to was the air compressor we used to keep the farm vehicles' tires properly inflated, but as its air reservoir bled down, it often fired itself up to recharge the tank. As the generator rattled up to speed, Deirdre, startled, spun backwards, and tripped over her own feet, landing on her ass in the moist grass. She spun on to her stomach, gathered her feet under her and bolted up the flagstone path toward the main house. When she flew by me, I was no more than five feet off the path, standing in the shadows next to the hedge. Again, her words from the first time we met came back to me: "We're trained to handle anything." *Oh, sister,* I thought. *You are a rank piece of work.*

Still, Deirdre Callas did not lack for courage. I fully expected her to hotfoot it back to her cruiser, but instead she crept up to the patio and began peering into the house windows. First the kitchen, then the butler's pantry, then Nora's apartment, where she paused. The lights were off, but the television was on, and the blue glow illuminated Deirdre's face. If Nora had looked over her shoulder, she would have seen the voyeur, but obviously she didn't, because Deirdre just stood there for several minutes staring at Nora. Then she moved on, and I glanced quickly into Nora's apartment; she was fast asleep in her chair.

Deirdre moved window by window along the outside wall of the living room, and when she had made it around the end of the living room wing, I stopped following her. I moved quickly into the house through the mud room and butler's pantry and was back at the inside of the front door only a few seconds later.

I peered out of the glass sidelight on the right of the front door and reared back, because Deirdre Callas' face was pushed up against the outside of the pane, peering in back at me. I recovered, flipped on the outside entry lights, and jerked the front door open. Deirdre Callas was still bent over when I shoved my little pistol in her face.

"Get your hands up!" I shouted, and, in a reflexive action, her arms popped straight upward. Then her look of surprise gave way to a condescending sneer, and her arms started to drop.

"Is that a real gun?" she asked.

Her tone was mocking, as if she was deriding the length of my penis. She looked down her long, straight nose at the object in my hand. "It looks like one of those toy cigarette lighters."

Her dismissive tone triggered an intense spasm of anger. I felt the color rise in my cheeks. After a lifetime of passivity in the face of being ridiculed and ordered around, I simply was not going to take this shit anymore. I suddenly felt a savage hatred for Deirdre Callas.

I had been aiming the pistol at the brass name tag on her uniform. Now I moved the barrel slowly downward and pointed it at the top of her knee.

"Yes, it's a real gun," I said, and pulled the trigger. The report was unexpectedly loud for such a little gun, and I jumped back in surprise.

Deirdre collapsed on the top step of the flagstone entry landing and then kind of salmon-flopped down the two steps to the driveway. She pulled her knee up to her chest and began a high-pitched metallic keening. It sounded sort of like she was saying, "knee, knee, knee," but maybe she was just sucking wind past clenched teeth, I don't know.

A peculiar calm now came over me. I said, "Oh, now look what I've done. I've damaged your nice trooper uniform."

"You bastard," she hissed. "You fucking bastard." She was rocking from side to side, her head lifted off the pavement, the cords in her neck taut and quivering.

"Oh, Deirdre, you just don't know when to shut up, do you?" I said. I moved the barrel deliberately to the right to aim at her other knee, this time just below the kneecap. I pulled the trigger again, lightly but firmly.

The first shot had made a small, neat hole, just next to the sharp crease in the left leg of her uniform trousers. Not much blood yet. The second shot made more of a mess, tearing a broad wedge in the cloth of her right pant leg, and blowing a clot of flesh and cartilage into the air. Deirdre Callas stiffened and grunted, her entire body spasming in pain.

I had just committed an act unlike any I had ever considered, much less acted on, even in my angriest moments at Moore River and Akers. I felt myself sliding into uncharted emotional territory, both immersed intensely in the moment and observing my actions from a distance. I felt both calm and electrically charged. The feeling was novel, but not... unpleasant. I confess, given all that had happened between us; Deirdre Callas' agony was gratifying to behold.

"You'll pay for this, you motherfucker," Deirdre hissed.

"Maybe I will, maybe I won't," I said, training the pistol on her nose. "But one way or another, you won't know what happens. Because you will be dead. And Deirdre, believe me, no one is ever going to find you."

Now Deirdre began sobbing and retching. Her eyes locked on mine, and she shook her head wildly from side to side, banging her face left and right on the Belgian block, her short brown hair flying wildly.

"Deirdre, Deirdre. Such a fuss." *Whose patronizing voice was this? Mine?* "They give you troopers such great training in the Maryland State Police, isn't that what you bragged to me? 'Trained to handle every situation,' you said. Well, what did they train you to do when you are certain you are about to die?"

✿   ✿   ✿

I KILLED DEIRDRE CALLAS WHEN SHE WAS STILL OUT COLD, FIRING A bullet into her brain at close range from just behind her right ear. She had been rendered unconscious when she made a frantic move for her holstered service pistol, and I had kicked her as powerfully as I could, directly in front of her right ear.

The shooting took place about thirty yards behind the tool shed, and Deirdre, in sitting position, was propped up against a small oak, held fast by the three coils of light rope that circled her neck and moored her, loosely but adequately, to the tree. The same type of cord formed a knotted loop around each of her wrists and was also wrapped around the tree, pulling her arms behind her. Her legs were untied, and both were twitching spastically. The clean bullet hole had scabbed. The more seriously damaged knee still pumped spurts of blood in time with her pulse.

Deirdre Callas' brain died instantly as the small-caliber round ricocheted around her braincase, but the rest of her body took longer. She groaned once, took one deep rattling breath. Her back arched. It took several minutes for the reflexes to stop twitching her arms and legs. Her eyes remained open, and I left them open. I don't go in for all that crap about gently closing the eyelids out of respect for the dead. I was content to let her stare blankly into eternity.

I had considered waiting for her to come around, waiting for the opportunity to lash her with vengeful words, giving her some time to contemplate her fate, letting her wallow in fear and horror. But I realized that I did not need a deep dramatic monologue. This was not a horror movie, and I was not a sadistic fiend, relishing the agony of the damsel in distress.

I had also seriously considered not killing her at all. I attempted some rational decision-making. On one hand, maybe a bullet in the head was a pretty extreme consequence for what was, on the surface, a pretty harmless nocturnal trespass. Maybe I should have just let her wander around our property and peer in our windows and spy on us. Maybe I should have just submitted.

But could I do that, just let her sneak back to her cruiser and drive off into the night? *No!* Because this wasn't harmless. This wasn't just one-time illegal prowling. It was a determined *attack,* a harbinger of invasions to come. This wasn't law enforcement; it was *rogue.* It was personal. Deirdre was coming after us. After *me.*

What in the world, I wondered, had been going through Deirdre's mind, skulking around my house like this? Obviously, I had hit a tripwire in Deirdre's personal mine field several times, and she clearly felt she had been grievously disrespected. So maybe her resentment flooded over the top and blinded her to the risks she was taking. Or maybe she thought there were no significant risks. It nettled me that I would never know.

As for me, when I looked at Deidre's unconscious body,

my little pistol pointed at her ear, I became aware of a strange prickly sensation coursing through me in time with my pulse, a feeling that went all the way back to being a seven-year-old in a stinking prison camp craving the power to punish and vanquish my tormenters. The feeling was almost mechanical, a kind of tick-tick-tick—like a string of dominos tripping and tipping inside me, clicking faster and faster as they fell. Falling all the way back to the Moore River Native Settlement. Maybe this echo of my past life was what people mean when they speak of "the arc of history."

Whatever it was, it now triggered a decision to act. I had been violated and humiliated by Deidre Callas several times now. She had wanted to make a show of using her authority to control and humiliate me, which for me had become the deepest, most visceral insult possible.

I was not going to let that happen again. The die was cast: Deirdre would die both because she had to die and because she deserved to die. She started it. I felt justified in finishing it. And thus, I completed my emotional reality check: *Yep, I am okay with killing her.*

When the last domino fell, and I pulled the trigger, I felt something akin to relief. Release. It just floated through me, like a soft passing breeze. I had never sought such a feeling—never suspected that one even existed—but now I felt a sense of... what?...satisfaction? Closure? It was none of these things, and all of these things.

Later, when talking to Tryg and Nora, I would keep these details to myself. Given my past, my demons, if you will, these little feelings and factors had meaning for me, and they were enough for me. But I wasn't out to gross anybody out or appear to relish the ugly stuff. It was just business, I'd say, regrettable but necessary business, now business done.

⚙   ⚙   ⚙

AS I WRAPPED DEIDRE'S BODY IN OUR BLACK LEAF-HAULING

tarpaulin, I wondered if Lon knew about Deidre's sneaking about like this. On one hand, the threat to us was greater if he did, because now this would be a conspiracy, not just a vendetta. But I was betting he didn't, not because he'd put a leash on Deirdre's angry impulses, but because he was too cautious to let himself get caught up in a warrantless search. In the crime of defiant trespass. In a piece of emotion-fueled misjudgment that could end up costing him his job. No, I concluded, Lon didn't know what Deidre was up to this evening.

I thought it important that I take care of Deirdre Callas' body by myself. I had no illusion that this would keep Nora and Tryg from being charged as accessories after the fact if the law ever closed in on us. But if Nora and Tryg did not know where the body was, they could not divulge where the body was.

❖   ❖   ❖

DEIRDRE CALLAS' REMAINS REPOSE SOMEWHERE IN NORTHERN

Maryland in a location that may or may not involve water or marshes or wetland, and she was disposed of in a way that may or may not have involved quicklime (calcium oxide, for you home chemists), cinder blocks, chain, and several padlocks. Deirdre Callas' uniform was disposed of at a separate place and in a different way that created the absolute assurance that it would never be found or identified.

As an aside, a useful bit of advice: if, when working to speed decomposition of a corpse, you choose to hasten the process with quicklime, watch out if, by design or accident, you add water. When you do this, it instantaneously creates something called slaked lime, and it releases an ungodly amount of heat. If you think that a marsh or wetland, perhaps way up some tiny tributary, is a good place to deposit a body where it is least likely to be found, all well and good. If you've watched a lot of crime shows on TV and think quicklime will help dispose of the evidence rapidly in your chosen wetland, by all means wear heavy rubber gloves and a good pair of muck boots. As I learned the hard way, if any of that slaked lime splashes on to you, you are in for a world of hurt.

By the time anyone reads this journal entry, Deirdre Callas' state police cruiser will have long since been found in an overgrown field behind that abandoned grist mill in Bear, Delaware. The keys will have been found in the ignition. The entire car, inside and out, including the keys, will have been found to have been meticulously wiped clean using bleach or some sort of industrial solvent. No attempt will have been made to clean up Deirdre Callas' blood in the trunk.

I had loaded my racing bike into the back seat because Deirdre occupied most of the trunk. The bike ride home from the grist mill, although long, was extremely pleasant. When I rode slowly back into Bohemia Manor Farm about 6:30 AM, Nora was up, fussing about in the kitchen when I walked in in my spandex biking duds.

"A bit early for you, isn't it, Hugh?"

"I couldn't sleep, for some reason. So, I finally thought, what the hell, why don't I just go out and pound some miles? Good decision. I feel good."

"That's nice," said Nora. "You want fried eggs or a western omelet?"

29

Fun and Games in Galena

TRYG TOLD ME THAT THE WORD WAS OUT THAT A FEMALE MARYLAND State Police trooper had gone missing. Given my prior run-in with Deirdre Callas at our interview, I was not surprised to receive a polite but firm "invitation" to come to the Galena state police barracks and answer a few questions. Surprisingly, the invitation came not from someone with the Maryland State Police, but from Bill Maroney of the Elkton Police Department, he of the impeccably pressed uniform. My command performance was framed by the usual meaningless false assurance so routinely given by cops in both real life and on TV: "You're not in any trouble."

No, not yet.

The room was pleasant enough, just an ordinary conference room with a large faux-walnut table and comfortable upholstered office chairs. No steel table bolted to the floor or welded steel loops for fastening handcuffs and manacles, no one-way mirror in the wall or spotlight shining into my eyes.

And lo and behold! There stood Colonel Bailey Suits, along with two other guys—clearly from Aberdeen, clearly his grunts— in olive drab. Then there were all the cops. State Trooper Lon

Santunas was there, looking sullen and none too happy to be present. One of the other three guys wore a discount outlet suit and K-mart tie, Maroney had on his Elkton Police Department uniform, and the last guy had neatly pressed olive-drab outfit— also Elkton Sheriff's Office, I was informed. *What an interesting crew,* I thought to myself. *I bet they're calling this a Task Force, except that if Aberdeen is driving this show you can bet your ass they're not calling it anything.*

Clearly, Suits was running this show. I forced a smile.

"Colonel Suits! We meet again."

"So we do, Mr. Ullam, so we do. Although this time for a different purpose. Please have a seat. The coffee machine is not running tonight, so we'll all have to do without. Sorry."

"Quite all right," I said. "I don't drink coffee." Actually, I love coffee and drink gallons of it, but I was not about to concede the least advantage.

Suits clicked on an 80's-vintage portable cassette tape recorder.

"As you know, Mr. Ullam. I am Colonel Bailey Suits. I'm head of Security and Military Police at the Aberdeen Maryland Research Center. I have been asked by the President of the United States and the Governor of Maryland to coordinate the activity of a joint task force investigating certain recent events on upper Chesapeake Bay. At the moment, this investigation is focusing on the disappearance of a Maryland State Police trooper named Deidre Callas. This is Bill Maroney of the Elkton Police, Bud Tinglestad of the Elkton Sheriff's Office, Special Agent Evan Gleason of the FBI out of Baltimore, and State Trooper Lon..."

I interrupted. "Oh, I've met Officer Maroney, and Trooper Santunas, and I know each of them very well. We go way back."

Santunas looked down at the table in front of him and said nothing.

"Do you know why we asked you to come in to talk to us?" asked Suits.

I decided the best defense was an aggressive offense.

"Well, I thought maybe it was to apologize to me for false arrest and false imprisonment by Maryland's state and local authorities, perhaps to offer me some compensation if I would agree not to sue for civil rights violations."

A priceless moment.

Suits' eyebrows shot up, while the rest of his face remained expressionless. Quite a feat, I thought. He looked around the table at his interrogation team, his task force, from face to face. "Does anyone know what he's talking about? Lon, what's this about?"

"I dunno," mumbled Santunas, still staring down at the table. His face had turned scarlet. Suits looked back at me and raised his eyebrows in an unspoken question.

"I assume you know what a show and go is, Colonel Suits?" I paused for effect. "Well, Trooper Santunas pulled the classic smash-your-taillight show and go on me awhile back and ran me into the Elkton sheriff's office for an overnight stay. There I was greeted cordially by Officer Maroney here, stuck in a cell overnight, denied a phone call or any outside contact, given the fabled white bread and processed cheese sandwich, and released the next day. No charges, no court proceeding. This all was just a little warning that I should mind my place. And of course, my taillight had magically been repaired by the time I got my car out of impound."

To my surprise, Suits did not say, "Is this true?" to Santunas and Maroney. He merely said, "This certainly warrants investigation. Did you report this incident at the time?"

I admit that I smiled, but to my credit I did not laugh out loud. "Well, I certainly told Mr. Sletland, our farm operations manager. He's the one who called the police when I went missing overnight and was told I was okay. I also discussed the incident with our housekeeper, Nora Dadmun."

"But you didn't make a police report," said Suits.

Now I did allow an edge to creep into my voice. "Make a report to the police about the police? Colonel Suits, you do not seem like a naïve man. What do you think would have happened to me or members of my staff at Bohemia Manor if I had filed a complaint or brought a lawsuit? I mean, really, sir. Do I look like an idiot to you?"

Suits flinched. He paused and then looked up at the ceiling. Without lowering his eyes, he said softly, "Santunas, you're excused."

"I'm *what?*"

"Excused. Instructed to leave. Wait for us outside."

Few of us ever experience moments of vindication and satisfaction as pure as this. It was enormously satisfying.

Although he had not exactly been rude before, Suits had been distant and formal, which I had assumed was standard operating procedure for intimidating interviewees. Now, although certainly not a picture of warmth, he seemed more friendly.

"Mr. Ullam, the issue you raise does not fall directly under my jurisdiction, but as I said, it certainly warrants further investigation. I intend to make a referral to the Office of the Inspector General of the Maryland State Police. This kind of crap has got to stop."

"With all due respect, Colonel Suits, I'd prefer that you didn't make that referral. Lon Santunas has been outed, and I think that's all the leverage I need to keep him from harassing me again. Let's let the sleeping dogs lie. If he has some bad dreams, that's enough for me. I'm not going to sue the police or bring a formal complaint."

Suits did not appear mollified by my act of charity. "Your prerogative, Mr. Ullam. You do what you see fit. As for me, I'll make whatever referral I see fit. My call, not yours."

At this point I realized we were at a fork in the road, a point where a major tactical decision had to be made: *Should I talk about the false arrest at the auction?* I was sorely tempted to pile on, to reveal that I had been victimized multiple times by the state police, that Santunas and his partner were well-known local racists. But to do so, I'd have to explain why we were shopping for electronic gear. *Do not feed the animals, Hugh.*

I had no doubt that Suits was more interested in the mystery electronic signals than in a missing state police trooper, but for the moment, the task force's investigative priorities were skewed by a human factor: a person was missing, perhaps in distress. Suits had been assigned to coordinate a number of different agencies and interests. He knew he had to show appropriate concern for the locals' interests. It was a matter of professional courtesy.

He jotted a note on his clipboard, then looked up at me, visibly changing gears. Cutting to the chase.

"Mr. Ullam, let me get this straight. You do know Trooper Deirdre Callas, yes?"

"Oh, yes."

"And you really don't know why we asked you to come here today?"

"Still waiting to hear, sir."

"As I said, Mr. Ullam, Trooper Callas is missing. For some days now, she has not reported in or reported for duty. There is no one at her home. Her state police cruiser also is missing. When we put together a list of people who might have some...animus toward Trooper Callas, your name came up on the list."

I suppose this was supposed to shock me into some inculpatory exclamation. Not going to happen; I had prepared for this moment.

I affected a stony coldness. "I find that statement to be deeply offensive, sir, not to mention defamatory. And we don't have to work very hard to imagine who put my name on that list, do we? Why, none other than the 'excused' Trooper Santunas, right?"

"I'm growing pretty tired of this harassment, Colonel Suits. But once again, I am willing to turn the other cheek. I'm not after a pound of flesh here, but I wonder if Trooper Callas' elopement is not part of a conspiracy, one that includes Lon Santunas, to avoid their accountability and to frame me. I need someone to prove to me that she hasn't just bolted before she and Santunas get their tits in a wringer."

I could see that Suit's wheels were really turning now. "Well, I don't think that we have to prove anything to anybody, Mr. Ullam. But let's all just amp it down a bit, shall we? We are not pointing any fingers at this point, we're trying to cover the territory, you know, just gather as many facts as we can. And given the cloud you've placed on Trooper Santunas' objectivity, it's all the more important that I get your perspective on your interactions with Trooper Callas."

He paused. "You okay with that?"

I cocked my head, then looked up at him. "We're okay." Please note how I said, 'we.' A little false bonhomie couldn't hurt. Here I was, suddenly the very model of reasonableness.

"Please tell me about your interactions with Trooper Callas."

That's right, Suits, I thought. Start broad, let me set the frame. And here's me, narrowing the frame. Sure, I could nail Callas on the false arrest at the auction, but maybe I wouldn't need to. I tiptoed in.

"I was interviewed by Trooper Callas after the plane crashed into the marina. She was sent out to interview a reported eyewitness to the crash. She thought that would be Hermann Bayard, and it turned out to be me. Anyway, I'm sure her notes of that interview are on file somewhere. In fact, they may be the basis for why I'm sitting here right now. And I'm quite sure my version of that conversation is quite different from hers."

"What's yours?" asked Suits.

"I found Trooper Callas to be rude, arrogant and unprofessional. I was being polite and cooperative, she was being aggressive and condescending. Without stating her business, she demanded to speak to Hermann Bayard, Bohemia Manor's owner. I told her that I was the one who witnessed the crash, and that Mr. Bayard was out of the country and could not be reached. She could not believe that, asked who was in charge. When I said that I was and showed her my legal documentation for that fact, she became overtly hostile and said she did not believe that a black person—that's not the word she used—would be put in charge of running a large working farm. She then wanted to continue our interview inside the house. I apologized, but said that was not possible because Mr. Bayard's daughter, who is severely emotionally handicapped, gets extremely distressed at the presence of strangers. Clearly, my refusal really pissed her off. I agreed to a complete interview in her police cruiser."

"Then what?" said Suits.

"We completed the interview in her police cruiser. I went through my observations of the crash in complete detail, and she took notes. Rather than going over all those details again, let me ask that you pull up the report from your side. Anyway, we finished the interview, she snapped her notebook shut, I got out, and she drove away. At the time I found her demeanor immature and unprofessional, but hey, her poor manners were no skin off my nose."

"So, what's the problem?" Suits said.

"Well, really no problem at the time, I'm a grown man and can tolerate ordinary rudeness, but it was only a couple of days later Santunas stopped me on Route 13 as I drove to Elkton. His comments to me suggested that he knew all about my interview with Trooper Callas. I inferred the two sets of events were ah... related."

"Well, that is indeed a problem." Suits' voice had softened, as if he was being overtaken by sheer curiosity. "What do you think was going on with all that, Hugh?"

Whoa! Sophisticated interrogator at work! Suits was moving beyond good cop-bad cop and into false rapport, mock deference.

"Well, Colonel," I said, "I cannot testify to Deirdre Callas' state of mind, and I don't know why she decided to disappear. To some degree, her actions speak for themselves, but what do they say about her motives? God, I don't know."

Suits made a come-hither gesture, which I took this as a signal that I should continue. I think he hoped I would make some slip and paint myself into a corner.

"Colonel Suits, it's not for me to make broad judgments about the trooper's character. My own opinion is that she is deeply racist. I think Santunas is, too, and I think they feed each other's hostility toward people of color. Generally. I also think there was something about me in particular that really got Deirdre Callas' goat, and that kind of surprised me. For my whole life I have made a point of not antagonizing people in positions of authority. I must have said or done something that set her off right from the start, but other than my position running the farm, I honestly don't know what that was.

"I'll be frank: personally, I hope I never see her again. But I also hope she's okay and that nothing bad has happened to her. I'll bet her friends and family are real worried. But sooner or later, I think you'll find out what happened. You know what they say: the truth will out."

Suits stood, so I stood, understanding the 'meeting' to be over. I was intensely relieved, but also wary: we had never touched on the mystery signals, the shark, the whale. Was this some sort of trick? Did they know about the auction and were skirting the subject, perhaps seeing if I'd inculpate myself or setting up a trap to be sprung later? I was relieved, but I certainly did not feel safe.

The four of us did not do closing pleasantries. Maroney—the guy from the sheriff's office who had jailed me as part of the show and go—Tinglestad and Gleason turned toward each other so they wouldn't have to look at me.

Suits walked me to my car, leaning on the roof as I slid in. He did not shake hands with me. "'Preciate your coming in, Mr. Ullam." Ah! Suddenly I was 'Mr. Ullam' again! The professional distance reset. "If we need anything more, we'll be in touch."

"That will be fine, Colonel," I said. "Always happy to help."

30

Mixed Messages

IN THE DARKEST DEPTHS OF NIGHT, GUNTHER SENKLER WAS standing on the dock in front of Schaeffer's, wearing blue-and-white vertically striped bell-bottom trousers, a naval officer's waistcoat with gold epaulets on the shoulders, and a Hornblower-style admiral's hat with gold braid. He appeared angry and agitated, gesticulating wildly, but I couldn't hear what he was shouting because of the repeated bang! bang! bang! of the pile driver driving in new dock pilings.

The pile driver itself shot a white plume of steam each time its massive cylindrical hammerhead dropped from a triangular derrick high above. The piles themselves were the diameter of telephone poles. They were striped red and white like old-fashioned barber poles, and they had been pounded in haphazardly at random angles. Behind them, Schaeffer's restaurant was bathed in a peculiar orange light shining down from the top of the 213 Bridge.

I was observing all this from high in the air, as if I was suspended weightlessly above the middle of the C&D canal. This did not seem unusual to me. I neither rose nor fell, I just floated, twisting slowly in an evening breeze. I was holding a camera, but

I couldn't get the lens to focus, so I was taking notes in a small spiral bound notebook so that I could make a full report to the Maryland Marine Police. The pounding was incessant, intensely annoying. I was wishing that Gunther Senkler would turn off the lights so that we could all just go home.

I was snatched from sleep by a piercing animal shriek, shrill, hoarse, intense. The pile driver rhythm continued, a repeated muffled report that could still be heard above another volley of full-throated screams coming from just down the hall.

I knew these sounds. I had heard them before. The yelling was what Nora and I call Rickey's banshee. It was the sound she made when she was taken by surprise or terrified. As a distress call, it was utterly unmodulated: regardless of what triggered it, it was screamed at full volume in a strange panting rhythm.

I also knew the pounding sound. Ironically, given my dream, it was what Nora and I call Rickey's pile driver. It was the sound of Rickey Bayard banging her head against a wall, floor, or some other hard object. This was a major danger signal: this meant Rickey was over the edge. This signaled the threat of severe bodily harm.

Dressed in boxers and a tee-shirt, I charged into the hallway that connected all the second-floor bedrooms and came face-to-face with Ray Hadley. He was wearing nothing but white jockey briefs, and from the looks of things, his hormones were rushing fast and pushing hard. He was panting, his eyes wild. He looked terrified. Behind me, Nora pounded up the stairs from her apartment, dressed in a sweatshirt and panties.

"You get Rickey!" I yelled. "I'll get him!" I threw my arm across Ray's throat and bull rushed him down the hall. He was so astonished, and my adrenaline dump so intense, that this involved no battle of strength. He backpedaled frantically to keep his balance until he crashed up against Tryg's bedroom door. With my left arm pinning him to the door, I flipped on the hall light. Ray's pupils were the size of saucers.

My scream tore at my throat; I knew I would have no voice in the morning. *"Ray! Ray! Ray! What the fuck did you do?"*

Ray's mouth moved soundlessly. My arm was still firmly across his throat. He pawed weakly at my wrist until I released the pressure. "She asked me, she asked me," Ray squeaked. "She said she wanted to try…"

I shoved him away from me, back against the wall, and spun into Rickey's room. Nora had switched Rickey's bedside light on; it shone a harsh halogen beam on a ghastly scene. Rickey was naked, her arms and legs thrashing and kicking. Her body was hunched up against her brass headboard. Her scream had become words: *"No, I said no, I said no, I said no, I said no!"* Each "no!" was punctuated with a bang of her head—*hard!*—against her brass headboard, which, in turn, banged into the wall.

Abruptly she stopped, collapsed. Rickey Bayard had knocked herself unconscious.

❂   ❂   ❂

THE ELKTON COMMUNITY HOSPITAL IS EIGHT MILES FROM BOHEMIA

Manor. It took me less than two minutes to pull a shift over Rickey's limp body and get her into the station wagon. As I clutched Rickey's limp body in the back seat, it took Nora Dadmun six minutes after that to reach the hospital's emergency entrance. Rickey regained consciousness briefly as we crossed the C&D Canal bridge, then turned her head to the side, vomited into the back seat footwell, and passed out again. She was still unconscious when we rolled up to the ER.

I carried Rickey into the receiving desk, yelled "Crisis!" at the top on my lungs, and was gratified by the instant response. I was helped by the fact that it is 3:30 in the morning and the ER was entirely empty, but still, there was not a moment's hesitation when this caramel-colored man carried a young white woman into a hospital and began yelling. The ER staff leapt into action.

On and off, Rickey had been unconscious for nearly ten minutes, a long time for what I had been assuming was a fairly routine concussion. The spittle oozing out of her mouth was foamy and red; she had bitten her tongue. Her legs were twitching; interestingly, her arms remained limp. A middle-aged nurse ran up with her arms spread, palms up, in a "What?" gesture. I shouted, "Autistic! Head-banging! Out ten minutes." She understood instantly, God bless her. She pointed at a gurney with fresh starched linen parked against the wall. When I put Rickey down, the nurse straightened her head gently, rolled up a towel and put it behind Rickey's neck, and then gently pried her mouth open.

"Okay," she said, "tongue's okay. Wheel her in the first bay over there." She took a black cylindrical light from a shelf in the ER bay and shone the light into Rickey's pupils. "Head trauma," she called to the nursing station. "Wake Dexter and get him up here, stat." She turned back to me. "We do not have an MD on duty right now. Dexter is a physician assistant. But do not wig out, he is absolutely the best there is."

A moment later, something threw a shadow across Rickey's face, and I turned to find my nose inches from the upper chest of the largest human being I had ever seen, or at least the tallest. I was sure he was well over seven feet tall.

His dark skin—almost purple—glistened in the ER's fluorescent light. He had short-cropped salt-and-pepper hair with a pronounced streak of white hair over his left ear.

He seemed curiously asymmetrical. He held his right shoulder markedly higher than his left, and when I glanced down at his feet, which were huge, I saw that his left leg twisted outward, while his right leg pointed straight ahead. He carried himself as if in pain.

There also was something asymmetrical about his face, and it took me a moment to figure it out. An eye patch covered his left eye beneath his rimless glasses, although at first, I didn't notice it because the patch was black and did not contrast with his face. His right eye, on the other hand, sunk deep into its dark socket, was startlingly white, a piercing bright laser.

He saw me reading his tag. He looked at me, and I saw that he bore an uncanny resemblance to Abraham Lincoln. He was like a huge, black Abraham Lincoln. His ears were disproportionately large, his aquiline nose equally oversized. His upper lip was narrow, his lower lip full, now pushed out slightly.

The name tag on his green tunic told me that this was Dexter Touré, P.A.

"Call me Dex," he said.

His hands, one now reaching to take Rickey's pulse and the other lifting one of her eyelids, were enormous, yet they moved smoothly and tenderly.

Dexter Touré, P.A., pulled his stethoscope into place, lifted Rickey's loose shift, apparently unsurprised at her nudity beneath, and moved the instrument across her chest and ribs. To my surprise, he also placed it against each of her temples and then reached it in behind the back of her neck.

Repeating the nurse's inspection, he too shone the light in Rickey's eyes. Then he scratched the bottom of her feet with a key he pulled from his pocket. After that he gently palpated the sides of her skull.

"So, explain," he said. "What is going on here?" He had the strangest voice: he both whispered and boomed, kind of a don't-fuck-with-me softness. It was distinctly African, but more notably, this was the voice of authority.

"High-functioning autistic," I said. "Asperger's. Extremely sensitive to noise, touch, light. Extreme startle factor. Got awakened abruptly about three AM by...by..." I faltered.

"By an unexpected sexual advance by a...houseguest," said Nora. "We don't know the details yet, but she may have encouraged him, either tonight or earlier. It may have seemed like she was inviting him. I may be wrong, but my guess is that things got out of control. When I got into her room, she was pounding her head against the bed frame, screaming and shouting. She was conscious, but she didn't seem to recognize me, and I couldn't get her to stop banging her head. Then I guess she just knocked herself out."

Dexter Touré exhaled slowly and nodded. "What was she shouting? Words?" he asked.

"At first it was just screams, like screams of panic. Then she began shouting, 'I said no!' over and over again."

"Good sign," said Dexter.

"How so?" asked Nora.

"If someone moves from uncontrolled vocalizing to words with appropriate meaning, that's a good sign. She was yelling at what she was afraid would hurt her. She has to be functioning at a pretty high level to do that. This does not sound like a heavy-duty fit or seizure, but she really was going to town on herself."

"I guess I figured wrong," whispered Nora, "I thought it was probably just a concussion."

"It probably is just a concussion," said Touré. "I'm quite sure. Basic signs point to it, blood flow in the upper body and head be good, reflexes are okay. Not good she's been out so long. How she acts when she comes to will tell me a lot. And, of course, we need to rule out any skull fracture with an X-ray. She ever do this before?"

"Well, Rickey does tend to lose it in various ways, but nothing ever quite as intense as this. She is not a chronic head-banger. She has other ways of stimming."

"Like what?"

"She talks to herself constantly, mutters quietly all the time."

He nodded. "Tell me, do I need a rape kit?"

"Don't think so," I said. "I think she went out of control before there was...penetration. When I grabbed him in the upstairs hall, he was still wearing briefs."

"Well, that's one less thing to worry about," Touré said, "medically and legally."

Touré put a cool compress on Rickey's forehead and asked the nurse to put an ice pack at the back of her neck. Then we all watched her silently for a few minutes until she started to stir and her eyelids fluttered. She popped back into consciousness abruptly, looked around her, and suddenly began thrashing wildly.

"It's not a fit! It's not a fit!" Nora yelled. "She's panicking! She's scared!"

Touré leaned calmly over the gurney, grasped Rickey's arms

below the elbow and pinioned them firmly to her sides. Rickey continued to writhe and pant. Touré let his arm fall across her diaphragm and began pressing down with his forearm, lightly at first, then harder. We all understood what he was doing: many autistic people feel calmed by firm, steady pressure.

In this case, however, Touré's firm pressure had a paradoxical effect. Rickey, still wide-eyed with fear, gasped and arched her back. She kicked her legs and rolled her hips from side to side, her upper body still pinioned in Touré's grasp.

She caught my eye, her own eyes wide, tears streaming down her cheeks. Her moan was deep and throaty: "Help. Help me. *Help.*"

I cannot really explain what happened next or quite why it happened. Her desperate cry triggered a seismic eruption of furious energy surging through me. I saw stars, then jagged blue lightning bolts. Years of pent-up anger exploded, years of pain and passivity broke the leash. That much I remembered later, then nothing more.

I am told that I howled and lunged at Touré, grabbing for his throat. Nora told me later that I landed a roundhouse right hand punch square in the middle of his chest that sent him reeling against the wall. She said Touré easily righted himself, grabbed me by the shoulders and spun me so that my back was to him. He then reached across my throat and pressed hard on my throat below the base of my neck. I was stopped instantly, Nora said, and then was out cold, collapsed unconscious at his feet.

Nora told me that Touré had looked at her calmly. "Jugular notch. Learned that in Iraq," he said. "He'll be out awhile, but he'll be okay." He then turned to Rickey, who had suddenly gone completely still, her eyes wide. He looked her in the eye. "Rickey," he said, his voice soft, "he's okay, and you going to be okay. I want you to lie quietly now. We going to take an MRI of your head and then send you home. You all right with that?" Nora said Rickey nodded, closed her eyes, and lay still.

I woke up on a cot in a small dark room illuminated only by a night light shining a dim arc down low on the floor. I swung my legs over the side and sat up, expecting a wave of dizziness or confusion. There was neither; I was simply awake in a small dark room. I stood and tried the door. Locked.

Before I could knock, the lock spun, the door opened, and I was cloaked in the great dark shadow of Dexter Touré. "Saw you on the monitor," he said. "Saw you were awake. How you feeling?"

"I feel better than I think I should, under all the circumstances."

"Jugular notch pressure point does that. You go out fast, come back fast. Usually not a lot of after-effects. Speaking of that, do you often go off that way?"

"Like what? I don't really remember what happened after Rickey cried for help."

"Well, what happened is that you went fucking ballistic, knocked me into a wall with a gut punch, and had to be restrained. I did that in the best way I knew how. You probably will be having a little short-term amnesia, but not to worry. But like I said, you go off like that often?"

"First time in my life. Holy shit. It was like a lightning storm, a tidal wave just took over."

"Yeah, well, that was some lightning storm. Guess a lot of negative energy bottled up, yeah?"

I looked past him toward the ER. "Rickey."

"Rickey has low-grade concussion, for sure. MRI negative, no skull fracture. Reflexes normal. Fully conscious, pretty subdued right now. Nora probably has her back to the farm by now. Rickey is going to spend the night in Nora's room with Nora. Don't want her to see the guy who visited her again, yeah? Rickey is likely to have a headache in the morning, she may not. She may be spacey. Good news is that because of her sensitivities, she going to naturally do the things people should do with a concussion—avoid noise, bright light, spirited activity. Stay calm, avoid stimulation. Look, all concussions cause some permanent damage, and that damage is cumulative. You can't let this happen again. But for the moment, I think she'll be okay, Hugh. Just watch her carefully and keep her off the rugby field."

"I gather you know my name."

"Oh, yes. Hope it's okay if I call you by your first name. I'm a pretty informal guy. And what am I thinking about you? So, *you're* the guy. There's a lot of talk about you in the black community around here, Mr. Ullam. You are our local mystery figure. Depending who you talk to, you're either the strange Abo monster or the arrogant prick who doesn't know his place. My black patients think you're pretty cool."

"So where am I, and how come there are no cops around to arrest me for assaulting you?"

"You are in the physicians' resting room and study. We crash here for a few Z's when time permits. And you are not going to jail because I see no reason you should be arrested. You landed a hell of a punch, yeah, clearly you intended no harm. Oh, there was harm—you should see the bruise!—but no foul. And I just thought you have had enough shit for one night. What's more, around here it's always good idea to keep non-white people and our local police away from each other as much as possible. Call the police? No point."

"But, man," Dexter grinned, "about that explosive behavior?"

"Yeah?"

"Maybe you should talk to somebody about that."

        ✿   ✿   ✿

RAY WAS APPALLED AT WHAT HAPPENED AND ASHAMED OF HIMSELF. He wrote guilt-ridden letters of apology to everyone—Rickey, Nora, me, even Tryg. They were simple, sincere, affecting. He owned up to his terrible lapse in judgment, his obvious misreading of all the mixed messages and sexual innuendoes—he called them "confusing social signals"—Rickey had been sending him for some months now. He said he really cares for Rickey—even *likes* Rickey—and thought she had given him a come-ahead to some sexual exploration. He said he knew that he had burned his bridges at Bohemia Manor and that being around the house in the future was likely be uncomfortable or alarming for Rickey. He said he would stay away.

In his letter to me, he asked if it was okay if he still helped Simone with the Bohemia Manor landscaping as long as he stayed outside and did not approach Rickey. In his letter to Tryg, he begged Tryg not to take his disappointment in Ray out on Simone, said he'd feel horrible if what he'd done came between them. In his letter to Nora, he confessed to feeling a great loss, "like a loss of friends and family both." He begged her forgiveness but said he did not expect to be forgiven.

It turned out that the abortive tryst was not the blind leading the blind, not just adolescent fumbling. Ray thought he knew what he was doing; it turned out that he just didn't understand who he was doing it with. Simone told us that although sexually experienced, Ray was not a predator, did not see himself as a young stud. She said he was unusually respectful of women for someone his age, said Ray expected a kind and gentle initiation for Rickey and instead triggered a frenzied overreaction. Simone said Ray's mind was pretty well blown.

Rickey wrote Ray back, a smudged letter in her atrocious handwriting. Ray showed the letter to Simone, who showed it to Tryg. It said,

> *Ray. Thank you for your letter. You didn't have to do that. I'm the one who messed things up. You are very nice. I thought that if I was ever going to have sexual intercourse with a man, my first time should be with somebody nice so I didn't have to figure out whether I was being fucked or raped. I know you were not trying to rape me. I did not know how to say what it was I wanted. Or didn't want. You only did what I said would be okay. Then when you came into my room, I got very scared. I didn't expect that sex would lead to a concussion, hah, hah. I'm sorry if I got you into trouble with your Mom and Hugh and everything.*
> *Your friend, Rickey Bayard.*

A couple of weeks later, I pulled Ray off the lawnmower and asked him to stroll with me for a bit. I said, "Let me not make too big a deal of this, but I'm not going to downplay it, either. We need to put things in perspective and also clear the air."

I faced him and took him by the shoulders.

"Goddamn it, Ray. I warned you. I was clear. And now you display a very serious lack of judgment. And it did some real damage, created some real danger for Rickey. And I'm not just saying that I think your dick ran away with your brain. Physically, Rickey is indeed stunning, and sexy. Whether she means to or not, she sends strong sexual vibes. I confess that I have thought unwholesome thoughts about Ricky on occasion. But you've seen all the different faces of Rickey, so you know that she is not really a mature woman who at age fourteen can make mature decisions about sex. When she came on to you, you should have sought the advice of your sister or Nora. You should have done a reality check, man.

"More to the point, Ray, *she is fourteen, for Christ's sake!* She's jailbait. Regardless of what she said she wanted, and she didn't really know what she wanted, having sex with her would have been statutory rape. Autistic or not, you should not have been getting involved with someone that young. That's playing around with pure dynamite.

"Bottom line, I know you are embarrassed at what happened and maybe you think you're dogmeat with all of us. That's not so, Ray. We all think you are a good guy, a solid guy. But I am going to ask you to stay clear of the house for a while. We all have to take some time to let the dust settle, to see where Rickey's head takes her.

"On one hand, maybe you'll always be toxic to her, and you're simply going to have to steer clear of her for good. I'm sorry if that happens, but maybe it will. On the other hand, this whole incident may roll right off her back. She'll probably never be able to look back and laugh at it, because Rickey has no sense of humor. But she may be able to look back on it and say, 'hey, no big deal.' We'll just have to see, Ray."

☼   ☼   ☼

BREAKFAST WAS WRAPPING UP. NORA WAS LOADING THE dishwasher, her back to us. Rickey was sitting across from me, her chin tucked into her chest.

"Hugh?"

"Yes, Rickey."

"I want to thank you for hitting Dexter Touré in the chest."

"Beg pardon?"

"I called for help. You tried to help. You're lucky that giant didn't kill you."

31

Dexter Touré

THE DEEP SOOTHING VOICE WAS FAMILIAR, BUT AT FIRST, I COULDN'T place it.

"Is this Hugh Ullam?"

"It is. May I ask who is calling?"

"Yes, this is Dexter Touré calling. I'm the physician assistant who treated Ms. Rickey Bayard in the ER for a concussion several weeks ago."

I laughed. "Of course! Dexter! Is this the same Dexter Touré who also assaulted me and rendered me unconscious?"

He laughed. "The very same! The same Dexter whom you assaulted first and who then did not call the police to have you thrown in the jail."

"Thank you, thank you, thank you for not calling the police. I do not get on well with the police around here."

"Oh, I know," Dexter Touré said matter-of-factly, as if my reputation with local law enforcement were a matter of common public knowledge.

"To what do I owe the honor of this call, Mr.…. Doctor…I'm sorry, what is the proper way to address you?"

"Please call me Dexter. Or Dex. Your choice. It would not

be appropriate to call me doctor. And I hope it would be all right if I were to call you Hugh."

"Fine. Fine on all counts. So, Dexter, why are you calling me?"

"I have three agenda items I would like to discuss. One of them is probably not a good thing to talk about on the telephone. Would it be a great imposition if I were to call on you at your residence?"

"Not at all. We all would be most pleased to see you again. How about this? Would you care to join us for cocktails and dinner this evening?"

"Cocktails and dinner! That would be splendid. Tell me, will the cocktails be served on the veranda by a polite chap in a little white servant's jacket?"

I was enjoying this. "Well, we call it the patio, and tonight is the veranda servant guy's turn to polish the Rolls Royce, so it's self-serve. But Ms. Nora Dadmun's cuisine will make you glad you came. We would be pleased to see you, Dexter. We live several miles south of the C&D Canal off Route 213—"

He interrupted gently. "Don't worry, Hugh. I know exactly where you live. In fact, I know a lot of things, relevant things, that you should know I know. What time shall I fall by?"

⚙   ⚙   ⚙

TO MY CONSIDERABLE SURPRISE, RICKEY WAS CLEARLY PLEASED when I told her that Dexter Touré was coming to dinner and suggested she don presentable attire. "Will I be allowed to talk, Hugh, or is this one of those times when I'm supposed to sit in a corner and play deaf-mute?"

"You are Dexter Touré's patient, Rickey. Of course, you may talk. I ask only that you take pains not to dominate the conversation."

"Hugh, you are such an asshole."

"Duly noted, Rickey. For the ten-thousandth time. He'll be here at six-thirty."

Dexter Touré drove a silly little English car called a Morris

Minor, mid-fifties vintage. In some peoples' hands, meaning properly restored, they were now regarded as classics. The one in Dexter's hands was a wreck. Dexter's was sort of a puke green color, accented with streaks of ochre rust along the bottoms of the doors. There was a big tear in the ragged convertible top above the rear window. Blue smoke billowed from the exhaust as he drove into the courtyard, and when he slowed, the car bucked as if the clutch was shot.

Watching this dark, black giant unfold himself from the tiny interior was like watching the clown car act in the circus: first one impossibly long leg was levered out the door opening, then his right arm appeared and swung up as he pushed his elbow down on the roof, then he swiveled and twisted his other leg out from under the steering wheel. Finally, in a kind of explosion of motion, the rest of him emerged into the sunlight, and he shook himself off to loosen up the kinks. These were moves that obviously had required rehearsal.

Rickey, Nora, Tryg and I were standing on the front door landing, rather like a receiving line for a foreign dignitary. Dexter Touré was dressed in white linen slacks, a light green polo shirt and white tennis shoes. The contrast with his purple-black skin was startling, striking. He was both an impressive and imposing presence, yet not scary. Just...*big*. He walked up to us with a pronounced limp. He smelled of lavender.

Somewhat to my surprise, he looked past me and walked first to Rickey. He clasped his hands lightly in front of him and bowed slightly. "Ms. Rickey Bayard, *Sawubona*."

To my utter astonishment—Nora and Tryg's too—Rickey reached out, touched his clasped hands lightly—that's right, *she reached out and touched him*—and replied, "*Ngikhona*."

Dexter Touré's smile could have illuminated a small city. "Ah..." he sighed, cocking his head. "That's very nice."

Then, in an insufferably patronizing tone, Rickey turned to us, explaining, as if to small children, "Mr. Touré is obviously Zulu. You may think he is Dinka or Masai because he is so tall, but he is Zulu. His greeting is the classic Zulu greeting. Sawubona means 'I see you.' The Ngikhona response means 'I am here.'"

"Do you speak Zulu, Rickey?" Dexter Touré asked.

"Well, just a little," Rickey said, lowering her head. "But I'm learning. I started after I first met you."

Dexter Touré was beaming.

"Are you Zulu, Dexter?" I asked.

"I guess I think of myself as pretty much American now, American enough to have fought in Iraq and picked up a Purple Heart. I do not crave to go back to Africa. But over there, the medical care, particularly for blacks, is oh, so bad. There are times when I think I should help. I came to the US to study philosophy and learn better English. You American blokes accepted me, naturalized me, took me into your military when I became broke, made me a medic, and sent me off to war. I no longer think of myself as Zulu, although I know and do many Zulu things. My parents are Bantu Zulu and still live in the KwaZulu-Natal region of South Africa. We are, how shall I say...not close."

Anticipating the next question, he said, "My father is five feet eleven, about average for a Zulu man. My mother is five-four. And yes, we are all very dark. Hugh, being so light-skinned by comparison must make you very envious." He winked at me.

God, I thought, this fellow and I are going to have some interesting conversations.

"So why are you so big?" asked Rickey. "I mean, your hands are fucking huge."

"Ah," said Dexter. "Marfan syndrome. You know Abraham Lincoln? Tall guy, big hands, long legs, huge ears? Appears on US currency?"

"Well, of course," said Rickey.

"Marfan Syndrome. Abe and me, we're both mutants, Rickey. Major gene anomaly. Really poor-quality connective tissue. And, at least in my case, great sense of humor."

✸   ✸   ✸

DEXTER SET HIS TUMBLER DOWN ON THE PATIO COFFEE TABLE AND rested his arms on his knees, which, spread akimbo, made a lofty inverted pyramid. The overall effect, with his head bent low, was of a large avant-garde garden art statue by Giacometti, the famed sculptor who poses long, skinny figures in oddly distorted positions.

He cleared his throat, as if quieting an audience slow to settle. "Ah, yes, the three items. One, Rickey, I wanted to check on you to see if you have recovered from your concussion. Since I got here, I have, among other things, been watching your pupils, at least in those moments when you do not have your sunglasses on."

Dexter's diction was crisp and precise, with very pronounced stops and pauses at the end of his sentences. Even outside on the patio, his voice had that same resonant echo I'd heard in the ER. African born, but evidently educated elsewhere: these were learned speech patterns and cadences.

"You are, Rickey, obviously very sensitive to light. I'd like to learn more about that. But as far as the concussion goes, I believe the effects of this most recent one have resolved. I doubt that you are having headaches, am I right?"

"You have it absolutely right, Dexter," she smiled. My God. Rickey Bayard, angry, autistic, profoundly isolated Rickey Bayard, was flirting.

"And I have to warn you, Rickey, in the strongest possible terms. You cannot let this happen again. The effects of concussions are cumulative, and they're permanent. Just because you're not experiencing symptoms, does not mean no damage has been done."

He looked at her sternly. "Rickey. No more head-banging. *Not okay.*"

She met his gaze. "Yes, sir. Message received." She smiled.

Dexter turned to me. "Second, Hugh, I must confess that checking up on Rickey was a pretext. I knew her symptoms would abate and that a trip all the way out here was not really necessary—except that I wanted to see her again because when she is not banging her head against the wall, I suspect she can probably be quite charming."

Jesus. Rickey was beaming.

"And I presumed to call, Hugh, because I believe you are a very interesting person and I wanted to get to know you better. I wanted, shall we say, to compare shades of black." He paused and cocked his head.

How can I describe my reaction to this? I think I maintained my outward composure, but I felt a powerful urge to weep. I could feel my breath catch and wondered if the others saw it.

I lived, and had always lived, in a tight, dark cylinder, so to speak. Barely enough air to survive in there. I could see out, but I could not move freely, could not open the windows, could not swing my arms, step out, or run out into the sunlight. I had to control my breathing: I could not expand my chest or take belly breaths or shout or sob. My existence felt constrained and minimal. But at least I existed. My cylindrical cell was the price of existence.

Dexter Touré's simple statement—*he was interested in me, he wanted to get to know me*—was unlike anything anyone had ever said to me before. As much as I wanted out, somebody actually wanted in. I was utterly taken aback.

The pause was long. Dexter was looking calmly up at me, his head held lower than mine. Nora had caught her breath; she too resonated with what Dexter had said, what he was offering: *an avenue out of isolation.* Tryg sat quietly, waiting to hear what I would say. Rickey was swiveling her head forth and back between Dexter and Me, trying to figure just what the hell was going on here.

"I think I would like that very much, Dexter," I said. "Let's see what we can do about that."

❂   ❂   ❂

DINNER WAS PESTO. NORA HAD PREPARED HOMEMADE PASTA, AND

she had used Italian parsley instead of basil. The meal, presented on whimsical hand-painted earthenware Italian plates, each with a different animal ringing its rim in various poses, was a visual feast: the pasta was ringed with quartered cherry tomatoes, chopped cucumber pieces, and—surprise!—crunchy wedges of Asian pear. Dexter ate slowly, chewed carefully, as if pulling the flavors apart with his tongue.

He looked at Nora, who looked back—far more directly than was her wont. "Nora," Dexter said quietly, "I assume you know how exceptional this is."

"If I may say so, I do," Nora smiled. "I'm very confident of this recipe. It never varies, never fails. I roll it out when I don't want to embarrass myself."

This is when I noticed something: Nora had pulled her hair back to show her full face, something I don't think I'd ever seen before. She was revealing herself to Dexter Touré. I thought, *something may be going on here.* Nora Dadmun was hoping that Dexter wanted to get to know *her* better. And she was taking risks. I sensed a vibe moving forth and back across the table. It looked like the risk was paying off.

"Hugh," Dexter said in an I'm-changing-the-subject voice, "the third thing I want to discuss. It may be serious, and it may be a bit scary for Rickey."

"The Hole in the Wall Gang knows everything, shares everything," I said, pleased to see Rickey nod in agreement. "She's not a child, she doesn't scare easy."

"Hugh, I believe you may be under surveillance."

I wanted to say, *duh, we know that.* Say that our closed-circuit system had revealed various kinds of monkey business wrought by various authorities. That we had found tire tracks at the end of the drive that did not belong to the pickup or the Ford. That we suspected prowling after dark, window peeking, that sort of thing.

Instead, I feigned ignorance. "What makes you say that, Dexter?"

"Last week Tuesday at the beginning of the graveyard shift, that state police trooper, what's his name, Santunas, brought in a guy with a broken leg. Nice clean snap of the tibia, straight break, simple cast, no pins. Guy was not a big talker. Patient billing tracking system said Garon Wilson, Naval Arms Research Laboratory, Silver Spring, Maryland. We were instructed to bill services to such-and-such address. Government address. No insurance.

"I had the guy out in an hour. He was hundred per cent military type, buzz cut, no-nonsense voice, told me he fell from a tree. Santunas was in uniform, this other guy was in some sort of fatigues, olive drab, army-type boots. But no marking or insignias. No branch, no rank markings. Stenciled name over the tit—excuse me, Nora—said 'Wilson.' Maybe I watch too much TV, but Mr. Wilson had spook, or at least military police, written all over him."

"Hmmm," I said.

"I stood in the adjacent ER bay, behind the curtain, to overhear them. Heard enough to make me want to come talk to you. Hugh, these guys are working together, or at least assisting each other. Santunas called Wilson a dumb fuck—excuse me, Nora—and told him that screwing up surveillance was like screwing up a free lunch. The guy got hot and told Santunas where he could shove it. Said the coordination on 'this whole project' was all screwed up and no one was really taking charge, that some guy named Suits was a self-important little dick. Said that this entire operation had turned up flat nothing in over a month, that he thought it was a huge fucking waste of time. I believe the phrase he used was 'goat rodeo,' but perhaps it was 'cluster fuck'—excuse me, Nora."

"You're excused," said Nora, laughing. "You can say 'fuck' any time you want around here. If you really want to learn to use all the grammatical variations of fucking this and fucking that, just call on Rickey. She's a complete fucking pro."

Rickey shook her head. "Nora, sometimes you're just a complete fucking cunt."

Dexter raised his eyebrows, realizing that clearly there was a long history here. "Anyway," he continued, "Wilson said he'd just been shifted over to Bohemia Manor from another house on the Sassafras River and no one had briefed him or given him a back story. He said, and I quote, 'I think your magical mystery signals came either from Summit Airport or from the Coast Guard station in South Chesapeake City.' Santunas said he was going to leave the reporting on this incident to Wilson, and the next time Wilson could just goddamned walk himself to the ER on his fucking broken leg. He, Santunas, left in something of a hissy fit, I'd say. Forty minutes later a white unmarked van stops outside and drives Wilson away. Any idea what this is all about, Hugh?"

"I know exactly what it's all about," I said, "and that's how I knew your trusty Morris Minor was on its way down our driveway two minutes before you pushed the doorbell. You see, Dexter, we've got their surveillance under surveillance, and besides, nothing is going on here that we care if the authorities see. We're clean livers here at Bohemia Manor."

"You lost me," said Dexter Touré.

"The whale in the canal, that plane crash where something jammed all the instruments, even that big shark they caught over off Turkey Point. They think all those things are connected, and that all were somehow related to a whole variety of goofy radio signals—some in the air, some in the water—that they think came from over on our side of the bay. 'They,' by the way, are the mystery men over at the Aberdeen Proving Ground, and if anyone knows anything about mystery radio signals, those spooks do.

"Anyway, somebody has organized the Maryland State Police, the FBI out of Baltimore and a bunch of MPs out of Aberdeen into sort of a task force charged with canvassing the whole upper eastern shore, with particular attention to houses on the water, because the whale lure signal was transmitted underwater."

"And....?" Dexter said.

"And they came over here and interviewed us. Twice. Santunas' buddy, Trooper Callas, braced me after the plane crash, and then a team from Aberdeen came for tea after the whale thing in the C&D canal. We knew nothing, of course, so we couldn't tell them nothing.

"But they really don't like us, or actually, they really don't like me. They can't figure out what the situation is here, and they seem offended that I've been given authority to run things when Hermann Bayard is away, which is almost always. The guys from Aberdeen were respectful enough, but Trooper Callas really gave me the whole 'I really hate black people' treatment. Twice, as a matter of fact.

"And you may know that Callas went missing a while back, no trace, no nothing. I don't know if they think we're good for that or not, but we're sure they continue to have some interest in us. That's why we have the closed-circuit TV and the electric eyes. We really don't care if they're around, but we just want to know *when* they're around. I admit that I'm surprised that Wilson was probably an Aberdeen guy, because I really thought they were done with us. So, I'm really glad you brought us up to date, Dexter."

❀   ❀   ❀

AS WE FINISHED OUR PLATES, THERE WAS A LULL IN THE conversation. Nora Dadmun was looking at Dexter Touré with uncommon directness. Something was definitely cooking here. Then Rickey dove in.

"Dexter?" Her tone was cautious, definitely a novelty with Rickey Bayard. "How did you lose your eye?"

He smiled as if to say, *hey, no problem talking about this.* "Short story, long convalescence. IED in Iraq. Improvised explosive device. We're just driving along, minding everybody's business, you know? And *Boom!* No more Hummer. Everybody else dead, me, major traumatic brain injury, smashed-up face. Left leg hanging by a thread. A lot of internal injuries. Hello, Purple Heart, good-bye military career. All the king's doctors and all the king's men did a fabulous job of putting me together again, but it took time."

A peculiar expression washed over Nora's face. "Where were you treated?" she asked quietly.

"After the first emergency surgeries in Germany, most of the treatment and rehab was at the VA hospital in West Philadelphia."

Nora had turned ashen. "Who was your physician?"

"Man, I really lucked out. I got the best. Brain trauma guy named Roger Hubey. Was there at the beginning, was there at the end, and every step in between. He brought me back from being a zombie. He was there when I learned to talk and walk again."

Nora dropped her crystal tumbler on to the middle of her dinner plate, breaking it neatly in half and spraying pasta and ice cubes all over the table. "Oh, my dear God," she whispered.

Jolted, I barked at her: "Nora, what the hell!"

"Before I came here, before I was hired to look after Rickey Bayard, I was a surgical nurse on Roger Hubey's service at the Philadelphia VA."

Dexter and I spoke simultaneously. "You worked at the VA hospital?"

"Eight years. All in med-surg. The last five under Roger Hubey specializing in traumatic brain injuries. Broken brains were my specialty."

"Did you shoot to become a PA?" asked Dexter. Physician's Assistant.

"No, I was happy being a plain old RN, but I had all the supplemental training for surgical nursing. I got my masters in brain physiology and rehabilitation from Temple. Let me tell you, I really know my shit when it comes to traumatic brain injuries."

Rickey seemed very surprised to hear this, putting her hands over her mouth. *Had she underestimated Nora Dadmun for all these years?*

Dexter and I again spoke simultaneously, only this time we said different things.

I said, "You never told me you were an RN."

Dexter said, "Did you treat me?"

Nora answered me first. "You always made it clear you weren't interested in my past, Hugh Ullam. You just treated me like I was nothing but the goddamned cook. But yes, I am an RN—who also graduated top of her class from the Fanny Farmer cooking school. Hermann Bayard thought it was a pretty dynamite set of credentials. He thought my brain expertise meant I'd be expert at working with autism. He was praying I could 'cure' Rickey. Dream on."

I saw Rickey nod in agreement.

She turned to Dexter. "As for you, no, I didn't treat you. I think I would have remembered, don't you think? You must have come through after my time."

"I came through when Roger Hubey had just been diagnosed with cancer."

"That was after my time," said Nora. "I was gone by then, although I did drive up to Philadelphia a couple of times to see him. But finally, I had to stop. The irony of a brain trauma expert getting brain cancer was simply too much for me to bear. Dear God, he did not deserve that agony." Now she was hanging her head, and her tears were bouncing noisily off the pieces of her broken dinner plate.

❖   ❖   ❖

AS DEXTER WAS STANDING IN THE FRONT HALL SAYING HIS THANK-
yous and good-byes and we were all doing the let's-do-this-again-soon thing, Rickey walked up to him. "Dexter," she said tentatively (*imagine Rickey Bayard being tentative!*).

He turned to look at her.

"All your injuries. Do they hurt?"

He inhaled deeply. "Yes, Rickey, all the time. The eye and face not so much, but the leg, yes. Lots of nerve damage. Some days are a lot worse than others. I don't know why. It's not seasonal or related to weather, but I certainly do have tough moments."

"Yeah, it's like that with me, too. Sometimes the pain is in the background, sometimes it just tears my face off. There's no telling what tomorrow will bring. Nobody understands what that's like."

"Well, now you know I do," Dexter said.

Rickey shifted her weight from one leg to the other. "Dexter?"

"Yes, Rickey."

"Would you be my doctor?"

Dexter was taken aback. I looked at Nora and Tryg. We weren't just taken aback; we were floored.

"Why would you want me to do that, Rickey?" Dexter said finally.

"Because all the jerks Nora—that renowned surgical nurse—has dragged me to are clowns or quacks. All my local docs do is prod me and shine light into my eyes and ask me the same questions over and over again. They hurt me, and they don't even know they're hurting me, and they don't listen. And that idiot who did the audiology test last year? Man, I wanted to rip her head off, she hurt my ears so badly. Only I'm not allowed to, because I'm a girl and an 'autistic person' so I have to be good or else they'll put me in an institution."

Dexter Touré looked stricken. "Oh, Rickey. My God. You stab me in my heart."

"Oh, yeah? Well, you should feel what it feels like in *my* heart, Dexter. What kind of battles go on in *my* head. And all the *grrreat* experts at the Center for Autism? All those neurologists at CHOP? What have they done for me? *Nothing.* They don't get anything, don't do anything, don't care about me. I'm just a curiosity to them."

Now Rickey's words came out in a torrent. Her voice climbed an octave. "They just like to test me, examine me, explore my threshold for pain. They love their little response-extinction exercises. They have all these endless, pointless debates among themselves, talking like I'm not even there. 'She's a savant.' 'No, she's just a high-functioning Aspy.' 'How do we test her intelligence?' 'Should we bother to test her intelligence?' 'Let's take her sunglasses and ear plugs away and see if she'll auto-adapt into relearned response patterns.' They talk and talk and talk, and then I'm sent home. Twice a year at Center for Autism, twice a year at CHOP. There's a term for this, Dexter. *It's called serial abuse.*"

She turned to me and smiled. This was not a kind smile, but a knowing smirk. Something savage was coming.

"And you, Hugh? You know *exactly* what I'm talking about, don't you? You know what it's like to be a lab rat. If Dexter really wants to get to know all about you, be sure to tell him all about Akers, about how kind and loving all the 'specialists' were."

I realized that Rickey had been listening intently every time I had ever dropped a comment or an anecdote about my upbringing. Hadn't missed a thing.

"Dexter, you want to know why I want you to be my doctor? Because you *see* me. *Sawubona.* I don't even care what doctoring you do on me. I just want a doctor who's not all wrapped up in his own bullshit. Someone who other people look at as some kind of freak."

Dexter crossed his arms across his chest and inhaled deeply.

"Rickey, if you're talking about routine healthcare and annual physicals, and things like that, you and Nora could make appointments with me for that. But I am not trained in the treatment of autism—in any form, including Asperger's. I don't have a bag of magic autism bullets. I cannot be your savior.

"And we've got to be really careful about professional distance. You have to decide whether you want a friendly doctor...or a friend. You've got good friends here. Regardless of whatever level of intimacy you can tolerate, they work hard to provide it, no? What could I—as a friend, rather than as a physician assistant—possibly add to the mix? Sure, I'd like to see more of you—just as I'd like to see more of all of you. But that's a selfish desire on my part. I'm interested as much in what I need as what I can give. Is that enough of a deal for you?"

Rickey looked down at her hands, then lifted her chin to look up into Dexter Touré's face high above hers. She breathed deeply. Very slowly, very carefully, she extended her hand, took his, and gave it an exaggerated shake. Given Rickey's aversion to touch, this was quite an extraordinary gesture.

"Deal," she said. Then she turned and walked out of the room.

Dexter looked at me and shook his head. "Hugh," he said, "I haven't the least goddamned idea what just happened."

"Neither do I, Dexter," I said. "But I guess we're all going to find out. Like the Good Lord, Rickey Bayard moves in mysterious ways."

32

The Lull Before the Storm

OKAY, I ADMIT IT: I GOT COMPLACENT. WE'D HEARD NOTHING FURTHER about the whale, had received no further visits from the friendly folks at Aberdeen. I thought we were home free.

For a few months, after the whale sensation blew over and the Aberdeen investigators drove away without putting us all in handcuffs, I thought Suzuki had it wrong: *things didn't change.* They calmed down, and for the moment an agreeable stability settled back over our lives.

Yes, the Hole in the Wall Gang seemed to have reacquired a stable equilibrium. And Rickey, while still not pleasant company, had now mastered a broader repertoire of rote social moves and responses, which made her seem a little less eccentric. Indeed, at times she seemed almost "normal," although her underlying tone of hostility, her constant edge, persisted. Maybe she had been brought up short by the consequences of her lab experiments. In any event, she became more subdued, a little less volatile.

Meanwhile, Tryg Sletland and Simone Hadley had fashioned a stable, kind and caring relationship, and they appeared utterly contented with their present lot. Simone now slept over at Bo Manor a lot, and Tryg slept over at her place a lot, but they never went through the motions of moving in together or creating a public display of affiliation.

Ray has been accepted back into the pack. He now spoke even fewer words than before, kept his eyes averted from Rickey at all times.

On another channel, Dexter Touré gradually but steadily laid claim to Nora Dadmun's heart and soul. As was the case with Simone, Dexter did not formally move in, but he came and went from Bo Manor with the ease of someone who had become an integral part of things. He brought news and bought groceries. He wasn't a great cook, but he was an eager helper.

Dexter made ever deeper inroads into Nora's heart and eventually her bedroom. Any way you looked at it, this was progress—in both their lives—and it was simply wonderful to see Nora's heart flower and bloom. I envied them.

Once Dexter's devotion to Nora appeared permanent and our trust in him had grown deep roots, we told him about Hermann's death and our determination to live happily ever after off Hermann's money. He responded calmly. "Well, that's certainly...*unusual*. Now that you've told me, does that make me a crook too? Let me say something. This...'situation' you all are enjoying. It seems very dangerous to me. It seems that you all are living right on the edge of catastrophe, every single day."

"Do you think we're all in denial, Dex?" asked Nora sharply, surprising Dexter with her vehemence. "Think we don't grasp all the implications of our situation, positive and negative?"

I raised a quieting palm. "I do not wish to discuss this here and now. Dexter, let me briefly address your concern, since our situation has potential consequences for you, if only as an accessory after the fact. Then let's move on. At this point, which comes a long time after our initial decision point—assuming that there really was a decision point and not just the pressure of unplanned events—*there is no choice*. The benefits are what they are. The danger is what it is. We shall see what we shall see. Rickey, if you know, please tell Dex what the Latin phrase *alea jacta est* means."

"Of course, I know. It means, 'the die is cast.' It's attributed to Julius Caesar as he was about to cross the Rubicon."

"Precisely," I said.

❖　　　❖　　　❖

FOR A WHILE FOLLOWING OUR DINNER TABLE DISCUSSION OF RISKS and rewards, we avoided further discussion of or planning for future events. Then one night, Dexter shifted gears while he and I sat in the living room savoring a fine single malt. Obviously, he thought it was time to get serious.

"Hugh, at this point, how would you characterize Nora's commitment to Rickey, her...*obligation* to Rickey?"

Uh, oh. Quicksand. "It sounds like you're asking me whether I think Nora is thinking of jumping ship."

"And if I am? If she is?"

"Well, Dexter, given your relationship with Nora and the intimacies you guys share, I'm not sure I should be the person answering that question. When it comes to Rickey, don't you know more about Nora's feelings and motives than I do?"

Dexter stood, stretched his arms over his head, and then rotated his head in a tight circle. He inhaled and held his breath. Readjusted his eyepatch. Finally, he snorted through his nose.

"I'm not sure. I do think Nora may be having a hard time separating the past from the present. For sure she has new things to think about."

"Look, Nora is not Rickey's mother...or relative...or anything. She is not Rickey's guardian. Rickey is not Nora's ward. When she signed on to be Marte Bayard's cook, Nora did not commit to a lifetime indenture. I certainly understand that. She is an employee—actually, *my* employee, and as my employee she has been treated fairly, no?"

I fought to find the right balance. "But having observed them in action for a lot of years now, I'm absolutely sure Nora has a deep, deep...*emotional investment* in Rickey. Rickey remains unable to take care of herself, and remember, Nora is a nurse. And

I'm sure Nora has a hard time with the picture of Rickey in some institution, banging her head against the wall.

"But it's really not just about Nora and Rickey, is it? Now it's about Nora and Rickey and *you*, because you, sir, have brought a light and hope to Nora's life that she never had. A life with you represents an alternative reality. A very desirable reality." I clapped my hands together for effect. Dexter flinched.

"And that certainly complicates things. Nora knows that Rickey has no choice but to basically mark time for the rest of her life, but Nora certainly doesn't expect *you* to mark time. Or, if in fact you are committed to each other, she doesn't want or expect you two to mark time.

"But that's not all, Dex. Nora is a felon, she just hasn't been caught and convicted yet. Maybe she's a victim of circumstance, but even so, she's boxed in. What are her risks? If we all are nailed, even if everybody piles on me and makes me the heavy—to which I completely assent, by the way—she's looking at some prison time."

Dexter raised his eyebrows, silently quizzing me.

I paused. "My guess? Sentenced to three years, out in eighteen months. Ordered to pay a shitload of restitution, because Nora has been extremely overpaid and she's just plunked it all in the bank. Given that prognosis, should she stay and pray, run for the hills, or 'fess up to the cops and get the shit over with? Except, oh yeah, when she gets out, she's a convicted felon, just like Sletland. And, she must be thinking to herself, 'if I'm thrown in the slammer, will Dexter Touré be waiting for me when I get out? Or when he gets out?'

"So, I think it is a very complicated situation. Perhaps we should not take Nora—or her role caring for Rickey—as a given in our planning."

33

Colonel Suits, On the Case

WHEN I PICKED UP THE PHONE, THE VOICE ON THE OTHER END WAS harsh, urgent. Familiar.

"Mr. Sletland?"

"Mr. Sletland is working outside. I'm sorry, but he is unavailable."

"Ullam." Said as a statement, not as a question.

"Yes, this is Hugh Ullam," I said.

"This is Colonel Bailey Suits. Remember me?"

"I certainly do. What can I do for you?"

"Well, the first thing you can do is to stop jerking us around. By lying to us, you people got yourselves into a lot more trouble."

"I had not been aware that we were in trouble."

"Well, you sure as hell are now. In the course of our investigation, we have now learned about your real role at Bohemia Manor Farm, your real authority. Now we know that Sletland is just your employee. We have heard all about your famed 'Constant Binder' and Hermann Bayard's famed 'to whom it may concern' letter."

"I hope you gave our regards to Troopers Santunas and Callas."

"This is not a good time to be a smart-ass, Ullam. You and Sletland misled us, made me think he was the top dog and that you were nothing more than the farm's bookkeeper. Now I learn that you are the brains behind the operation. Why in the world would you deceive us that way?"

"Because I thought we would be accorded more respect and courtesy if you were dealing with a white man rather than a black man."

There was a long pause. "I take offense at your implication."

Time to pivot off the back foot and push. "Colonel Suits, I frankly don't care if you take offense or not. You know I'm speaking the truth: we were a lot less likely to be bullied and pushed around if you thought the farm's general manager was white. In fact, you have already proven that in this phone call."

Suits was caught off guard. "And just how is that?"

"When you rang, you asked for *mister* Sletland. When it came time to address me, suddenly all the *mister* business disappeared. I was just 'Ullam.' I notice things like that, Colonel. Disrespecting me is obviously perfectly comfortable for you. Unfairly or not, I attribute a racial motive to it."

Suits started to speak, but I cut him off. "Hear me out, Colonel Suits. You and your goon squad appear at our door unannounced and without prior notice. Before you even hear that we will voluntarily grant you access, you threaten to get a search warrant if we resist your search. You play the heavy.

"And what do we do? We invite you to conduct a thorough search, inside and out. No protest, no huffing and puffing. Just, 'sure, c'mon in. Let us show you around.' And we do. We guide you through the house. We let you examine Hermann Bayard's office. Nora Dadmun submits to a pretty aggressive interview without complaint. Despite our telling you how fragile she is, you were introduced to Hermann Bayard's handicapped daughter. I have to tell you that your intrusion was, as we warned you it would be, extremely upsetting to her."

Suits again started to speak, but again I talked over him. "And what did I do? I drove your squad all over the farm in *our* vehicle. Let 'em scour the fields, let 'em go over Hermann's airplane hangar with a fine-tooth comb, let 'em look at anything and everything. Your guys will tell you that I was helpful and cooperative.

"And what did you find? *You didn't find a goddamned thing!* And that's because there was nothing there to find. You used up a lot of our time, and because we thought your purpose was legitimate, we accommodated you. We were polite, right? Did it matter whether I was in charge or Sletland was? Hey, as the saying goes, 'no harm, no foul.'

"And as we wrapped up, Colonel Suits, there's one other thing I remember about your visit."

"And just what is that, *Mr.* Ullam?" I admired the restraint of his tone.

"When you were leaving, you politely shook Mr. Sletland's hand. And you politely shook Nora Dadmun's hand. But you could not be bothered to shake my hand. How do you think that made me feel?"

I'll give Suits this: he rebounded quickly and counterpunched well. "Mr. Ullam, I intended no disrespect to you, but I regret if any of my behavior came across as insensitive. For that, I apologize to you, sir. But I must tell you this: *your* behavior has aroused our suspicion, and I advise you not to think that we are engaging in some wild-goose chase. We play for keeps, Mr. Ullam, and I want to tell you something, else man-to-man. *I* play for keeps."

34

Shatters

NEUROLOGISTS NICKNAME IT "THE SHATTERS." IT DESCRIBES A sudden disintegration of your eyesight in which your visual field suddenly fractures into unconnected pieces, as if someone has shattered a mirror with a hammer and rearranged all the pieces randomly. If you were sitting at a table in the safety of your own home, the effect would be frightening and profoundly disorienting. If it happens when you're driving a pickup truck at fifty miles an hour on a rain-slicked rural two-lane country highway, as I was, the effect is overwhelmingly terrifying.

As Nora and I pulled out of Galena having scored four cases of canning jars, I sensed something amiss. At first my vision merely blurred, and I thought it was just the pickup's ancient defroster failing to keep the windshield from fogging up. Then my entire field of vision began shrinking, as if someone were closing down the iris of a camera.

"Nora," I said, "I think something is very wrong. Something's wrong with my eyes, and I feel as if I am sliding out of my body."

Nora's response sounded as if it was coming from the end of a long tunnel, muffled and alarmed. "Hugh, I can't understand what you're saying. You're talking gibberish."

"I'm blind, Nora, I'm blind!" I remember screaming. Nora remembers only a strange low wail. With peculiar detachment, I realized that I could not feel my left hand or arm. Then I realized that I couldn't feel my left foot, either. My right hand still gripped the wheel, and the weight of my hand and arm now pulled the wheel downward, turned the truck's wheels hard right, and threw us into a sweeping right turn. We "swapped ends," as the locals would say, spinning through a hundred and eighty degrees.

We flew off Route 213 backwards, our speed undiminished, all control lost. We rocketed backward through a shallow ditch, and the truck was thrown through the air into the empty parking lot of the Galena municipal baseball field. We slewed through the loose gravel, still speeding backward, even though we were in gear and my right foot had the gas pedal floored. We bounced off a handicapped parking sign and caromed into the chain-link backstop behind home plate. The pickup was jerked to an abrupt stop, wheels spinning, the engine roaring, and the occupants scared shitless.

It must have been Nora who switched the key off because it sure wasn't me. I was too busy screaming. Waves of searing pain were shooting from the base of my skull, radiating down the left side of my body—first neck and shoulder, then arm, then down to my leg and foot. My field of vision was still a shimmering kaleidoscope, and I could not orient myself. I was vomiting and shaking and sobbing. It felt like I was trapped, helpless and afraid, in some bizarre horror movie.

❂　　　❂　　　❂

A DAY LATER THINGS SEEMED FINE. THE PICKUP HAD BEEN OPERABLE after hitting the backstop, and Nora had driven us back to the farm, the front wheels shimmying wildly like a scene out of a Buster Keaton movie. It also turned out that both rear shock absorbers had been ripped out, so every time we hit a bump the truck gave out an alarming crash.

But in the course of our short drive, surprisingly, things got better. My eyes, I mean. By the time we turned down the drive at Bo Manor, my vision had cleared and stabilized. The searing pain had at the base of my skull abated abruptly, as if someone had switched off a light switch. My left side still was all pins and needles, but I was not paralyzed. I could again move my fingers and grip things.

Nora tells me that at that point I suddenly began laughing uproariously, which scared the hell out of her. I remember that part. I was laughing because I had just recalled an insult I often heard leveled at rednecks in Cecil County: "that damn fool don't know whether to shit or go blind."

By the next morning, even the stinging sensation on my left side was gone. I was normal. Unhurt. Fully operational. I tried to kid myself: *Maybe this was just a neurological fluke, a singular hundred-year storm that would just blow out to sea and leave me and my life alone.*

❂   ❂   ❂

YET I COULD NOT BANISH SHEER TERROR AT THE PROSPECT OF AGAIN subjecting myself powerlessly to doctors and diagnostics. I was afraid of what they might do to me, and I was afraid of what they might find. Tears did not work, did not vent the fear, or wash away the pain. At times, alone, I wept until I was out of breath. No catharsis, just exhaustion.

Nora watched my optimism wither. "Hugh, what's wrong?"

I felt a sudden flare of anger ignite and spread through my entire body. I was pissed off that I was so transparent, furious that things were so out of control. "I just can't handle this. Not now. Twenty years without a seizure, and suddenly this happens! Does this mean I'm going to have to go through the whole seizure diagnostic torture again? Well, that ain't happening! I've had enough of that to last me forever."

Nora being Nora, I expected a sympathetic response and was surprised when I didn't get it. Instead, her response was cold, fierce.

"You think your silly denial puts you in control? Do you

think denying that anything's wrong is going to stop you from having another seizure? Any good control freak has to admit when he's not in control, Hugh, and you don't even know what happened or what's going to happen next! You really need to find out what's going on, Hugh. You owe that to all of us because we depend on your being functional."

"Thank you, Nurse Dadmun, for your opinion. Very professional, very compassionate. I will take it under advisement."

Nora ratted me out to Dexter, described the whole seizure episode and told him about my refusal to seek help. He drove down from Elkton, sat me down in the living room with Nora. He came down on me hard, pushing me to get an MRI and to write to Australia to see if I could get a copy of my medical records. I resisted, stubborn and surly, and now both Dexter and Nora moved into a full court press, dragging me into the living room lecturing me as if I were Rickey. All the cliches: *Think of the risks. You're in denial. This is childish. You're being immature, irresponsible. Don't you want to know the truth?*

Fuck you, I thought. *I know truths you'll never know.*

Nora played the guilt card again: "It's for your good, but it's also for our good. You know how much we depend on you." One of Dexter's quiet comments hit hardest, cut deepest, made me both want to cry out and punch him in the face: "This isn't Akers, Hugh. That was then, this is now. This is not the time to play old tapes. Get real, man. This is truly serious shit."

We fell silent. There I sat, my fists clenched, my chin tucked tight against my chest, letting the silence sizzle like a burning fuse. Probably no more than a minute had passed when I realized I could not bear this any longer, could not withstand the pressure, could not bear to have my friends ally against me...and could not stand my ground.

But I could not capitulate either, even if I wanted to just to make peace. There was no explaining, no way to make them understand. I stood and ran my hands over my scalp. Inhaled very slowly, very deeply.

"I thank you both for your concern. I know you think you're

doing the right thing. You just don't know what the hell you're talking about." I crossed my arms over my chest and tucked my chin sullenly into my chest. "Discussion over."

In the following weeks, I withdrew unto sullen isolation, unable to communicate the revulsion triggered by the idea of again letting doctors mess around with my brain. I missed meals, spoke in monosyllables, was persistently churlish. I was being impossible, and I knew it. But I couldn't help it, could not stop it, could not shake it.

❂   ❂   ❂

A MONTH WENT BY WITHOUT INCIDENT, AND I FELT A GLIMMER OF optimism: maybe the Galena shatters had indeed been a one-off event, simply a grim reminder of events long past.

So much for self-delusion: I awoke one morning and could not roll over. Could not stand. Could not speak intelligibly. As before, the symptoms resolved after a few hours, but not before Dexter Touré had scheduled an emergency consult at HUP—the Hospital of the University of Pennsylvania.

❂   ❂   ❂

SCORE ONE FOR SUZUKI. EVERYTHING WAS ABOUT TO CHANGE: I WAS about to receive a diagnosis that would alter everything, that upset the whole fruit basket. Basically, and not particularly tactfully, I was told I was on the road to death.

Doctors Sonia Rosenblatt and Kyle Cosworth at HUP were regarded as among the best docs in their specialty, graybeards who had seen it all, the maestros of differential diagnosis. On an expedited basis, they ordered a quick series of MRIs, and to my extreme surprise, Australia immediately accommodated their request for all my medical records. Evidently, Dexter had been leaning hard on people.

Everyone should have a good Jewish mother, and if you're offered a choice, order up Sonia Rosenblatt. In her sixties, I guessed, ash-blond, ruddy complected, she radiated health, looking hale and outdoorsy, like a true Sabra, even in her white clinical coat. She looked like she should be on a kibbutz in Israel, not delivering bad news in Philadelphia.

After asking me to sit down, she smiled warmly and reached unselfconsciously across the table and put her hand over mine as she sat down next to me. It seemed like the most natural thing in the world. Evidently, she was the people-person on the team, and Cosworth was the no-nonsense science guy. He was much younger, rather WASPy looking, a prominent jaw, prematurely balding, hawk nose. Kyle Cosworth was the bad cop, the teller of hard truths.

Rosenblatt spoke first. She had a tendency toward mid-sentence pauses. "Hugh, we've thoroughly researched your history of...significant cerebral events. I'm sure you know your history, but...because we're tape-recording this meeting, let me just summarize for the record.

"Age seven, massive skull fracture from being fallen on by a horse. Actually, three massive skull fractures, basilar, diastatic and depressed. Evident frontal lobe and parietal lobe damage. Some temporal lobe, occipital, and basal trauma. Comatose for over thirty days. Expected to die...didn't. Subsequent history of seizures from age seven to eighteen, undoubtedly secondary to the brain trauma. Looks like there were...five. Two mild... half-way between *petit mal* and *grand mal* in intensity. Two severe, with delayed recuperation, some retrograde amnesia. One very severe. Life threatening. Evident...major residual brain damage. Significant partial memory lapses. Does this seem correct to you?"

I nodded.

"Also, we understand the...researchers...at Akers subjected you to four electro-convulsive 'therapy' experiences, even absent a diagnosis of depression. That's very curious. Kyle and I think these may have further weakened the integrity of your...mental architecture.

"It is hard for us to tell what...cumulative effect the brain trauma had, because there were no baseline data relating to your intelligence, memory or...*unusual faculties* before the horse fell on you. Your records show, however, that after you came out of the coma you rapidly developed or displayed—they didn't know which—exceptional intelligence, a superior memory, and an amazing facility with mathematics. All of these faculties got higher and better over the years, and that probably was not just the result of your rigorous home-schooling regimen. By the time you were an adolescent, you had developed a robust synesthesia."

"This is old history," I interrupted. "Look, until my two recent seizures, I had not suffered a seizure in two decades. I thought myself a pretty healthy guy, in both function and cognition. I am very, very unhappy that I have begun experiencing seizures again."

Kyle Cosworth crossed his arms across his chest. "You haven't," he said. "They weren't seizures, Hugh. They were... *strokes.* Or, more precisely, *transient ischemic attacks,* often called TIAs or ministrokes. Unlike a hemorrhagic stroke, where a brain artery leaks or ruptures, TIAs are triggered by blocked or crimped arteries. Usually with a TIA, the blood flow to the brain is blocked only for a short time, usually no more than five minutes. Your two TIAs, although short in duration and consequences, seem to have been unusually severe. That's one reason...Sonia and I wanted to learn more about your history."

"You're telling me that at my age I'm having strokes?" I whispered.

Rosenblatt took over, looked up at the ceiling, and then looked me directly in the eye. "We think your past history of significant brain trauma created some cerebral vulnerability that has begun to manifest itself."

"So, they weren't seizures?"

"Nope." Rosenblatt said. "Seizures are neurological. As you've experienced, they are electrical storms. Strokes are circulatory. They are a malady of the brain's plumbing, not its electrical system."

"Which is worse?"

"Well, the effects of seizures can be cumulative and result in various kinds of amnesias and even…'gifts' like yours, so your seizure history is a serious issue. But, as in your case, their effect can ameliorate over time. As I'm sure you know, a lot of epileptics lead pretty normal lives if their seizure activity can be controlled.

"But strokes do structural damage, and big strokes do big damage. They really wreck the machine. Paralysis sometimes. Or aphasia—that's loss of speech. Paralysis. Disruption of autonomic functions like blood pressure, breathing, balance, swallowing. And frequently they kill you, immediately or consequentially."

I had begun to shiver.

For some reason, Kyle Cosworth now stood—*Was he uncomfortable? I wondered*—and leaned against the wall. He sighed, then spoke softly. "In anyone, TIAs are bad news because they tend to recur and sometimes grow more severe. Prognostically, they are often precursor events to major stroke activity."

"In your case, I'm sorry to say, it's even more serious than that. In a man your age, Hugh, TIAs are very problematic, signaling something other than early-stage arterial blockage. Structurally, something bad is going on. In your case, we think we know what that it is. The huge amount of trauma your brain has experienced, coupled with the damaged circuits of all that repeated seizure activity at a relatively young age, mean, simply put, that your brain has become, very frail. Your TIAs, if I may use a blunt metaphor, are tremors signaling the high likelihood of an impending earthquake."

I didn't know what to say. For some reason, I chose to try to take the edge off by making a stupidly comic gesture, holding my arms out, palms up, shoulders shrugged, as if to say, "Well, whaddya gonna do?"

Dr. Rosenblatt gently pushed my hands down. "We know this is an enormous shock, Hugh, and Kyle and I discussed how much we should tell you. Given the gravity and uncertainty of your situation, we decided on full disclosure, however painful that may be. Under the circumstances, it's only fair."

"What are the circumstances?" I said, deciding to sit up straight in my chair and take my medicine like a man.

"Your MRI is very clear and, frankly, very troubling. We see large lesions both in areas that control motor function, executive function—that's judgment and decision-making—and those that control cognition. Your parietal lobe—the back of your brain—is relatively intact, but your frontal lobe, temporal lobe and occipital lobe all appear to be compromised and vulnerable. Frankly, we are surprised that you have been functioning as well as you do and have been largely symptom-free until recently."

"What does this mean in practical terms?"

Cosworth's turn. "It means that the next time you experience a TIA, or, almost equally likely, a major stroke, there's no predicting what part of your brain will be involved and what effects you might suffer. On the function side, could be wheelchair stuff. You could become paralyzed—probably more on one side than on the other. You might lose motor control of a hand, a leg, or your trunk. Your language centers and language skills might be impaired, and you could lose the ability to speak altogether.

"On the cognition and perception side, the possibilities are all over the place. You could lose your sense of taste or smell. You could become blind. You could lose your sense of balance or your ability to swallow. You might lose the ability to tell where your body begins and ends. You might suffer lapses in your premotor sequential thinking, that is, the ability to organize your thoughts. You could suffer the loss of your ability to recognize word sounds, to read letters, to understand symbols, to articulate language.

"As you are aware, your memory already has gaps and sometimes is unreliable. That could get still worse. Some people lose emotional memory—their lifelong collection of feelings and emotional inner life. You might become impulsive or uninhibited. If the left side of your brain suffers severe damage and the right side takes over, you might totally lose your sense of self and drift along in a kind of sweet euphoria.

"The point is, Hugh, that we can't predict what will happen, when it will happen, or even if it will happen. And neither can you. There is no treatment regime—not prophylactically, anyway.

We can't treat this, any more than you can treat a building with a crumbling foundation.

"If you do suffer a stroke, then we can do rehab—and that has to be done absolutely as quickly as possible, by the way—but nothing you can do will tip the odds at this point. What will be, will be."

"My, God. What do I do?"

Sonia Rosenblatt's voice was soft, as gentle as her message was hard. "The first thing, Hugh, is that you must come to grips with the reality of your situation—the absolute unpredictably of your life from this point on. You must get your mind around the notion that you may abruptly lose the ability to operate physically, mentally, or emotionally, and you should try to protect those around you from the consequences of that loss. For their sake, you need to put your affairs in order."

"What do you mean, 'put my affairs in order?' You make it sound like I'm going to die any second."

"That's not what we're saying. But we are saying that you are at heightened risk of a cerebral accident that could do anything from giving you a mild headache to killing you on the spot. You can't stop or even direct what happens, Hugh, but you can prepare for it. You can make yourself and your family ready for whatever happens. That is your responsibility right now."

The conference room begin to spin. I felt myself begin to tremble, and I pushed my palms down hard on top of the conference table to steady myself—to try to steady everything. "I'm sorry, I need to leave. I gotta get out of here."

"That's completely understandable. This probably is a good time to wrap this meeting up. We should be meeting regularly from now on and refreshing your MRI frequently. Even if we can't affect what's happening, we can at least know what's happening. We also have a very fine psychological counseling group who works with our patients. They can help with both perspective and planning. They're really good, Hugh."

I stood and started to put on my jacket. I couldn't seem to get my arms through the sleeve holes and stood there wrestling with my parka. I tried to smile.

"Am I having a TIA?"

"No, Hugh," Dr. Rosenblatt smiled back. "You are suffering a very harsh dose of reality."

I finally got my jacket on and started for the door. Kyle Cosworth put out his hand like a barrier. "One last thing, Hugh. Did you drive here today?"

"Yes, I have the farm truck."

"Well, we're going to call you a limo to get you back down to Maryland. Someone from the farm can come pick the truck up later, or we can arrange to have it dropped off. But Hugh, we have to make one thing absolutely clear."

He took me by the shoulders and looked me sternly in the face.

"You must never, ever drive again."

❀   ❀   ❀

MEANWHILE, BACK AT THE RANCH, WE WERE ALL SITTING IN THE living room, everyone except Rickey and Ray, when I told Nora and Dexter and Tryg and Simone the news.

"Wow," said Dexter. "I really had it wrong. I sure thought it was seizures. Because you are so sharp, I had forgotten about your heavy trauma all those years ago. This diagnosis changes everything. Hugh, you can count on us to help in any way possible. It's just that at this point, there's no telling what is possible."

Dexter rose, walked over to me, took my hands in his giant mitts, lowered his head as if in great pain. "I am really, really sorry, man."

Several days later I was sitting in the kitchen eating a tomato and cucumber sandwich. Rickey was seated across from me, spreading crunchy peanut butter on Ritz crackers. She was gulping them down, chain-wolfing, so to speak. She was lubricating the whole process with a tall tumbler of Kombucha, a probiotic drink that tastes like turpentine.

"Hugh. Can we talk?" Rickey had been watching a lot of Joan Rivers on TV recently, relishing, and often mimicking, Joan's savage wit.

I finished the last bit of cucumber and licked my fingers. "What's up, Rick?"

"That's what I want to ask you. I may be autistic, but I'm not dumb. All this nudge-nudge, wink-wink shit going on between you and Nora, and Tryg suddenly spending all his time at Simone's. I'll tell you what I think."

Rickey had never been comfortable looking people directly in the eye, and now I was struck by how forcefully she held my gaze.

"I think…." She paused to take a deep breath. "I believe that you are suffering from some sort of crisis, maybe in your brain, and that you are working hard to hide it. From me. Not from me and Tryg and Dexter. *Just from me.* I think they know what's going on. But you are treating me like an idiot, and I want you to know I seriously resent it."

I sighed. "Okay, you win. Here's the scoop. TIAs. Transient ischemic attacks. Ministrokes. Two so far, likely to be more."

She did not appear surprised. "What's the prognosis?"

"Almost sure to get worse, high probability of a major stroke. When and how bad not certain, but the handwriting is on the wall. Because of the unpredictability of what might happen to me, we have to start planning for what we're all going to do. Right now."

"Wow, that's a heavy load just to drop on me."

"Well, isn't it nice to make this all about you."

"It's my privilege to be an asshole. I'm autistic."

I burst out laughing. Startled, she dropped her Ritz cracker, the peanut butter gluing it to the front of her jumper. She brushed it on to the floor.

"Rickey, I believe that may be the funniest thing you have ever said."

"Yeah, well, I've been watching a lot of Joan Rivers."

"We're dancin' here, Rickey. Shall we cut to the chase?"

"*Yeah, tell me what you're going to do with me.*"

A long pause. "Do you have thoughts about that?"

"Yeah. *Stay here forever.* Build a new lab. Eat Nora's cooking. As usual, avoid you clowns as much as possible, in exchange for which I promise to be as polite as possible when we do have to interact."

I sighed. "Not gonna happen, Rickey. All this too must end. You and Nora and Tryg, you all have your strengths, but you can't run this enterprise. We have to plan how we're going to wind down the Hole in the Wall Gang."

Rickey waved her hands dismissively. "Easy, you buy us each a gun, like a Glock or a .357 or something. We all stand in a circle, aim at each other. Circular suicide. Count of three, one, two, three, bang! End of problem."

"That sounds like something Joan Rivers would say," I said.

"Fuckin' A," Rickey Bayard said.

35

Causa Mortis

PUT YOUR AFFAIRS IN ORDER, SONIA ROSENBLATT HAD SAID.

Just think about that for a moment. What does that mean? How do you do it? What ground does that cover? What action items does it require? Do you just make a checklist and tick things off, like going shopping? Do you pray? Do you ponder the great imponderables?

Samuel Johnson is reputed to have said, "Nothing so focuses a man's mind as the knowledge that he is to be hanged in a fortnight." Well, here I had the gallows in sight, and my mind remained resolutely unfocused. I knew neither what to do nor what to feel.

As one for whom survival has always been the highest priority, I had never seriously tried to get my mind around the idea of my own death. I was a being who simply could not process the notion of...*not being*. I could find no emotional niche in which to deposit the idea of simply *ceasing to be*, of being annihilated, of becoming nothing.

Forever.

I was completely terrified. Sick-in-the-stomach terrified. *No! No! NO!* terrified. I suffered periods of hyperventilating until I grew dizzy. I found that I did not progress through the classic DABDA cycle supposedly common to those facing death—Denial, Anger, Bargaining, Depression, Acceptance. I just went straight to depression and stayed there. My prognosis kept leaping out and slapping me in the face: *You are soon going to die, which is going to be bad, and then you're going to be dead forever, which is worse.*

One day I took myself to Hermann Bayard's gravesite, not to seek companionship or communion with the dead, but simply because it was a place to go. I sat on a hillock overlooking the place where Hermann's physical disintegration was probably still in progress. God, Jesus Christ, and I had never been within miles of one another, but suddenly, involuntarily, that old child's prayer popped into my mind:

> *Now I lay me down to sleep.*
> *I pray the Lord my soul to keep.*
> *If I should die before I wake,*
> *I pray the Lord my soul to take.*

Tears suddenly flooded down my cheeks. "But I won't have a soul! There's nothing to keep, nothing to take! How can this be? How can this happen to me?" I cried for a long, long time. I did not feel better afterwards. Just hollow, just empty.

❖   ❖   ❖

I KNEW THAT PUTTING MY AFFAIRS AND THE FARM'S AFFAIRS IN order was going to involve a lot of gifts and transfers, and so for a while I fretted over whether, in my current diagnostic state, I was operating "in contemplation of death," what lawyers call *causa mortis,* or whether I still qualified as a living person making *inter vivos* gifts to other living persons, that is, transfers between the living who expected to keep living. The distinction was relevant in terms of estate taxes.

Then one day, over a stiff scotch, I realized that I was doing all these mental gymnastics over nothing. I experienced a real

God-am-I-ever-stupid moment, and laughed out loud. In wrapping things up, I might be the architect of various gifts and transfers, but they weren't *my* gifts or my assets. Other than some clothes, I didn't have any assets! I wasn't even going to write a will, because I had nothing to bequeath and nobody I wanted to bequeath anything to.

Everything I utilized in my daily life and treated as a possession was really Hermann Bayard's! The trick was going to be to give a lot of his assets away, and the odds against doing that successfully were long. The trick was going to be to make Hermann Bayard's transfers, to the extent anyone saw them at all, look like *inter vivos* transfers. The kind of challenge I could really sink my teeth into.

36

Think Fast, Again

COLONEL BAILEY SUITS DID NOT BOTHER WITH A GREETING, OPTING instead for a full body slam. His voice issued from the phone in a hoarse bellow.

"Ullam, you are in big, big trouble. I really don't have to call and tell you this, but I wanted the satisfaction of letting you know that we are on to you."

Nothing so focuses a man's attention as the knowledge that he will be hanged in a fortnight.

"You have my attention, Colonel Suits."

"Do you know a Navy lieutenant named Denver Pullen?"

"Certainly do."

Suits seemed surprised that I admitted knowing Pullen so readily. "And just exactly how do you know him?"

"C'mon, Colonel. You already know exactly how and when I met him. Now you're just jerking *me* around. Denver Pullen was in charge of the government surplus equipment auction down in Stevensville where we bought some electronic equipment for Hermann Bayard. Oh, and once again, tell Santunas and Callas I say hi."

Suits ignored the last gibe. "Bought for Hermann Bayard?"

"For Hermann Bayard." Suits had not expected this, I bet.

"Why were you buying electronic equipment for Hermann Bayard?"

"To replace all the electronic equipment that was destroyed when Mr. Bayard's daughter accidentally set fire to his workshop. She was screwing around with his stuff when he was away, and something overheated and started a fire. Total write-off. Everything had to be replaced. So, we did."

"Bayard's equipment."

"Bayard's equipment."

"And where did he get *that* equipment?"

"Originally, I think he bought much of it from Washington College in Chestertown after they closed their electronics major and made it surplus. And, if your crack investigators had enough sense to sniff their own asses, they would have found that he bought much of it from *you guys*. Hermann purchased some things from Aberdeen's Procurement and Surplus Sale Director, I remember. He also got some stuff from DuPont, as I remember. Your investigation seems to be going hot-and-heavy, and soon your crack military investigators will track the details of those transactions down, I'm sure. None of it's a secret."

"What kind of equipment?" Suits' voice had taken on an *ah-ha!* tone. Some JAG lawyer had evidently given Suits the crash course in cross-examination 101: *Never ask a question you don't know the answer to.*

"I'm no expert on all the technology Hermann bought, I just wrote the checks. But I know that much of it involved radio receivers. Very sophisticated receivers. And antennas. There was a lot of power equipment and recording equipment and other related items, but Hermann's basic interest was in high-technology listening gear."

"And just what was Hermann Bayard listening to?"

"*You*, Colonel Suits. *He was listening to Aberdeen.* For a while a few years ago, Hermann Bayard became obsessed with listening to Aberdeen, with electronic eavesdropping, if I may call it that. He was receiving and recording all those weird signals you spooks are always transmitting. He does not like you guys much. Matter of fact, I think he has a Freedom of Information Act request in on you Aberdeen people. He's something of an anti-government Libertarian."

There was a pause, and I swear I could hear the gears whirring. Clearly Colonel Bailey Suits and I had entered into a high-speed chess game, each of us thinking about our next move as fast as we could.

"Did he transmit signals?"

"Can't say. I was never in the workshop with him when he was using the equipment, except once, and that time he was busy recording some kind of jamming signals you guys were sending that were fucking up all the boat instruments and compasses all over northern Chesapeake Bay."

Suits put down his bishop, so to speak, and started a different gambit with his knight. "When we inspected the hangar, there was no electronic equipment there. Just a bunch of rusty farm junk."

"That's right. The replacement equipment is long gone. As your guys found, we now use it to store an old combine that Tryg Sletland hopes to bring back to life and sell."

That's it, Hugh: divert, digress, overload his circuits, stifle his strategy.

"Where is the electronic equipment now?"

"Landenberg landfill, Landenberg, Pennsylvania."

"Buried in a landfill?"

"Well, I'm pretty sure the first set of equipment was totally buried, because it was all destroyed in the fire. It was nothing but junk. The second round of stuff, I don't know. We carted it up there, and they have a shed where people drop used TVs and computers and monitors and stuff. We dropped it there, and I think the gleaners may have taken a lot of it, because it was very good stuff. After a while, the landfill just buries anything that isn't taken. Maybe some of its still there. Your guys could check."

"What's gleaners?"

"Scavengers, junk pickers, the 'secondary market.' A lot of

people make their living picking through things other people get rid of. Then they sell it on."

"You're telling me thousands of dollars' worth of sophisticated equipment was just dumped at a...dump in Landenberg, Pennsylvania?"

"Yes, that's basically what I'm telling you."

"The generators, too?"

"The generators, too, except for the generators we've kept to provide back-up power at Bo Manor if the power is interrupted to the house or the hangar."

"Why would you just dump all that stuff at Landenberg?"

"Because the landfill in Bear, Delaware is for municipal trash only. Contract trash collection, big trucks, all that. Landenberg is open to the public. Pay your money, drop your stuff."

"They charged you to drop your equipment? You bought it and then paid to dump it and it was perfectly good equipment?"

It seemed to me that Suits' chess game was going badly.

"Well, let's just say we made a financial accommodation with Landenberg. They knew they could get pickers to pay under the table for a lot of it. So, they cut us a deal on their rates. Still, yes, it cost us some money to clean out the hangar."

Suits paused to get his bearings. I thought I heard him inhaling through his nose, sort of sniffing, which I took to be a good sign—maybe my sleight of hand was confusing him. "This is beyond belief, Ullam. So, enlighten me," he said sarcastically, "*why* did you get rid of the replacement electronic equipment?"

"Because Hermann Bayard ordered us to. And now you're going to ask me why he ordered us to, and I am going to tell you he was *furious* when he learned about the fire and furious when he learned that we had bought replacement stuff for the workshop without clearing it with him first.

"Rickey burned her arms and hands in the fire, mostly first degree, but some second degree on her chin and throat. She's healed, but there's scarring. But she could easily have been killed in the fire, and Hermann Bayard went absolutely apeshit when he came into town, learned about the fire, saw Rickey's scars, and then saw the replacement workshop. He fired Nora Dadmun for not supervising Rickey well enough. He fired me for writing the checks for the new stuff. He fired Tryg Sletland for 'aiding and abetting,' as Hermann called it. He demanded that the equipment be disposed of immediately, and I mean *immediately*. He was livid. Out of control, really."

On the phone, I thought I could hear Suits licking his lips. I wondered what that meant.

"Hermann did not care about the money, the costs, Colonel Suits. He cared about the idea of having his autistic daughter burned up in a fire. I think the workshop fire left Hermann a little unhinged. After a few days he rehired Nora and me and Tryg. Then he packed his bags and said not to expect to see him for a while. Frankly, that's the last we've seen or heard of him."

"And just when did all this happen?"

"I don't know the exact dates—you know, the fire, the auction, rebuilding the lab, and then dismantling it—but I can reconstruct all that for you if you insist. I can ask Tryg and Nora, and I can check my checkbook stubs. But I can tell you this: that equipment was out of here long before the whale went into the canal and before the mysterious power surge. We still think all of these events are Aberdeen's doing, and you guys are just throwing up a smoke screen."

"Why didn't you tell us all this when we searched the farm?"

I forced a laugh, hoping it sounded spontaneous and genuine. *"Are you kidding?* Well, I could say, 'because you didn't ask,' but that would be a little precious. So, I'll tell you a couple of real reasons. First, because you just barged in and sort of told us to sit down and shut up while you did your tough-guy military inspection. We may have acted helpful, but we sure as hell were not feeling helpful. You military cops do not have such hot people skills. Including you, Colonel Suits.

"Second, and more important, we did not think you'd believe what we told you about the equipment, even though it's true. We thought you would harass us further and maybe frame us for something that Aberdeen, or maybe someone else, actually had done. And we knew we were pretty vulnerable targets. We were hoping we could avoid being hassled any further and dragged out into the sunlight. We believed, and we still believe, that the government wouldn't hesitate to set us up."

There was silence so long it was painful. I itched for Suits to say something. Finally, he spoke, his voice flat and hard.

"Let me be clear. I do not believe you, Mr. Ullam. We have reexamined our own tracking and radio direction-finder traces for the times these transmission anomalies occurred, and they cast a shadow directly over your farm."

"But not *solely* over our farm, I bet. Besides, a shadow is a shadow," I said, hoping that sounded profound. "It is neither a reality nor a proof of reality. Who do you think carried out all this electronic skullduggery? A farm manager with a felony conviction? An indigenous Australian accountant? A cook? A profoundly autistic teenager? You've got no credible suspects, Suits, no motive, no proof. You guys are chasing your tails. So don't give me this bullshit about shadows."

"Ullam, *Mister* Ullam, we believe you are the most likely culprits, and we are going to work to bring you to justice. And we don't use the usual criminal justice system. We don't need to convene a federal grand jury to issue subpoenas to force you to testify. In the military, we have our own compulsory process, our own lawyers, and, at the end of the day, our own judges. Perhaps you should consider retaining counsel."

"Knock yourself out," I said and hung up.

37

Hidden Money, Hidden Gifts

NOW THAT YOU KNOW WHERE HERMANN BAYARD'S BODY IS AND sort of know where Deirdre Callas' body is, I bet you want to know where the money is. How much there is. How I set up the finances. How I moved the dollars around. But you know, of course, that a magician never reveals the sleight-of-hand techniques that the audience aches to learn so that they too can be "in on it." Sorry, you can't be in on it.

I was thinking a lot about what to do with the money. Beyond attending to the Gang's present and future monetary needs, I had other fish to fry. Hermann Bayard had far too much money and made poor use of it. Many worthy organizations and worthy purposes have far too little money and, if they had more, could use it splendidly. This was a situation that cried out for redress, at least to my limited abilities and limited time.

Now, I know what all the trusts and estates lawyers are going to say: even if Hermann Bayard died intestate, Rickey Bayard was his sole heir, and even after the government munched a huge hunk of Hermann's bucks for estate taxes, Rickey stood to inherit many millions. But who would administer those millions, tend the money bin? Rickey was a minor, and a manifestly legally incompetent minor at that. No one had been formally appointed to see to her welfare, attend her legal needs during and after distribution of the bucks, and manage her financial affairs after distribution.

Obviously, neither Nora nor I could apply to be her guardian or trustee without revealing that we had been behaving illegally and had been guilty of embezzlement from the moment Hermann dropped dead. That fact would probably preclude either of us from being appointed to protect the interests of the poor little rich girl.

When, at some point, a court made Rickey the ward of someone who did not know her, someone had no reason to care about her, someone who would have disposition authority over an enormous amount of money, I thought the odds were high that Rickey would fare badly, would have little or no voice in the utilization and distribution of her wealth. As Mr. Bumble so aptly put it in *Oliver Twist,* "the law is an ass—an idiot." I resolved not to leave Rickey's welfare in the hands of some idiot, even at the cost of committing some legally dodgy moves to get her—and Nora, and Tryg—a better outcome.

Accordingly, if in this journal I told anybody where the money was, obviously they'd just try to appropriate it. Still, I can sate peoples' curiosity about The Big Number. All in, all up, all subject to varying degrees of liquidity and offshore account rates and redemption rules, I had about $211 million to work with. The investments were diversified: I had spread the bucks around offshore accounts in the Caymans, Bermuda, private banks in London and Zurich. I had cash on hand, CDs, mutual funds, tax-leveraged investments, gold and silver bullion, sheep accounts.

I will not reveal who all is getting gifts and donations. I cannot trust anyone to endorse and support my donative intent, and some of my chosen donees are pretty far out, pretty radical, particularly as white people would see it. But here's the bottom line: I, Hugh Ullam, using Herman Bayard's resources, began giving a lot of money away, as fast as I was able. I would write to some entity I considered worthy in my capacity as Hermann Bayard's agent and offer an immediate lump sum donation. Sometimes I would earmark a purpose—a new library or an indigenous school lunch program in the outback—and sometimes these were unrestricted grants. Each donation was conditioned on the donor's name being kept anonymous and on assurance that the donation would be entirely used up by a specified date.

I got a few requests for further information and assurance that the donations were legal and legitimate, but mostly the beneficiaries of Hermann's generosity asked few questions, just took the money, and ran. Good for them.

38

Da Plan, Boss, Da Plan

IT FELT STRANGE TO SIT IN THE PASSENGER'S SEAT. I WAS accustomed to driving, not riding.

"You okay? How ya feelin'?" Nora's voice had a tinny brightness to it, as if this were an innocent inquiry. I felt myself bristle.

"God damn it, Nora. Don't you do this to me. Don't make a cripple out of me before my time. We both know the score."

"Whoa, Mr. Ullam. Whoa. I am not patronizing you. You think this whole situation is easy on us? This unpredictability is new to all of us, and rushing around to deal with everything has us all stressed. We are all going to have to figure out the best way to navigate day-to-day. Please, do not take your frustrations out on me."

We were in the Ford wagon, just Nora and me, just "going for an afternoon drive." Dexter was on call at the ER, so it was just the two of us. Just like old times. No destination, just diversion, just trying to get away from it all. Warm day, blue sky, a few clouds.

We drove for a half hour in silence, listening to soft jazz

on Chestertown's bush league FM station. Easy listening, easy driving. Finally, Nora turned to me.

"So, what are we going to do, Hugh?"

I laughed. "That reminds me of that old joke where the Long Ranger and Tonto are surrounded by hostile Comanches, and the Lone Ranger says, 'Well, Tonto, old friend, looks like we've had it,' and Tonto says, 'What you mean *we*, Kemo Sabe?' Yeah, we may have been living in the same boat before, Nora, but from this point forward, we are all certainly not in the same boat."

"Well, what *are* your plans?"

"Plans? How can I plan? At the moment, my plan if you can call it that, is to sit and wait. When fate strikes me down, I just hope it's fast. My plan is to die, hopefully with some grace and dignity, hopefully without a lot of pain. But of course, I don't have a lot of control over that."

"And the rest of us are just supposed to just fend for ourselves? Maybe I'm wrong, but there must be some pieces we can put in place, no?" Nora said quietly.

"We'd all have a lot more options if Hermann hadn't croaked. Then we'd just be a bunch of moochers, and we could all claim that we were sucking down a ton of his dollars in exchange for the care and feeding of his handicapped kid. You and Tryg and Dexter and I could just say, 'Bye, bye,' and that would be it. As it is, all of us, except Rickey, are players in a long-running game of theft-by-deception and probably numerous other crimes. Even if we did not have to concern ourselves with Rickey, at this point we cannot simply leave the key under the front doormat and say, 'Ta.'"

I put my feet up on the dashboard, waggled my feet to and fro, like windshield wipers.

"You want to know the basic plan? Even before I can't manage the farm and the finances anymore, all the rest of you are going to have to get out of town. Right away. There is no way your life at Bohemia Manor Farm can be sustained if I become incompetent or am not around at all."

I heard a sob. Nora turned away from me.

I plowed on. *Okay, Hugh, let's get this over with.*

"Nora," I said, "please pull off over into that rest area over there."

We sat quietly for several minutes, steeped in one of those big-things-are-coming silences. You could almost hear the ominous drum roll in the background.

"As I think about it, Nora, I see two main priorities. We have to stay ahead of the law, and we have to stay alive. Someday the cops—state, federal, Suits' Aberdeen goons, whatever—are going to have a lot more questions for us, particularly if we just vanish. We have to find a way to assure that they never get a chance to ask those questions, right?"

Nora nodded.

"Obviously, I'm not concerned about that for me. But as for the rest of you, I think you have to separate. So, we don't need one plan, we need a bunch of plans, each independent of all the others. Perhaps hidden from all the others.

"Each of you has to have enough money to get by. For good. And there's the rub. I'm the only person authorized to deal with the money, and I'm the only one qualified to manage the money. And I'm not going to be here. So, my challenge is to find a way to set each of you up—probably different ways for different people—once and for all.

"I worry least about Tryg. I just say, 'Your employment is terminated, thank you for your service and commitment, and here is a huge bucket of money. Go forth, maybe change your name, and build a fully funded new life somewhere. Buy a little farm in Wisconsin, whatever.'

"Now you. You asked what I've been thinking, and I'm telling you. This all isn't cast in stone, Nora. It's just preliminary brainstorming around damage control.

"Here's a major planning stumbling block for me. Shall I assume that you're going to continue to care for Rickey or not? If you are, it seems to me that I can't set her up without setting you up. But that's doable. Without Hermann's approval, I don't see any way to make you Rickey's legal guardian, but maybe that wouldn't be necessary anyway. No one is ever going to accuse you of kidnapping her, so my initial thought is to buy you and Rickey a nice house somewhere, create a trust that provides for her care for the rest of her life, and create another trust for you that makes it worth your while to continue as her caregiver. The only challenge there is to figure out what will happen down the road when you die."

Nora darkened. "And just where might this house be?"

"God, I don't know," I said, impatient. "I haven't had a lot of time to think about that yet, but someplace far away from Cecil County Basically, what you need is privacy and security and stability, right?

"One possible idea: my financial contact at Hoare's Bank in London has a second house at a gated community called The Landings on an island just south of Savannah. Very private, very secure. By our standards up here, housing is cheap, maybe forty percent of our prices for the same size house. There are lots of houses with three car garages, so Rickey could have a workshop and library. It's got a big health club and social membership gets you into four different clubhouses, and…"

Nora interrupted, glaring at me. "Whoa, whoa, whoa, Mr. Toad. You're really getting ahead of yourself here."

"You're right, you're right. There are thousands of possibilities where you two could safely hole up. I'm just so eager to get things set up that when a one-stop shop comes along, it looks super attractive to me."

Now Nora was breathing deeply, almost panting.

"I gather I'm missing something."

"You sure are, Hugh." Her knuckles were white on the wheel.

"From day one you have taken it for granted that Ulricke Bayard, having been dumped in my lap for years, should *stay* in my lap. For the rest of my life. You want to tell me when I signed on for that? Did I ever tell you I would be content to be a permanent indentured servant?"

Idiot that I was, I had actually permitted myself the flawed assumption that Nora would continue to care for Rickey for the rest of their lives. Now I proceeded to pile stupid on stupid. "But don't you like Rickey, feel something for Rickey?"

"I honestly don't know how you can you ask me that question. Don't you think I have demonstrated my commitment? But Hugh, you know as well as I do that there is no respite from Rickey. She's the gift that keeps on taking. Day in, day out. Year in and year out. I can see why the suicide rate is so high among people who have to care for permanently disabled people, especially those people who don't care back."

Now Nora fired a head shot.

"Hugh, you are not a mean-spirited man, but, God, you operate like a *machine*. An organized, responsible machine, but still, a machine. So, Rickey the machine doesn't bother you the way she bothers me. And when she gets on your nerves, you just go into your office and close the door. Just leave Rickey to me, as always.

"Until Dexter came into my life, I could not do anything about it. I was locked in. With Dexter, slowly but surely, I'm making progress in unpacking my baggage. It's scary, Hugh, but it also is wonderful. We may be a freak show, the seven-foot Zulu and the wine stain girl, but we've got something going. And now you want me to put away my chance of salvation so I can baby-sit a cripple for the rest of my life? Wow, *that's* some choice."

"You done?" I asked.

"Not by a long shot, Mr. Ullam. If you think I'm going to live in a cage with Rickey Bayard, now and forever, you've got another thought coming. You better consider *that* in your plans."

Nora threw the car into drive and peeled out of the rest area, spewing gravel.

I found a handwritten note on my pillow that night. Nora's handwriting. It said, "Hugh, I have had this tucked into my personal papers for years. I do not know who wrote it or where I got it, but I think it speaks to the present situation." Paper-clipped to her note was a single page, obviously typed on an old manual typewriter.

"We need other people, not in order to stay alive, but to be fully human, to be affectionate, playful. To be generous. How genuine is my capacity for love if there is no one for me to love, to laugh with, to trust tenderly, to be trusted by? I can love an idea or a vision, but I cannot throw my arms around it. Unless there is someone to whom I can give my gifts, in whose hands I can entrust my dreams, someone who will forgive my deformities, my aberrations, to whom I can speak the unspeakable, then I am not human. I am a thing, a gadget that works, but has no meaning."

39

Rickey Testifies

THE REGISTERED LETTER, ADDRESSED TO ME, WAS FROM COLONEL Bailey Suits. The embossed letterhead read *United States Department of Defense, Special Investigations Division.* Below my Bo Manor address, it said, *In Re: Northern Chesapeake Electromagnetic Anomalies, 145-3287.*

I will spare you all the introductory statutory citations and threatening legalese. The point of the letter was that Suits was requesting—*insisting on*—an interview, under oath, with Ulricke Stuhlmann Bayard, conducted by one Colonel Sylvia Matthes, Ph.D. The subtext of the letter was you can do this the easy way, or you can do it the hard way.

The easy way was to make Rickey available for an "informal" conversation—sworn, under oath, recorded—at Bo Manor. The hard way would involve compulsory process—the equivalent of a subpoena in the military justice system—lawyers, written pleadings, hearings, and, after the bad guys won, an interrogation at a military facility, in this case Aberdeen.

Nora, Tryg and I convened in the living room. "Well," I said, "I told you the Aberdeen feds were going to play hard ball. I knew Suits wasn't going to buy the story about the equipment being Hermann's, but I thought it would buy us a little time to think things through. Looks like time's up."

"Speaking of the equipment," Tryg said, "what are we going to do with all that stuff in the storage lockers?"

"We don't do anything with it," I said. "I'm simply going to stop paying the storage fees. Eventually, they'll declare us in default, cut off our padlocks and auction the contents."

"If Aberdeen is so hot about this equipment, won't they investigate all these sales and find out who bought our lockers and then pressure the buyers?" asked Nora.

"I don't think that's likely," I said. "First of all, there are a lot of these auctions, because a lot of people who rent storage lockers just abandon their stuff. Second, no one inventories the contents of the lockers. They just open 'em up, the bidders bid, they pay cash on the barrelhead, and cart their purchases away the same day. Someone's going to be thrilled at the deal they got on our stuff. I can't guarantee our stuff will never be tracked back to us, but I must say I'm not all that anxious about it. Now this interview thing with Rickey—*that* makes me anxious."

Tryg leaned in, his elbows on knees. "Can't we just refuse? I mean, taking a deposition from a severely handicapped and obviously incompetent adolescent? No court is going to stand for that. The Aberdeen people, they've seen her, we've showed 'em how frail she is. What they are doing is cruel."

"Tryg, that is exactly the point. They are not trying to get a lucid deposition from Rickey Bayard; they are trying to bust our chops. If we protest and refuse, they bring out their lawyers, drag us into some kangaroo court, and cry to their judge about some pressing national security emergency. We pay for a lawyer of our own, he screams in outrage about harassment and cruel and unusual this-and-that, and then we lose. Even if we win, which is highly unlikely, they will have forced us to subject Rickey to all this bullshit, and they know we don't want to freak her out. So, they hold the heartless-and-cruel card.

"Oh, and one other card they hold. The fuckers can call in the Social Services people. Say Rickey's parents have abandoned her, and she is living with a bunch of people who have no legal responsibility for her welfare. When they threaten to remove her, we can't complain because we have no legal standing. They'll emphasize that they offered us this kind, gentle home interview with their lady shrink, and we're the ones who forced things to get ugly.

"Furthermore, Rickey's obvious incompetency doesn't mean shit. They are not asking whether or not she's competent to stand trial. They'll claim she's some sort of fact witness who may be able to provide some kind of useful information, no matter how impaired she is. Tryg, prosecutors have elicited testimony *from dogs!* 'Was this the man who was holding the gun?' *Arf! Arf! Arf!*'

"I don't believe they think Rickey's responsible for the transmissions. Would *you* believe she could do that? No, they think that one of us or all of us did it, and I believe they're hoping that Rickey will blurt out something or reveal something that throws us under the bus. We are holding only one card. We say, 'You guys are child-abusing assholes, but we have nothing to hide, so okay, go ahead and interview her. Then maybe you'll finally get off our backs.'"

"You're saying this is like going to Plan B," said Nora.

"Plan B-squared," I said. "If you can believe this, we are going to have to put our fates in Rickey's hands, see if she's capable of some serious performance art under some very stressful circumstances. We have to prep her on the story that it was Herman's equipment in the hangar, but we don't want to rehearse her so much that it looks like she's reciting lines at the school play. Look, Rickey knows what's at stake for all of us. I think we have to take the risk that she can keep her cool, play the role, remember her lines, stick to the point, and throw them off track. Nothing else we can do will get them off our back."

"Sweet Jesus Christ," said Tryg.

I SUSPECT COLONEL BAILEY SUITS WAS SURPRISED WHEN HE

received our prompt return registered letter saying that we had no objection if their Dr. Matthes wanted to talk with Rickey. We did ask that Dr. Matthes respect Rickey's frailties and refrain from aggressive or abusive interrogation.

We chose the kitchen for the "conversation." That's where Rickey hung out much of the time, and she was most comfortable there; the living room was formal and alien to her. Suits' tech guy set up their video recorder; we set *our* brand-new videocam, the Kmart price tags still dangling. This upset Suits, who tried to tell us we couldn't record. "Why not, Colonel?" Nora asked innocently. "None of us is hiding anything, are we?" It was finally agreed that Nora could sit in and that Tryg would handle our camera. Without being asked, I volunteered to step out in order to avoid any suggestion that I was signaling or coaxing or threatening Rickey.

I was introduced to Colonel Sylvia Matthes, MD, Ph.D. and was impressed. She was dressed in civilian clothing, provided a warm smile and a gentle handshake, and had a round, pleasant face framed by a cowl of sandy hair with a curtain of bangs across her forehead. She provided me with a one-page biography that was above reproach: Psychologist, Psychiatrist, Columbia, Columbia again, Afghanistan, on loan to NATO for interrogation training, architect of a respected PTSD program, Guantanamo Review Board, adjunct professor at the University of Maryland, side-gig as profiler for the FBI, author of numerous books and articles. She seemed to keep busy.

Later, after Suits and Matthes had left, we all watched Tryg's video, including its dramatic conclusion, applauding loudly as Ulricke Stuhlmann Bayard won her Oscar.

On the tape, Rickey was guided into the kitchen by Nora, wearing a pair of Nora's gray flannel pajamas and a pair of headphones. No sunglasses today. She walked rigidly, her eyes darting.

Before she could sit down, the front of Nora's pajamas darkened at the crotch. The stain ran down the front of Rickey's right leg, and a pool of urine spread around her bare foot. Nora gasped and grabbed for a dish towel. Rickey stood immobile, her expression blank.

Sylvia Matthes kept her cool, extending her hands out toward Rickey, palms up. "That's okay, Rickey. We know this is pretty stressful, right? All these outsiders who want to talk to you? I'd probably pee myself too." Rickey looked her in the face and nodded.

When Nora and Rickey returned from a costume change, Rickey was wearing a pair of blue jeans and one of Tryg's faded blue polo shirts. She wore Nora's sneakers. The headphones were gone. Without being directed, she went over to the kitchen table and sat down across from Colonel Matthes.

Matthes again extended her hands, palms up, but did not try to touch Rickey. Rickey looked at her unblinking. "Are we okay, Rickey?" Matthes asked. Rickey looked away but nodded.

Their tech guy then stepped forward, with the tape running, and asked Rickey to raise her right hand. She complied, cocking her head, curious.

"This deposition is being taken under oath," the tech recited to no one in particular. "Do you, Ulricke Stuhlmann Bayard, swear that the testimony you are about to give under oath is the truth, the whole truth, and nothing but the truth, so help you, God?"

"I don't believe in God," Rickey said.

"In that case," the tech said, "do you aver and affirm that your testimony will be true and complete?"

"Autistic people always tell the truth. We don't know how to lie," said Rickey.

"I'll take that as a yes," said the tech.

An amused smile played over Sylvia Matthes' lips, and then she turned to Rickey, making firm eye contact.

"Rickey, some pretty...unusual things have been happening around this area recently, and our job is to try to find out all about it. We've been talking to a lot of people who live around here, including Hugh and Nora and Tryg. They've been very helpful. I was hoping you might be helpful, too."

"Helpful, okay," said Rickey.

"Rickey, to start us off, would you tell me a little bit about yourself?"

Rickey stared at Matthes blankly. "What do you want to know?"

"Well, let's start with the basics. How old are you now, Rickey?"

"I am over fourteen years old. Chronologically, that is. In terms of knowledge acquisition, I'm much older. The fucking shrinks say my social age is about six. Idiots."

"Do you go to school?"

"I have been home-schooled for many years, and now I have a high-school equivalency diploma. I took tests so they would know I was not cheating or slacking off. I am an autistic person, so Nora was allowed to give me extra time to take the tests. I didn't need it. My education continues. Now I am self-schooling in my chosen fields of interest."

"How are you doing?"

"I am doing very well, thank you. How are you doing?"

Matthes laughed easily. "Oh! Yes, well, I am doing well too, Rickey, thank you for asking. What I meant was, how are you doing in your continuing education?"

"Now that I take no tests and receive no grades, my level of achievement is impossible to ascertain objectively. But I am satisfied with what I'm learning and how fast I'm learning it. I am a quick study, yes."

"What things do you like?"

"STEM stuff, particularly math. The new math. Calculus is fun. And languages. And discourse analysis. Also, biology, particularly Hegelian taxonomy. And the social hierarchies of great apes and gorillas interest me."

"Are there any things you don't like?"

"I don't like poetry. And I don't like history. And I don't like loud noises, and I don't like being touched, and I really don't like bright light, and I don't like unfamiliar places, and I don't like people who ask me what I'm feeling."

"Ah, ha. Okay, I'll try to stay away from those things. Is it better if I just stick to facts, Rickey?"

"Much better. Helpful."

"I understand your mom doesn't live here anymore, is that right?"

"That is correct. She's in the wind."

"When did she leave?"

"When I was seven."

"Why do you think she left?"

"Because I am an autistic person, and she couldn't stand autistic people, so she got drunk all the time and then she left."

"Do you miss her?"

"You said you wouldn't ask me how I felt. Are you a social services person? Are you here to take me away?"

Caught off guard, Matthes recoiled. "Oh, no, Rickey. *No.* Like I said, I am here to help Colonel Suits find out about some strange things that have been happening."

"You are not being helpful. You said we were supposed to be helpful," Rickey said.

"So I did. Sorry. Can I ask about your dad?"

Rickey turned rigid, and she stared up at the ceiling. "You mean my *father?* What do you want to know?"

"Well, for a start, where is he?"

Rickey began slapping her palms on the table, and her answer came in a peculiar rush.

"I don't know where he is. I never know where he is. I don't know where he is going, and I don't know where he has been. And I don't care. My father means less than nothing to me. Nothing to me. Nothing to me. You are not being helpful."

I'll give this to Dr. Sylvia Matthes: she knew how to pivot.

"What if we went back to your schooling, Rickey. Would that be okay?"

"The facts, just the facts, just the facts." Rickey was shaking her head vigorously back and forth. "Helpful."

"Have you ever studied anything about electricity or electronics?"

"Well, which one? They're not the same, you know."

"What's the difference?"

"Electrical devices convert electrical energy into another form of energy like heat, light or sound. Electronic devices control the flow of electrons for performing particular tasks." Rickey recited this in a hollow monotone, as if her voice were artificially generated.

"Rickey, do you know what those words mean?"

"Yes. No. Well, sort of."

"Then where did you learn to say that?"

"In a book. But I didn't read all of it because I didn't like it. It was very abstract."

"Do you have any electronic devices?"

"Yes, a TV set and my electric toothbrush. Our telephone is electric. You might say my calculator is electric, but I think it's electronic."

"Did you ever build any electronic equipment, Rickey?"

"No way, Jose. I'm a kid."

"Do you know anybody who did?"

"My father had one mean motherfucker of an electronic surveillance console. But he didn't build it. He bought it from a college."

"Oh, that's interesting. What did he use it for?"

"Listening. For a while there he was one mean motherfucker listener."

"What did he listen to?"

Rickey stood up abruptly from the table, threw her arms out, operatic fashion, and burst into song, her voice shrill and tinny. "Aberdeen, Aberdeen, prettiest town I ever seen, people there don't treat you mean, in Aberdeeeen, my Aberdeeeen." She bowed and sat down.

"Did you ever use your father's surveillance equipment?"

"I wasn't allowed to touch it."

"What happened to it?"

"It all burned up."

"How did that happen?"

"I touched it." Rickey clasped her arms across her chest and looked up at the ceiling.

"I don't understand, Rickey."

"He was away. I wanted to see the oscilloscope. I loved watching the oscilloscope. One day when he was there, he let me watch it for three hours. It was very soothing. So, I wanted to watch the oscilloscope."

"Do you know what an oscilloscope does?"

"It makes wonderful wavy lines that dance, dance, dance. When I watch it, I can feel my mind dance, dance, dance."

"What happened when your father was away?"

"I didn't know how to switch just the oscilloscope on, so I turned all the switches on. But then everything went on all at once and made this terrible whining noise and something in one of the cabinets was going boom-boom-boom and I was very frightened and the things in the hangar got too hot and the wires started on fire and the automatic sprayer system went on and the fire got worse because you're not supposed to use water on electrical fires, and I tried to beat the fire out with my smock but it caught on fire, and I started to catch on fire, and Tryg Sletland wrapped his coat around me and put me out, and Tryg Sletland saved all of our lives because he sprayed foam on the fire but everything was burned up and wrecked so they took it out and threw it away."

Now tears were streaming down Rickey's face. Her shoulders were shaking. Sylvia Matthes impulsively reached out toward her, and Rickey recoiled, toppling off the kitchen stool. Behind Rickey, Nora was shaking her head in warning: *Do not try to touch Rickey.* Tryg Sletland suggested that everybody take a break.

After Rickey had had a few Ritz crackers with peanut butter and caught her breath, the group reconvened, and the video cameras were switched back on. Now Suits was sitting next to Sylvia Matthes, and Rickey clearly was uncomfortable with that.

"Rickey," Matthes said, "it's too bad all that equipment got burned up. Before it burned up, did anyone else use it besides your father?"

"How would I know?" Rickey responded. "Why don't you just ask them? Turn on your video machine and ask them. They're adults. They can talk." The hostility in Rickey's voice was stunning. This was not the same adolescent who have been submissively responding to Sylvia Matthes minutes before.

"I think that's a good idea, Rickey. We should interview them, too, just like you. That's only fair."

"Helpful," said Rickey, looking down.

"Now at some point there was new equipment, right?"

"*At some point*, yes," said Rickey sarcastically. "But I never saw it all put together. Hugh and Tryg said I couldn't go in the hangar anymore."

"So, you don't know if there were new oscilloscopes?"

"There were six oscilloscopes. Two Westinghouses, two Raytheons, one Wei Lung, and one from Sundstrand."

"If you didn't see the equipment, how do you know there were six oscilloscopes?"

"I went to the auction with Tryg. I saw his list. I got to wave the bidding paddle. We got everything on the list. Tryg said we screwed 'em blue."

Bailey Suits leaned in toward Rickey. "Now, this new equipment. Did Hugh or Tryg or Nora use the new equipment?" he asked sharply.

Rickey froze. She looked petrified.

Suits lost his patience. "Oh, c'mon, Rickey, just answer the question!"

On the spot, Rickey invented a new behavior, something we'd never seen before: she moved her face to within a couple of feet of Bailey Suits and shrieked at the top of her lungs. Suits jumped to his feet and leaped back, his eyes wide. In the next room, I heard Rickey's cry, felt the blood rush to my head, and rushed into the kitchen, my arm pulled back and ready to throw a punch.

I was stopped by a stop-action tableau: Suits was frozen in

a crouched defensive posture with his fists balled, Rickey was gasping with her forehead down on the table, Nora rested her hands gently on Rickey's shoulders, and Tryg was still running video. Matthes looked surprisingly composed.

"I'm very, very sorry, Rickey. We weren't helpful. I think it's best if we wrap up this conversation now." She signaled their video tech to shut the camera off; I noticed that Tryg kept our camera running.

Colonel Sylvia Matthes, MD, Ph.D., stood and smoothed her skirt. "Thank you for your help, Rickey. I know this was not easy for you." She took Bailey Suits by the elbow and headed for the kitchen door, their tech following with their camcorder and tripod. At the door, she stopped and turned back to Rickey, as if she had suddenly thought of something. "Rickey, can I ask just one more thing? When your father came back, did he like the new equipment you had gotten for him?"

To my astonishment, Rickey demeanor had completely changed. She had calmed, and now she made eye contact with Matthes. She answered deliberately, her affect flat. "When my father came back to Bo Manor and saw my burns, he just went crazy. He rushed out to the hangar, and when he came back in, he was waving his hands and shouting. He yelled in Hugh's face and hit him across the back of the head with this hand. He told Tryg he was fucking fired. He said to Nora that she was...was... *grossly incompetent.* I was hiding in the corner. My father came over, pulled me up and grabbed me by the wrists, right where my burns were. Then he slapped me across the face. Right where my burns were. He was pretty out of control.

"That was the only time my father ever hit me in my life. I ran out of the house down to my secret place in the orchard. I came back in after dark. By then he was gone. So no, I don't think he liked the new equipment."

40

An Intentional Community

"I MAY HAVE FOUND SOMETHING," NORA SAID OVER BREAKFAST.
Tryg was there. Rickey was not.

"What's that?" I responded.

"There is an 'intentional community'—that's what they call it—called Winston Hills Village up on four hundred and fifty acres in Chester Country, Pennsylvania. I sent away for their materials. It's sort of like a commune, I guess, except that it's a not-for-profit corporation and it's been around a long time. The village has eighteen houses, and about a hundred adults of all ages live there. About forty have some sort of developmental disability, twenty are elderly. The rest are resident volunteers and their families."

"What's their 'thing?'"

"Their thing?"

"You know, their religion, their philosophy, their belief set, their 'guiding values.'"

"Apparently this place is pretty well thought of in the mental health world, and it's certainly well-endowed financially. There are several different Winston Hills communities, and yes, they all talk about cultivating inclusion, tolerance and a rich spiritual life."

"Oh, boy," said Tryg. "Sounds like the woo-woo fringe."

"All the communities adhere to something called Anthroposophy. Created around the turn of the century by an Austrian named Rudolf Steiner. They use an approach to education called Waldorf, and all the communities put a lot of emphasis on what they call a 'biodynamic' approach to agriculture. They also have their own views on medicine, therapies, and the arts. They run some sustainable small businesses that collaborate in co-ops with other local businesses. They sell their produce, sponsor cultural festivals, like that."

"Does this sound like Rickey to you?" I asked.

"I'm not sure exactly what it sounds like," said Nora. "If you talk about 'a common dream of social, cultural, and economic renewal, which is what their materials describe, and I'd say no, it does not necessarily sound like a great fit for our autonomous little anti-social savant. They preach inclusion of people with mental handicaps, but not exactly Rickey's kind of mental handicaps."

"Then why are we talking about this?"

"Because, Hugh, if I may say so, we're a getting little desperate at this point. Maybe this actually is an option. It's a community run by caring people, it has a lot of farm space and running room, it supports people who can't fit in elsewhere, and it believes in putting everyone to work. I'd at least like to give it a look."

So we did. We made an appointment for a tour and orientation. Now all we had to do was to explain the trip to Rickey. I decided the most effective approach was to bull-rush her, to ask neither permission nor forgiveness, to keep it short and matter-of-fact. And vague. We convened in the living room.

"Rickey, we are looking at alternative places to live, after it's not possible for us to stay at Bo Manor anymore. There's this place up in Chester County we heard about and want to see, an unusual community that runs a big farm, as well as a lot of little businesses. They've been around a long time, and they're well known for how well they accommodate people with special needs."

"People like you and Nora?" Rickey said innocently.

I could not help but smile. But I pressed on. "No, Rickey, people like you."

Her eyes narrowed. "Is this an institution?"

"No, Rickey. It's more like a town. Actually, it's a corporation. A non-profit corporation that runs a farm, owns a bunch of houses, runs its own school, provides social and medical services. Pretty unique place, actually."

"How many people live there?"

"I think about a hundred. All ages. All kinds of interests."

"And you want me to go with you to see this place."

"Yeah. We could go ourselves and then come back and tell you about it, but it would be better if you were able to check it out yourself."

"For sure. You guys wouldn't know what to look for. Look, is this a done deal and I'm just being dragged in after you've already made a decision?"

"No. This is not like that."

"Will my opinion matter?"

"Not only will your opinion matter, Rickey, your opinion will be decisive."

"How long will this little adventure take?" asked Rickey.

⚙ ⚙ ⚙

BEFORE HEADING UP THROUGH CHESTER COUNTY'S GLORIOUS FARM country, we sent the Winston Hills people a brief summary of Rickey's medical and developmental profile, authored jointly by Nora and Dexter. We let Rickey read it before sending it off, and she said it seemed fine to her, although maybe it understated her mathematical skills and language aptitudes.

To my surprise, Winston Hills Village was only about thirty miles from Bo Manor. Rickey, surprisingly, kept her opinions and reservations to herself, riding quietly in the back seat during the drive up. Was she being coy? Why not? After all, Nora and I were being coy.

We were met by Winston Hills' director of development,

a singularly laid-back gentleman named Robert Sklar, dressed casually in chinos and a striking blue loose-fitting Amish shirt. Probably in his sixties, he was engaging and personable. No apparent hard-sell or wild-eyed religious zealotry. The hardest he pushed was to say, "I've been here thirty-five years, and I've seen what this kind of community can do—and can't do. It really works for the people it works for, but I'm not going to pretend it's a utopian community that works for everybody."

"Are there any autistic people living in the community?" Nora asked.

"Well, we don't use diagnostic labels, but we have five residents you could describe as 'neuro-atypical.' One very high-functioning, three functional, but non-verbal. All five look pretty well-adjusted to me, within their personal limits."

I relaxed my defenses a bit.

The village was clean and attractive in a 1950's kind of way, the houses modest and rustic. No white picket fences, but an abundance of rocking chairs on the porches. No TV antennas. We visited the communal barns and nurseries, the crafts production building, the combination school building and community gathering center. If Tryg had been with us, he would have been impressed. This place was run right.

I was pleased that Sklar spent more time talking to Rickey than to us. He treated her like an adult, and he respected her questions. She seemed to warm to the attention. Out of the blue, she said, "I want to know more about Rudolph Steiner. Was he for real or some fringe thinker?"

Sklar smiled. "In his time, which was from about 1900 until he died in 1925, he was considered the real deal, both in Europe and in the U.S. In Austria, he was a respected architect and economist. However, mostly he became known as a social reformer who focused a lot of his thinking on how kids learn and develop. But he also was a very spiritual guy, and his philosophy, which he called Anthroposophy, sought to combine moral, spiritual, and creative values. Anthroposophy is not a religion, Rickey, it's a mind-set.

"We are not a cult here, Rickey. As an 'intentional community,' that is, people who come together by choice, our intentions put a lot of focus on acceptance and inclusion. We place greater emphasis on collaboration than on competition. We're nice people, and the kids who come out of our Waldorf schools are nice, responsible kids."

"Thank you," said Rickey. "That was really very helpful."

During the rest of the orientation, Rickey comported herself politely and appropriately, if a little woodenly. She showed strong interest in the machine shop and the farm tractors. Finally, she said to Nora, "If it's all right, I'd like to head home now." To Sklar, she said, "Thank you. You've given me a lot to think about."

We piled into the Ford and headed south. After a few miles during which Rickey said nothing, Nora turned to her and asked brightly, "Well. What did you think?"

"Not on your life," said Rickey. "I'd kill myself first. Seriously."

41

Endgame

TRYG AND SIMONE ASKED IF THEY COULD SPEAK WITH ME AND NORA in the living room. Nora and I were already seated when they walked into the room. Holding hands. Looking...edgy.

"We have good news and bad news," said Tryg, deadpan. Simone stood close by him, looking up into his face, looking loyal.

"Why not start with the good?" I said.

"Okay, the good news is that Simone and I are getting married."

"That's wonderful!" Nora and I said simultaneously, only Nora said "wonderful" and I said "terrific."

"You really are a marvelous couple," Nora said, "and of course we wish you every happiness. When's the big day?"

"Doesn't matter. Pretty soon. No big ceremony. We want to be married more than go through all the rigmarole of getting married, if you catch my drift."

"So, where you gonna have the wedding?" Nora asked.

There was a dead silence. Tryg and Simone looked at each other. I saw him squeeze her hand.

Tryg shuffled his feet. "Hugh, Nora...we're not going to tell you. I know it sounds shitty, but we are not going to give you any information that someone could use to track us down. Can you understand that?"

"I understand it and agree with it," I said. Nora was shocked, reeling.

"It will be a small ceremony. Like probably just the two of us. And Ray, of course. It will not be in the United States. After we get married, we'll go house hunting...or farm hunting."

There was a long pause. Nora and I looked at each other: *Well, this is it.*

"I see," I said. "I guess that's the bad news."

"Yes, Hugh, I guess that it is."

I can't say that I hadn't seen this coming. When I considered Tryg's risks and options as we wound down the Hole in the Wall Gang, leaving the states seemed high on the list of good ideas. Why the obviousness of marrying Simone and leaving the country hadn't previously occurred to me, I honestly don't know. Denial, perhaps.

"Okay, then!" I said with forced enthusiasm. "Let's talk details later. Right now, let's crack a bottle of Hermann Bayard's best champagne and drink a toast to the future."

❂   ❂   ❂

THE FOLLOWING MORNING, TRYG AND I HAD A LENGTHY BUSINESS meeting.

"I'm sorry just to spring it on you as a surprise, Hugh."

"There was no way not to spring it, Tryg. Either the decision was made, or it wasn't. No bigger surprise than my blind-siding you guys with all the TIA stuff. And Tryg..."

I paused and smiled. "It is absolutely the right decision, the best course of action. You have my full support, and I am going to do everything in my power to turn things into a 'happily ever after' thing for you and Simone. One question. What's Ray going to do?"

"All I know is that he won't be with us, and he won't be in the United States. He knows the score, and he doesn't want to

303

go to jail any more than we do. We've told him we'll fund him for three years, then he's on his own. He's pretty freaked, but we think he's cool."

Tryg had brought a checklist of action items. First, he suggested that Bohemia Manor Farm cease farming operations, that we just let the fields lie fallow. He knew the tenants were going to be surprised and upset, and he suggested giving each one $25,000 as compensation for their unexpected loss in income. I shrugged an okay.

And so it went: we worked down Tryg's list for another hour—all the farm's vendors and service people, where the warranties for the household appliances were kept, who to contact for reshingling the garage. Tryg had schedules and timelines for everything, and if only someone would adhere to them, Bohemia Manor would stay in tip-top shape.

We both knew that no one would, and that Bo Manor wouldn't.

When he was done, Tryg stood and started to leave. I gestured him to sit down.

"Tryg, you have delivered on everything you ever said you'd do. Now it's my chance to deliver. But my delivery has some conditions."

He raised his eyebrows.

"I want you to move fast on this. First, I want you to change your name here in Cecil County. Officially. File a petition with the court. Use a nice ordinary name—the kind where there is bound to be hundreds of them, like Bob Jones or something. Get a new driver's license. Even more important, get a new passport. As soon as you can.

"When you settle wherever you've decided to live, and my opinion is that it should be a country that has no extradition agreements with the U.S., you should change your name again. Again, choose a common, unremarkable name, okay? Oh, when you guys get married, have Simone legally change her name, too. Jane Smith, or whatever. Then, and only then, use this."

I handed him a five by seven note card that I had laminated.

On it was typed the name of an offshore private bank in Grand Cayman, an account number, and a contact name. And a current account balance: $3,477,990.

"Tryg," I said. "Almost all Hermann Bayard's money is now in offshore accounts. All except for some small working accounts here in the US. It's all in private banks with numbered accounts. All different kinds of accounts, all kinds of assets. As we go our separate ways, Hermann is going to provide well for all of us. Except me, of course. I can't take it with me."

Tryg winced.

"Sorry. Bad attempt at gallows humor. That card is your exit visa, but don't screw up how you use it. When you are legally Joe Blow of Kokomo and happily married, you call up the guy on this card in Grand Cayman. He will know who you are, even if he does not recognize your new name. I will give him a recognition code. It will be 'John Deere.' That's your door-opener, the account number alone won't do it.

"This place is a first-class offshore tax shelter. The best. It's clean, it's legal, and it is impenetrable. I think it probably is the most secure and most discreet of all the institutions I use, and that's saying a lot, because no one is going to get into any of Hermann Bayard's accounts, even if somehow they get his account numbers. I recommend you use this institution as your bank for the rest of your life—and Simone's.

"So anyway, when you're all set, you call this guy. You tell him you want to withdraw every last dollar. You open a new account under Simone's name, put all your money in it. They will charge you six thousand dollars to start and three thousand a year for account maintenance. It's a bargain, just for the security. This guy will be your man. Whenever you like, you call him up and say, 'Hi, I want some money, please.' He'll get it to you, lightning fast, nice and liquid, no questions asked.

"Now the amount on that card is just your working capital. You two will have to find a place to live, right? If you agree to live out in the country, on some estate or farm with lots of acres and a few recreational sheep, maybe a workshop with lots of nice equipment in it, you call our friend at the bank and have him call me. If I am still alive, I will put another two million dollars into that account. But you must use it for real estate. No blowing it at the casino in Monaco or Singapore."

Tryg's head dropped, and his shoulders began to shake. There was an audible plop as a tear hit the coffee table.

"Hugh, I don't know what to say."

"I don't want you to say anything. I just want you to understand that loyalty and competence have their rewards. You know I don't do emotion real well, Tryg. I think I'm a good friend, but I know I've never been a friendly friend. But I want you to know that I have valued…I have *treasured*…our relationship. Hermann and I give you our thanks.

"Oh, and one more thing. If you and Simone have a boy, name him Hugh. If you have a second son, name him Hermann."

❂   ❂   ❂

I HAD PUT MYSELF ON A FITNESS REGIMEN, WHISTLING PAST THE graveyard, so to speak. I had been extending the length of my daily walks, and now walked out to 213 and back every day, about a mile. If it wasn't doing me any good, it wasn't doing me any harm, either.

I was just starting back down the driveway when I saw a white van on Route 213 switch on its right turn indicator and turn into Bo Manor. The painted letters on the side looked like a giant monogram. The letters on the top, blue, in a squared-off modern font, said MSF in capital letters. Then there was a broad black horizontal dividing line, and underneath that, in the same font, only in red letters, it read DWB.

The van stopped next to me, and the driver reached over to roll down the passenger window.

"Mr. Touré?"

"No, I'm Mr. Ullam, the General Manager of this farm. Mr. Touré doesn't live here, but he's certainly a good friend. Was he expecting to meet you here?"

The man reached into his pencil pocket and pulled out a business card. When he spoke, it was in a thick accent I could not identify. It sounded like he said, "I'm Mickey Wrench-in. I was asked to meet Ms. Dadmun and Mr. Touré here this afternoon."

What his card said was, *Mikal Roentgen, Chief of Operations, Doctors Without Borders.* It listed a New York City address.

"Oh! Roentgen!" I said. "As in the inventor of the X-ray."

"Ja! My great-great uncle Wilhelm," said Mikal, beaming. "Pretty bright guy. Am I making a disturbance?"

"No, not at all. You say Nora is expecting you?"

"Ja, Nora and Dexter both. Shall I give you a lift to the house?"

Nora seemed calm and composed, but Dexter was clearly flustered when Roentgen and I walked in together. We repaired to the living room. Dexter spoke first.

"Hugh, we think we have most of our plans nailed down, and we asked Mikal to come down so we could explain everything to you."

I confess I was peeved. I don't like having machinations going on behind my back. "Oh, and just what are your plans?"

There was a long silence. Roentgen seemed undisturbed, sitting back in his chair with an amiable smile.

"Okay. Here goes. Nora and I are leaving the country together, and we are going to be working for *Médicins Sans Frontières.* You may know it as *Doctors Without Borders.*"

"I know it under both names," I said. "Fantastic organization. Out to save the world and does a pretty good job of it."

Mikal Roentgen beamed. I turned to Nora.

"Well, I must say, this takes me by surprise. You're going …together?"

Nora leaned forward and rested her hands on her knees. "I'm sorry. We didn't intend to blind-side you, Hugh. It's just that when we first reached out to MSF to see if they had a need for an emergency room doc and a registered nurse, things began moving really fast."

Roentgen sat up in his chair. "Is true, Mr. Ullam. When

I'm hearing their backgrounds, I'm putting a lot of pressure on them. I confess, I was doing everything I could to hasten a decision because we have an immediate, desperate need for them. Still, I'm not thinking I overrode their will. They are ready and committed, ja."

My head was spinning. "You're going together."

"Yep," said Dexter.

"You getting married?"

"We may, we may not," Nora said. "But we're together, Hugh. This is not a job decision, this is a life decision. It's been forced on us sooner than we'd like, but it's a good decision. We're going to be together, and if it turns out we can work together in something rewarding, that's a lot more than just frosting on the cake."

What did I feel at that moment?

Too soon! Too soon!

I felt like I was suddenly losing my footing, as if the solid floor of my world was tilting, as if all the walls of my life were tumbling down. Yes, I knew that things had to change at some point, but so soon? *So soon?* I was not ready for this, not prepared to be confronted with a *fait accompli*, a decision in which I had had no voice.

"Where? Where will they be going?" I said to Roentgen, then caught myself. "Wait a minute, wait a minute, don't tell me. I should not know where they can be found."

Roentgen looked at me curiously. "Why shouldn't you know? Are they running from the law or something?"

Oops! How do I get out of this one?

"Mikal, due largely to serious health issues I have, our situation here is deteriorating. We have to make some quick decisions about what to do next. Also, our employer, Hermann Bayard, is not popular with his German family, and we've been getting signals that they're planning to take legal action against him, basically to try to take his money away. If that happens all of us here could be involved as witnesses. We are very loyal to Hermann, and we've agreed that to help protect him, we will make it as difficult as possible for anyone to find us and subject us to legal process."

If this explanation triggered alarms, Mikael Roetgen didn't show it. "I see, I see. Okay, as you wish. I can say this. As for where they go, there are a number of places where Dexter and Nora can be very valuable. Incredibly valuable. All of them are war zones. Places with open conflict. Places where there are hundreds of casualties monthly. Africa, the Middle East, several African countries. Dexter and Nora will be allowed to choose their poison."

I tried to picture these places. Hot, brown, dusty, *crazy*. Bullets and bombs and fire and insane amounts of depraved cruelty. I tried to juxtapose my mental picture of ER service in the midst of open warfare with Nora cooking coconut pancakes with walnuts in the Bohemia Manor Farm kitchen on a Sunday morning. I could not help but shudder.

"When?"

"I gave two weeks' notice to the Emergency Room Service this morning," said Dexter. "I'm going to be working every day until I leave."

"And that's when you're going, Nora?"

"I'm going to stay on a few weeks longer, wrap up loose ends. Then I leave to join Dexter."

A wave of nausea washed over me, then a wave of intense anger. I slapped my hands on the arms of my chair.

"*A couple of weeks?* Well, the hell with that! You're abandoning me just as all the shit drops on my head? After all our time together, is this the loyalty you show? Christ! You're just going to drop Rickey in my lap?"

I expected Nora to soften, to tear up, to back down. Instead, it was the opposite. Her jaw tightened, she sat up in her chair, and she looked me straight in the eye. She brushed her hair back from her face, almost flaunting her birthmark.

She spoke slowly, deliberately. No tiptoeing, no uptalk.

"I know Rickey is going to...to...take this very hard. She's going to make a scene. I know she's likely to lose control and yell and curse us—curse me, of course, but curse you, too, because you've always represented safety and security to her. Rickey has been in denial, and it's going to be horrible when her all-encompassing security blanket is torn away.

"*But…it…cannot…be…helped.* It rips me apart that your life is at such great risk, and it pains me that you're going to conclude that I am betraying your trust as well as abandoning Rickey.

"So be it. Tryg is taking care of himself, and I get to take care of myself, too. Instead of just pampering a single handicapped person, I have the chance to make a huge impact, to save a lot of lives, to add deep meaning to my work and my life. And I get to do it standing alongside a man I dearly love and deeply respect.

"Can you possibly be so selfish that you expect me to walk away from that?"

❁　　　❁　　　❁

NORA PADDED QUIETLY INTO MY OFFICE AND SLID INTO THE CHAIR across from my desk. It was three days after Mikal Roentgen's visit.

"Don't worry, I'm not going to take your head off," I said. "I think I've gotten back under control, gained a little perspective."

"Hugh, I am sorry. I wish there were some other solution."

"Other than dying? Yeah, I wish there was some other solution, too."

"I've talked to Mikal. Dex is still leaving in two weeks, but I am staying here for another month. I've signed the papers and approved our first assignment, but Mikal says our situation warrants a compassionate leave for me. During that time, we've got to bring Rickey into the loop, interview someone to serve as her full-time caregiver, and find a place for them to live."

"Sounds like a plan," I said.

"Please don't be sarcastic, Hugh. I really am trying to help in any way I can. I'm sure that there are scores of possible living arrangements, but for something that can be done quickly, that place you mentioned in Savannah sounds like it pushes all the buttons. I have a list here of a group of medical practices and social service agencies in the Savannah area that specialize in working with handicapped adults, including three that focus particularly on people on the autistic spectrum."

"The what?"

"That's what they're calling it now—the autistic spectrum. Rather than simply saying, 'yes, you're autistic or no, you're not,' they recognize that autism does not have convenient diagnostic boxes. A person's symptoms can fall somewhere along a continuum, and you provide support and services based on where they fall. As one expert put it, 'If you are dealing with an individual with autism, you are dealing with an individual.'"

"Where do *you* think Rickey falls on this spectrum?"

"I bet you couldn't get two experts anywhere to agree on that. She really is unique. As I told you from the moment you arrived, Rickey bridges a whole lot of categories."

"So, what's your point?"

"I'm going to look for referrals to caregiver candidates in and around Atlanta and Savannah, but I've got to be careful of running into people who stick autistic adults in rigid categories. We both know that Rickey needs a lot of structure, but she also needs all the running room she can get. I agree with you now. The best solution for Rickey at this point is to buy her a house and hire a full-time companion. It just won't be me. So, we have to find someone knowledgeable about the spectrum."

"So, what are you going to do?

"I'm going to get on the phone full time and try to get a list of qualified candidates from referral sources down south. Then I'll fly to wherever they are and interview as many as I can. If I find a stand-out candidate, I'm going to offer her—and for sure it will be a her—a job and a lot of money. And I'm going to pray."

"Pray for what?"

"Hugh, we're trying to set all this stuff up as if it were a clockwork machine that will run by itself forever. But if something goes wrong, you're going to be gone and I'm going to be gone and no one's going to be around to do damage control."

"Well, it will be the trustee's job to do that."

"You can't expect some trustee to go beyond handling Rickey's financial affairs and maybe step in to do crisis management, hopefully years and years down the road, if ever."

"All we can do is the best we can do, Nora. I know there's no fail-safe. But I am going to call one of my offshore guys and ask if he'd like to be the trustee for Rickey's personal affairs. For a flat fee of, say, a million dollars. If he says yes, I can rest a little easier. Die a little easier."

❂   ❂   ❂

I DIALED THE NUMBER ON MIKAL ROENTGEN'S BUSINESS CARD. HE answered on the first ring.

"Roentgen."

I took a deep breath. "Mikal, this is Hugh Ullam down at Bohemia Manor."

"Yes, Hugh." I sensed no tension, no defensiveness in his tone.

"First, I want to apologize for subjecting you to my outburst last week. Dealing with explosive anger should not be in your job description."

He laughed. "Actually, it is, Hugh. If you imagine the stresses and crises and insanity that surround our work, you must see that explosive anger goes with the territory. We're all mad all the time, even when we got our peace faces on. At MSF, we live in a world of explosions, ja?"

"Still, I'm embarrassed. I don't think that's what you expected when you drove down to sign a few papers with Nora and Dexter."

"Hugh, it's okay. We all are making hard decisions here. I didn't know the news would come out the way it did, but Dexter and Nora had explained their difficult situation to me. You know who it was that said, 'you can't make an omelet without breaking a few eggs?' Josef Stalin. We had to break a few eggs, Hugh. I knew that sometime you would be put in an untenable position regarding Rickey and Nora. I knew that, and I pressed hard for

Nora to leave anyway. MSF needs her more than Rickey Bayard needs her, ja?"

I took a deep breath. "How can I argue with that, Mikael? You are an angel of mercy, you and your people, and what you need is support, not being pissed on."

"Thank you, Hugh. Thank you for understanding. For accepting."

"Done deal. Enough said. On another note, Mikal, and the main reason I called, do you people have too much money?"

His laugh was a sharp bark. "Ja, Hugh, we have so much we're giving it all back, ja. What, you want to make a contribution?"

"Mikal, what I want is for you not to ask me a lot of questions. Just let me say that I am in a position to make sure that a significant contribution is made to MSF, subject to certain conditions."

"Uh-oh, this sounds skeevy. Should I be suspicious?"

"Well, let me put it this way. When you were a kid, or even a young adult, did you ever play the game where someone challenged you to imagine what you would do if you won the million-dollar lottery but had to spend it all in one day?"

"Hugh, I play that game every day. But now both the stakes and benefits are higher. I beg for donors to let me play that game."

"Mikal, if MSF got an unrestricted lump sum grant of, say, five million dollars, could it spend it all in a year?"

Roentgen snorted. "What, you joking with me?"

"Just answer the question. Unrestricted grant, anonymous at the outset and remaining anonymous forever after, paid in cash in a single up-front payment. Five million dollars."

"Yes, Hugh. I could spend five million. Easy."

"What about ten million?"

"I think maybe you are trying to make me cry. We are desperate, all the time desperate. You have no idea how tight our budget is, how constantly short we are of all the things that cost money. Ten million would have a huge impact. Beyond huge. A staggering impact."

"Okay. What about twenty million? Remember, you'd have to guarantee that you absolutely would spend it all in one year.

If anything was left over, the penalty would be that you'd have to give the remainder back. Could you spend twenty million?"

"Try me," Roentgen said.

"Okay, I will," I said.

❂   ❂   ❂

I HAD THE SENSATION THAT THINGS WERE REALLY ROLLING—LIKE A rolling deck on ship caught in a storm-ravaged sea. It was unbearably sad, but the sheer momentum of events kept the sadness from taking hold and immobilizing us. We knew we had ground to cover. Tryg, Simone, Dexter, Nora, me—we were all chugging along. All except Rickey, of course, whom we allowed to live in the library and spend all her time in her present pursuit of Sanskrit and thence to the Upanishads.

Then I had had another TIA, this one strange because I had no awareness that it was happening and, afterwards, no recollection that it had happened. I found myself tucked in bed with Nora hovering over me. When my mind cleared, I learned I had lost three days of my life. Out cold, or at least out to lunch.

This time there were residual symptoms. I began to feel noticeably weaker, not just in specific limbs, but generally, like I was dragging a hundred pounds of chains around in a backpack. I was sleeping more. I was aware that I simply was not…sharp.

I was napping one afternoon when Nora came in and shook me awake. She was positively vibrating.

"*What did you do!*"

I was groggy, confused. That is exactly what Giala Billimoria used to yell at her Dalmatian puppy when it pissed on her carpet at Akers.

"What did you do!"

Click. I grasped what Nora was on about. "Oh, that. I asked Hermann Bayard if he would give Doctors Without Borders twenty million dollars, seeing as how he wasn't using it anymore. In his own quiet way, he agreed. His only requirement is that they spend it fast, so no one could come and take it away from them. Actually, he's giving the money to *Médicins Sans Frontiĕres* in Geneva, not Doctors Without Borders in New York. That way we get the money out of the country. No wait, the money is already out of the country. We—Hermann and me—we're funding the grant from an offshore account, so actually, nothing is coming from the US."

I sat up with effort, slowly rolled my legs over the side of the bed and put my feet on the floor.

"Mikal Roentgen seemed quite pleased," I said calmly. "He gets the drill, knows how I'm doing this. He's okay with it. I like a man with a good set of situation ethics."

"I am speechless. Can you imagine how much good that will do?"

"Well, I'm only sad that I probably won't be able to match that grant year after year until every last one of Hermann Bayard's dimes is gone, but *que sera, sera*. And, of course, I have to leave enough to provide for Rickey."

Tears began streaming down Nora's cheeks. Her sobbing came in soft hiccups. She reached for my hand, and, to my surprise, giving it to her came easily.

"Wait," I said. "I'm not quite done with you, Nora Dadmun. Would you go over to my desk and bring me that red plastic folder?"

From one of the back pockets of the accordion folder I pulled out a laminated card, nearly identical to the one I had given Trygve Sletland.

"Listen carefully to me," I said sternly. "I don't want to have to repeat this. First, I want you to call the bank that's listed on this card and ask for the contact listed on this card. This is serious banking business, but you will find him very jolly, sometimes even a little silly. But always respectful. Say my name, then say your name, then recite the account number on this card. Then say, 'Transfer.' He'll say, 'How much?' You say, 'Sixteen and a half million pounds.'

"He'll say, 'Do you realize that's the whole account?' You say, 'Yes.' He'll say something like, 'Destination?' You'll give him the name of this other bank in the Caribbean, tell him the account number, tell him the name of the account rep. He'll read the Caribbean account number back to you. He'll say 'Thank you very much. Do you want us to keep the account open here?" You might as well say yes. Never know when you might need an extra offshore account. He'll say, 'Well, all right, then,' and 'How's the weather in Earleville, Maryland?' and you'll say, 'Just fine, thank you,' and you'll say, 'G-day,' and bingo, you'll be comparatively rich."

Nora screeched. "What?"

"Then you call the guy at the Caribbean bank. Rather stuffy chap, but you could put flaming bamboo sticks under his fingernails and he still would not divulge any confidences. After the account is set up, you'll get to know him well. He's your personal banker. You just call up, say, 'Hi, this is Nora again, would you be good enough to wire me another three thousand pounds, just to tide me over to the end of the month?' Easy as pie."

"But Hugh, I have money. I've been saving whatever I've been paid for years."

"How much?"

"Now up to a little over two million dollars," Nora said proudly. "I invested well."

"Well, now you've got more. I'm not going to tell you to use it wisely. I'm just going to tell you to use it. Use it all, Nora. And when you make some big, silly expenditure, think of me. I meant well."

    ✿   ✿   ✿

THEN THINGS GOT REALLY TENSE, REALLY FAST.

Rickey was waiting for us as Nora and I drove in from the airport. She had been sitting on the front step, evidently waiting for us. Now she stood with her hands on her hips. As we pulled to a stop, she stalked over toward the Ford Nora and pounded her hands on the hood.

"Where have you been?" she yelled.

Nora stepped out of the car. "Didn't Hugh tell you?"

"All he said was that you had to take a trip on 'family business.' You always told me your family is somewhere out in Wisconsin and that you hadn't had contact with them for years. *So, what takes you out there now?*"

Rickey was shouting at the top of her lungs.

Nora turned to me. "Oh, no, Hugh, no. For heaven's sake, is that really all you said to her?" Now she too was shouting at me.

I respond poorly to yelling, and I was not about to be bullied. "There is a time and a place for full disclosure. I wanted Rickey to hear it from you, hear what you had learned."

Nora tipped her head back and closed her eyes. Sighed deeply. She looked out over the golden fields that separated Bo Manor and its courtyard from the steely gray of the Bohemia River, today rippled with whitecaps.

She sighed again and turned to Rickey. "I was in Savannah, Georgia, Rickey. Trying to find a new place where you can live without being disturbed. Let's go inside and talk about it."

At the breakfast table, I spoke first. "Okay Rickey, you know the score, but I need to remind you that with Hermann's death you were left with no legal guardian, and the moment the social services people found you and found that you were a dependent minor, which you are, they could place you an institution of their choosing.

"We were not going to let that happen. With no legal right to Hermann's money, we have used it anyway. Basically, I became a criminal, and Nora and Tryg also became criminals—although Tryg was already a convicted felon—so that you could preserve your life here.

"Not to be melodramatic, Rickey, but I could die—or be totally incapacitated—at any moment. At that point, not only will you all lose the only person who is capable of managing the finances of this farm, you will lose the figurehead who has been claiming to be legally in charge all these years. The Bo Manor years are coming to a close, Rickey. The members of the Hole in the Wall Gang now have to go their separate ways, and pronto.

Nora and Tryg, and even Dexter, because he knows we've been perpetrating a fraud. They all have to go someplace they can't be found.

"And, of course, we can't leave you unprotected. We have to take care of you. And to the best of our ability, we will. Do you understand?"

Rickey looked down at her placemat, drumming her fingers on the tabletop. She said nothing.

"Tryg and Simone are getting married. They are going far, far away. They will have new names and a new life. And Rickey, after they leave, you can't ever see them again, can't ever talk to them again."

Rickey's eyes grew wide. "*What?* You mean I won't be able to call them or talk to them and go visit them? Oh, no way. You can't do that to me."

"We're not doing it *to you*, Rickey. We're just doing it. Because we have to. No choice, unless you want to lead the police to them. So, no forwarding address, no phone number, no Christmas cards. New names. They will be leaving soon, and that will be good-bye. I'm truly, truly sorry, but that's the way it is.

"As for you, we heard that there's a place away from here, a gated private island community just outside Savannah, where we could set up permanent housekeeping for you. Establish a medical and social services network. Provide for all your needs…safely, securely and for as long as you live."

I turned to Nora, who had been staring at her hands. To my utter astonishment, she reached under the table to her handbag and pulled out a pack of Marlboros. Nora had never smoked, none of us had. She pulled out a cigarette, tamped it on the side of the pack, pulled out a Bic lighter, and lit up. She saw my surprise, my disapproval.

"Screw it. I'm under stress. This is not a good time to pass judgment on me."

She turned to Rickey. "Actually, I am very encouraged. We have to act fast, Rickey, but I think we've found a very workable arrangement. It's not Bo Manor, but it's pretty nice. The Landings is a private community on an island just south of Savannah. It's kind of like a big, big park. It's very beautiful. It is surrounded by the ocean, and it has huge marshes and wetlands. It is a gated community, and it has very tight security. There is a gatehouse people have to pass through to get in, and they have security patrols driving around all around the clock."

Nora pulled a brochure from her handbag and pushed it across the table to Rickey. It was all greens and blues, fairways, greens and ocean and puffy white clouds, aerial views of sweeping vistas, shots of golf courses, lagoons, marshlands, herons, and huge live oaks draped with Spanish moss. Rickey pulled it to her, turned over several pages, dwelled for a moment on a picture of a huge health club, and, expressionless, pushed the brochure back toward Nora.

Nora was trying to keep this from sounding like a sales pitch, but her voice became artificially animated nonetheless. "The island is about twelve miles long. It's got roads for cars, but it also has a network of paths for golf carts. Some people never drive, they just go wherever they want on the island on their golf carts. We would get you your own golf cart. There is a little village on the island, with a supermarket and a fast-food store. So, you could get around on your own and buy some of your own food and kind of do whatever you want. The town also has a library. A lot of people spend time there.

"The Landings Club has four separate clubhouses, all linked to the same membership. You can go to any of the clubhouses, order whatever you want, and just sign a check. No tips, everything gets billed to your account. I had a great conversation with Sue Rosen, who is the manager of one of the clubs called Marshwood. I told her about you, and she said she would be happy to make sure you got good attention and were seated away from other people and that nobody bothered you. She's really nice.

"If you're interested, there's a big health club. It has two Olympic swimming pools."

Nora had run out of breath, and she paused. Rickey remained impassive, her fingers still drumming on the breakfast table.

"I looked at several houses. The prices are very low by northern standards, Hugh. Five hundred thousand gets you a lot of house, like thirty-five hundred square feet. The houses tend to be quite traditional. All the ones I looked at were move-in ready, and they all had big kitchens and three garage bays. One whole bay could be used for a shop for Rickey's tools and equipment."

Rickey looked up.

"Three of them had three bedrooms, one had four. One of the bedrooms could easily be turned into a library and office for Rickey. They all had a large master suite..."

"Who would get the big bedroom," Rickey interrupted. "You or me?"

Nora paled. I saw her hands begin to tremble. I could see the wheels turning: *What to say? How to say it?*

I saw her gather herself, come to a decision point. *This was it.*

"Rickey, I will not be there."

Confusion and disbelief washed across Rickey's face. "What do you mean, you won't be there?"

"Rickey, Dexter and I are leaving the country. Together. We are going to work with a medical organization called Doctors Without Borders. They provide humanitarian medical services in crisis situations around the world. They can desperately use an ER doctor who has worked in war zones and operated with inadequate supplies. They obviously also can use an experienced nurse, too. Rickey, Dexter, and I are starting a new life. I can't tell you where, but it will not be in the United States."

Rickey was struggling to keep herself together, struggling to process the implications of all she was hearing. She began waving her hands randomly in the air.

"But what about this Savannah house? You're not going to be there with me?"

"No, Rickey, I'm not."

Tears sprang from Rickey's eyes and ran down her cheeks, into the corners of her mouth, which were pulled tight with anguish. Her voice cracked. "You can't just leave me alone!"

"We won't, Rickey. We would never do that. Hugh is going

to create an offshore trust to buy the house and pay all your expenses. There will be a financial trustee who will handle all your money needs, an utterly confidential business guy. Just as important, I've been interviewing women to find someone who can be your helper and companion. Just like me. Whoever we get will have to be willing to live with you, cook for you, see to your medical needs and appointments, be your advocate. A permanent, full-time position.

"I interviewed six. I got their names from people active in the local autism services community. I was very impressed with all of them, with their kindness and their sense of commitment. There was one I liked the most, Carolyn Flowers. She is terrific. She's a licensed social worker. She's single. Her husband was killed last year in an auto accident."

Nora paused, clearly struggling to control her emotions. "Her son is seven. He was in the same accident." Nora stopped. Gathered herself. Inhaled sharply. "He is in what they call a permanent vegetative state. He's not going to recover, Rickey, he's never going to wake up."

"I'm very sorry to hear that," said Rickey flatly.

"Rickey, before the accident, her son was on the spectrum."

Rickey blinked. "So?"

"So, Carolyn is an expert on working with autistic people, on understanding them and their needs. Much of her present work is with autistic clients. She said that if you liked, she would be pleased to fly up here to meet you, to get acquainted. I said I'd have to check with you."

A strange change had come over Rickey. She'd hardened and grown rigid, as if someone had poured cement over her, and now it was setting up. She seemed to be looking neither at Nora nor me. The room fell silent.

Finally, Rickey responded. "Sure. What the hell? Bring her up."

I turned to Nora. "I'm assuming she's working. What would we do about that?"

"I told her that I was asking her to serve a single client, to commit to a single client. I told her that her compensation would be paid through a fully funded trust and would exceed anything she could imagine. I also said that the trust would provide at least some of the funding for the care of her son. That did it. Believe me, she's fully on board with all this."

"Does she realize that I will be unavailable and that she will have no further contact with you? That basically, she'll be operating on her own?"

"She does, Hugh. I spelled it all out and I —"

"*Just hold on!*" Rickey burst out, sobs coming in choking gulps. "Is this going to be like Tryg and Simone? Everybody gone forever? You're just going to dump me, and I won't be able to see you again, either? Oh, no you don't! *Oh, no, no, no. NO!*"

"Rickey," I said. "We cannot risk having you and Nora and Dexter stay in contact. To keep them out of jail, we're going to have to get them out of the country. Far, far away. Someplace where the authorities here cannot find them and force them to come back. Somewhere where they will completely start over. They'll probably change their names" – Nora's eyes widened— "and we can't give you information that the cops could squeeze out of you to track them down."

"But I won't tell," Rickey wailed. "I promise I won't tell."

"I appreciate your promise. I'm sure you mean well. But it's just not good enough, Rickey. First, we have to make it hard for anyone investigating what happened here to find you. We have to do everything we can to keep you from ever being pressured to reveal things that would help them find Nora and Tryg and Simone and Dexter. I'm sorry, but we have to keep each other in the dark. All of us."

⚙   ⚙   ⚙

TRYG WORKED FAST. IN A SURPRISINGLY SHORT TIME, THE STATE HAD officially given him, Simone and Ray nice bland new names. Each had a new driver's license, and the passport expediter in

Philadelphia said their new passports would arrive within a couple of days.

Our going away party for Tryg and Simone wasn't much of a party. We grilled a huge beef tenderloin out on the patio, had some salad, baked potatoes. Nobody wanted dessert. We shared a bottle of champagne, except Rickey, who had poured herself a healthy shot of Canadian Club, four fingers, taken neat.

We spoke little; there was little to speak about. Obviously, Tryg and Simone did not share a forwarding address. We said little of the future, both because I didn't have much of a future and because any information they shared represented some level of risk.

Neither Tryg nor I could predict what kind of investigation there might be in the future or who would conduct it. Tryg was not on parole, so there would be no parole violation to pursue, just plain old fraud and theft by deception. But I worried that his status as a convicted US felon would fire up some zealous Interpol type who would resolve to run Tryg to ground with the zeal of Javert in *Les Misérables*.

Was Tryg the hotter target, I wondered, or was Nora? Would anybody seriously try to charge Dexter as an accomplice and accessory after the fact, way after the fact? Would Rickey be found, harassed, assigned criminal culpability? Found, maybe, I fretted, but where would the justice be in prosecuting her?

I knew, of course, that in this whole scheme I was the prime cherry, and I supposed a lot of people would be pissed that I, an admitted murderer and big-bucks embezzler, might escape justice. To which I would reply, *do you call dying at my age justice?* I would call it a sad end to a bizarre play with an offbeat first act, a pretty boring second act, and a really disappointing final act. Going out with a whimper, not a bang.

Would anybody really care that we had used up a lot of Hermann Bayard's money? Had we not really just committed victimless crimes? Or would some distant Bayard relative in Germany feel a strong urge to exact a pound of flesh or attempt to recoup lost monies? Tryg and I agreed that we just didn't know. Tryg made it clear that he intended to keep a low profile and avoid any spending or acquisition that would raise local eyebrows. "I'm just going to keep on doing what I've been doing," he said quietly.

I noticed a very interesting thing: No one asked me what I was going to be doing in that time between their departure and my death. My demise seemed certain—but unpredictable. Two months? Six months? Ten years? Everybody else's plans were locked and loaded, but no one asked what I intended to do, where I intended to go. How I would manage.

I suddenly was reminded of the ill-conceived policy the Clinton administration had implemented regarding homosexuals serving in the army in the 90's: *"Don't ask. Don't Tell."* Well, nobody asked, and I didn't tell. My silence was a very lonely place, my private vacuum, empty beyond description.

❂   ❂   ❂

WHEN THE TIME CAME, WE DROVE UP TO THE PHILADELPHIA International Airport. Actually, Tryg drove. Damn the rules, I was going to drive home. If I had a TIA on the way, well, tough darts.

Simone had a small suitcase, Tryg nothing but a back pack. They really were going to start fresh, from soup to nuts, strangers in some strange land. We rode in silence, content to just let things wind down without a lot of speechifying or drama.

At the airport, we faced each other briefly outside the car. This wasn't closure. It was murder. There was really nothing to say, nothing to add.

But I tried. "Thanks, man. Really," I croaked.

"Thank you, Hugh. Thanks for all you've done."

And that was it. Tryg took Simone by the elbow and turned to leave. Then he turned back. "If you die, Hugh, I think they should place you on a flaming pyre on a john boat and float you down the Bohemia River in an Aboriginal Viking farewell. If the tide was right, you might make it all the way to Baltimore."

"Tryg, you are not a real funny guy, and that is unquestionably the funniest thing I have ever heard you say."

He did his aw-shucks shrug.

42

Master of My Fate

THE AFTERNOON TRYG AND SIMONE LEFT, RICKEY ASKED NORA AND me to join her in the formal dining room. She walked in carrying a stack of several white bath towels. Nora and I sat next to each other. Rickey sat down across from us on the other side of the table.

Nora sniffed the air. "Rickey, have you been drinking?"

"Goddamn right. I'm loaded. Absolutely...shit...faced. I'm also really pissed off."

I sat back in my chair. "What are you pissed off about?"

"Dexter is gone, and I didn't even have a chance to say goodbye to him."

"That's because you wouldn't come out of your room when he called to you."

"Fuckin' never see him again," she mumbled. "Or Tryg, or Simone or pretty soon you, Nora. Losin' everything. *Fuckin' losing everything.*"

I noticed she hadn't mentioned me.

I learned forward. "Everything changes, Rickey. It's a tragedy, but there's just no way we stop it. I'm not pleased about it either, but we ran a pretty amazing show here for a long time. We hid in the tall grass, dodged the bullets, lived the life we wanted to live. And we are doing everything we can to keep you protected and stable."

"Oh, I'll take care of that," said Rickey. She appeared noticeably unstable, propping herself up on her elbow. She turned to Nora.

"Nora, would you excuse us for just a couple of minutes? I have something I need to show Hugh, and I'd prefer if it was just him and me."

"Of course," said Nora. "I'll come back in about ten minutes, that okay?"

After Nora left, Rickey lifted the top towel off her stack. Laying there between the towels was Hermann's .357, dark blue and shiny against the fluffy white terry cloth.

"Bet you thought I didn't know about this, didn't you?" she said.

"You'd win your bet. I thought we respected each other's personal property around here."

"Yeah, but these are terrible times. And terrible times call for extreme action." Suddenly Rickey wasn't slurring her words anymore. She spoke firmly, precisely.

She picked up the pistol and set it to the side—definitely out of my reach, even if I tried to pounce across the table. Rickey picked up the towel, flapped it in the air, and draped it over her head. It looked like an Egyptian headdress. She looked amazingly like that famous bust of Nefertiti. "Don't want to make an unnecessary mess," she said calmly.

Rickey picked up the .357, steadied it with both hands, and pointed it directly at the middle of my forehead. "Did you like my poem, Hugh? Remember? The one that went, *Beyond this place of wrath and tears, looms but the horror of the shade.* She clenched her teeth, fixed me a fierce glare the likes of which I had never seen before. Her voice was steely.

"*I am the master of my fate; I am the captain of my soul.*

"Invictus, Hugh," she said softly. "Fucking Invictus."

Rickey looked at me, and in that moment, she looked dead

sober. She sighed. "You guys didn't think us autistic people experience emotions, did you? Well, fuck it. And fuck you. Fuck all of you."

Slowly, steadily, Rickey re-aimed the pistol. Away from my forehead, tipping the barrel upward. Then she pushed the pistol's long black barrel up under her chin, back where her graceful throat curved down into her neck.

She reached up and pulled the towel down over her face. Then she pulled the trigger.

43

The Parting Glass

AS STATE TROOPER ARLON SANTUNAS TURNED THE LAST PAGE OF Hugh Ullam's journal, a note fell out, two pages, attractive feminine handwriting. Written with a fountain pen. Santunas picked it up gingerly.

"Hugh," it said, "a departing note as I take my leave. This Scottish song has also been a staple in Irish and Welsh households since the 1770's. It was sung before Robert Burns wrote *Auld Lang Syne*. They sing it in Wales, we sang it in our family, both over there and after we came to the U.S. Except that one time at our brunch, I don't think I've ever heard you sing, but I can imagine you—hear you—reciting this as a poem as a quiet commentary on fate. Goodbye, and God bless you. Love, Nora."

The Parting Glass

Of all the money that e'er I had
I spent it in good company.
And all the harm that e'er I've done,
Alas, it was to none but me.

And all I've done for want of wit
To memory now I can't recall
So fill to me the parting glass,
Good night, and joy be to you all.

Of all the comrades that e'er I had,
They're sorry for my going away.
And all the sweethearts that e'er I had,
They'd wish me one more day to stay.

But since it fell unto my lot
That I should rise and you should not
I gently rise and softly call,
Good night and joy be too you all.

Yes, fill to me the parting glass,
And drink a health what e'er befall
And gently rise and softly call
Good night, and joy be to you all.

Epilogue

From the *Cecil Whig*
"The Independent Voice of Cecil County"
June 7, 1997

Mystery Journal Leads to Cop Convictions

Elkton, MD. In an outcome that resembles the ending of an offbeat suspense movie, a mysterious personal journal has led to the conviction of two Cecil County law enforcement officers charged with multiple civil rights, hate crime and conspiracy offenses. After a co-conspirator, Elkton police officer William Maroney, pleaded guilty and testified against his co-defendants, a federal jury in Baltimore of eight women and four men deliberated less than two hours yesterday before reaching their verdict. Convicted on all counts were Maryland state police Trooper Arlon Santunas and Elkton Deputy Sheriff Bud Tinglestad. Santunas and Tinglestad did not take the stand in their own defense. A second State Trooper, Deirdre Callas, listed in the indictment as an unindicted co-conspirator, has been missing since 1993.

The officers' prosecution stemmed from a Pulitzer Prize-winning *Atlantic Monthly* article in June 1996 about a mysterious journal written by Hugh Ullam, General Manager of Bohemia Manor Farm in Earleville, Maryland before he committed suicide in 1994. A photocopy of the lengthy journal was delivered anonymously to noted investigative journalist Susan Southwick in January. Southwick's award-winning article, *Down Wind and Out of Sight,* chronicled the tale of an offbeat "found family" who lived on illegally at Bohemia Manor for several years after its owner, Hermann Bayard, died unexpectedly.

Southwick, who writes frequently on issues of racism, racial equality, and social justice, said that she did not know and had never met Ullam. "One day I simply found the journal sitting in a box on my desk. I don't know how it was delivered or who delivered it. But it was a uniquely compelling story, so I researched and wrote the *Atlantic Monthly* article. I contacted the military investigator from the Aberdeen Proving Ground described in the journal, and he helped verify dates and events. It was he who referred the civil rights violations involving the law enforcement officers to the United States Attorney's Office in Baltimore."

The journal revealed that Ullam, an indigenous Australian financial expert, relocated to Cecil County after being hired by Hermann Bayard to manage Bayard's farm and financial affairs. The journal chronicled the strange, secluded life of the "Hole in the Wall Gang," as the farm's four residents called themselves, as well as experiments by Bayard's autistic daughter, Ulricke "Rickey" Bayard, described in the journal as a 'savant,' in which she used underwater radio signals to lure a whale up the length of Chesapeake Bay to the Bohemia River. The disoriented whale was struck by a freighter in the C&D Canal, resulting in the death of a person whose boat was struck by the out-of-control ship.

As military investigators investigating the unusual radio signals closed in on them, both Ullam, fifty and suffering from life-threatening health issues, and Rickey Bayard, then fourteen, committed suicide. The other two group members, Trygve Sletland and Nora Dadmun, disappeared and are believed to have left the country. Their whereabouts are unknown.

The civil rights and hate crimes charges against Santunas and Tinglestad, as well as Maroney's guilty plea, stemmed from a series of incidents, chronicled in detail in the journal, in which Santunas, Callas, Maroney and Tinglestad repeatedly conspired to subject Ullam to racial harassment and intimidation, including subjecting him to false arrest and false imprisonment.

Maroney has been released on his own recognizance pending sentencing. Santunas and Tinglestad will remain free on $50,000 bail until a scheduled September sentencing. Both have been suspended without pay with intent to discharge. Neither had any comment on the charges, their convictions, or on the mysterious journal.

Supplemental Author's Note

THIS BOOK IS A WORK OF FICTION. ALL CHARACTERS AND EVENTS ARE products of the author's imagination.

On the other hand, the geography described in *Down Wind and Out of Sight* is accurate and true to life, and if one were inclined, one could drive around Cecil County and see Elkton, Cecilton, North and South Chesapeake City, Georgetown, and Galena pretty much as described. A few minor adjustments have been made for the sake of plot, but not many.

It may be of interest that "the real" Bohemia Manor Farm was originally listed for sale in 2008 at $13.8 million. The price was then dropped to $9.3 million. It was put up for auction in 2010. Here is an excerpt from the actual auction listing:

NOTICE OF ABSOLUTE AUCTION
BOHEMIA MANOR FARM

Bohemia Manor Farm, a 12,750 square foot manor house set on 368 acres of waterfront property on the Bohemia River, will be sold, without reserve, at a live auction on October 12, 2010.

The waterfront property features 3,600 feet of water frontage on the Bohemia River and 2,900 feet on Manor Creek, hundreds of acres of tillable fields, and waterfowl impoundments. The home, built in 1920 following a fire in the previous house, has 11 bedrooms, 11 bathrooms, a grand ballroom, period wall coverings and 10 wood burning fireplaces as well as a guest/caretaker's cottage, a four-bay main garage, an airplane hangar suitable for general aviation, with a nearby cultivated field easily converted back to grass runway.

Bohemia Manor was founded in 1661 by Augustine Herman, a Czech cartographer, who named it as a tribute to his homeland of Prague, Kingdom of Bohemia. It was built on land granted Lord Baltimore, Cecil Calvert, in recognition of Herman's creating a map of the Chesapeake Bay coastline. The estate remained in the hands of Augustine Herman's descendants, most recently the Bayard family of Delaware, for more than 350 years, until 1993, when the current owners purchased the property and then extensively restored it in 2003-2007. "This is one of the most historically significant properties in Maryland," said Daniel DeCaro of DeCaro Luxury Real Estate Auctions. "The beautiful and expansive landscape creates a private setting that respects the historical legacy, while a bevy of amenities add the luxurious comforts of modern living."

The auction did not go well. The property was most recently sold in 2014 for $3,775,000. Today Bohemia Manor Farm is a winery, Chateau Bu-De, and it offers tours and wine-tasting events.

✿　　　✿　　　✿

IF YOU'RE INTERESTED IN THIS BOOK'S BACKSTORY, IT BUILDS ON five elements. First, for years my family spent weekends at a small vacation cottage on the Bohemia River, directly across the river from Bohemia Manor. It stood as a large and imposing red brick presence looking down to the river over an expansive, impeccably manicured lawn. In all the years we had our cottage, we never saw a single human being at that big house across the river. Obviously, someone was mowing the grass, but we never saw anyone living and breathing. It was all pretty eerie, and we all wondered what was—or wasn't—going on at Bo Manor over the years. Ultimately, lacking a story, we made one up.

Second, a big bull shark really was caught off Turkey Point the 1980's, a most unusual event.

Third, when I was in my early teens, I was given an LP record called *Sounds of the Humpback Whale*. It was a collection of hydrophonic recordings gathered deep at sea, along coast lines and in waters of various temperatures. Some "songs" had deep booming statements, others had light seductive trills that might be attributed to the mating season. Then there was a variety of juvenile squeaks that I thought were probably humpback whale puppies. The jacket said that biologists had concluded that there were distinct patterns of communication in the whales' songs, and that phrases and even whole songs often were repeated over and again in the course of days or even months. That is to say, the scientists believed that the whales' sounds were not random and had some communicative purpose.

Fourth, everything that Rickey said about Humphrey the whale is absolutely true, including the part about the J-11 underwater transducer.

Fifth, on July 28, 1942, the oil tanker *John M. Reed*, being towed by a tug and heading south toward Chesapeake Bay, smashed into the highway drawbridge then spanning the C & D canal directly adjacent to Schaeffer's Restaurant (this was not the present Route 213 bridge depicted in the book). The crash plunged the entire bridge structure into the canal, completely blocking it. No one was injured, but the crash punched a large hole in the *Reed*. The aerial photos of the accident are very exciting and inspired the description of the ship crash in the book.

Several years before this, a ship had plowed into the St. Georges bridge further east on the C&D Canal in Delaware, killing three. And more recently, on a foggy morning on the Elk River in February 2002, a large tugboat was run over by a 520-foot freighter. The tug capsized and sank, killing four crewmen.

It seems there's always something happening on the northern Chesapeake Bay.

Acknowledgments

UNTIL YOU HAVE WRITTEN A BOOK, PARTICULARLY IF YOU ARE A first-time novelist, you probably have paid little attention to the acknowledgments authors frequently include at the end. But let me tell you, they mean a *lot* to the author.

Writing is a solitary endeavor, and authors, often excessively in love with the fruits of their own creativity, really do need a candid reality-check provided by diverse sources of objective feedback. In addition, the emotional support that a fiction writer's network of contributors provides is as important as their ideas and suggestions. I am deeply grateful to my merry band of beta readers, hand-holders, critics, cheering section and marketing strategists, whose input significantly changed and dramatically improved *Down Wind and Out of Sight* as it evolved.

My support group bridged generations and professions, disparate personality types, wide varieties of intimacy and distance. These folks gave me lot of perspectives, a lot of ideas, a lot of tough love and candid criticism, a lot of practical advice. I wish everyone could experience the warmth of such support.

So, thank you to Wendy Kaplan, a professional legal newsletter editor who early on stoked my motivational fires by opining that she thought I had created a "unique, stand-alone genre." VJ Pappas, my first Dow Jones editor and for three decades a fast friend and candid critic, gave the novel's pace a kick in the ass. My daughter Hollis Richardson put her Georgetown Master's degree in Language and Communication to fine use, providing astute observations about form and substance and balking not at critiquing her own father. James Diorio, Ph.D. knows a ton about fluid dynamics and the electromagnetic spectrum. Any absurdities in my description thereof are the fault of my comprehension and not his explanations.

And thanks too to a wonderful cross-section of beta readers helped refine the novel's voice, pointed out anachronisms, and contributed detailed copy-editing. Dr. Karol Wasylyshyn, Kate Richardson, Andrew Price, Tobey Chier, Patricia Dobrinska, Dr. Nicholas Scharff, Jackie Scharff, Harriet Ruffin, Megan Niño, Felicia Greenberg, Pamela Bridwell Cain, David Richter, Julie and Elan Aqua—thank you all.

And to my professional editor, John Paine: It was tough love, John, but you got it right. Thanks for your judgment, your candor, and the advanced course in fiction writing.

❁   ❁   ❁

IT'S COMMON FOR WRITERS TO EXPRESS GRATITUDE TO A SPOUSE or partner for their patience and love, and I hereby do so— heartfelt—to my extraordinary wife, Pamela Woldow. *But wait! There's more!* Lucky is the author whose wife also is a skilled copy editor, as well as a seasoned marketing consultant, website builder, social media expert, avid researcher, and networking extrovert. Pam has pulled me from the introvert's cave, and I am much the better for it: *"So, Doug, here's what we're going to do…"*

Bless you all. People like you make me want to write more. The next novel is complete, and the third is underway. God, this is fun.

About the Author

Douglas Richardson is a former Assistant U.S. Attorney, legal counsel for Pennsylvania's mental hospitals, and an award-winning Dow Jones columnist for over twenty years. In *Down Wind and Out of Sight*, he combines a deep understanding of human psychology, a wealth of experience in criminal investigations, and the ability to create unforgettable characters.